FLAMES OF GOLD

LIZ DELTON

TYTAN
THE HOLLOW ISLES
ROKHOLD
MAR NEVAN
THE TWIST
KING'S MOUNTAIN
AREM
THOAN
GHORVOST
GREEN'S TAVERN
THE GOLD WOOD
CARRIAGE HOUSE
RAYVA
BELTA
NOVA ISTRA
THORNKILL
HOLVDAN
THE SALT SWAMPS
BARD'S REACH
VIREN
SOUTHMARCH
RESBROK MANOR
ASHBROK MANOR
VERINDAS

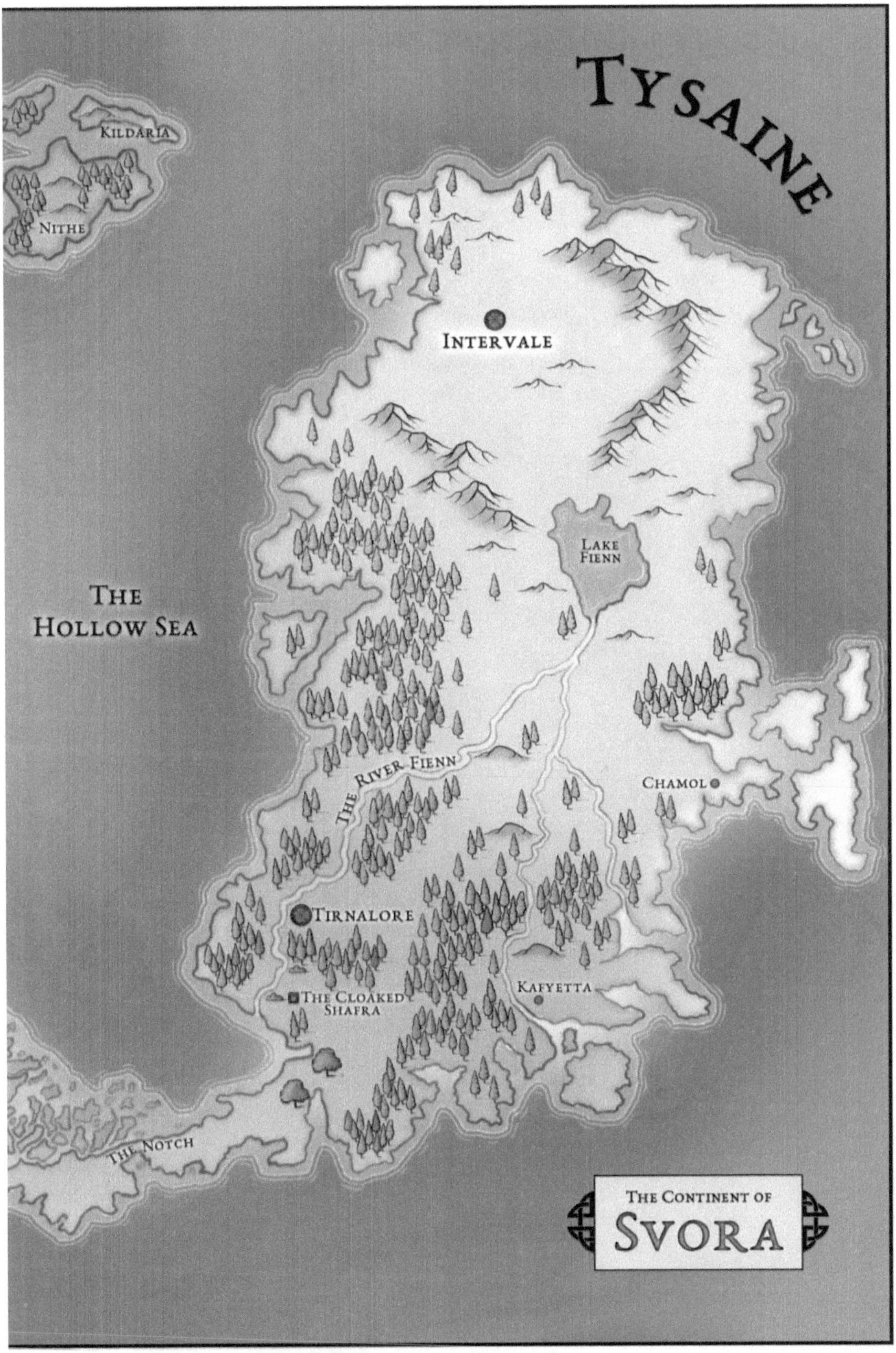

TYSAINE
KILDARIA
NITHE
INTERVALE
LAKE FIENN
THE HOLLOW SEA
THE RIVER FIENN
CHAMOL
TIRNALORE
THE CLOAKED SHAFRA
KAFYETTA
THE NOTCH
THE CONTINENT OF SVORA

THE GOLD WOOD

"Fairaleigh Veil, you're wanted by the king." A gauntleted hand landed heavy on her shoulder.

Fig groaned and took a last swig from her tankard, then set it down on the bar. She spun on her barstool to face the silversword, his armored bulk blocking her view of the rest of the tavern. Fire surged through her veins, and she let a small flicker of flame dance across her knuckles to show him exactly who he was dealing with.

The silver helm hid most of his face, save for his silver-ringed eyes and lightly bearded chin. The blondish hair along his jaw matched the straight strands spilling over his pauldrons. Outfitted in plate armor worth more than enough coin to feed a family for a year, he looked like a wall of muscle and metal.

"Fine," she said, narrowing her eyes. The king had sent only one man, which she found curious and slightly insulting. She was fairly confident she could take one of the king's men, their enchanted blades and abilities notwithstanding. She eyed his sword, noting the intricately forged details on the hilt and the faint hint of metallic magic that tasted like copper across her tongue—much like the blood they spilled.

He hadn't said she was under arrest, so she decided to

acquiesce...for now. The king of Tytan wasn't a tolerant man, but he followed the laws, and she had done nothing illegal. She couldn't pretend she hadn't seen this coming, however.

She'd left the Carriage House two years ago and had been on her own ever since. The enclave of silverswords that ruled Tytan didn't like that. Few people did; most preferred to keep the mages under the crown's watchful eye, hidden away at the Carriage House, away from everyone else, even after they'd finished their training. But Fig didn't want to live in a gilded cage.

"Let's go," the silversword grunted, jerking his head in the direction of the door.

Fig sighed and stood, but the man kept his hand on her shoulder, intent on leading her out of Green's Tavern. Green, idly drying tankards behind the bar, swiveled his gaze in her direction. Fig shook her head and shrugged. She could handle herself. She had managed on her own since leaving the Carriage House, scraping by as a mage for hire. And by the Bard, she was finally living her own life. Why was the king interfering now?

Outside, the cool night air kissed her skin, and a light breeze off the Gold Wood brought the taste of honeyed gold to her tongue as the magic that dwelled there wafted close. She could see a faint glimmer of the gold leaves even from here. That was why she favored Green's Tavern: its proximity to the Gold Wood, a place forbidden to her kind unless she pledged her life to the Carriage House. A mistake she had only made once. Perhaps she was paying the price for that broken promise now.

She glanced over her shoulder and grumbled, "Mind taking your hand off me, 'sword? I'm about to sink into the muck with your heavy hand weighing me down."

The silversword grunted but didn't release his grip.

"What, you think I'm going to run? I've had dealings with the king and his ilk before. I'm not afraid."

"Perhaps you should be."

Despite her confidence that the king would do her no direct harm, the silversword's quiet words drew a shiver up her spine.

No silverswords awaited them outside the tavern, and the man leading her headed not for the lean-to where horses were tethered, but directly to the dirt road.

"What, am I supposed to walk the entire way to Rayva?" Fig demanded crossly. "I've got a job tonight, you know." He didn't answer, merely gave her shoulder a slight push as they kept walking.

She stretched out her senses, uneasy. All she caught was the magic sifting through the trees of the Gold Wood, the leaves of which glittered like their namesake. Her captor—or escort, she hoped—and his enchanted sword were the only other thing she registered, a strange coppery red signature the man and his weapon shared. She turned and studied his helm again, but it wasn't one she recognized. So he wasn't one of the 'swords who thought it was their responsibility to harass any mages who dared to live on their own.

When the tavern was well out of sight, she realized he wasn't leading her down the road toward Rayva, but on a road that wound around the Gold Wood. She halted in her tracks. Quicker than should be possible for a man wearing full plate, he whirled in front of her, grasping both her arms.

"Where are you taking me?" she demanded.

"To see the king," he replied, not releasing his grip.

She scoffed. "What does he care about me? I'm not going back there. Let me go. I'm supposed to be meeting a blacksmith—"

There was a hiss of sliding silver, and his sword was drawn. But his attention wasn't on her. He had shifted his body partially in front of her, and now she could see what he was looking at. They stood with their backs to the Gold Wood, facing the wide valley that lay before Rayva. High above the valley, a ball of light shot through the inky black. A shooting star, bigger than any Fig had ever seen. It was followed by two more, shooting across the sky. A chill went through Fig as she watched them over the silversword's armored shoulder.

"A portent?" the man muttered.

She took a swift breath of cool night air into her lungs, glanced at the sky once more, and slipped away, running straight toward the Gold Wood. Portent, indeed. It was time for her to go. She got six steps before he lurched after her.

Though the shooting stars had caught him off guard, he was, of course, unnaturally fast. She had hoped the silverswords' superstitions might slow the man's footsteps, but he showed no reservations about entering the Gold Wood.

"Morgha take you!" he cursed, barely audible over the clanking of his armor.

Of course, *now* she was breaking the law, something she hadn't considered when she started running into the Gold Wood. Now the king actually could hold something against her.

With the taste of honey on her tongue and glittering gold sifting from the trees, she ran. It was easy to wind a path through the trees, their trunks spaced so widely one could probably even drive a carriage through. A blanket of golden leaves draped above her, emitting a golden glow even this late at night.

Though her ancestors of Old Svora had tended these forests for millennia, the Gold Wood had been property of the throne for some two hundred years now. Anyone with the blood of Old Svora— mages like her—were only allowed in the forest if they served the crown. And though the Carriage House deep within the forest was an opulent estate with opportunities to learn and work, in truth, it was a marble and gold cage. She had spent eight years of her life there before she'd noticed the bars.

She needn't run as far as the Carriage House to lose the silversword, though. She just needed to outrun him long enough to lose him. *That shouldn't take long, given all that armor*, she thought with a smirk. Gold leaves whipped by as she darted around another auran tree.

Her lungs were filled with a heady sensation they hadn't felt in a long time. *Don't let it get to your head*, she told herself. She wasn't used to the magic of the Gold Wood sinking into her skin, coating her tongue, and setting her head spinning. She tried to focus on her feet, on the crunch of the golden leaves underfoot, on the beauty she could see in the faint golden glow of the woods.

The next thing she knew, she was flying forward, her feet taken out from under her. Perhaps all those muscles under that armor weren't just for looks. She had just enough time to throw her hands out before she slammed into the ground.

The silversword crashed down with her, his arms flung around her calves. She twisted, fingers scrambling in the dirt and leaves. Panic erupted in her chest as he surged up, sword drawn. She had broken the law, regardless of what the king had originally wanted her for. She was trespassing in the Gold Wood, a crime punishable by death. And here was one of the king's men to dole out the punishment.

On instinct, she pushed out her hands, sending billowing flames toward him. Plumes of golden fire lit up the trees around them. They both recoiled. She yanked her hands back, and with them, the flames. It was too much. She had underestimated the inherent magic of the Gold Wood.

She glanced around the clearing to ensure the nearby trees weren't on fire—the plumes had gone twice as high as she'd intended—and the silversword took that moment to strike.

Brandishing his sword as if it were an extension of his body—rumors were, the enchanted blades of the silverswords acted as such—he lunged at her again. With her gaze locked on the heavy sword, she didn't see his other hand reach out for her arm.

He yanked her toward him, crushing her to his chest. She jerked her head from side to side, but she was trapped in his arms.

"That's enough of that, *goldfire*," he said. "You burn me, you burn yourself now."

Breathing heavily, she still entertained the idea for a moment, but with the strength of her flames, she couldn't risk it. Normally, her flames wouldn't burn her, but here, surrounded by the magic of the auran trees, her magic was unstable. Luckily, she hadn't set fire to any of the endangered trees, but she didn't want to risk using her flames again.

To add to her list of crimes, she now had attacked a silversword with fire magic. *By the Bard, what have I done? Only ten minutes ago, I was having a drink in the tavern...*

He growled, "I don't want to have to carry you out of here, but I will. Are you done?"

Rage simmered in her veins, but she nodded, and he finally pulled away.

She let the rage burn away as he pointed a gauntleted hand in the direction they had come. Pursing her lips, she started walking again, gold sifting down gently from above. She retraced their hasty path through the golden trees, then he began to guide her in a slightly different direction.

As she finally caught sight of the edge of the forest, she savored the sensations around her. The glittering gold. The scent of honey thick on her tongue. The feeling that she was glowing just beneath the skin. Would she ever feel it again? Would they lock her up in a dungeon in Rayva, or was it a gilded cage the king wished for her? There would be no freedom, either way. At least if they sent her back to the Carriage House, she would live in the heart of the Gold Wood. A political pawn in exchange for a life in the forests of her ancestors.

True night met their eyes at the edge of the forest, but the sky was clear, and the moon and stars bright enough to see the road. They had come out by a small bridge over a brook, which looked somewhat familiar to Fig, but she couldn't quite place their location. Just as the silversword led her near the bridge, she spotted the carriage parked in its shadow.

She allowed the silversword to lead her to the carriage, and he opened the door for her. Inside, her gaze fell upon the man sitting on the cushioned wooden bench, a man she hadn't seen in two long years. He had smooth tanned skin and brown hair, one strand of which fell casually into his eyes. He wore an elaborate purple waistcoat, trimmed in gold and black, with a stiff collar running parallel to his perfect jawline. The perfect jawline of Prince Devryn Verrence.

Finally, she met his eyes, then looked down again.

"Fairaleigh Veil, Your Majesty," the silversword announced.

"Fig," the prince said, his mouth quirking up in half a smile.

She swallowed the lump in her throat and looked back up at

Prince Devryn. "Dev," she said, her stomach doing a little flip. "Your man here said I was wanted by the king. What in the Bard's name is going on?"

Dev's gaze lingered on her eyes for a moment, then he looked down at his hands. "My father is dead. And I need your help."

Fig stared at Prince Devryn from her seat in the parked carriage, letting his brief explanation sink in.

"Murder? How can you be sure?" she said. They still sat on the outskirts of the Gold Wood, and the soft breeze that rustled the gold auran trees brought a hint of magic to her senses even in here. Oh, how she missed it. *I need to find new digs closer to the Gold Wood,* she told herself. *Maybe with the job I'm supposed to get tonight, if I ever get back to Green's Tavern...*

"I am *quite* sure," Dev said, running a hand through his chestnut hair. "They tried to kill me, too, and Vaelor saved me." Dev jerked his head in the direction of the silversword, who remained vigilant outside the half-open carriage door. Every so often, he looked their way, and his silver-ringed eyes glinted in the darkness.

Fig clutched her elbows, hugging herself. "Well, I'm sorry, Dev," she said in a low voice. *King Devryn,* she realized with a jolt to her stomach. "But what do you need my help for? You've got silverswords in scores in Rayva, the command of the entire enclave. How come you only have one man with you, anyway?" she demanded, eyebrows furrowed. Dev was smarter than that, unless...

"It *was them,*" Dev said with ire. "The silverswords."

Fig sat in silence for a moment. She rubbed her fingers together, unconsciously producing tiny sparks. *The silverswords?* King Haemond had control of the enclave, as had his forefathers. He had a veritable army of enhanced fighters with their enchanted swords at his command—not to mention King Haemond himself had been a silversword.

"They turned on him? Why—?" She cut herself off with a wave of a hand. "Wait, what about..." She nodded at Vaelor, his silver armor glinting in the moonlight.

Dev gave her the ghost of a smirk, and said, "Oh, I can trust him."

When she furrowed her brow, he continued. "He's fairly new to the enclave, and I have my reasons. Besides, he saved my life," he added, as if that settled it.

Fig glared at him to go on.

Dev obliged. "It was this afternoon. I didn't think anyone even knew I'd left the castle. But five of them cornered me in an alley in Blac—er—"

"*Black End?*" Fig said, eyes rolling as she took a breath for patience. "What in the Bard's name were you doing in Black End, and with only one guard, you idiot?" She pressed her lips together. Maybe she shouldn't be calling the heir to the Rayvan throne an idiot.

Dev shrugged, his famously playful demeanor surprisingly absent. It had been a long time since she had seen him, that much was true, but it was apparent he had suffered much by his father's murder and the subsequent attempt on his own life.

"How did you get away?" she found herself asking next.

"Vaelor," Dev said. "He had them on their backs in a matter of minutes, faster than a Black End lady of—"

Fig held up a hand to halt the salacious comment. Perhaps the old Dev *was* still in there. "One silversword," Fig said under her breath, "against *five?*"

Dev leaned back, propping an ankle over his knee, a self-satisfied smirk rising to his lips as if he himself had been the one to hold them off. "Five. They wore no armor, so I recognized them all. Did they think I wouldn't? Niel Ganivan from Thornkill; we used to play marstones in the castle courtyard when we were children! Liess Astor, from Southmarch—she's Weld to a formidable axe—she got a good hit on Vaelor. Anyway," Dev went on, "five silverswords in full armor wouldn't exactly be stealthy, marching through the city to murder their heir, so they went without it. It was Gan Wroghsley—the knave—who held his pathetic short sword to my throat and hissed in my ear, 'You're dead, never-to-be-king. Your father lies in a pool of blood, and you're about to join him. The likes of your blood will never sit on the throne.'"

A sickly feeling slithered through Fig's core at the words. *Your blood...*

The blood of his mother, Queen Eileigh.

The blood of Old Svora, that not even the king had expected in his bride from the Hollow Isles. Blood that blessed its descendants with rich magic. Magic that was completely useless in the eyes of the silverswords, or in the eyes of some, a curse.

Dev paused, perhaps also thinking of the tragedies surrounding his family line. Finally, he went on, "It was his downfall, though, those clever words of Wroghsley's. It gave Vaelor time to disarm him."

Fig let out a small gasp. Their weapons were bonded to them in some arcane ritual no one outside of the silversword enclave and the Sisters of Morgha knew about. Taking another's Welded weapon was said to be akin to ripping out their heart.

"I flung his sword to the side," Vaelor said in a low voice. "I had two more coming at Prince Devryn from either side. *King* Devryn. My apologies." Vaelor made the correction with a deep bow of his head.

Dev nodded once in acceptance. He had always looked regal—even now, hiding out in a carriage in the shadow of the Gold Wood. Poised, perfect, and now an heir without a throne. The throne had never quite seemed his, ever since the truth about Queen Eileigh had been revealed. All the mages at the Carriage House had whispered about it. Fig wasn't one to gossip, but she couldn't pretend she hadn't wondered: Would King Haemond truly make Devryn king? With the blood of a mage? With the blood of Old Svora, no mage could be turned a silversword, and the silverswords had held the Rayvan throne for over two centuries.

"So why do you need my help?" Fig said, drawing the words out.

His gaze meeting hers, Dev said, "Who do you think is sitting on the throne right now?"

"I truly have no idea," she said, shaking her head.

"I do. Rhivven, the butcher of Viren."

"Even if that's true," she said slowly, "what in the Bard's inky fingers makes you think I can help you get the throne from that bloodthirsty briigard?" She had never met the man, but one of her more memorable tasks at the Carriage House had been to go to the recently conquered country of Viren after the Silver Slaughter to help put out the fires raging up and down the highlands. She'd seen the aftermath of his work. And so had Dev.

"That's not exactly—" Dev began. "It's not as easy as that." His tone was infuriatingly patient.

"You call that easy?" she demanded, sudden ire rising. "I haven't seen you in two years, Dev, and you pluck me out of a tavern—where I was supposed to be meeting a legitimate lead on some business—and ask me to help with this? The Bard will laugh until his sides ache when he writes this tale for the gods."

Dev crossed his arms. "The Bard can laugh. I'm not giving up my throne. Even if all the silverswords hated me for my mother's blood, my father still cared! He swore up and down that he would never cast me down for it. He had no qualms about installing a mage on the throne. After my brother died, he raised me to rule. Besides, I would be good for Tytan, not some blood-lusting soldier like Rhivven. But now? Now Rhivven's taken the country instead of following my father's wishes. That's why they killed him."

Dev went on, "And you think I should just run off and give up? Forget about the life I've been building since I can remember? The life my father wanted me to have? Of course, that would be *your* advice, Fig. You're an expert at giving up and running away." He scoffed, his handsome features furrowing into a frown.

Heat flooded Fig's cheeks, and she fought to keep flames from erupting out of her fingertips. Sparks flickered despite her efforts, singeing her seat. She stood—a feat not as impressive as she intended since she had to duck to keep her head from hitting the ceiling. "Goodbye, Dev—*King* Verrence."

He gaped at her, but she already had one foot out the door and was soon standing on the road in the cool darkness. The silversword made no move to stop her, so she stalked past him.

"Fig—" Dev called.

She kept going, the subtle glitter of the Gold Wood to her right. She should return to Green's Tavern. Perhaps her client had been late or was desperate enough to wait for her. She was highly skilled, after all. Not many fire mages were available for hire. But any mage working outside the Carriage House had a bad reputation, and she was still fighting tooth and nail to find legitimate work. Of course, Dev had come to throw it all into the fire.

She took a deep breath, the scent of honey thick in the air. Careful not to let the proximity of the Gold Wood get to her head, she made it back to the tavern uneventfully, though she kept an eye out for Vaelor. She wouldn't put it past Dev to try to kidnap her again, but it wasn't as if the man in full armor could sneak up on her in the dark.

Boisterous calls and a shouted refrain from a bawdy song filtered from the tavern when it came into view. She stopped twenty paces from the door and closed her eyes, trying to calm her senses. The walk in the dark had done little to soothe her ire at Dev's words. *Of course, that would be your advice, Fig. You're an expert at giving up and running away.*

After a deep lungful of night air, gathering up all the outrage that had flooded through her, she let it all out in twin bursts of gold fire from her hands, burning bright as if her own negative thoughts fueled it.

When the flames ran out, she forced a smile and said, "Now, to find that blacksmith."

Intending to ask the tavernkeeper if the blacksmith had shown up looking for her or left his information, she reached for the door handle and yanked it open.

She was met with a wall of steel and silver-colored armor.

For a split second, she wondered how Vaelor could have possibly gotten back so quickly. Then she realized it was *not* Vaelor, but three silverswords, one of whom held a wicked looking axe in her hand.

"Fairaleigh Veil?" the woman said.

This again? she thought, her heart racing. "It's Fig," she blurted. Evidently, she *hadn't* burned off all her anger.

Eyes shadowed by her helm, the woman smirked. "The mage who quit the Carriage House, Fig. Yes, that's what they call you, isn't it? A nickname from your Carriage House days? You're a long way from there. That's where your kind belong, you know, not out here tainting the rest of us with your cursed blood." The woman stepped forward, and the other two filled the doorframe behind her.

"I don't belong there," Fig insisted. "I got my discharge papers from the headmaster."

"Oh, but you do," the woman said. "*King's* orders. It's unsafe to have untrained mages running around Tytan. Particularly those with your set of skills, fire mage."

Fig thought back to her outburst of fiery emotion just before opening the tavern door and cursed.

"I—"

She ran. Sprinted back toward the Gold Wood just like she'd done to try and lose Vaelor earlier. *Fine. If they want me in there so badly...* But no, she couldn't get out of control. She wasn't used to the forest's raw magic anymore, and if she burned even one auran tree, she was a dead mage. She veered to the other side of the road, and hurled herself into a ditch, hoping her head start had afforded her enough time to hide. While the Gold Wood would boost her magic, she was a danger to herself—and the endangered trees.

They charged. The clanging of three sets of full armor rang out across the night. The noise changed, and she clutched her fingers to her mouth as she lay in the ditch. She couldn't fight three silverswords. How had Dev's man fought off *five*? Sure, they hadn't had their armor, but still...

A moment later, she found out why the clanking sounded different. Out of nowhere, one of the silverswords crashed right into the ditch after her, as the other two ran in a different direction—a distraction. They were aware of how loud their armor was and had used it against her.

Her attacker grappled to hold onto her hands, which now glowed like coals, flames licking her fingers. Before she could fling the fire at him, pain exploded in her jaw as the man's gauntlet collided with her face. Reeling, she didn't have time to think before he grabbed her hair and yanked her head back.

She gasped and flung fistfuls of flames into the man's face without pity, wondering if her jaw was broken from the blinding pain. She earned her freedom from his crushing arms. She rolled away, the ripe smell of leaf mold rising to greet her, when two hands landed soundly on her back. The other two must have flanked her.

But the two hands that lifted her from the ditch belonged to none other than Vaelor. She extinguished her flames, eyes wide.

Steel came between them as the silversword attacked again. Vaelor flung Fig away to safety, and she scrambled on her hands and feet, clutching her jaw in pain. As she staggered up the side of the ditch, she saw Vaelor ram his attacker away with his shoulder before drawing his own enchanted sword.

Her heart beating painfully fast, she looked around for the other two silverswords, but all she could see on the dark road were two lumps twenty paces off. "Huh," she said to herself, scrambling farther from Vaelor's fight.

Vaelor wielded a two-handed sword, perhaps a claymore, like the Virenish lowlanders used. He swung it through the air as if it weighed no more than a feather.

The other silversword was on the ground in a matter of minutes, a dark pool of blood growing visible in the dim light.

"We better go," Vaelor said in a low baritone.

"B-But what about the bodies—" Fig stuttered. Despite the bad reputation mages had, Fig had done her best to stay on the right side of the king's laws these past two years. Though she occasionally saw Tytan's underbelly, murder was never an option. Not for her. Her refusal had gotten her into plenty of scrapes and lost her plenty of jobs. But even if she was a quitter and didn't finish her training, she wasn't about to throw away her morals.

Vaelor's mouth twitched. "There's no time. And they're not all dead, anyway. Just him." He jerked his hand at the attacker in the ditch.

Without further ado, Vaelor strode off in the direction of Dev's carriage. Fig stood there, torn. *Must* she go with them, to be hunted with the ousted heir until they were all dead? Or could she go back—

No. There was no going back. The silverswords at Green's Tavern had been looking for her specifically.

Did they know Dev would go to her? Or were they simply seeking all mages who dared set out on their own? Of course, the crown already had most of the mages under their thumb at the Carriage House, but until now she had been free to live her life as she pleased, whether that was a good decision on her part or not.

She took a step toward Vaelor's retreating back, when she heard one of the silverswords from the ground call, "You're dead! You're a dead mage, Veil!"

Fig rapped her knuckles on the carriage door, but there was no answer. She glanced over at Vaelor, who said, "It's us, King Devryn."

The door swung out, revealing Dev's sheepish face, his hands raised as if he were about to summon his magic. Part of Fig wanted to punch him for what he'd said before, but she knew he was in a tough spot right now. Not to mention his father had just died.

She gave him a nod and turned away, swinging up onto the driver's seat. The two horses danced at the shift in weight but settled quickly.

"What are you—" Dev sighed loudly, then leaned his torso out of the door to address her. She couldn't help thinking how handsome he looked hanging by one arm holding onto the roof of the carriage. "Very well. We ride for Nova Istra. The Bard's Road will be fastest from here. Vaelor, will you..."

Fig inspected her jaw with a tentative hand. She knew she was still able to talk and move it around, so it must not be broken. But *gods*, the bruises that were surely forming would be legendary. "Look," she said. "I turned you down the first time. I had work to do—a real job. I don't expect you would know how hard it is for someone like me to... Well, is this a job or what?"

Dev bobbed his head slightly. "Of course. I will compensate you. And once I take the throne, you'll have everything you ever want. You can live in the Gold Wood or not. Your choice. Mages should have the choice."

Choice.

"Very well," Fig said. That would have to do. It wasn't as if she *had* a choice anymore, now that the silverswords were hunting her.

But if Dev took the throne, life could be better for mages all over Tytan.

Vaelor mounted the other side of the driver's seat, and Fig cleared her throat. "We're not taking the Bard's Road. The silverswords were already looking for me at the tavern. What makes you think you can take this polished piece of pomp down the Bard's Road without getting killed?"

Dev opened his mouth, palm raised in protest. Fig cut him off, "We're taking the Mountain Road."

"The Mountain Road?" Dev said, "That's practically in the opposite direction of Nova Istra."

Fig rolled her eyes. "I know where Nova Istra is. But we need to make a stop first. You said you need to get to the Hollow Isles?"

Dev swung down, coming closer to address her. She straightened her back a little.

"Yes. I hear there's someone of my mother's blood sitting on the Hollow throne in Nithe, a distant cousin or half-uncle or something. They're the only ones who might be able to help me stand against this coup. Tysaine won't help—they made it clear they weren't interested in our war with Viren. And with the enclave fully against me now, the Hollow Isles is my only hope."

She nodded. "Fine. Well, if you want to sail out of Nova Istra, we're going to need papers. I don't think anyone's going to let you go anywhere once Rhivven declares his rule across Tytan and announces that the Verrence heir is on the run. Everyone will be looking for you." *Every 'sword will be trying to kill you*, she thought to herself. *And me.*

"See?" Dev said to Vaelor. "This is why I needed Fig."

Vaelor shifted, looking nonplussed. She was used to the attitude from silverswords. Brutish, bloodthirsty, and secure in the knowledge that they ran Tytan.

Fig shook her head. "We'll take the Mountain Road. The woman I live with, Bruna, she owns the cottage. She can get us papers by morning, I'm sure of it. She owes me, anyway."

And Fig wouldn't mind picking up some of her things if they were to travel to Nova Istra, then on to Tysaine, and finally, the Hollow Isles. No ship out of Tytan would sail directly to the Hollow Isles anymore, not since the revelation of Queen Eileigh's blood and the resulting devastation to the Verrence family. It would be a long journey, and she would quite like another change of clothes, at the very least.

"Fine," Dev said, "Let's see if the carriage will even make it down that rickety track."

Fig snorted. "Are you sure you need this contraption? We'd be less noticeable if—"

Dev's shoulders straightened. "They're going to notice us whether I ride in a carriage, on a horse, or naked on top of a Virenish tagor— they're searching for me, so the quicker we get to Nova Istra, the better."

"I'm trying not to picture you riding a tagor," Fig muttered as Dev got back into the carriage with a snort, though the image in her head of Dev riding one of the scaly beasts persisted. "Let's go." She handed Vaelor the reins. "I'll watch the trees."

Sparks danced on her fingers as the carriage lurched into motion. Now that she was sitting, the night finally began to catch up with her. Exhaustion leached into her bones, but she watched the forest on either side of the road as they trundled through the night. She wasn't sure how long it would take for the two silverswords near Green's Tavern to recuperate, but it was safe to assume more of them would soon follow. How they knew to find her at the tavern, the Bard only knew.

Night wouldn't be upon them much longer. In a few hours, all of Tytan would awake and news of King Haemond's death would spread up and down the country. And who knew what rumors they would spin about the flight of the heir Devryn. Now Fig was a part of that tale, whether she wanted to be or not.

With only minimal instructions to Vaelor, they made their way up the Mountain Road without incident, save for all the swearing from the occupant of their carriage on the tumultuous ride. The Mountain Road was made for farm carts and was therefore riddled with a series of ruts at any given stretch. But Fig didn't mind. With the Gold Wood on their right and the muscled yet haughty silversword on her left, she was quite content. The scent of honey on the breeze was enough to keep her alert, despite her exhaustion.

They parked the carriage on the other side of the small woods behind Bruna's cottage, hidden by some bushes. Dawn's light remained hidden, for a little while longer, anyway.

"You might want to stay here," Fig told Dev as he lurched out of the carriage. With a quick flick of his hands, an amethyst-tinted wind brushed down his clothes, making him appear more put together than he was. "The last time Bruna met you, you almost dumped her in the well."

"Bruna?" Dev said, his mouth quirking up in a smile. "*That* Bruna? What in the Bard's name are you doing living with her? Last I heard of her, she was forging notes for brothels in Black End."

Fig gave him a pointed look. "And we need forged documents, do we not? Besides, there's not many of us mages outside of the Carriage House. We tend to stick together, and Bruna's work is as innocent as a priestess's compared to some of the things I've seen."

"Priestesses aren't as innocent as you think either," Dev quipped. "Fine. I'll stay here. The carriage is better when it's not moving, anyway. Vaelor?"

"With you, Your Majesty."

"Actually, I was going to ask you to accompany Fig. Since they were looking for her at the tavern, they might come here too. I've no idea why they were there, and that troubles me."

An empty pit opened in Fig's core. They very well might come here. "We better be quick and warn Bruna. I still don't know how they found me at the tavern. Did anyone else know you were seeking me out?" she demanded of Dev.

He shook his head vigorously. "I swear, we left Rayva right after the assault in Black End—"

"How did *you* know I was going to be at Green's?" she said.

"Well, I—" Dev began, and the slightest flick of his lowered gaze tipped her off.

"Have you been keeping tabs on me?" she asked incredulously, her mind reeling. "Never mind. I should go get Bruna."

They left Dev in the carriage, which, at least for his safety's sake, looked discreet enough from afar. If any silverswords got near it, though, it would be hard to miss the silver Verrence crest embedded in the center of each wheel, the quality of the wood, or the plush padding of the driver's bench.

Vaelor went first, his sword sheathed and his eyes alert. Fig followed, watching the cottage through the trees. Dawn had begun its slow approach, but the light remained murky.

A goat bleated from somewhere on the small farm next door as they reached the edge of the woods and stopped. Vaelor glanced at Fig as she lifted her cowl to cover her head.

"Bruna sleeps in a loft over the main room," she said quietly. "We should get her out if the 'swords are coming here, but she'll probably need to grab some supplies first."

"They could be here already," Vaelor said, his deep voice low. His gaze was still trained on the cottage. "I'll go first."

They could see through several windows, and nothing looked amiss, but her hand shook a little as she pulled out her big iron key. She handed it to him, saying, "Go ahead."

Vaelor moved through the tall grass at the back of the cottage with a sure grace. She wasn't sure if the fluid movement was something granted to him as a silversword or something that came naturally. Every silversword had different enhanced attributes; whatever arcane ritual they underwent to cross over somehow enhanced their natural abilities or gave them new ones. Whatever it did, it made them more than human, linked intrinsically to their weapon.

Crouching lower in the bushes, she watched him open the front latch with the key. The hinges complained loudly, as they always did. Bruna intended the noise to warn of intruders, so she let the hinges get rusty and avoided oiling them. Fig half expected to see papers shooting out the door at Vaelor as Bruna realized who wielded the key.

When Vaelor calmly stepped inside with no immediate assault, Fig leaned forward, watching and idly rubbing her bruised jaw. The sinking feeling in her gut twisted a little as she waited. *If they knew I was going to be at Green's Tavern, they must know where I live, right?*

Were they looking for me in particular? Or just any mage?

When Vaelor beckoned to her with his gauntleted hand, she leapt through the tall grasses and bounded for the door, eager to get moving.

"Is she still slee—" Fig began, then stopped in her tracks. Cold seeped into her core, as if a flame had gone out, scoured by a bitter wind.

Furniture had been knocked aside. Papers were strewn everywhere as if a maelstrom had struck. Blood spattered many of them. And in the center of the room lay the body of the closest person she had to a friend.

Fig's knees hit the floor. She reached out a hand for Bruna's, brushing the woman's fingertips. They bore scores of paper cuts from Bruna's defensive attack. She was a paper mage, and though she normally used her skills to manipulate things *on* paper, Fig knew she could do whatever she wanted with the substance, including defend herself.

But against how many silverswords? Fig swallowed hard, then grabbed Bruna's hand. She clenched her eyelids shut tight, bowing her head as hot tears leaked out.

She was brought back into the moment by the soft muttering of what sounded like a prayer behind her.

Looking over her shoulder, she saw that Vaelor had unsheathed his sword and was down on one knee with the weapon before him, both hands on the hilt. She caught him muttering, "...return to Morgha swiftly and without pain."

When he looked up, Fig nodded her thanks, blinking away the tears as best she could. She turned back to Bruna and brushed some stray black hairs from the woman's round face.

"We should go," Fig whispered, not looking away from Bruna's lifeless eyes.

She had only lived with the woman for half a year, but it had been the time that Fig was finally figuring out what to do with herself. She'd been an outcast after she'd left the Carriage House, struggling to make a living, going from village to village, harassed by silverswords at every turn. But she had her discharge papers; she was allowed to practice magic outside the Gold Wood, beyond the eye of the crown.

Plenty of people had wanted her services, except they weren't the kind of people or "jobs" Fig agreed with. Arson. Death. Threats. That wasn't how she wanted to live her life. Finally, she'd met up with Bruna, who'd taken her under her wing. Bruna had connections with honorable people who would employ a mage like her. Bruna showed Fig how to live without throwing her morals aside or getting involved in anything over her head.

"Too late for that," Fig muttered to Bruna, cracking a watery smile. *I'm in way over my head now.* She took a shuddering breath, then closed Bruna's eyelids, and stood. Fire licked Fig's fingers as she turned to face Vaelor.

"We should go," Vaelor repeated.

Fig looked around the cottage that Bruna had welcomed her into. The massive desk covered with all sorts of pens and different types of paper; the bookshelves lining the walls, filled with books from all over the Svoran continent, not to mention the Hollow Isles, even as far as Pan Vidda.

She stepped over some fallen papers near the door that led to her room. Formerly a lean-to against the side wall of the cottage, they had converted it into a room that was almost—but not quite—draft-free. She eased the door open, quickly collected some clothes into a satchel, and grabbed a dagger Bruna had given her last Morgha's Day. What use it would be against the silverswords, well, the Bard could laugh about that later when he wrote down the tale of her life.

Her gaze immediately went back to Bruna in the center of the blood-splattered papers when she returned to the main room. Fire sparked at her fingertips, and she tried to slow her breathing to calm her senses.

Vaelor stood just outside the door, keeping watch. Fig gave the cottage one last look, not wanting to leave Bruna here, but seeing no alternative.

They had nothing to get them through the port at Nova Istra—a trivial problem now, it seemed. However, Fig's desire to get as far away from Tytan as possible was growing exponentially by the hour. Not wanting to leave empty-handed, Fig strode over to Bruna's desk and searched the drawers for something they could use. Official-looking fake work titles. Merchant registrations. Even a counterfeit wedding certificate. All forged with Bruna's paper magic.

The Tytan crest jumped out at her as she shifted some envelopes on the top of the desk. Four envelopes, each with fake names and titles inside. Her heart lifted slightly.

"Thank you, Bruna," she muttered, clutching the papers to her chest. They only needed three, but she wasn't about to look a gift shafra in the mouth.

She backed toward the door, tucking their new identities into a pocket. She stepped over the strewn papers until she crossed the threshold into the dawning sunlight. Vaelor mirrored her, following a few paces in front of the cottage.

Inside, Bruna lay amid her papers. Fig couldn't help but wonder if this was all her fault for siding with Dev. But the silverswords couldn't possibly have known that when they attacked her outside the tavern. Right? *Why* were they looking for Fig? More harassment from the 'swords? Or did they have some other sinister plan for mages now that Rhivven was on the throne?

And here, Bruna had only had her paper to defend herself.

Fig took a deep breath, and golden flames circled her fists. They felt good against her skin, not burning, but invigorating. She looked over at Vaelor, and their eyes locked for a second. He nodded.

It came from her heart, but the flames burst forth from her hands. She flung her fire at the cottage, two great plumes surging through the open door. The dry wood quickly ignited, and soon the flames feasted on the papers rustling about inside. They burned away in seconds, scattering ash and embers as they floated in the heat drafts. A whirlwind of burning paper.

Bruna had been hesitant about letting a fire mage live with her for a reason.

Fig turned her back on the crackling golden flames, her bag slung over her shoulder. She rubbed her fingertips together, and tiny sparks rained down on the long grass. She didn't care what else burned.

"Come on," she told Vaelor. She listened for the roar of the flames as they headed back into the woods, a sick feeling in her stomach. That could have been her in the cottage, lifeless eyes staring up at the ceiling.

Her footsteps must have slowed, because Vaelor was now several paces ahead of her. He halted, holding up a hand. An unnatural wind whistled through the brush up ahead...right where they had left the carriage.

A jolt ran through Fig as she darted to the left, mirroring Vaelor's movement to the right. Then, they both surged out from the brush on opposite sides of the carriage. Dev stood five paces from the carriage door, fending off half a dozen silverswords.

The bottom dropped out of Fig's stomach. She only hesitated for a moment, drawing in a deep lungful of air. Her nostrils stung with the coppery scent of the silverswords' enchanted blades, each moving at an unnatural speed as they advanced on Dev. He held them off surprisingly well, but the silverswords repositioned and trapped him with his back against the carriage.

"It's about time you two showed up," Dev called. "Where's Bruna?"

"She's not coming—"

The silverswords lunged, and Fig sent a burst of flame at the nearest man, who stumbled back and ripped off his helm, which had caught the brunt of the heat. Vaelor launched himself forward, swinging his massive sword right at Liess Astor, one of the 'swords who had accosted Fig last night. Liess held him off with her axe, but she was forced back several paces.

Before anyone else could move, Vaelor swung around and struck the second attacker with a sharp clang of metal that Fig could practically feel in her teeth.

"Right," Fig said, dropping back to Dev as she rubbed sparks between her fingertips. "Let's get you out of here."

One of the silverswords broke through Vaelor's defense and lunged right for Dev, sword arm raised high. Fig caught sight of runes etched down the center of the sword as the blade came right between her and Dev. She shoved Dev farther to the side—toward the horses—and threw a fistful of gold flames at the silversword.

He shrieked, though she wasn't sure where she hit him. His sword came down wildly on the carriage's coupling, freeing the horses from their restraints. Not appreciating the violence in the slightest, the two already white-eyed horses took the opportunity to dance forward.

"Dev, grab the reins!" she called, looking around. Vaelor was still fighting three silverswords; one of whom was Liess, who landed a heavy blow with her axe in the center of Vaelor's chest plate. Vaelor staggered a few steps back, his plate dented. Regaining his balance, he hefted his claymore and charged at Liess. Fig backed away on shaky legs.

Thankfully, Dev still had his head—literally and figuratively—and had already grabbed the loose reins before the horses could completely free themselves from the carriage harnesses and this nightmare.

Dev threw himself onto the black mare with ease, a burst of amethyst wind aiding him. Fig managed to hurl a fireball at one of the silverswords whom Vaelor had just tossed to the ground. Dev threw Fig the reins for the white mare, and she turned to mount the horse, but balked. The creature towered over her, its withers taller than the top of her head. She wasn't exactly known for her height, either.

"Fig!" Dev called, recognizing her predicament. He motioned upward with his hand in question. "Ready?"

She nodded, and a burst of wind bloomed under her feet, giving her the lift she needed. She managed to swing her leg over the side of the horse without too much awkwardness, though it had been years since she'd been lifted on a horse in this way. "Thanks!" She quickly settled herself and turned the massive mare to face the fight.

Liess was bearing down on Vaelor with her axe again, and Dev and Fig both sent magic at her in a blast of amethyst wind and gold fire.

Vaelor took the opportunity to extricate himself from the fight, kicking a man in the chest as he backed toward Fig and Dev.

With a panicked glance around, Fig realized their immediate predicament. There were only two horses.

Liess recovered with inhuman speed and was now striding their way; Fig swore she could smell blood on the silversword's axe, even though she saw nothing on it.

Fig held out a hand to Vaelor. "Get on!" she cried.

He didn't think twice and lurched up onto the mare behind her easily. His armor jutted into her back, but as she turned the mare and urged them east down the Mountain Road, she figured it was better to be slightly uncomfortable than dead.

<hr>

"I think we're safe," Fig said an hour later. These were the first words anyone had spoken since fleeing the carriage. A muscle twinged painfully in her neck as she checked behind them again, but the silverswords hadn't caught up.

"They must have been combing a nearby village on foot," Dev said, bringing his horse beside hers.

"I wouldn't mind going on foot from here," Fig muttered. Vaelor's armor had bruised a couple of places in her back in their hasty canter away from the village. She already had enough bruises. She hadn't seen the damage yet, but she could feel several that had formed on her jaw from last night's fight with the silverswords.

They slowed to a walk in the grass beside the Mountain Road, the road itself too dangerous to ride the horses very fast lest they snap an ankle in the deep cart ruts.

An edge of Vaelor's armor jabbed into her again, and Fig said, "Let's stop for a quick rest, shall we?"

Without waiting for an answer, she pulled the mare to a halt and slid off, her stomach swooping at the unaccustomed long drop.

"Where did you get these horses, anyway?" she asked Dev. "They're *massive.*"

"Well, when you're the height of a child..." he jested. She gave him a look. "They're Virenish Eifdales."

Fig raised an eyebrow and glanced at Vaelor, who she was pretty sure hailed from Viren. She had noticed the small braids in his fair hair, the same kind she had seen on the bodies of men and women in Viren after the Silver Slaughter. Before the funeral pyres had been lit, anyway.

The fact that a Viren had been made into a silversword was surprising to begin with, but to be directly guarding the crown prince? She'd give a gold vikker to hear the Bard's tale about how that came to be. How could Vaelor even stand the Verrences or the enclave after the silverswords had conquered Viren? And how could Dev trust Vaelor? If Fig had been taken from her country after the silverswords had slaughtered everyone who defied them, she'd fight tooth and nail to get revenge against whoever had ordered it. But he'd protected Dev so far, and even kept her from getting killed by the other 'swords. She'd just have to trust him for now.

Fig took a swig from the waterskin she'd grabbed from the cottage, then offered it to the others. She swallowed and wiped her mouth with the back of her hand. "We can loop around the Gold Wood and head south to Nova Istra this way."

"Why don't we just cut straight through the Gold Wood?" Dev said, handing the skin to Vaelor.

Fig snorted, hands on her hips. "Why—seriously? Because if I'm caught in there, they can execute us on the spot. Just because you're crown prince—"

"King," Dev corrected in a sing-songy tone. "And I'm not that dense, *Fairaleigh*. I don't know why we have that stupid law in the first place. Mages should be allowed in the Gold Wood whether they work for the crown or not. But here's my point: they just *tried to kill us*. So what does it matter if we go in there now or not?"

She opened her mouth and quickly closed it, warmth flooding her cheeks. "Right. Well. Yeah. Let's do it then. Hopefully, the place isn't already crawling with 'swords."

"Let's hope they know you're desperately paranoid and wouldn't want to step foot in there."

"Yes, yes," she drawled. "Congratulations, you outwitted me. In my defense, you robbed me of my sleep last night."

"Let's get moving then," Dev said. "Though how we're going to get on a ship—"

"I have them," Fig blurted out, taking the white mare's reins and walking ahead toward the forest. Everything that happened at the cottage came flooding back, and her throat began closing up. She had almost forgotten to tell him about the papers in the heat of their fight and flight. She swallowed, focusing on the gold leaves glinting in the sun ahead, a subtle glow ringing them, the magic almost calling to her.

"Have what?" Dev called, following with Vaelor.

"Papers."

"But you said Bruna wasn't coming..."

Vaelor muttered something, and Dev stopped asking questions.

Fig's stomach ached, and she tried to focus on that sensation instead of the memory of Bruna, lying on the floor amid her papers. She led her mare over to the line of trees at the edge of the woods and looked up. The auran trees towered over her, and the scent of magic wafted on the wind toward her like the sweetest honey.

There was only one road in and out of the Gold Wood, and it led directly to the Carriage House. But the trees were spaced far enough apart that they should be able to navigate it just fine. And unlike other parts of the Gold Wood, there were no fences here. Not many people used the Mountain Road by the abandoned King's Mountain.

Besides her brief foray into the woods last night, it had been two whole years since she'd been inside the forest—the place where it was rumored that Old Svoran magic originated.

Fig believed it. Her magic was always stronger even at the edges of the forest. The auran trees weren't just beautiful, they had a mystical quality about them. It wasn't like her magic *only* worked near the Gold Wood; she had traveled as far as the Notch, and her magic was the same as always. But something about the Gold Wood seemed to amplify it. It was too bad the trees only grew in this one place and not over the entire continent as they had in times of old. Their numbers only seemed to be dwindling as the years went on.

She took a deep breath, reveling in the honey scent that permeated the air. *The smell of magic.* At least, that's what it smelled like to her. Some mages thought it simply smelled like trees in here, and Bruna swore it smelled like apple blossoms.

"You know, I heard they're studying aurans in Tirnalore," she said, forcibly ignoring the cold that gripped her heart at the thought of Bruna.

Dev came up beside her, leaving Vaelor to trail behind with the black mare. "They study *everything* in Tirnalore."

"I'd love to go there someday," Fig said.

"Well, we might have to," Dev replied. "Depending on where the ships out of Nova Istra are bound. I say we take the first one heading for Tysaine, regardless of the city."

"Agreed. The sooner we get out of Tytan, the better."

They walked on in silence for a peaceful moment, though exhaustion was starting to creep back up on her. She had been up all night; her meeting with the blacksmith had been scheduled much later than she had wanted. She couldn't help but wonder where she would be right now if she hadn't shown up to Green's Tavern at all.

Dev caught her sighing, and said, "Look, I'm sorry about all this. And I'm really sorry about what happened to Bruna."

Her chest constricted. She nodded and continued staring straight ahead.

"Perhaps we should get some rest," Dev offered. "I know I—"

Rustling overhead drew them to a halt. Fig brushed sparks from her fingertips as she surveyed the trees, chin pointed up. She heard a lone bird, but farther off, somewhere above the trees.

"It's nothing," Fig said. "But let's keep going. We can rest later."

After that, they kept their footsteps as quiet as possible, ears alert for any sounds. Though the silverswords held an unusual superstition about entering the Gold Wood, they did frequent patrols for outlaws. It was the king's land, after all.

Vaelor seemed to harbor no ill will toward the woods, and he kept a keen eye on their surroundings as much as she did. *Maybe between the two of us, we can keep Dev alive,* she thought.

But how long would it take for him to reclaim his throne? Surely he wouldn't be safe until then, not unless he wanted to start a new life as a commoner in Tysaine or sail all the way to Pan Vidda or beyond. She couldn't picture him settling down to work basic magic—powering sails or working a dwarven blacksmith's bellows or something. She shook her head. No, ever since his brother had died, Dev had been groomed for the throne, even after they had discovered he had Svoran blood and couldn't be turned a silversword like his father.

She had always known he would make a fine king someday, a fresh start for Tytan. She just hadn't realized how soon that *someday* would come—and how quickly that future would be stolen from him.

After a little while, Dev dropped back to walk with Vaelor, leaving Fig to lead the way. She picked a path through the trees, hoping her calculations were correct and they were keeping enough distance from the Carriage House as they worked their way southeast. She brushed her arms every so often, marveling at the way they almost glowed with the magic of the woods. She could feel it coursing through her, as if the magic sang in her blood to use it. But she had to be careful. All the warnings from her training days surged back into her head. *Self-control is power. Your magic is nothing without control.*

When the sun began to set behind them, something darted out from behind a tree, heading right for Fig.

She held her hands up in front of her face. Fire burst from her skin, but she worked hard to keep it close. She didn't know exactly where Dev and Vaelor were and didn't want to risk an unexpectedly intense blast. The flames came frighteningly fast, licking up and down her skin harmlessly until she focused it into her hands.

Something sliced through her arm, a tiny stab of pain. She staggered a few steps back. Whatever was attacking her was small, but it was still right on top of her. Snarls and growls were coming from somewhere between her elbow and a flapping leathery wing.

"Hold!" Vaelor called.

Fig stopped flailing her arms, and tamped down on the sparks, though a few drifted from her fingers to dissipate before they even hit the ground. "What—is it?" she ground out. It was clinging to her forearm now that Fig had stopped moving. She thought she might be bleeding somewhere.

"Some kind of..." Vaelor began. "Ah..."

"Dragonet," Dev supplied.

"Dragonet?" she whispered. Arms frozen at an awkward angle in front of her face, Fig tried to peer around them to look at the creature, who was shaking and continually adjusting its position. All she caught sight of was a flash of green and gold. She was surprised its claws didn't hurt her as it shifted about.

She had only ever heard stories of dragonets. Someone might claim to have spotted one, but no one could ever prove it. The king's men said there weren't any around, and most everyone believed them. The size of birds, they could be just as dangerous as any fire mage. But this one looked afraid.

"What's the matter?" Fig asked the creature, though she didn't expect an answer. It was cowering on the back of her forearm, shifting from claw to claw.

Grieva.

The word filtered into her brain as if it had been spoken there.

"Oh," Fig gasped. "You can..."

The dragonet skittered around the other side of her raised arms, giving her a wide look. *Grieva!* it shouted in her brain.

"What's a grieva?" Fig asked Dev, still reeling from the shock of having it speak into her mind. "And did you know they can—"

A shrieking cry came from the direction the dragonet had flown from, and the three of them staggered back. Vaelor drew his sword in a sharp ring of steel. Fig clutched the dragonet to her chest, but it scrabbled its way up to her shoulder, finally freeing her arms.

Grieva! That's a grieva, you daft Svoran!

Fig's gaze hopped between the dragonet and whatever was crashing through the foliage toward them. What in the Bard's name was a grieva?

A shriek rang out again, and they all looked up. The horses danced, nervously picking up their hooves. The leaves rustled, and something massive and feathered burst toward them. Fig ducked, still harboring the dragonet. Dev threw a burst of amethyst wind at the creature.

The horses whinnied in terror, struggling against Vaelor's grasp as the creature sailed behind them and circled back. It clipped Vaelor's shoulder, knocking him into the white mare. The mare reared up, its hooves flashing dangerously in Vaelor's face, before dashing back the way they had come; the black mare crashed after her. Fig barely had time to register her shock as she whirled to face the creature.

The thing halted for a moment, hovering menacingly midair and readying to charge them again. By the brown and white feathers and wickedly sharp beak, Fig recognized it as a Vorse Eagle, albeit a massive one; the dragonet must have its own name for the thing. Its wingspan the size of a man, with sharp talons that could do some serious damage to anyone not wearing armor, the eagle flapped its wings, studying them for a brief moment.

Fig summoned a ball of golden flames with her fingers, meeting the eagle's menacing gaze. This thing had cost them their horses and terrorized this poor creature.

It shrieked and soared straight toward them. Fig turned her feet, preparing to hurl a burst of flame. But it soared straight over them, giving up on its quarry. At least it was smart enough to realize it was outnumbered. It disappeared, flying over the thicket and into the shadows of the auran trees.

Fig looked down at the dragonet, who was still shaking, curled into her elbow. It stared up at the fingers of her other hand, still engulfed in flames. "Oh, sorry," Fig said, extinguishing them.

It chirped at her. In her mind, she heard, *I take it back, Svoran. You're not daft after all.*

Fig snorted. "Thanks?"

"Um, Fig?" Dev said, waving at her with a quizzical smile. "Are you talking to that thing?"

The dragonet scrabbled around her elbow, releasing a low growl at Dev, who took a step back.

I'm not a thing, Svoran. And I can burn you just as well as she can.

Dev locked his eyes on Fig's, and she was sure he, too, had heard the words this time. Apparently, the dragonet chose who heard his words.

A smirk rose to Fig's mouth. "That's right, Dev, you heard—" She glanced down at the dragonet. "I'm sorry, can I address you by a name?"

The dragonet bobbed his green and gold head. *I am called Emrah. And I should thank you for saving me from the grieva. They are a menace when they think they can get away with it. But I had to pass through this part of the wood for—well, that's not important. And you are?* He let out a friendly chirp at her.

"Fairaleigh Veil, but I prefer Fig."

"Of course she does," Dev said, stepping forward, and lowering his voice. "Because *I* gave you that nickname."

When Dev didn't introduce himself, Fig felt a twinge of sadness.

Surely, he had never had to introduce *himself* in his entire life. "Emrah," she offered, "this is King Devryn Verrence, the proper ruler of the Rayvan throne. And Vaelor, though I don't know his surname—"

"Resbrok." Vaelor stepped forward, his hand still on his sword, and gave Emrah a respectful nod.

Emrah chirped, while Fig studied Vaelor a little closer. Resbrok? She had heard of House Resbrok. One of the last to fall during the Silver Slaughter.

The dragonet lifted his head and peered around at the golden auran trees before scurrying up onto Fig's shoulder with surprising familiarity. She guessed Emrah was too nervous to light on a tree branch just yet.

Since you saved me from the grieva, I will offer you something in return, Emrah said to them.

"Passage to the Hollow Isles would be great," Dev quipped, an annoying glint in his eye.

Emrah let out a growly chirp that somehow sounded condescending to Fig.

They heard something in the distance behind them, and Fig and Vaelor spun around. Her heart thudded in her chest, though her eyelids blinked heavily as she studied their surroundings. Had the silverswords finally caught up? Lack of sleep was *certainly* catching up with her. But after a moment of waiting, they dismissed the sound. Perhaps it was the horses crashing through the brush on their way to find safety.

"You know," Fig told the dragonet, "somewhere safe to hide would be great, until we can get our bearings."

Dev sighed wearily. "I could use some rest, too, but our priority is to get out of Tytan."

"I agree," Fig said, "but we've already lost the horses. You really up for a walk all the way to Nova Istra right now? Because I'm not. We need somewhere safe to hide out for a bit. Just a few hours, maybe."

Emrah flitted off her shoulder and clung to the side of the nearest auran tree, his claws navigating the seemingly smooth surface with ease. He had a curious glint in his eyes.

You need somewhere to hide? he said, the tone scratching scathingly across Fig's brain.

"W-well, yes, we just need a place—" she stammered, unsure as to why this request had drawn sudden ire from the tiny creature.

I should have known. Red sparks sifted down from his wings as he backed higher up the tree. Fig could feel power coming off him, a scent reminiscent of a forge reaching her nose. *The Feijowa sent you, didn't they? I don't have it! And even if I did, I don't owe them anything!*

"What?" Fig blurted out in confusion.

Emrah's eyes glowed like embers as he backed farther up the tree. *You're just trying to find my place, aren't you? And if you expect me to believe he's a king with the blood of Old Svora with only one guard, I'm a bird's ashes.*

Flames licked at Emrah's claws, and Fig knew she had to do something. She took a step forward, empty palms raised.

"I promise you, no one sent us. I-I don't even know who the Feijowa are. Do you?" she asked Dev and Vaelor. They shook their heads, staring up at the glowing dragonet.

"See?" she continued. "We just needed somewhere to lay low for a while. Dev truly is the king, but there was a coup, which is why we're on our way out of Tytan."

The fire licking Emrah's claws extinguished, but his eyes still glowed hot, so Fig went on, "Never mind. We don't want to bother you. We can find somewhere else to go."

She backed up, bumping into Dev's shoulder. "He kind of reminds me of you," Dev said in her ear, making her shiver. "All fire and spark."

"Shut up," she muttered.

But the dragonet wasn't giving up, not entirely. Sparks sifted down from him like a firework caught in the tree. Fig pushed Dev backward, gaining distance from the fiery creature. Vaelor crept alongside them with surprising quiet.

"We'll just leave," Fig said. Though she could probably protect herself from his flames, she had no desire to let the situation escalate that far. She had no idea what powers dragonets had. None of the stories she had read had prepared her for the creature to talk inside her head, after all.

They put a few trees in between them and the dragonet, and Fig felt a pang of loss for the horses. Wracking her brain for somewhere safe they could stop and rest or acquire some mounts, she took another step back, thinking it might be safe to turn and leave. She was disappointed the encounter with the dragonet had turned sour. What were the chances of coming across such a fascinating creature? How many people had ever spotted one before?

Dev was right, though; they needed to keep moving. She knew a mage in Ghorvost through Bruna, but she wasn't entirely sure she could trust him. She was about to suggest it to Dev when the dragonet darted toward them.

Fig froze, flinging a hand in front of Dev.

Wait! I won't hurt you, Emrah said, hovering at eye-level, green and gold scales glinting. *I'm sorry. But I'm fairly sure the grieva was sent by the Feijowa clan, and you three showing up looking for my place right after it had chased me seemed far too coincidental. But the Feijowa and those they employ wouldn't back down like you did. They kill or be killed.*

"Oh," Fig said. "Why are the Feijowa after you?"

Ashes, that's not important, Emrah said, snapping sparks from his wings with some finality. *I'll take you to the tower.*

"Do you think we can trust him?" Dev asked her an hour later. They were still following Emrah, watching for glints of gold and green scales between the leaves of the trees ahead.

"I mean," Fig said, rubbing her neck, "I suppose we don't have to go with him. I have a contact in Ghorvost, but he might rob us in our sleep."

Dev's chuckles died when he saw the look on her face. "You're serious?"

Fig rolled her eyes, not entirely sure herself.

"What do you think, Vaelor?" Dev asked.

The silversword behind them gave a soft grunt, perhaps surprised at being asked for his opinion. "I think a dragonet will have less political avarice than any person we might encounter."

Dev held up a finger. "Very true. And Fig can protect us if he gets too fiery—or are you forming a bond with the little guy?"

Fig stared ahead, looking for Emrah. She found him right away, even though he was a mere glint of green scales flitting east. "I think we're safe for now. He's just distrustful, a trait that is more likely to help us than hurt at the moment."

Just through here, Emrah told them a moment later. *Watch out for the whorlthorns.*

"Ahh!" Fig cried, the warning coming too late as a spiral-shaped thorn pricked her in the arm. She carefully extracted the thorn and flung it away.

Sorry. Planted them myself a few years back from some seeds I nicked from a thieving peddler. They keep most things out, though mostly just animals pass through this region of the Gold Wood.

Emrah had flitted back to hover a few inches away from Fig as she removed herself from the whorlthorn bush. When she was free, she inspected her arm, finding a small bloody hole from the thorn as well as what looked like a small bite mark with dried blood trailing down from it.

Oh, uh, sorry about that, Emrah said, flying closer. *I thought that grieva almost had me. I was out of my wits—*

"It's fine," Fig said with half a smile. "It's nothing."

Dev let out a low whistle, and Fig turned to see what had caught his attention. They stood at the edge of a small bright clearing that housed an old stone tower. Three levels of windows were set into the cylindrical structure, and it had a faded red tile roof. The sun shone down on the clearing, indicating it was later in the day than Fig had realized. A wave of exhaustion rolled over her. She would settle for a moldy patch of blankets or a bed of leaves at this point. Everything since the tavern last night was becoming one awful blur.

With a chirp, Emrah led the way toward the tower. They went down a sharp decline, as the tower was in the center of a dip in the land. The towering auran trees surrounding it hid the building from view. Dev beelined for the door, but Vaelor cut him off, a hand on his sword.

"Ah, right," Dev said, stepping aside.

Wordlessly, Vaelor entered through the arched wooden door first to scout the building. Emrah had disappeared, perhaps through an open window, leaving just her and Dev outside. Fig took a moment to scan the surrounding trees. Aside from the leaves of the aurans gently fluttering in an invisible breeze, they were alone. She took a deep breath, filling her lungs with the power of the Gold Wood and, for the first time that day, feeling a sense of calm.

Dev was staring in the other direction—toward what Fig thought was the way to Rayva. He looked tired, uncharacteristic exhaustion etched into his face. He had gone through much more than her in the last day, between his father's assassination and his own flight from Rayva.

His gaze still directed toward the capitol city, he said, "Do you think I'm doing the right thing?"

She swallowed, a big lump in her throat. For once, the facade of the cocky prince had slipped, revealing the boy she knew underneath. She reached out, paused, then put her hand on his arm. "I...I don't know. But I'm glad you came to me for help."

He snorted. "No, you're not. You're wishing I left you alone, not tangled with all of this."

She tightened her grip on his arm, and he finally looked at her. Something leapt in her stomach when his eyes met hers, but she pushed through. "I *am* glad. Besides, who else would you have gone to?" she ribbed. "You never got along with anyone else at the Carriage House from what I remember."

"Ah, well, difficult not to be jealous of a prince, I always thought," he said, and she was glad to see the humor glinting in his eyes again, making things seem almost normal.

But Dev had to go and dash that, adding, "Maybe that's why Rhivven turned on me—jealous, I expect. I mean, silverswords have their own benefits, but mages are superior."

"I agree," Fig said, crossing her arms. "And who wants to be magically bound to a weapon all their life?" she scoffed lightly, not wanting to offend Vaelor, who actually seemed all right for a 'sword. "Though the Bard knows I never expected to get up close and personal with so many silversword weapons."

Dev cringed and shook his head. "Yes, I never wanted that either. I didn't ask for any of this."

"I know."

Fig's worries about whether or not the silverswords still hunted them were forgotten when Vaelor returned and beckoned them into the tower. Fig gave Dev one last glance before they headed inside.

"I don't remember us commissioning any buildings in the Gold Wood," Dev said, gazing around the round room.

"Older than your father's reign?" Fig questioned. It was possible; the place did look quite old. The raised hearth on the other side of the room was massive, large enough to roast a whole pig. And in the center of the room there was a water pump and basin in the floor, though it looked bone dry. She doubted Emrah had been the one to keep the place looking as good as it did. Perhaps some humans had kept it up before him; there was no rotting wood or crumbling stones.

"Where did Emrah go?"

The dragonet flitted down from the second level and hovered by the staircase which curled around the inside of the tower walls.

Fig's bag slipped down from her shoulder. "I don't suppose this place has any cots? Though I'd settle for a soft bit of floor at this point..."

Dev gave her an incredulous look, but Emrah snapped his wings and zipped upstairs. *Come look at this!* he told them.

Shrugging, Fig headed up after the dragonet, running a hand along the stone wall as she rounded up the stairs to the second floor. She saw Vaelor secure a large bar over the tower door before she reached the next level, and her shoulders relaxed a little.

The second floor's walls were lined with dark wooden alcoves, each the size of a person, stacked two high. "Was this a barracks of some sort?" she wondered aloud. She approached the alcoves, frowning at the ropes woven into what looked like a net or hammock in each of them.

I don't think so, Emrah said. *I've always thought maybe it was a post for the Sisters of Morgha, but it's older than any of the modern places of worship I've seen.*

Dev tapped a finger over his mouth. "It's no Mar Nevan, that's for certain. I'm surprised the silverswords never discovered this, though. It would make a fine guard tower."

"Well, let's hope they never discover it," Fig said, using a hand to test the web of ropes on the nearest bed. They seemed sturdy enough and softer than sleeping on the wooden floor. Whoever had bunked here before might have put a thin mattress on the ropes, but she could sleep in it like a hammock. "If you don't mind…" She yawned.

"I don't," Dev quipped, "Vaelor? Do you mind?"

Over by the stairs, Vaelor nodded, falling into a guarding stance.

Relief swept over Fig, and she crawled into the nearest netted bed. She didn't even care that Dev chose the next alcove right at her feet. The last thing she saw before losing the fight to sleep was the glint of green and gold darting upstairs.

A stretch pulled through her body, and her foot caught in something. No wait. She was tied up! Her eyes flew open as she struggled to get free. Panic seized her. Why were her feet restrained? The silverswords must have found them!

She twisted, trying to free herself, and tumbled to the floor. As her hands hit the hardwood, remembrance slammed into her. These were only the ropes from the bed. Throwing a dirty look at the netted bed frame, she tried to gracefully get to her feet, hoping Vaelor hadn't noticed the extent of her struggle. He remained motionless by the stairs, which was just as well. The man was guarding the king after all; at least, he was competent.

Dev was still asleep. She smirked, wondering if he would suffer a similar awakening, since one of his hands had slipped through a gap in his bed's netting. But she let him rest, studying the peaceful look on his face for longer than was strictly necessary.

A few slit windows let in a dose of dusky light, and she wandered up the staircase, hoping to find their host.

The top level of the tower was lined with more bunks, but the windows were larger, and Fig spotted the sun setting over the auran trees. It was the ceiling that made her pause in wonder. Her mouth dropped open as she took everything in; the wooden slats lining the top of the tower were embedded with a random pattern of gemstones from garnets and rubies to affervatz and lyrestone, with scorch marks all around them.

She gazed at it for several moments before realizing that Emrah was indeed elsewhere. This must be his collection, like the legendary gold and silver hoards of the mythical dragons that dragonets were supposed to have descended from.

She was drawn to a window facing the sun, which had just set in a burst of gold on the horizon. The Wood spread out before her, and the view still took her breath away, no matter how many times she had seen it from the Carriage House. The golden leaves of the auran trees glinted in the remains of the sun's rays, twinkling as they swayed in a gentle breeze. She glanced south.

What would her life have been like now if she had just stayed at the Carriage House?

King Verrence would still be dead, she reasoned. But what of her...and Dev?

She turned her back on the woods and gazed up at the gemstones, her attention catching on a large black and white stone at the center of the ceiling.

She thought back to her earlier conversation with Dev, and her cheeks warmed. Why had she told him she was glad he asked her for help? Her life had been torn to shreds since that moment. Even if the silverswords weren't after *all* mages, Fig had most certainly been identified as someone Dev would seek for help; she would never be safe in Tytan until Dev was on the throne. And then there was Bruna.

Crossing her arms over her chest, she shut her eyes briefly. It wasn't Dev's fault Bruna was dead. It was Rhivven's, and Liess Astor's, and all those other bloodthirsty briigards.

Tytan deserved a better king. It deserved Dev.

The flap of leathery wings drew her attention to the stairs, where Emrah was zipping up to the top floor, sparks dripping from his claws.

We have a problem.

Heat surged in her veins at the sudden fear his words instilled, and she had to yank back the flames that leapt to her fingertips. Now was not the time for her amplified magic to jump out like this. "What— they found us? We should go wake Dev—"

"Awake, actually," Dev said, bounding up the stairs. "And confused." Vaelor came up hastily behind him. "I'm awake in spite of the bed that tried to strangle me, and confused as to why *we* have a problem. I looked out the window just now and saw a group of dwarves encroaching on the tower; last I checked, I only mortally offended the silverswords by my existence. Explain," he demanded of Emrah.

The dragonet's wings darkened to a deep emerald, but the edges were rimmed in glowing red. *I—the Feijowa—I told you they were after me—*

Fig rushed back to the window, keeping out of sight. "I'm surprised they would enter the Gold Wood."

"A great hideout," Dev said dryly to Emrah, "when no one would trespass onto the king's land, unless your pursuers were desperate enough. Why are they after you?"

The dragonet swooped over to Fig's window, not landing on the sill, but clinging to the side with his claws to remain out of sight.

It's personal, he told them, bristling.

Vaelor shifted to look out the next window, armor clinking slightly.

"It's about to become real personal," Dev said, "for *us*. We shouldn't have come here. You said it was safe."

Emrah hissed. *I thought it was safe, too, Svoran. But it's not you they're after.*

"And yet when they find a king, plus a king's ransom"—Dev glanced up at the gems in the ceiling—"I don't think they'll be picky about who they're after. I can see why you're not into having visitors."

A snort of sparks almost like laughter came from Emrah, and he looked up at Fig.

If this is the Feijowa, and they find him, they won't let anyone leave alive, he said, and somehow Fig was sure he was speaking only to her. *You need to get him out of here. I saw his magic. He can leave by these windows.*

Fig nodded, her gaze flicking between Dev and Emrah as her heart raced. Sparks danced at her fingertips as she wondered what the dwarves might do when they discovered the Verrence heir and his allies here. Whose side would they choose? The bloodthirsty silversword currently on the throne? Or the heir to two centuries of 'swords? Considering it was Tesvier Verrence who took the Mountain from the dwarves those two long centuries ago, the odds weren't in their favor either way. They needed to leave.

She glanced at Emrah, thinking of how he spoke in her mind. *What if she... Can...Can you hear me?* Fig tried.

Sparks burst from the little dragonet, and he stared at her, golden eyes growing wide. *You...You're talking in my head. H-how are you doing that?*

She snorted, then said, *Same way you do it, I expect. It was...surprisingly easy. You've never had a human in your head before?*

He lowered his eyes, shaking his little head. *No, actually. But a matter for another time. Get King Devryn to escape out the window. I'll go down and try to settle with them. This is my tower after all. But if the oil hits the flame, you and the warrior will need to fight your way through the front.*

"The front?" she blurted out. "How many of them even are there?"

Dev and Vaelor looked up at her, startled, unaware of her secret conversation. They were both gazing out separate windows at the forest, no doubt watching the approach of the dwarves.

"A dozen," Vaelor said, "but they've slipped into the shadow of the tower now."

Fig sidled away from Dev and over to Vaelor, and Emrah dropped onto her shoulder. "These Feijowa or whoever, they're not going to let us go if Emrah can't placate them," she told him quietly. "We might have to go out the front."

Incredulous, Vaelor stared down at her, the almost haughty look on his face partially obscured by blond braids.

But your boyfriend can go out the window, Emrah told the two of them.

Fig twisted to look at him. "What? Dev? N-Not anymore, you nosy dragonet."

A faint snuffling sound came from him as he darted over to Dev's window.

"You and the king?" Vaelor whispered, his voice low.

"Not anymore," Fig all but growled. "Let's just do this. Dev isn't going to agree to leave us easily. Have you ever fought dwarves before?"

Vaelor grunted. "I've fought all manner of men. I don't think it matters what they look like."

"It doesn't," Fig responded. "It matters what they can *do*, and what they *know*—" A thump came from downstairs. "They're trying the door. Emrah, are there any other entry points down there?"

Another bang. Fig somehow felt all the way up on the third floor. What were the dwarves doing to that door? She locked eyes with Vaelor.

Emrah grumbled, *They're going to break my blasted tower, that's what they're doing. I'm going down.*

"Are you sure?" Fig blurted, suddenly worried. Sure, this was his mess, and sure, he seemed like he could defend himself with fire, but he was so little.

Sure as a fire burns, he said with the sound of his wings snapping together.

In a flurry of glittering gold and green, he flitted down the curving staircase grumbling so all could hear, *Wait! I'm coming, don't break the damn door down.*

The pounding immediately ceased. Tension rippled over Fig's skin as she sidled over to the top of the stairs, where Vaelor had positioned himself. A wave of a metallic scent wafted over her, and she eyed his claymore. She couldn't explain it, but she could feel some kind of magic at work near him and his Welded weapon. A slight chill ran up her spine, and she looked toward Dev, who was still at the windows, surveying outside.

A faint mechanical sound came from downstairs, a gear turning, followed by several light thumps. Fig exchanged a confused glance with Dev, and then they heard the door open. Emrah must have some kind of mechanism to open the door.

"Where are you, you little flying snake?" a deep, resonant voice spoke first.

I'm right here, you dolt.

"Who are you calling—"

Another dwarf interrupted, "Calm yourself, Collis. Where is it, dragonet? That's all we're here for." The voice was just as resonant, but not as deep.

I don't have it. I never had it. And I didn't take your money, so I don't know what you're doing here trying to break down my door.

The first dwarf, Collis, snarled. Fig heard scuffling and the sound of Emrah's wing's fluttering. "Ballast! We know you went into the Mountains. Our scouts saw you."

Fig frowned. What had the dwarves engaged Emrah to retrieve? And in the Mountains that the dwarves were forbidden from returning to? She heard more scuffling and a squeal from Emrah.

I did! I went in. But I couldn't get to the chambers you told me—I— there were those fire-blasted silverswords in there.

"In the Mountain. *Inside the Mountain?*" Collis demanded. "More ballast," he spat. "Even the king knows the swordsmen are useless in the Mountain. Only the dwarves have any power there! The little flying snake's got it around here somewhere, probably with all his other treasures."

The other dwarves were silent, and Fig knew they were probably imagining what Emrah's hoard might hold. Tension spiked up from her gut to her chest, and she allowed the slightest slip of fire to flicker on her hands, working hard to control the fiery burst that *wanted* to come out. *This gods-blasted amplification,* she thought. *I'll be lucky if I don't burn down Emrah's tower if it comes to a fight.*

"This isn't our fight," Dev said close to her ear, somehow appearing at her shoulder. Her flames took that opportunity to try to double, so she extinguished them quickly.

"I know, but if they're about to search the tower, we can't be discovered up here. *You* can't."

More footsteps downstairs, and a strong scent of earth pervaded the tower, even on the third floor. Fig wondered if all the dwarves were now inside.

No. I swear to you, Emrah was saying, *I never retrieved it! I never even* saw *the ash-blasted thing!*

"He probably wants to sell it to the king for a higher price!" Collis raged.

"Aye!" several booming voices agreed.

"Oy!" the somewhat calmer voice interrupted again. "Pipe down, all of you. You'll draw the 'sword patrol with that racket. They're not far off through the wood. Dragonet, no harm will come to you if you just give it to us or let us search the tower. But if you resist..."

Vaelor and Fig shared a look. The silversword strode over to Dev, stopping a foot from the king, and said quietly, "Sir, it's time for you to leave. Now. The mage and I will meet them in arms while you go out this way—" He gestured to the window on the opposite side of the tower from the front door.

Dev narrowed his eyes. "No. I'll stay with you—"

Fig imagined she could feel Emrah's nerves buzzing with tension. She had never crossed arms with dwarves before, but their uncanny knowledge of metalsmithing and anything earthen made Fig wonder if they were somehow connected to the magic of Old Svora too.

She waited, breath held, for Emrah's response.

No.

The calmer dwarf sighed. "Very well. Feijowa, take it all."

Fig put her palm on Dev's chest, and pushed him toward the window, but he planted his feet. "You can't risk yourself," she hissed. "Listen, *you're doing the right thing.*"

Unspoken words hovered between them from their conversation earlier. She watched his eyes, and she could see the realization there. He was king. If he were to reclaim his throne, he would need to be *alive* to do so. And they had no fight with these dwarves.

"Fine," Dev said, finally looking away. "I'll meet you at our spot—"

She opened her mouth, shut it, and nodded. She knew the place, deep in the Gold Wood.

A deep cry of pain rang out. It was a cry she had heard before when flames met flesh. Emrah was fighting.

"Go, now!" she told Dev. He hesitated for a second. Something heavy crashed downstairs. Fig took a deep breath and flung her arms around Dev, evoking memories she had long ago suppressed. His arms went around her waist, and he said, "Fine. Looks like I'm the one leaving now, eh?"

She pushed him away. "Maybe that makes us even. Now get out of here! Vaelor and I will handle this. And I'll see you soon."

Dev nodded at Vaelor, squeezed Fig's arm, and flung himself out the window.

Crashes echoed up from the second floor, quickly followed by the sound of feet on the stairs leading up to the third floor. Without hesitation, Vaelor descended, his armored bulk filling the stairway.

Fig followed, not wanting to get trapped alone on the top level—*she* certainly wouldn't survive a jump from the window. She leapt off the curved staircase halfway down, avoiding Vaelor and the dwarf he crossed swords with. Even though Vaelor was much taller, the dwarf was holding his own, his thickly muscled arms expertly wielding a wide short sword. Fig summoned flames to fling at the dwarf searching the alcoves, scorching the bed she had slept in and just missing the dwarf who lunged out of the way, rolling across the stone floor. In one fluid motion the dwarf rose, hefting an axe in a battle-ready position.

"Treachery!" Collis, the dwarf fighting Vaelor, intoned. "I told you as much, Firth!"

The dwarf ready to take Fig's head off—Firth, evidently—replied, "I can see that, Collis, no need to point out the obvious." The dwarf grunted, swinging the axe again.

"Wait!" Fig said, her fingers sparking with flames. "We don't want to hurt anyone. We're not even involved with Emrah!"

"On a first name basis with the little piece of ballast, though, ey?"

Collis said through his teeth as he shoved Vaelor back up a step.

Firth finally lunged at Fig with the axe, and she sidestepped, releasing a shower of fiery sparks and making the dwarf back off.

"We only just met him!" Fig insisted, holding up golden flames in defense.

The dragonet in question darted up the stairs, a pair of dwarves pursuing him, their weapons raised. Fear shuddered through her. The windows on this level were too small to escape from, even if she wanted to. And there was no way through the half dozen dwarves at the head of the staircase. They all moved toward Fig, weapons glinting in the faint light that trickled through the windows. She didn't think her flames would hold off this many.

"Fairaleigh!" Vaelor called. Sensing the danger, she whipped her head around. He held out a burly arm, hand outstretched toward her. At that moment, a searing pain ripped through her middle.

Firth's axe sliced down in a whirl of movement, causing her to spin toward Vaelor. As she lost control of her lower body, she felt Vaelor grab her hand and lift her up onto the open staircase. Pain like she had never before experienced sliced through her. It was as if the lower half of her body had been torn off entirely.

Out of her mind in pain, and not caring about the amplification of her powers, she gathered flames in her hands and flung them down at Firth and the other dwarves advancing on their retreat.

They had nowhere to go but up.

She didn't mind Vaelor's armor poking into her as he carried her up to the top floor; in fact, she could barely feel it, could barely feel anything but the taste of honey on her tongue.

Her eyelids fluttered, and she spotted a gold and green glimmer on the ceiling, prying off some of the stones embedded there. She let out a deranged snort. *Is now really the time to save your precious stones?* she called to Emrah.

Before you burn the place down, yeah, he shot back.

With another snort, her head lolled onto Vaelor's dented chest plate. Then suddenly her whole body was jostled violently, and more pain ripped through her middle. She opened her eyes—when had she closed them?—to see that she and Vaelor were perched on the windowsill.

"Wwwhat?" she slurred. "N-no, we won't make it."

Vaelor had already sheathed his sword—probably when he was jostling her—and now prepared to jump. "We will," he grunted, and jumped.

Awareness jolted her back to her senses in the most unkind way. She clutched him painfully as wind whipped around them. Her brain felt like it had been ripped out of a drunken slumber with a freezing bucket of water, as fearful thoughts reeled through it. *Were silverswords really so powerful that they could survive a third story drop? What if she fell from his arms upon impact?*

And most troublesome of all, *why couldn't she feel anything in her torso or legs?*

The wind howling around them as they fell had the faintest amethyst color to it. The moment she realized that, she passed out, only to be enveloped in velvety blackness.

Her eyelids floated open, and she saw a canopy of gold leaves. They were under the aurans, Dev sprinting beside Vaelor as the silversword continued to carry her. Fig's eyes fluttered closed once more, but not before catching sight of green and gold scales above them.

The next time her eyes opened, Vaelor had slowed his pace to a walk. He looked down at her, and she shifted around to look for Dev, who was still walking beside them.

"Can you walk?" Vaelor said. "It doesn't look—"

"No, I don't think I can," Fig said shakily. "T-thank you."

Vaelor merely grunted.

"Perhaps we should stop," Dev said, a hint of fear in his voice.

"What?" Fig mumbled. "Is it the Feijowa again?"

"No," Dev said. "It's you..." His face loomed over her.

"Wwwhat?" she slurred.

Dev's hands were covered in blood. "Set her down," Dev told Vaelor.

"Why din—*didn't* you g-go to the meeting place?" Fig demanded drunkenly.

"By the Bard, we need to do something for this wound," Dev said above her. Somehow, there were leaves in her fingers. "Do you have anything?"

"Not me," Fig said, with a deranged giggle. "Left my bag at the tower. Dwarves'll take it. Pro'lly stealing Emrah's gems too."

"Shh, love," Dev said. "I was asking Vaelor."

The leaves in her hand got all soft and fuzzy. In fact, even her face felt soft and fuzzy, like a newly spun blanket. One of her hands stroked her face, and she was about to tell Dev to give it a feel, too, when Emrah darted into her vision. He was *so* sparkly.

"Do it," Dev said to Emrah, causing Fig to furrow her eyebrows.

What were they doing again?

Vaelor stood a pace away, his back to them, no doubt watching for the dwarves.

Emrah hovered over her stomach, and a red glow emanated from his center. Fig smiled at the beauty of the creature. She was so glad they had found him. But when sparks began to pool at his claws, and he opened his mouth, her chest sank in fear and all feelings of softness became jagged shards of reality.

"W-wait—"

Fire burst from Emrah's mouth right to Fig's stomach, where pools of blood seeped from the wound. She tore her gaze from the gore, her brain ripped from the pleasant void she had been sinking into and tossed into a cold reality that burned like frostbite.

Abruptly, the fire stopped. Though she had looked away, she hadn't been able to shut her eyes through the ordeal, so she had stared at Vaelor's feet planted a few paces away.

Emrah fluttered up a little higher, an apologetic look on his scaly face. He landed on Dev's shoulder, and they both looked down at her expectantly.

"I'm really s-sorry about your gems," Fig slurred to Emrah, before everything went black.

A gentle swaying rocked Fig, enveloped as she was in a fuzzy blackness. But the fuzziness brought back a sour memory, which jolted her into consciousness.

Her body was no longer in that awful drunken state from the dwarf slicing an axe through her stomach. She wanted to be thankful for the return to her senses, except now her entire midsection was wracked with pain. A groan escaped her, and she clutched her stomach.

Opening her eyes, all she could see was scuffed silver metal, and she became aware of arms wrapped around her. She lay across Vaelor's lap, and the rocking sensation she had felt before was the horse they rode upon. "Did the horses come back?" she muttered, blinking.

"Oh, by the Bard, she's still delirious, isn't she?" Dev said, concern in his clipped tone.

Fig raised her head to look around for him. He was walking beside the horse—apparently there was only one—and Emrah flitted above them, gold and green scales dull amid the green leaves of the trees.

Green leaves?

She struggled to sit up. Vaelor caught her movement and lifted her with a steady hand until she was upright. She had to lean against him with his armor once again poking into her back, but relief that she could sit outweighed any annoyance. With the pain of the cauterized stomach wound assailing her, she hadn't even noticed the lack of magic from the Gold Wood. Gone was the gentle glitter raining down from the aurans. And gone was that feeling of truly belonging to a place of beauty, despite what it did to her magic.

"Where are we?" she demanded. "And I'm not delirious."

Emrah chirped from above them, something Fig took for a laugh, and a smile rose to her lips. But when her hand drifted to her stomach, which was bare, the edges of her tunic torn and burned, her face went blank. She yanked her hand away from the skin, having felt the ragged, burned skin there—cauterized by dragonet fire.

"Just outside Nova Istra," Dev answered hurriedly, tearing his gaze away from her stomach. "Does it hurt?"

Without looking at it, she tried to survey the damage. It was nowhere near as painful as before, when she lay delirious on the forest floor, but now it hurt in a different way. She had traded one wound for another. At least, she wouldn't bleed out. And none of her organs had come spilling out; she didn't think they would have cauterized it if anything on the inside had been damaged.

The memory of Emrah's flames scorching her skin suddenly burst to the forefront of her mind, and she flinched. Dev put a hand on her leg in concern.

"No, it's fine," she said. "Well, it's still painful, but it's manageable."

"You're not just saying that, are you?" Dev said.

She met his eye. "It's manageable compared to the pain I was in before. Thank you all for saving me." Sudden emotion welled up as the words came out. They had saved her—there was no doubt in her mind that those delirious moments in the Gold Wood could have been her last, her blood spilling out of her.

Vaelor grunted in acknowledgement, and Dev muttered something unintelligible—rather unusual for him.

Emrah, though, circled back nearby, and said, *You're very welcome, Svoran. It was the least I could do considering the situation you all ended up in.*

"Please, just call me Fig."

Emrah chirped and darted onward. She had to admit, it was nice to have the little dragonet around—he was funny, and he kept a sharp eye on the woods, which were getting murkier by the minute. She stared after Emrah, wondering. In the tower, she had reached out to him in her mind, just like he did. Could she do it again? Or was that part of the delirium? At this point, she couldn't recall.

I'm sorry about your tower, she tried.

Emrah bobbed in the air and shot a glance back at her. *Ashes, I forgot you could do that! Well, I suppose it's my own fault for getting tangled with the Feijowa.*

Fig shifted her position. *What were they after, anyway?*

Just some dwarven dagger. I thought maybe I could pull it off, but like I told the dwarves, I ran across some silverswords…inside. I've only ever seen them patrolling the entrances. And even I dare not get caught in there by the king's men.

She glanced down at Vaelor's arm still wrapped around her, keeping her from slipping off the horse. *I wonder what they were doing there? Well, Dev's king now. We can find out when we get him his throne back.*

Oh, Emrah said. *Is that all?*

Fig snorted, and Dev looked up at her, a crease between his eyebrows. "Something funny?"

She darted a look at Emrah. "Oh, just something Emrah said." She wasn't sure why, but she didn't want to tell him about her newfound discovery that she could speak into Emrah's mind.

He cocked a hand onto his hip. "He telling you secrets now?"

She chuckled weakly but couldn't come up with a clever retort.

Dev shook his head, returning his gaze to the rapidly darkening sky they could see between the lacework of branches and leaves.

"How long since the sun set?" she asked. "Any idea how much farther?"

"Not long," Vaelor rumbled from behind her.

She clenched her stomach accidently when she tried to shift to a different position, and she hissed, drawing a hand to her torso while avoiding the damaged skin.

"We should get you to one of the red sisters as soon as we get into the city," Dev said.

"If we have time," Fig responded, "and we might not. I'll be fine. Burns have to heal on their own."

"*Fine,*' she says," Dev chided her. "You just had your stomach sliced open and then cauterized by dragonet fire!" He blanched at the look on her face. "They'll fix you up in an instant."

"I'm sure they would," she said, "however, I don't particularly want to go anywhere near the Sisters of Morgha at the moment. How do you know they're not aligned with Rhivven and his coup? Close as the red sisters are to the 'swords."

Dev shook his head, *tsking.* "I doubt it. The 'swords have always had the greatest respect for the sisters."

Fig pressed on. "Well, obviously. They need the sisters for their rituals—so why wouldn't they include them in their schemes?"

Dev cleared his throat and gave Fig a pointed glance toward Vaelor, as if she were offending him. She wrinkled her brow, side-eying the silversword.

"The sisters are safe," Vaelor said, adding his say in the matter. "Even in Tysaine, they have them, but they're on no one's side but their own. And Fairaleigh's right, the silverswords *do* need them. If anything, Rhivven will be at their mercy."

"What do you mean?" Fig asked. She spotted a slight haze of lights in the distance, peeking out of the ever-darkening sky. "There it is." She pointed. The lights from Nova Istra dissipated the gloom where the Hollow Sea met land.

Panic filled her core as she thought about the bag she had left at the tower, but after frantically patting her pockets, she located the papers she had taken from Bruna's desk, with neither blood nor burn marks on them. A melancholy relief swept over her, and she patted them again.

"The silverswords need the sisters more than the sisters need them," Vaelor explained. "The ritual to make a silversword can only be done with the blessing of Morgha. Though, of course, all the blood the silverswords spill is good for the sisters' practice too. So either Rhivven will be begging for Mother Savidah's favor, or he'll make the mistake of demanding it."

"Huh," Fig said. "I suppose so." Her only experience with the red sisters had been on the few occasions she'd been injured badly enough to require a real healing—the kind that only magic could fix or, as the sisters would say, only the healing waters of Morgha could fix.

Unlike Fig's mage blood that allowed her to use her own unique magic—every Svoran-blooded mage was different—anyone could join the sisters and be taught to heal. But it was all a mystery, how common folk without a drop of mage blood could use water to heal people. Of course, the sisters always demanded coin for their healing services. Any respectable village had a fount blessed and maintained by the sisters, holy wells said to contain a drop of water from great waters of the holy city of Mar Nevan, which had been blessed by Morgha herself when she walked the Svoran continent.

But not everyone could afford the services of a red sister, nor reach them in time.

Fig had thought it all nonsense until she was ten and broke her arm, only to have it healed at the village fount in the time it took for the sister to pour water over it.

Her stomach twinged as she moved again, and she resisted touching the mottled skin. "If we have time, maybe we can visit a fount," she muttered.

"This is perfect," Dev said as the gates of Nova Istra came into view. Darkness had fallen, obscuring their faces. "We'll go straight to the docks, maybe barter the horse for a meal and a change of clothes, if we can."

Fig looked down at the creature in question. It wasn't one of the Virenish horses. "Where did this horse come from, anyway?

"I had Vaelor borrow it from a farmhouse," Dev said.

"Borrow?" Fig chided.

"If they knew who they were lending it to," Dev said with an impish smile, "they would have gladly gifted it to me. They would have also been glad to give me this." He held up what looked like a horse blanket.

Fig squinted at him. "Which is...?"

"In the dark, it'll pass for a cloak," Dev said, tossing it to Vaelor. "And I'm glad it's dark. I don't think it would disguise all that armor during the day."

Vaelor caught the blanket and slowed the horse to a stop. A surprisingly gentle gauntleted hand landed on her arm, making her suddenly very aware of Vaelor's proximity. "Do you think you can ride alone?"

"Um...oh!" Fig blurted out. "I will try."

Dev looked worriedly up at her.

"Shouldn't Dev ride, though, so he can escape quicker, if it comes to it?"

Vaelor murmured. "Too obvious a target."

"Of course," Fig said, side-eyeing Dev as he watched her. "I'm not going to topple off, you know."

He held up both palms. "Forgive me for my concern."

A twinge of guilt rippled through her, and she frowned. "Sorry. And thanks. I'm just...disoriented is all. And *starving*," she said, suddenly realizing it. "Farmhouse didn't have any food you could borrow?"

Dev frowned. "We tried, but the farmer chose that exact moment to let his dog outside. But a tavern meal will fill our stomachs much better than the stale bread and cheese I was trying to *borrow*."

Fig's mouth watered at the idea. She stayed atop the horse just fine, though the ache in her stomach was growing. It was hard to tell the hunger pains from the burning.

Perhaps we should get you to the Sisters of Morgha first, Emrah said to her. *Or at least, find some silversap to treat the skin.*

Her eyes darted to Emrah, who was flitting through the trees, looking almost like a bat. *What, you can't read my thoughts, can you?*

Aloud, Emrah snorted, sparks sifting down from him. No. Definitely *not* like a bat.

No, Svoran, I merely saw the look on your face.

They reached the edge of the trees, and Emrah swooped down onto Fig's shoulder. Even his light weight made her wound twinge. She hadn't had a burn this bad in a long time.

She looked across the field toward the twinkling lights of Nova Istra, the port visible over the city's low buildings. Light danced on the waters of the Hollow Sea, reflected from a few lanterns hanging from the heavy forms of ships that appeared like sleeping giants.

"Is he coming with us?" Dev asked, pointing at her shoulder.

Fig looked at Emrah. "Oh. I had assumed—"

It's never intelligent to assume, dear Svoran, Emrah said. *But I would like to come with you. I'm not sure what I have left at the tower to go back to, and I need to let things cool off with the Feijowa. And you're an entertaining lot.*

"Happy to entertain," Dev said wryly. "But stay hidden, if you don't mind. The last thing we need is to draw unwanted attention."

A twinge of melancholy struck her at the reminder that Emrah had lost his home to the Feijowa. She gave him a sad smile. Just like she had lost her home to the silverswords—for that was exactly how she thought of it. They had come looking for her, not Bruna, she was sure of it, but it was all her fault Bruna had been caught in the crossfire.

We can be homeless together, Fig told Emrah.

He bumped his head against her neck, something she took as an endearing agreement. But then he told her, *Oh, I have every intention of getting my tower back, someday. And maybe even that sword the Feijowa want so badly.*

Fig frowned, but kept her thoughts to herself, not at all sure that was a good idea. But he was his own dragonet, and who was she to criticize?

They crossed the field, Fig still mounted. Emrah tucked himself into the swathes of fabric from her hooded tunic. She was again surprised that neither his claws nor scales did anything to irritate her skin.

Vaelor had donned the horse blanket, securing it as a makeshift cloak, and stowed his helm in one of the horse's saddlebags. Now Fig could see the sides of his head were shaved, and the thin blond braids woven throughout his hair. Some had metal beads braided into them, while others had small decorations she couldn't quite make out in the darkness silhouetting him.

The gates of Nova Istra were growing ever closer, the lanterns now blazing down at them. The lack of silversword presence at the gates was normal and confirmed that word of Rhivven's coup hadn't traveled far yet. Then, a little thought wormed its way into her head; would *anything* change with Rhivven as king?

Sure, King Haemond had been a silversword, intolerant, bloodthirsty, and condescending—or at least, that was how Fig had seen him. Would Rhivven be any worse?

She shook her head. Of course he would. King Haemond had had at least one scrap of tolerance in his body: he had kept Devryn as his heir. He had wanted his mage son to ascend the Rayvan throne. And they had killed him for it.

As she watched Dev nervously adjust the hood of his cloak against the blinding light spilling from the gate lanterns, she had no doubt in her mind that Dev would be a better king than either of those silverswords, and she was doubly glad that mages couldn't be turned 'sword.

Despite the darkening hour, Nova Istra was alive with light. Lanterns hung from shops, and silver glinted from the eyes of the few patrolling silverswords they passed. But they were most interested in the bobbing lights of the harbor. Vaelor pointed out that they should trade the horse first, in case they needed more money than the three of them had scraped together for their passage.

Fig had shifted her tunic around to hide the hideous cauterization. She was coming to forget about the pain unless the tunic brushed the burned skin. They had more important things to take care of first. It wasn't the first time she'd been burned.

She held her breath as she approached a man outside a fairly respectable-looking stable. Everyone had agreed she should be their spokesperson; both men were too noticeable should anyone come questioning later. Vaelor hung back with Dev, and Emrah nestled further into Fig's hood; he was so light she often forgot he was there.

After exchanging the reins for a handful of coins—a little less than she wanted, but considering it wasn't actually *their* horse, she let it go— the three of them headed straight for the harbor, drawn to the glow.

There were three ships in the water, so the chances of one going to Tysaine seemed rather good.

Fig was again elected to speak to the harbormaster. "I guess I'll do all the work, ey?" She elbowed Dev in the ribs.

He rolled his eyes. "Hey, if you think they won't recognize me, I'll be glad to go."

Fig darted a look at Vaelor, whose Virenish presence would be noticeable even without the armor bulging under his horse blanket. She patted her papers and coins before heading to the harbormaster's office: a small wooden stand in the center of the docks with mullioned windows on all sides and a large lantern sitting atop, which shone out over the waters.

"Good evening," Fig said to the harbormaster.

The man grunted. "What?"

"We're looking for passage to Intervale," Fig said. "I don't suppose any of these ships are heading there?" She had decided to name the northernmost city of Tysaine, considering that "anywhere out of Tytan" would sound a little suspicious.

"At this time of night?" the harbormaster nearly growled.

"Oh, no, whatever you have leaving next," she said, trying to infuse her words with nonchalance. She started to twitch her fingers but thought better of it. She didn't want to accidentally summon sparks here of all places.

"Well, why didn't you say so," he muttered. He thumbed through a massive ledger, the papers thick and somehow crispy from the salty air. Fig wondered what Bruna would have thought of the paper—she always had an interest in how paper aged.

"No Intervale. Sorry. But there's a rig heading for Tirnalore at dawn. Tirnalore'll have more ships going up to Intervale than you'll get here."

"Oh, right," Fig said, her face brightening. "That works. Thank you!"

A smile actually crossed the surly man's face, and Fig's smile widened.

"Passage for three?" she asked.

"Aye, sure, they've plenty of room. That'll be nine vikkers."

Nine gold vikkers lighter, Fig joined Dev and Vaelor, with three sheaves of parchment bearing their false names and the name of the ship, the *Narrow*. The harbormaster had pointed out the ship in question, and it certainly lived up to its name, though what it lacked in width, it made up for in length. Fig could see why they were eager to take on more paying passengers. Probably not much cargo fit in its hold.

"We've got til dawn," she told her companions, waving their tickets.

Dev's eyes lit up. "Thank the Bard," he said with a sigh. "Shall we find a red sister for you next?"

"Let's just go collapse in a tavern for a bit," Fig said. The idea of having a proper meal and a seat perked up her senses. The burn wasn't bothering her right now, but she was sorely in need of some food.

"You don't have to ask me twice," Dev said, steering Fig off the dock, Vaelor a hulking shadow behind them.

Are you sure you don't want to get healed first? Emrah said, and she somehow knew he was only talking to her. His tail twitched inside her hood, wrapping itself around her neck.

Are you worried about me? Fig replied, hiding a small smile. *I'm fine. It's twinging a little, but it can wait an hour. I'm starving.*

Dev quickly steered them to a tavern a few blocks over, evidently having spotted it on the way to the docks hoping they would have time. "And if the food's as good as the smell promises it to be," he said, "perhaps we can purchase some to take with us. I abhor ship fare." He shuddered.

"I'm more interested in finding some extra clothes if we can get some." Someone had tried to clean Fig's tunic while she was unconscious, but the bloodstains hadn't fully washed out. "You couldn't steal any of those from the farmhouse?" she muttered to Dev.

"Vaelor looked," he said, opening the door to the tavern. "There wasn't anything nearby."

Fig glanced at Vaelor, suddenly wondering exactly *who* had cleaned her tunic.

A snort came from her collar. *Your neck is flaming*, Emrah said to her. *Something got you all bothered?*

She ducked her head and darted her gaze away from her companions, looking toward the bar. Her mouth watered at the smells drifting on the air. Before she could take it all in, Dev was handing her a pint of ale. She accepted it with both hands and followed the two men to a table in the back corner, one of the few open ones. Fig somehow ended up with her back to the door, which she didn't like one bit.

"I sent for some food," Dev called over the chatter of the other patrons.

Fig nodded mutely and sipped her ale. She would eat anything at this point, but the smell of the tavern was promising. The ale had an immediate impact on her empty stomach, the fuzzy feeling stealing over her far quicker than usual. She set it down to wait for her food. Dev had no such reservations and was halfway through his by the time three steaming plates arrived. The twisting hunger in Fig's stomach had only been made worse by the lone sip of ale.

Nothing for me? Emrah voiced.

Dev sent a panicked glance at Fig, his gaze darting to her neck. Fig smirked.

"Uh...sorry...I..."

I jest, Svoran. I caught my meal in the woods.

Snorting, Fig grabbed the bread roll from her plate, sliding it through the gravy slathered on her meat and vegetables. A groan escaped her as she swallowed, then tucked into the rest of her meal. The ale was fresh and washed the fare down perfectly.

Calm settled on her shoulders; it was a wonder what a full stomach could do for one's nerves. That, and having their tickets secured to cross the Hollow Sea and only a few more hours to wait in this gods-forsaken country. She could probably even buy some silversap elixir for her burn from one of the vendors before they boarded the ship and skip the trip to the red sisters.

Fig took a swig of ale and wiped the remains of the gravy from her plate with the last of her bread. "I don't know if it's because I nearly died or if this is the best tavern in Tytan, but—"

The tavern door banged open. "Oh gods," Vaelor muttered.

She froze. "What? What is it?" The noise level of the tavern hadn't changed, so she desperately hoped it wasn't the silversword crew that had been following them. That was the last thing they needed.

By Drakioryn's scaly claws, Emrah cursed. *I'm sorry.*

Fig grasped at her connection with Emrah. *Sorry for what? Can you see who it is?*

It's them again. The Feijowa. Only two came inside.

Fear seized Fig's gut—the exact place where her mottled wound rippled across her stomach. *Are you sure?*

Dead sure, Emrah replied, his tail tightening around the back of her neck and sending a shiver down her spine.

Fig saw Vaelor move his hand toward his sword, and she reached across the table to grab his arm. She caught his eye, the unmistakable silver glint sending a jolt through her core. "Wait," she said. "Maybe they don't actually know we're here. Lower your hoods, the two of you."

They complied, Dev slumping in his chair like a drunkard—the sight believable since his second tankard was long since empty. A wave of copper-tinged restraint wafted from Vaelor, but he remained still, picking at the food left on his plate, while attempting to look casual.

The dwarves're hailing the barman, Emrah reported. Fig could feel him twitch beneath the curtain of her hair. She hated having her back to the door, but at least she had Emrah to look out for her.

We're in a public place, she said, *they can't do anything to us here.* She was unsure who she was reassuring—the dragonet, or herself.

The food in her stomach had turned sour—or maybe it was the ale; either way, a powerful stomachache had her clenching her gut. Maybe it *wasn't* the best tavern in Tytan after all, she thought to herself.

The patrons around them continued their carousing, while everyone at Fig's table sat in tense silence, waiting.

A minute passed, though it seemed like twenty, when Emrah blurted out, *They're just getting ale. They wouldn't be getting ale if they thought we were in here, would they?*

Fig looked at Dev, uncertainty on his face. "Maybe they don't know we're here," she said carefully.

"They might if we keep acting like someone died," Dev said. "We're drawing more attention than a tagor at a tea party."

A snort rippled from Fig, then she clenched her stomach, face scrunching in undeniable pain.

"What is it?" Dev demanded.

"I..." She could no longer form words. The pain lanced through her insides like her guts were being wrung by an iron fist.

Suddenly she didn't think it had anything to do with the quality of the food.

Hands shaking, she brought her fingers to the wound under her tunic. The outside felt fine, if horribly disfigured. The problem was on the inside.

Emrah, she called weakly. *Something's wrong with me.*

His tail tightened, and she could tell his words carried to the others. *We need to get her to the Sisters of Morgha. Now!*

Fig bowed over her middle, barely registering what was going on around her. This was even worse than the initial pain, probably because this time she wasn't delirious with blood loss.

"But the dwarves—" Dev began.

Don't know we're here, Emrah said.

"How do you know?"

I don't, Emrah snapped. *But if we don't get her insides healed now, she'll be dead on the floor before they do notice us.*

Vaelor stood, going to Fig's side and lifting her in his arms. Pain lanced through her gut like knives.

"Vael—" Dev sputtered, "Are we really—" He glanced around at the patrons beside them, then hurriedly changed his expression. "A bit too much to drink, I'm afraid," he slurred. "Best be getting some fresh air for the lass."

Then a whirl of colors and light passed through her vision, as she buried her head in Vaelor's hard, armored chest.

Hurry, Emrah's voice flitted through her head.

Suddenly, everything was dark. But her stomach still ached like it was about to rip itself apart, so she didn't think she was asleep. *Outside. We're outside*, she thought.

"Wh..." The effort to speak was too much. Too painful. *What about the dwarves?* she asked Emrah, immensely glad for their mental connection.

Didn't notice a thing, Emrah said, worry coating his words, but she didn't think it was about the Feijowa from the way he clung to her shoulder.

A whiff of blood reached her nostrils, except it wasn't blood at all, only a group of passing silverswords, their coppery scent assaulting her nose in the night air. Her gut clenched again. Would Liess Astor and their crew be looking for them in Nova Istra? It was the nearest port city from their most recent encounter. They must know Dev was going to flee Tytan.

Gods, I can't wait to get out of this chapter of the Bard's tale—and this country, she thought, unsure if she sent her words to Emrah or the gods themselves.

MAIREAD

Mairead Joiros wiped the tears from her eyes with the sleeve of her red robe, then crammed her journal into her bulging leather satchel.

She had nowhere to go. She was no longer welcome in her own chapel, let alone in the order of the Sisters of Morgha. The brand now burned into her hand would forever remind her of her failure.

"I should have stayed in Mar Nevan," she whispered to herself. Now she could never return. She took one last look over her chapel and the holy fount she had served for less than a year. She hadn't even made it a year outside the convent. All because of *the incident*.

The holy mother's letter had made it clear she wasn't welcome back at Mar Nevan. Hidden magic in the letter had also slowly burned a brand into her palm as she read it. The holy sisters at Mar Nevan knew how to do many more things with the sacred waters than just heal.

She eyed the tears on her sleeve. These were sacred waters, too, she'd always thought, much like the waters resting in her fount here inside the chapel. She put a hand on the side of the round stone fount. It wasn't the grandest in Tytan, but it had been hers to serve. She had blessed; she had healed.

But she had also questioned far too many times. Such was her curse, since she was little. It had earned her many a beating; she should have learned a lesson by now, but somehow she couldn't. Now, after *the incident*, she shouldn't be surprised that they burned her out of the order.

She squeezed her eyes shut, keeping those memories at bay. The incident only revisited her in nightmares now.

She went to the open door to extinguish the red lantern hanging there, but her heart seized. The paper lantern she had painted when she first arrived, its intricate designs derived from long hours of meditation in front of the fount. A beacon in the night for those who sought Morgha's holy waters. She swallowed the lump in her throat and decided to leave it burning. Morgha's light shouldn't be extinguished even if Mairead's had been snuffed out.

As she stood in the doorway of the chapel, someone turned down her alley—a group of someones, actually. Two people held up a third. She groaned. It wasn't the first time she had seen such a sight.

"Help!" one of them called. "She needs help!"

Mairead pulled back in the doorway, out of the red lantern's light. She looked at the fount, tears springing to her eyes again.

"I—I can't," she tried.

The group passed into the red lantern's light, and she could see they had shifted the girl into the big man's arms. She was seized up around her stomach in a bad way. And something she had never seen in all her eighteen years curled around the woman's shoulder—a green and gold scaled *dragonet*.

"What in the Bard's—" she began, then clamped her mouth shut. "No, I'm sorry, I can't—"

"We'll pay anything," the other man said, lurching up close to her, the faint scent of ale on his breath.

"What's wrong with her?" The words slipped from her mouth before she could think. Curiosity always got the better of her. Always to her detriment.

"A stomach wound," the large man said in a resonant voice. "It was cauterized, but we think the inside—"

The injured woman groaned, hunching over her stomach even more.

The little bird-sized dragonet shifted to the top of her shoulder, and the most curious thing occurred.

Will you help her or what?

The words burst into her head, but they weren't her own thoughts. Somehow, she knew it was—"Y-you? Did you just...?"

"Yes, yes. It was him," the second man said. "Will you help her or what?" He repeated the dragonet's words.

"I-I can't," she hedged.

"You keep saying that," the second man said, "but you're a red sister, aren't you? The fount's right there! Why in the name of your goddess of healing and death won't you help her?"

She looked down at the palm of her hand, at the brand burned there. These people didn't know what it meant. The brand shouldn't stop her from healing this poor woman. Except...

Had the blessing of Morgha left her, or was it simply the blessing of the holy mother at Mar Nevan?

Weren't they one and the same?

"All right," she snapped, then said more gently, "All right. Bring her to the fount." She could at least try.

The man carrying her rushed inside, and Mairead heard armor clinking. She tried to peer at his eyes, but his hood was pulled over them. She didn't think the silverswords would want anything to do with her after *the incident*—they had clearly already gotten their revenge by forcing the holy mother to strip her of her title. Perhaps this man had nothing to do with them, considering he was hiding his armor. But that didn't mean Mairead didn't give him a wide berth as she surged around to the other side of the fount.

The man laid the ailing woman on the stone floor by the fount. Mairead strode over, reaching for the wooden ladle resting there. She scooped up the water and poured it over each of her hands, cleansing herself for the work she had been tasked with. Her heartbeat thumped a deafening rhythm in her ears.

Was she still able to heal?

The poor girl would likely die soon if Mairead couldn't.

There were two other founts in Nova Istra, but the nearest was a thirty-minute walk up Cere Street. Mairead took a deep breath, and dipped her ladle once more, drawing up the waters.

One of the men had pulled the woman's tunic aside, revealing blotchy, burned skin over a hideous wound. From the way the woman curled in on herself, groaning anytime her position was changed, Mairead knew that whatever was wrong was inside her guts.

Mairead passed her left hand over the water in the ladle, not wanting to use the hand with the ugly brand on the palm. The backs of both hands displayed red tattoos she had been given at Mar Nevan, a string of sigils and runes that helped her call upon Morgha for aid—or so she had been told. She whispered the words as she passed her hand over the water, closing her eyes briefly, and sending a silent prayer to Morgha, the mother of them all. *Please, please help me heal her.*

She pulled away her hand and poured the water over the woman's stomach.

"Fig, please be all right," the smaller of the two men said, crouching by the woman and holding one of her hands. There was something familiar about his voice, but a hood covered his face too.

Mairead got to her feet and retrieved another dipper full of water. Curiosity getting the better of her, she tried to peek under the smaller man's hood.

The dragonet flitted into the air at that moment, and his voice penetrated her mind once more, *Well? Is it working?*

Mairead crouched beside the woman. The burns and the wound were completely gone, revealing the soft skin of her stomach. But Mairead's surprise that her healing magic still worked was short-lived, because the work wasn't done; she still had to save this woman. She placed her left hand on the skin and poured a ladleful of water over her hand and Fig's stomach. Mairead whispered the words again, willing the magic of the waters deeper, deeper into the body, into the tissues, and into the organs.

The sigils on the back of her hand flared a glowing red, and Mairead closed her eyes. She repeated the chant, sending it deeper. Crouching by the woman, she thrust the ladle at the swordsman. "You—fill this."

Without question, the man did as she asked, holding the full ladle with reverence upon his return.

Mairead repeated the process twice more, until Fig's eyelids fluttered open, and she rolled onto her side. Immediately, she vomited onto the cobblestones.

The reek of beer and partially digested food assailed Mairead's nose, and she politely turned away to retrieve one of the many cloths folded on the shelf behind her. The large swordsman took it from Mairead and wiped Fig's mouth.

Coughing, Fig took the cloth and wiped her own mouth, raising herself so she could sit, and then draping her arms across her knees. She looked around, as if suddenly realizing where she was. Then a hand flew to her stomach, and she caught Mairead's eye with a panicked expression.

"Water closet's through there," Mairead told Fig, helping the woman stand and pointing her toward the washroom. Mairead watched Fig walk away, and her chest swelled with emotion. Her magic still worked. She still had Morgha's blessing.

The questions that flooded her brain increased tenfold, but they would have to wait for another time. For now, it was enough that she could heal. Except she was still not welcome in her own chapel.

The men glanced at each other as Fig disappeared, and Mairead got more white towels to clean up the mess on the floor. "I've seen worse from stomach wounds," she said while she wiped, "but I've never seen the outside cauterized like that. My guess is that her guts got nicked, very slightly, and maybe when food tried to go through them...?"

"Ahh," the smaller man said. "Guess we really should have come here before the tavern, eh?" he said to the other man. "Now I know not to trust her when she says she's 'fine.'"

No kidding, the dragonet said.

Mairead snapped her gaze to him. "And him..." She trailed off in wonder, finally getting a good look at the dragonet. Covered in tiny green and gold scales, he was about the size of a bird, but from the stories she had heard, a hundred times more dangerous. "What exactly are you doing with—"

At that moment, someone else shuffled into the alley, a group of two this time. And between their armor and the silver glint from their eyes, she knew exactly who they were.

CHAPTER
10

Fig splashed water on her face, feeling remarkably fine. Well, as fine as a person could feel after heaving up the entire contents of their stomach. Twice.

The washroom had no looking-glass, but she could see and feel her stomach, her smooth skin somehow softer than before her axe wound. Her insides seemed to be working as well; everything came up, but without any lingering pain like before. She was certain the hollow feeling in her stomach was because it was completely empty and tender after ejecting its contents, but she wasn't ready to put food back into it just yet.

She heard raised voices outside the washroom and smoothed her tunic back down; Dev and Vaelor were probably worried about her. The way they had looked when she had returned to consciousness would haunt her for more than a few nights. It was clear she had been on Morgha's door.

When she opened the door to the washroom, several things happened at once.

Emrah spoke in her head, *Trouble—careful!*

Two men had appeared—silverswords. One grabbed the red sister by her flaming red hair, and she squealed. Dev and Vaelor stood frozen, the fount and silverswords between them and the door.

The other silversword spotted Fig coming out of the washroom; he raised his blade toward her, and she held her hands halfway up.

"Mairead, you little red kirich," the silversword holding Mairead said. "I was told you wouldn't be practicing anymore this side of the Notch, eh? What's going on here?"

"I—" the girl squeaked.

The other silversword glanced away from Fig and yanked one of the red sister's hands up. A strange round rune was burned into her palm that Fig had never seen before. The red sisters typically had tattoos on the *backs* of their hands. "Oh, see this, Maelchior? They've burned her out of the sisterhood. She *isn't* supposed to be practicing."

Fig furrowed her brow, unsure what this was about. She spotted Emrah, who was perched on the top of a tall shelf. She looked away, so as not to give away his location, then pushed into his mind, *What in the Bard's inky fingers is going on?*

These two just burst in—I have no idea, he replied.

She knew this wasn't really her business; this girl seemed to have history with these particular silverswords. But Mairead had just pulled Fig from the brink of death, out of Morgha's outstretched arms, practically.

Fig took a hesitant step forward, still careful to show her hands. "She...she wasn't practicing," she lied. "It was my fault. I had too much ale and needed a washroom. That's all we were here for."

"Ballast," the stout one spat. "What's this on the floor, then? We've seen healings before, we're no fools."

Fig's gaze slid to the dirty towels in the red sister's hand, and the wet cobblestones. Her expression twisted wryly. "It's vomit, gentleman. I didn't make it to the washroom...the first time, anyway. You can check back there to see the second round, if you like." She jabbed her thumb toward the washroom, and a deranged part of her hoped they would. It would clear her exit, at least.

The stout one rolled his silver-ringed eyes, and Fig thought maybe they'd just leave. Then he put his hand on his sword, and that bitter copper scent rose to Fig's nostrils. Damn.

Emrah, she called, on edge.

I'm ready, the dragonet replied.

Vaelor shifted infinitesimally, ready to guard Dev.

The other silversword sniffed, and his nose wrinkled. "It does smell like puke, Maelchior."

"Shut it," Maelchior snapped, and threw the red sister to the ground. Mairead caught herself on her hands and knees. "Either way, this little red kirich is done here, stripped of her station. And she's currently trespassing at the temple of a sacred fount. I think she needs to come with us to the barracks."

Still on her hands and knees, Mairead's eyes filled with terror. There was no way Fig could let these silverswords take the girl. She didn't know what Mairead had done to wrong them or what that brand on the girl's palm meant, but Mairead had healed Fig. Even if she *had* been kicked out of the sisterhood, she deserved better than whatever ill-doing these men clearly had planned. But as usual, the silverswords took what they wanted.

Sparks ignited at her fingertips, but before Fig could do anything, both Vaelor and Dev stepped in front of Mairead. Fig darted forward to grab Mairead's arm.

The girl got to her feet, looking around at the three of them. "You shouldn't—" she hissed.

"Shh," Fig said, pulling her another step back. "You saved me. Let us save you."

"But you don't know what—"

"Don't worry," Fig said with a ghost of a smile. "We're already doomed."

"Step aside," Maelchior growled. "This doesn't concern you." All four men had their swords drawn, but Fig could see the idiocy of it all. There was no room for any of them to maneuver in the small chapel. She pushed Mairead around the other side of the fount. Then she had an idea.

Emrah? Tell Dev and Vaelor to back down. We need to get out of here.

The two silverswords surveyed Dev and Vaelor, who were still hooded. "And who are you two, anyway?"

I told them to back down, Emrah said, *but it doesn't look like they're going to.*

No kidding. They can't talk back to you, eh? I wonder, why is that? she asked, knowing now really wasn't the time.

Maelchior lunged forward, bringing his sword around in a neat half arc, which was heading right for Dev. *I guess they can maneuver in here just fine,* Fig thought.

Vaelor protectively elbowed Dev aside and met the blade with his own, his bulk easily throwing the other man's sword off. But they weren't silverswords for nothing, their bodies and minds enhanced by the connection to their weapons. Suddenly Vaelor was locked in a close fight with the two men. A whiff of copper emanated from the 'swords, making Fig think of blood, though none had been spilled. Perhaps the copper scent was what caused the rumor that the silverswords' weapons craved blood.

Dev inched backward until he found Fig, and the two of them crept closer to Mairead, who was shaking, alternating her gaze of terror between the fight and the brand on her palm.

Maelchior rammed his shoulder into Vaelor, throwing him into the side of the fount, where Vaelor's back struck the stone. He righted himself, roaring as he cocked a fist back and sunk his gauntleted hand into Maelchior's face.

The silversword spat out blood and responded with an elbow to Vaelor's face, which threw off his hood.

At the sight of Vaelor's silver-ringed eyes, Maelchior let out a roar. "I thought as much! Who are you? What are you doing interfering here?"

Vaelor didn't answer; he only blocked the other man's blade which had come swinging from the other direction. Vaelor caught it with his armored forearm and threw him off. The other man went clanging into a shelf, knocking towels all over the floor. It was clear Vaelor's gift as a silversword was in his strength.

Fig glanced at the open doorway. The two silverswords seemed distracted enough by Vaelor—who Fig knew could hold off half a dozen more silverswords. She would have to trust him.

Emrah still hid at the top of the shelf. She didn't blame him. In the middle of a city, surrounded by humans, this was probably the last place he wanted to be.

Go, Emrah told her. *While it's clear.*

What about you? Fig asked, giving Mairead a push toward the door. "Let's go," she hissed aloud.

The red sister snatched a bag by the door, then she, Fig, and Dev dashed outside. They got a few steps clear of the door when a crash rang out, the force sending a shock up through Fig's feet.

Vaelor lay on the ground in the doorway, half in and half out of the chapel. Maelchior loomed over him, but Vaelor wasn't moving. Maelchior raised his sword in both hands, ready to deliver a final blow. Vaelor wasn't wearing his helm, and his exposed throat panted with the strain. Sparks leapt to Fig's fingertips without a thought, as bile rose in her throat.

"No!" she cried. Gold flames burst from her hands. She flung them at Maelchior. Though she was out of the Gold Wood, her flames still felt off. She reined them in, not wanting to set fire to the chapel. Through the flames, a little shadow flitted outside into the night air, impervious to the heat. Emrah landed on Fig's shoulder and bumped his head against her neck. She released the flames, and Maelchior stumbled backward, falling to one knee. He had shielded his face with his forearms, but instead of getting up, he remained crouched over, groaning.

Fig lunged over to Vaelor and yanked on his hand. "Get up, you big Viren. Let's go."

Vaelor lurched to his feet, uncustomarily stumbling as they shuffled out of the alley. "Thanks, goldfire," he mumbled.

"Where to?" Dev asked when they reached the corner.

"Think we can make it to the ship?" Fig said as they turned right. "Hide out nearby until it departs?"

"As long as they don't suspect we're headed there," Vaelor said in a low voice, still quieter than usual.

"Are you all right?" Fig asked.

"Fine," he grunted. "Knocked my head on the door."

"There's a ship?" Mairead asked hopefully. They had reached a street near the tavern and slowed down to blend in with the few passersby going about their business. Vaelor adjusted his makeshift cloak, draping it as best he could around his head again.

Fig nodded, her face brightening. "And I don't know if you need it, but I've got a fourth identity you could use—"

"Identity? Why would I— Who are you people, anyway?"

Emrah snorted. *Uh oh*, he said gaily.

"Uh—well—we can talk about that later," Fig said. "I—er—mistook the situation. I thought you were wanted by the silverswords or something."

The harbor was in sight now. Fig could see the *Narrow* sitting at the dock. She glanced back at the street they had just come out of. Still no sign of the two silverswords. Of course, she didn't know how badly Maelchior had been burned, but his companion might have gone to raise an alarm.

"I didn't *think* I was wanted," Mairead said, also glancing over her shoulder as she absently rubbed the brand on her palm. "I just... The holy mother... Well, I'm no longer a red sister," she admitted.

"We gathered as much," Dev said, patting her back.

It was late enough in the night now to be considered early morning, and dawn was probably only an hour or two off. Barely discernible pre-dawn light had begun to creep up on the sea's horizon. Nervous relief washed over Fig. They were almost there. They just needed to get on the sea, and they would be clear of this mess—for a while, anyway.

The wide docks were wreathed in shadows, except for the harbormaster's cabin with its guiding light shining out at the sea. After slipping through just a few more aisles of cargo, they would reach the *Narrow*.

"It doesn't look like they followed us," Fig said as they stepped onto the edge of the docks. "We can just get on the ship. It's not like they know who we are."

No, but they *do.*

Fig turned just in time to spot the group of dwarves heading down the street. Five of them this time. She pulled everyone into the shadows.

"Bard strike it! What have we done to deserve this?" she muttered to no one in particular...or perhaps to the Bard himself.

The dwarf with the axe strode at the front. Firth, Fig remembered. She clutched her newly healed stomach, wondering if she was imagining the pain again. She shook her head. No, it was healed. She was better than new.

"Who're they?" Mairead asked.

"Shh," Fig hissed. *Emrah, why don't you tell her?*

Several moments passed as Emrah silently filled in Mairead, who stared at Fig with wide eyes, except when she glanced down at Fig's belly. Fig grimaced at her, shrugging.

What are you telling her? she demanded of Emrah.

The dwarves were slowly trawling the lane by the docks. Nova Istra was the nearest port to their altercation in the Gold Wood. Of course the dwarves would assume this was the first place they would run.

"*More* silverswords?" Mairead griped.

A jolt went through Fig, and she followed Mairead's gaze. A large contingent began filling in from the northern end of the lane, silver glinting in the pre-dawn light.

We really shouldn't have come here, she thought.

A hand grasped Fig's shoulder; it was Dev.

"They can't possibly know you're here," she said, trying to soothe both their worries. She covered his hand in hers briefly. "Maelchior and his friend probably just summoned the rest of the 'swords at the barracks after we attacked them." As soon as the words left her mouth, she knew there hadn't possibly been enough time for that. But Dev already looked panicked.

Vaelor shifted closer to Fig, and the sight of his silver-ringed eyes sent a chill down her spine. "It's the most logical port," he said in a low voice.

Fig clenched her fists. He had come to the same conclusion as she had. It was the most logical place to look for anyone fleeing Tytan—particularly a recently overthrown monarch. This could very well be a force sent from Rayva. *How could we have been so stupid?*

Emrah's voice came in, *Do you want me to scout over there? It looks like whoever is leading them stopped to argue with someone.*

No, Fig replied. *It's not safe for you. Not for any of us.*

The dragonet let out a snarl and left her shoulder, swooping among the shadowy cargo on the docks.

"Damnit, Emrah," Fig muttered, eyeing the mass of silverswords congregating. It seemed like they were waiting for something.

"More've been arriving every day for the past two days," Mairead said, eyeing the crowd.

"Two days?" Fig echoed. She shot a glance at Dev.

He shut his eyes for a second. "Briigards. *Briigards!*" he hissed.

"What's—" Mairead began.

Fig put a hand on Mairead's arm. "Well, Mairead, since it seems like you're in just as deep as we are, I'd like you to meet King Devryn Verrence."

"K-King? Devryn?" Mairead stuttered. "B-but what about—?"

"My father was murdered by the silverswords," Dev said quietly.

Just as Emrah swooped back onto Fig's shoulder, a clang of metal rang out near the head of the silversword gathering. Civilians who had work to do before sunrise had already begun to fill the streets by the harbor.

A heavily armored man grabbed hold of a streetlamp, swinging with unnatural ease onto the stone base, sword held aloft.

It's nothing to do with us, Emrah told them.

"Like hell it isn't," Dev growled.

"Who's that?" Fig said.

"Djuren," Vaelor said in disgust.

At the same time, Emrah said, *He's one of the 'swords I saw in the Mountain.*

Standing above the crowd, Djuren pulled off his helm, tucking it under his arm. His face was meaty, and his thick graying eyebrows furrowed. Raising his sword, he called, "People of Nova Istra! Hail! Our new King Rhivven of Rayva demands your allegiance this day. The briigard Haemond who would put polluted blood on the throne is dead. And his son with Svoran blood has fled Tytan like a coward, putting shame to the long line of silversword ancestors who ruled from the Rayvan throne for centuries. He is no longer prince. And he will *never* be king. A new dawn is here. Long live King Rhivven!"

Strangled yelps and cries rang out from those assembled. Fig scanned the silverswords in a panic. *Rhivven isn't actually here, is he?* she asked Emrah, terrified.

Emrah growled. *I didn't see anyone with a crown. I think they're just here to spread the news and assert their dominance.*

The people of Nova Istra who had wandered over to see the commotion appeared torn. Fig could barely make out their faces, but the cries ranged from actual tears to the occasional shout of agreement. The tang of fear was thick upon the seaside air.

Either way, she didn't see how they were going to get out of this. There was no way they could defend themselves from that many silverswords, no matter how skilled Vaelor was. And the Bard only knew how they would get on the *Narrow* in all this mess. The light on the seaside was growing weakly, at odds with the dark malevolence taking place on the edge of the docks.

The crowd stopped clamoring, and Djuren seemed satisfied with their obedience.

"Is that it?" Dev muttered incredulously. "That's *it?*"

Fig could see why he was outraged; but how was a crowd of unarmed citizens supposed to disagree with a massive gathering of silverswords who could cut them down in an instant?

As Djuren shifted his position to get down, a sharp movement occurred in the crowd. An axe flew straight for Djuren's unarmed head.

The entire mass of silverswords churned like a deadly whirlpool of blades and death, moving first to defend Djuren, then to seek out the attacker.

Mairead clung to Fig's arm, and Fig grasped the girl's hand. They were a mere twenty paces from the maelstrom, and if discovered, would be just as dead as the attacker surely was now. At least *someone* disagreed with Djuren's pronouncement.

"Wait, is that..." Fig trailed off, spotting the man at the center of the silversword's ire. "No." It wasn't a man at all, but a dwarf.

It is, Emrah told them, letting out a squeak. *It's Firth.*

Firth stood alone, a surprising five feet from the 'swords. Fig could see more than a few men nursing injuries a few paces away—silverswords whose skills likely lay in their strength, rather than their speed. Her respect and fear of the dwarf grew.

"Treacherous louts!" Firth called. "The lot of them! You can never trust a silversword. They'll cross ya soon as kill ya! Rhivven killed King Haemond to get the throne for himself, not for some ballast about protecting it from mage blood! If you don't believe that, you're just as softheaded as these silvery briigards!" Firth's voice then lowered, no doubt uttering a personal insult or threat to the 'swords nearest him.

Dev grabbed Fig's shoulder again. "Now would be a good distraction to get on the ship, eh?"

Fig glanced at the ship, the glow of the horizon becoming even more evident. They were losing their shadows, but surely all eyes were on the dwarves.

Emrah landed on her knee, and she hesitated, glancing between him and Firth, who was now swinging widely with the same axe that had almost killed her.

"Wait, you aren't seriously considering—" Dev said.

But the thought of what Emrah had told her about silverswords in the King's Mountain—what had long ago been the dwarves' ancestral home—gave her pause. What *were* the silverswords doing there? Firth had said the silverswords couldn't be trusted. Did it have something to do with the artifact the Feijowa had wanted Emrah to procure?

She turned to look at Vaelor, who was staring at the scene with a wary eye.

"What do you think?"

A low grunt rumbled from his chest, and he met her eyes. "I think it would be safer for all of us if these dwarves didn't make it."

"Right?" Dev agreed, clapping a hand on Vaelor's armored shoulder.

But Emrah was looking at her curiously. *Actually,* he said to all of them, *I'll never get paid for that artifact if they're all dead.*

"What?" Fig hissed, nearly searing him with a glance. "You said you didn't have it! You almost got me killed! Twice!"

Emrah chirped, flapping backward off her knee. *I don't! I don't have it! Yet. Relax, Svoran. But I do know exactly where it is. Do you really want to turn down an invaluable bargaining chip with the dwarves when you're trying to reclaim your throne?*

Dev groaned, rubbing his hand on his forehead. "Fine." He made to stand.

"No," Vaelor said, "Not you, sire."

Dev rolled his eyes. "I'll just stay here alone, shall I?"

"What about me?" Mairead cried, indignant.

Dev frowned at her. "I'm sorry, love, you're a capable healer, but can you protect a king from a horde of 'swords?"

Mairead's pale face turned almost as red as her robes and hair. With a huff, she folded her arms.

We're running out of time, Emrah said, landing on Fig's knee and kneading it the way a cat would with his clawed feet.

"Dev, you stay here with Mairead and Vaelor, and I'll go—"

"Forgive me, goldfire," Vaelor said, and she opened her mouth at the nickname, "but I have a better chance of—"

"He's right, Fig," Dev interrupted. "Let him go."

"But..." she huffed, unsure why she even wanted to go in the first place. Firth *had* almost killed her. "Emrah, go with him," she said, crossing her arms.

The little dragonet swooped over to Vaelor, but after glancing at Vaelor's expression, hovered near his shoulder instead of landing on it.

The three of them watched Vaelor go, easily blending in with the mixed crowd of Nova Istrans and silverswords.

"You sure you trust him?" Fig whispered to Dev. "He could turn on us the second he gets to the silverswords."

"I trust him," Dev said softly.

"Maybe one day you'll tell me why," she muttered. Fig watched Vaelor slide in among the silverswords, dropping the horse blanket from his shoulders, and melding in seamlessly with the armored men and women milling about. He *was* the better choice to send.

What's it look like over there? Fig called to Emrah after giving him and Vaelor a minute to get a bit farther through the crowd.

They've got Firth bound with rope, and they're talking of a public execution.

"Execution?" Fig muttered aloud.

"What did you say?" Dev said.

"Nothing."

Mairead shrunk farther into the shadows when a pair of silverswords patrolling the outside of the crowd passed by.

"Who're they?" Fig asked.

The ex-priestess hesitated. "Oh, just more silverswords I got on the wrong side of," she said quietly.

"Seems like something you do often," Dev remarked.

Something shifted in the crowd. Suddenly the silverswords were organizing the Nova Istrans away from Djuren's lamppost, forming an open space. Kneeling in the center of the space were five dwarves, hands bound behind their backs.

"Bard's broken quill," Fig swore. "Whose idea was this again?"

Vaelor stood at the edge of the group of silverswords; he was acting as a guard and holding the crowd back. But he had forgotten his helm in the saddlebag, which was looped around Dev's shoulder, making him more vulnerable than most. Particularly with his Virenish hair on display.

"Where's the dragonet?" Mairead asked, still clutching Fig's arm.

"I don't know, let me ask him," Fig muttered.

"Hah! I knew it," Dev said under his breath. "You've been talking back to him somehow, haven't you?"

Fig's expression slid off her face. "Oh, well—yes. Sorry, but a lot's been going on, and—"

"Just ask him where he is," Dev said, a sly smile on his face. "You can tell me about it later."

I slipped behind Vaelor's neck, in the shadow of his armor, Emrah replied grumpily when she asked. *I'm waiting for the signal.*

Signal to do what? Fig demanded.

The silence that followed seemed to stretch on forever.

"I can't watch this," Fig huffed, turning to look at the *Narrow.* The sky behind it was growing lighter by the minute, and their hiding place was no longer hidden. Anyone who passed by the ships would see them immediately, but the docks were surprisingly empty—everyone had been drawn into the crowd. It wasn't every day that silverswords showed up to announce that Tytan had a new king, then followed their announcement with a public execution of dwarves.

Well, not if we can help it, she thought.

"Maybe we should move," Fig said, glancing around at the other crates. The dockmaster's stand, too, was empty. Just as she was about to suggest moving to hide behind the stand, she spotted another figure lurking near the cargo. A dwarf.

She poked Dev sharply. "That's one of the Feijowa!"

"What, where?"

As Dev looked, she got a quick look at the dwarves kneeling on the cobblestones. The silverswords were still getting something set up, and Djuren was yet again arguing with another 'sword.

The lone dwarf crouched by the cargo, staring at the scene of horror unfolding in the streets. Djuren and the 'sword finished their argument and started shoving the dwarves into a stricter line. They would all be dead soon, the only ones to stand up to the news of the coup.

Fig rubbed sparks from her fingers, and with a backward glance at Dev, darted over to where the dwarf was hiding.

"Fig!" Dev hissed quietly.

But it was too late. She was almost upon the dwarf, who hadn't seen her approach, his gaze so intent on his comrades. Coming up from behind, she had her fingers on his neck in an instant. And at the edges of her fingers, sparks danced, letting him know that she was playing with fire.

"Who are you?" he said gruffly.

"Doesn't matter," she said. "But I've got a man in the square ready to help your friends. What are you doing lurking back here?"

"Not getting killed," he huffed.

She recognized his deep voice. "Collis?"

"How in the name of the Mountain d'you know who I am?"

"Your friend Firth put an axe through my gut."

He made to turn and look at her, but at a fresh burst of sparks, seemed to think better of it. "They put their axe through a lot of people."

Impulsively Fig snorted, though inside she was trying not to think about what that axe—and its aftermath—had felt like. "Listen, I only just met Emrah. We had nothing to do with whatever artifact you were looking for. But he's in that crowd with our man, willing to help them for some reason. Will your people be ready to move?"

Collis hesitated, still trying to look back at her. She loosened her fingers, letting out a few sparks to remind him she was still there, still ready.

"Oh, aye, they'll be ready," Collis replied darkly. "The silverswords have betrayed us too, mage blood."

"What do you mean *too*?"

A roar erupted from the square, and Fig twisted to see Firth standing, arms wide with the rope around their hands burned to cinders. They held a crude dagger in one hand.

A glimmer of green and gold flitted behind the dwarves. 'Swords darted forward, clearly wary of the dwarf who appeared to wield fire to escape their ropes. Emrah still hadn't been spotted.

Though they were free from their ropes, they were surrounded by silverswords and curious onlookers. "They still need an escape," Fig muttered.

Collis grumbled, "That's what I was trying to do, mage, until you interrupted me."

"What?" Fig demanded, pulling her fingers away, without taking her eyes off Vaelor.

At the same time, she called to Emrah, *What's going on? I found another dwarf, but I'm not sure what—*

Collis elbowed one of the small crates he had crouched near. One of the wooden slats had been pried off, revealing a crumbling black substance inside.

"Firejack?" Fig said, squinting at it. A clang rang out from the square, Vaelor's sword striking another. Firth had somehow gotten their axe back and was protecting the four unarmed dwarves. It was only Firth and Vaelor, with the dwarves behind them, surrounded by a sea of silver.

And somewhere in there, Emrah, who Fig only just realized hadn't answered her.

Emrah? she called, frantic.

Collis was speaking to her. At her blank stare, he repeated, "I *said*, do you have a flint? Mine got soaked in the bay."

Passing over what he'd been doing *in* the bay, she grinned at him. "I can do you one better," she said, snapping her fingers and producing a bright flame at the tips.

Collis recoiled, eyeing her warily. "Careful with that, will you!" he growled. She snuffed out the flames, her cheeks warming.

"It's not just this crate," Collis hissed, "but the whole pallet. You'll blow the whole port to dust. I wasn't going to light the whole thing!"

"Sorry," she muttered. "Then what do you want me to do?"

Collis glanced over her shoulder, eyeing the ever-rising sun. "Not getting us killed would be a good start."

"I said I was sorry," she grumbled, flexing her guilty fingers.

"And mages wonder why we don't like them," Collis said so quietly she didn't think she was meant to hear. "We need to create a distraction. Fast. Though I hate to waste all of the firejack. It's the whole reason we came—never mind."

They both glanced over at the commotion. Firth and the other dwarves were all in the fray now, many of the dwarves having somehow acquired weapons. Vaelor fought like a devastating whirlwind of steel, though his face retained its calm. The reek of copper emanating from the mass of riled up silverswords overwhelmed Fig's senses. How was anyone to survive that fight? Even if Vaelor possessed strength beyond what he was born with, all the other 'swords did too.

"Right. A distraction," Fig agreed, licking her suddenly dry lips and glancing around, her brain void of thought, let alone any brilliant ideas.

Before Collis could speak, a breeze flitted around them, and Dev appeared behind her. "What are you two doing over here?" he demanded. "Chatting about the weather?"

Fig's face burned in embarrassment. "We're going to create a distraction with the firejack," she snapped.

"Firejack?" Dev replied with mischief in his eyes. "Excellent. How? Place a few crates scattered down the docks and set them off?"

Dev looked at Collis, and they both nodded, as if that had been their plan all along.

Collis began trying to pry a board off another crate to get at its contents. "That should do it. Won't damage much, if we space out the crates. Nowhere near this stack, though."

Fig nodded at the crate he was trying to open, "Don't bother. I can blast right through that."

She couldn't tell if the stare he gave her was disbelief or fear, but she didn't care. It wasn't exactly thick wood.

"De—you," she said to Dev, "stick with Mairead. If something happens to you, she can heal you, all right? I saw a skin of that holy water on her belt. Head toward the ship after you set the crate. I'll run down the line and set them off."

"I'll be fine," Dev said, hefting up a crate of the flammable powder.

Shouts came from the center of the silversword battle; citizens had joined in, and the rallying cries filled her heart with a mix of pride and fear. How in Tytan would they survive that whirling mass of silver death? They had to stop this. The citizens had either rallied to fight or been swept into the madness and were fighting for their lives.

She grabbed one of the crates and rushed to the north side of the port, while Collis went to the south. "I'll start setting it off at the north, and—" she whisper-shouted at the two of their departing backs, but they were already gone. *The Bard only knows how I'll signal anyone. If only—*

Emrah! she called in her mind. *Are you all right? What's going on?*

Silence—only in her mind, though. Her ears ached with the sounds of death and violence coming from the open square. She picked up the pace, sprinting across the openings between stacks of crates. But no one seemed to be paying attention to the harbor.

Maybe they should have just given up on the dwarves and secured their place on the *Narrow*.

She glanced at the ship in question, longing to be safe under its decks with her friends by her side. But Emrah and Vaelor were still caught in the center of that battle. Judging by the cries reaching her ears, and the chokingly-thick coppery scent that she suspected wasn't just the wafting aura of magic, the citizens weren't faring well against the bloodthirsty silverswords.

"Right," she muttered to herself, tearing her gaze from the *Narrow*. She shook her head, not used to being so unsure. "Gotta stop this." She set her firejack down behind a tall stack of crates, and with a quick apology to whoever owned said crates, summoned flames to both hands.

Something slammed into her shoulder, and she reeled to the side, off balance. It wasn't something, it was—"Emrah! Thank the Bard you're all right!"

She crushed him to her shoulder in an awkward mage-to-dragonet hug, but he didn't seem to mind. He nuzzled her neck for a split second, then reared his little head back.

You need to get out of here! Where are the others? You're not going to like what happens next, he told her.

W-What do you mean? she thought back to him.

Suddenly the crowd of silverswords parted. Vaelor rushed through in a burst of strength and steel, crashing through anyone in his way. Directly behind him were Firth and the other dwarves.

Despite the terror at the shear strength of Vaelor's charge from the fight, Fig's heart lifted. "What's wrong with that?" she said. "They're getting out!"

Emrah chittered, dancing his claws along her shoulder as if hopping from foot to foot.

That wasn't what I was talking about. You need to go, now. Where's Dev? We have to get him out of here!

Vaelor charged straight toward the large stack of firejack where Fig had first found Collis—where all the firejack was stored. Collis had said it would blast the whole port to dust if they blew the whole stack.

"No!" she screeched, reaching out an impotent hand. Tiny claws clenched on her shoulder.

Go! Emrah said, lifting his wings as if trying to drag her away.

Her heart lurched into her throat. But Dev and Collis had run to the south of the port—she couldn't get to them unless she ran right through the center—where Vaelor and the dwarves were about to set off the firejack...

She swallowed hard and set off running.

Though she wasn't completely impervious to fire, she could withstand far more than a normal person if she focused hard enough, convincing the flames not to burn her. And though Emrah's flames had burned when he cauterized her wound, she had been out of her mind at the time. Besides, that had been the worst burn of her life, and she'd been through flames countless times. She would make it—but would the others?

And then all thoughts flew from her head.

She caught sight of a spark of flame just as the sun rose over the port of Nova Istra. Then the burst of flames collapsed all sound around them as the crates exploded.

Emrah clinging to her shoulder, Fig sprinted through the flames, connecting her senses to the fires around her to keep them from burning her. She fought her way through a rushing current like a sailor through the crushing waters of stormy seas.

She couldn't stop to think. She saw Vaelor and another dwarf dashing away in the wrong direction—back toward the silverswords. One dwarf lay dead on the docks. The others were nowhere to be seen, and she only hoped they had headed for the water.

Crashing into Vaelor's side, she pushed him and the dwarf toward the water, their only hope. She used her own gold flames behind her to ride the current of fire.

Vaelor's armor was hot—impossibly scalding—though it didn't hurt her as much as it must be hurting him. How could he move his legs in all this? But he stumbled forward, her small arm wrapped around his waist. She wrapped her other arm around the dwarf's, who was somehow still limping along.

Then, her feet ran out of dock, and she was falling.

She had barely enough sense to draw an extra breath before the cold burst of the Hollow Sea washed over her, an explosive sensation after bathing in the flames. She would have reveled in it, but something was dragging her down, fast.

Vaelor.

Her arm was still wrapped tightly about his waist—caught, in fact, in a crevice between two plates of armor. And they were sinking straight down. His heavy claymore was still strapped to his back, only a fraction of the weight of his extensive armor.

He didn't move.

Bard strike it! she screamed in her head. She squinted her eyes open, and they stung a little as she tried to glimpse what was going on above her. Though the rising sun was evident among the clear waters, the flames consuming the docks painted a horrifically vivid image of her underwater nightmare.

Timbers, crates, men, and dwarves littered the waters as ships moved unnaturally in the water. A particularly narrow one was keening dangerously to one side.

Eyes bulging in panic, she tried to disentangle her arm from Vaelor's armor.

Fig! Emrah burst in her mind. *Where are you? I can still feel you—*

About to drown under Vaelor's armor, she shot back, jiggling the clasps of the plates at his back. *The big Viren's going to be the death of me!*

Finally, she got the clasp undone and freed her arm. Her lungs strained. She looked up toward the surface, ignoring the sting of salt water in her eyes. They were getting farther and farther away as each second ticked by. Every part of her body screamed to save herself and swim upward toward the precious air.

The dwarf she had dragged in was swimming away from the dock, showing Fig a clear path to an empty spot by the shore.

She looked at Vaelor's unconscious face, pale hair floating about his head. She couldn't leave him.

Hastily finding the next clasp, she removed the piece of armor entirely. Once free, the armor sunk to the depths, where she and Vaelor were still headed. *Gods!*

Only seconds had passed since they'd plunged into the water. She found the next biggest piece of armor and got to work, fingers fumbling. Thankfully, many of the leather clasps had been damaged by the flames. She was able to rip some pieces right off, while she had to locate the metal clasp on others and work it loose. Finally—finally!—they stopped sinking.

But now she needed to get to the surface with an unconscious, massive Viren and his enormous sword in tow. She couldn't very well separate him from the weapon. It would be just as bad as leaving him for dead.

Marking the direction the dwarf had gone, she awkwardly wrapped her arms around Vaelor's wide chest, using only her legs to move them. She kicked. It was like swimming through honey. Were they even moving?

Her chest constricted; what little air remained in her lungs felt like poison, killing her much as the water would.

As she squinted above again, there was a rush of movement in the water near the surface. She kicked fruitlessly, clutching Vaelor. The ship—the *Narrow*, she was sure of it—was keeling to the side, falling right into the docks, which had been reduced to flaming flotsam crashing about.

She kicked with all her might, squeezing Vaelor to her.

Kicking, kicking, her legs started to feel like honey themselves, her head just as sticky and slow.

Then Vaelor's limp arms clutched her back. She nearly let out a scream but managed to keep her precious—though poisoned—air inside her lungs.

She couldn't see his face, but his legs were moving; they were both swimming, both kicking.

Their heads crashed through the surface of the water, and suddenly the deafening silence Fig had been drowning in was brought to a painful stop, replaced by screams of terror and pain, of crashing wood, and of hungry flames.

They both gasped together, their breaths mingling. Sopping wet, they clutched one another, floating at the surface, finding precious, precious air. She raised her eyes to meet his silver-ringed ones.

"Over here," Fig gasped, one arm still flung around Vaelor, as one of his was also around her. She felt as though she would sink all over again if she lost her hold; her limbs were so weak. The new air hurt her lungs, but she cherished every painful breath, gasping as they swam in the direction she had seen the dwarf seek safety.

Both panting as they kept their heads above water, they awkwardly swam toward the shore.

Emrah? Emrah? she called.

Thank Drakioryn! You're alive!

Warm relief spread from her heart, and she stopped kicking for a moment. It barely mattered, as Vaelor's strokes had overshadowed her own pathetic attempts to swim.

Where are you? she called, peering around at the smoky edges of the port. Random screams and the occasional sound of fighting echoed from the depths of the smoke-filled harbor.

A flit of shadow caught her eye, and she saw Emrah land on someone's shoulder.

It was Dev's shoulder. She let out a sigh of relief, a gasping laugh with it.

"What is it?" Vaelor asked, his arm clutching her torso tighter.

"It's Dev," she said, raising a weak hand to point.

Vaelor grunted and altered their course slightly. Beside Dev stood Mairead and two dwarves.

Only two? she wondered. But as Vaelor swam them over to the shore—Fig had given up, her strokes were barely worth the effort—she spotted a third dwarf emerging from the trees, a small wooden craft in tow. It was Collis. Firth and the other dwarf helped him pull it to the shore.

Her feet met land, and she nearly cried in relief. Land. Tumbled pebbles under her waterlogged boots. She gazed back at the destruction of the bay and shuddered, knowing how close it had come to being her grave.

Vaelor ushered her forward, and she gladly lurched from the waters, sopping wet and nearly sobbing.

"Fig!" Dev said, flinging his arms around her. She squeezed back just as tightly, her tears coming in earnest now.

"How did you..." she began. "Where..."

Dev stepped back and clapped Mairead on the shoulder. "She didn't let me stick around to make sure you lit the crates. What were you thinking, anyway, blowing that whole stack, Fig?"

Fig looked scandalized. "It wasn't me! It was these idiots!"

"Idiots?" Firth grunted. "We stopped the battle, and—"

"And destroyed the only way out of Tytan from here," Fig said, jerking her chin toward what was left of the *Narrow*. It was rapidly sinking. The other boats were in no shape to set sail either.

"We had it handled!" Fig said. "Collis and I were only going to set off a few crates for a distraction—"

"That true, Collis?" Firth said, crossing their stout arms. "Working with a mage, eh?"

Collis grunted, aiming a kick at the vessel he had acquired. "We had it covered."

Surprise stained Firth's features, then they shrugged and said, "Well, let's get on with it."

Fig froze. *Get on with what?* she wondered. Her chest tight, she gazed at Firth's axe, hanging from their belt. Vaelor shifted closer to Fig. She noticed with surprise how different he looked without his armor.

Dev was the first to speak, "I hope you mean all getting out of here," he said carefully. "We helped you all escape—Fig and Collis worked together to come up with a plan, and Vaelor went right into the scrum for you, Emrah at his side."

Firth grunted, narrowing their eyes. "Oh, aye. That's what I meant, all right. I'm no *idiot*," they added, cutting their gaze at Fig with the ghost of a smirk on their lips.

A chill ran through Fig as the wind shifted, and suddenly she was ice cold. "Too bad we can't row across the Hollow Sea, eh?" she said, stepping into the boat. Dev hopped in eagerly beside her.

Everyone found a place in the boat except Firth, who stood on the shore, a meditative look on their face. They reached down and picked up a fistful of sand and rocks, holding it in their palm for a moment.

Fig tried not to stare as Firth whispered a few words in the direction of the harbor and tightened their fist. A fine mist spiraled down from their hand, a glimmer Fig could barely see, floating on an invisible breeze toward the harbor, where Firth's dead lay.

To Fig's immense surprise, Dev offered to row. Dry as a bone, having fled the dock by foot thanks to Mairead's chiding, he was the least ruffled of them all. But with the length of the boat and the sea's current, he couldn't do it alone. With Dev toward the back, and Collis up front, Vaelor gave the boat a push from the shore, then hopped in beside Fig, as they rowed as fast as they could from Nova Istra. Fig hardly recognized the vessel, but it must be some kind of Virenish craft, meant for navigating the waterways of the lowlands.

"Too bad there's no sail," Dev muttered to Fig. The chill of the air on her skin felt worse since she knew Dev could dry her off. But the dwarves apparently had no idea who Dev was, and it was best it stayed that way.

She could wreathe herself in flames without burning herself, but there was no way she would risk that in the boat. And creating warmth without flames was something she had never mastered.

Mairead took the prow, Firth and the other dwarf, Silva, just behind her. Fig and Vaelor sat toward the back. It was cramped, but no one complained, not even Dev.

Collis glanced back over his shoulder at Vaelor. "Good thing you've done away with your armor, mate, or we wouldn't be able to take ya on."

Vaelor looked annoyed at the remark.

Was he mad she had lost him his armor? Fig's temper flared. "You were going to drown us both!"

He made a noise of surprise, glancing behind him at the bay, where billowing smoke blocked out the entire port. The *Narrow* was gone, and Fig knew she probably shouldn't show her face in Nova Istra for a very long time.

Then Vaelor shook his head. Was he smiling? "No, it's... I didn't think I'd make it past setting off the firejack crates, let alone get out of the water unscathed. Thanks, goldfire."

She ducked her head upon hearing the nickname, then narrowed her gaze toward the edge of the port. She nudged Vaelor, and he turned to look where she was pointing. Silver glinted from the place they had disembarked. It fluctuated in the weak morning sunlight, like whoever stood there was crouching close to the ground. Then more silver appeared, tripling the glints of light. Smoke wafted in and out, making it impossible to see any details, with their increasing distance.

"*Mir* Morgha," Vaelor muttered. If that was a Virenish swear, Fig seconded it.

Was it Djuren himself? Or Liess Astor, finally catching up to them? Or merely a trick of the smoky dawn light...

On edge, she whipped around as she heard Emrah clatter to land on the front of the prow. "Can't you row any faster?" Fig hissed at Dev and Collis.

Firth looked up with keen eyes to where Vaelor's attention was still drawn. "Silverswords? Do you think they sighted us?"

"I don't know," Fig said in earnest, unhappy that Firth had drawn the same conclusion so quickly.

Vaelor turned back around, and Fig saw him clenching his knees and staring at Dev.

"I think he can handle it," Fig said in a low tone.

"What?" Vaelor answered, his silver-ringed eyes finding hers.

"Dev can handle rowing. You almost just drowned."

He shrugged, but his hands relaxed.

"All Dev had to do," she said, louder, "was run down the dock with a crate of firejack. But you all had your own plan." She threw the dwarves and Vaelor a slightly accusatory glance. "You should have told Emrah to tell us the plan."

"He was already in the crowd," Vaelor said. "I couldn't—"

"Oh, yes, Fig," Dev piped up. "Tell us how *you* can talk back to Emrah in your head, when *we* can't."

She speared him with a look, and he shrugged as best a man rowing a boat could shrug.

Firth was leaning on the side of the prow, looking at her. Everything had grown quiet all of a sudden.

"I don't know," she admitted. "Do you, Emrah?"

Everyone looked at the dragonet, perched on the prow like a green and gold figurehead. A glittering of sparks sifted from his wings, and he shook his little head. *I don't know,* he told them. *It's never happened before.*

Gazes turned to stare at Fig. This time, Mairead came to her rescue. "I don't think this really matters right now. We should focus on getting as far from here as we can."

Firth eyed the former red sister. "And who are you, and how did you get entangled with this gang of thieves?"

"*Thieves?*" Mairead demanded, pale face blank.

"Thieves?" Fig repeated, her ire rising. She could barely keep the sparks from her fingers. "We've stolen nothing! *You* wanted Emrah to steal something for you, and he didn't even find it! He doesn't have the gods-forsaken thing, and you know it! And—*And!* Let's not forget the fact that you almost killed me!"

Fig crossed her arms, staring down Firth, glad that men and dwarves sat between the two of them.

Mairead drew as far away from them all as she possibly could. Staring open-mouthed at Firth, she said, "You're the one who sliced open Fig's stomach?"

Firth shrugged. "She looks in perfect health to me."

"No thanks to you," Fig shot at Firth. "Mairead healed me and was going to come with us on the ship—"

"Till you dwarves burned it down," Dev added.

"I don't recall asking you," Firth said. "And who might you be, anyway? Seem a bit more refined than these other two." Firth waggled a hand at Fig and Vaelor.

"Ask the Bard on your reckoning day," Fig retorted. They *certainly* didn't need the dwarves finding out who Dev was. That was the whole reason they had fled the tower in the first place. "We don't need to go any farther with you dwarves. You'll just as soon kill us over some trinket Emrah never even acquired for you—"

"I'd quite like to get out myself," Mairead said in a high-pitched voice.

"I don't blame you," Firth muttered, but the words elicited no warmth from the ex-priestess.

"Pull to the shore," Fig told Dev, who tried to steer inland. But Collis went on, his strokes keeping them parallel with the shore.

Then a burst from Emrah startled them all. *Djuren has it!*

"Has what?" Fig asked.

He has the sword of Morin.

"H-How could he possibly—" Firth spluttered.

"That briigard!" Collis swore.

"That silversword back in Nova Istra?" Fig said. "He has the artifact the dwarves sent you to find?"

I saw him in the Mountain, Emrah told them, launching deftly into the air to circle nervously around the boat like an energetic bird of prey circling its meal. *When I went to retrieve it. I was in the Chamber of Morin-Song, like you said, Firth, when the silverswords came in.*

Both Collis and Dev kept up the pace as they glided along the calm waters, willow branches leaning over the shore.

"You were in the King's Mountain?" Mairead asked Emrah in a hush.

"It's *our* mountain," Collis blurted. Firth and Silva both grunted, "Aye."

Mairead bowed her head, cheeks reddening to match her robes and hair. "My apologies."

I was there, Emrah said for Mairead's benefit, *looking for something for the dwarves. But the silverswords came in, Djuren at the head. Drakioryn only knows how they got into the chamber. All the tunnels I went through could barely fit a svorcat.*

"It *belongs* to us," Firth broke in.

"No one's saying it's not yours," Dev muttered.

"Well, apparently, Djuren is!" Collis burst out, jolting the boat. "I've heard of him. Practically licks the ground Rhivven walks on, doesn't he?"

"So Djuren is Rhivven's man," Fig said, "No surprise there. The silverswords—" She cut herself off. "Present company excluded. They're all in league together. Rhivven's been planning this—perhaps planning something bigger than just the coup."

"*Just* the coup?" Dev said weakly, a deranged chuckle slipping from him. "Oh, yes."

Fig gave him a pointed look.

"We'll be getting that back from him, then," Firth said, gazing up at Emrah. "And you'll be helping us."

The dragonet dropped a foot in the air, then recovered. *What? Why me?*

"You're still on contract, aren't ya?" Firth said. "Hence why we came to remind you of that at your tower."

Remind me, Emrah repeated darkly, sparks sifting down from his wings, which fizzled on the water's surface.

Fig couldn't bear the thought of Emrah going with the dwarves. First of all, Emrah clearly didn't want to. And a second more selfish reason, she liked the dragonet. "No," she said, glancing up at Emrah, "he's working with us now."

"Yes," Dev drawled. "Special contract."

"Ballast," Firth swore, thumbing the axe clipped at their belt. "He's ours."

I'm no one's, you daft dwarf! Emrah shot back, zipping high into the air. His belly began to glow like hot embers, and Fig barely noticed herself leaning closer to Vaelor.

"Ah, well, I thought Knoll would like living in that cozy tower of 'yorn," Firth said loudly, ignoring Emrah's display of aggression. "He'll be pleased it's a permanent situation."

Who? What? Who's in my tower? he demanded.

Fig thought back to all those gems embedded in the ceiling and wondered how long Emrah had been collecting them. And then there was the peaceful serenity of the tower nestled in the Gold Wood, an unquestionably magical place. What she wouldn't give to call that *her* home. Free from the political maneuvering of the Carriage House, but still part of the woods that sang to her blood.

"There must be—" Fig began, but Dev cut her off.

"Like I said, we have a special contract with him."

Fig looked at him sharply. He gave her a half shrug, as if to say, *how much worse could it get?*

She shook her head in a definitive *no*. It could always get much worse.

Dev, of course, ignored her. "Emrah is coming with us. By order of the king." He looked like he was enjoying this.

"Oh, aye?" Firth said, tone rising, "So ye're all working with Rhivven too?"

"Oh gods, no," Dev said, chuckling. "The true king."

"But—"

"Bard save us," Fig muttered. "The true king," she repeated in annoyance, "is sitting right in front of you. King Devryn Verrence, the last surviving heir to the Rayvan throne."

Collis stopped rowing.

Firth's eyes narrowed. "S'pose you did look familiar." An awkward pause filled the silence as Firth and Dev stared at each other, the boat gently going off course, Collis's paddle now forgotten in the water.

The dwarf backed down first, and finally said, "Well, King Devryn, how do you propose the dwarves reclaim the sword of Morin from the bloodsucking silver briigards? You know, the only sword made from the one metal that will make them damn-near immortal?"

THE SOLANSE

The small fire crackled in the dark, its woody scent and warmth bringing ease to Fig's ravaged body and soul. It had been a long, terrible day. She sat slumped against a fallen log, somewhere in the Virenish highlands. No silverswords had pursued them—not by sea, anyway. But that didn't mean they couldn't still be coming.

Most of them sported an assortment of burns. They all turned down Mairead's offer of healing, however. The ex-priestess only had one small flask of the holy waters. Dev only had a few burns, and Fig could tell by the look on his face that he didn't want to seem like a pampered prince in front of the dwarves, who had outright refused the healing.

Fig desperately wanted to sleep. Though she only had a small burn on her arm from losing focus a few times in the flames, she had been near death far too frequently for her liking in the last few days, but they needed to come to terms with the dwarves before any more blood was spilled, and Dev was proving difficult.

"I've never heard of bloodril," Dev insisted again. "How could there be some dwarvish sword made from a mythical metal?"

Firth paced back and forth outside of the firelight. "Why in the holy flight of Heubrin's axe would *you* know about it? It's a *dwarvish* sword."

Dev rolled his eyes, spearing another piece of meat from the spit roasting over the fire. Fig had sampled some of the meat already, and though ravenous, she was quite scarred from her last meal. Mairead had assured her the wound was healed, but Fig didn't want to risk eating too much.

The ex-priestess was already asleep beside her, curled up on the ground with her head resting on her leather satchel. She looked the most out of place in their group. A weight settled on Fig's chest. They shouldn't have gotten Mairead involved.

Vaelor had insisted the meat was from a couple of vorse eagles, but based on Emrah's chuckles as the two of them brought the meat to the fire, Fig wasn't so sure. From the little she'd tried, it did *taste* like vorse eagle.

"Why would *I* know about it?" Dev said, crossing his arms. "Because I'm a Verrence. My father, the Rayvan spies, and all the knowledge in Tytan—"

"Pardon me, Prince Devryn—" Firth interrupted.

"It's King."

The silence between them became thicker than the starless night. Fig knew she didn't really have any place in this conversation, but she longed to give Dev a good smack. He was being bull-headed, and he knew it.

"If you say so," Firth said. Fig practically saw Dev's hackles rise.

Gritting her jaw, she decided to wade in. "Dev," she said gently, "perhaps the dwarves have their own secrets. And Firth"—the dwarf didn't pause their pacing, but threw her a look—"stop antagonizing him. None of us want Rhivven on the throne. And I don't think anyone wants the silverswords in possession of this bloodril blade."

"Oh aye," Collis said around the knife he was using to pick meat out of his teeth. "Strongest metal ever found on the continent since the age of Heubrin himself. Should one of those silvery briigards Weld with one, their enhancement would be terrifying. And they're practically death-proof anyway."

"Not all of them," Dev said quietly.

Firth finally stopped pacing. "Listen lad—Your Majesty—the Feijowa had no love for your father, but it weren't nothing personal. Since the time of King Bailemor, when our mountain was taken from us, no dwarf will ever truly belong in this king's country—not while the maps say what they say, not while we can't step foot inside the Great Mountain."

An almost invisible cloud of dust rose around Firth as they talked—Fig wanted to think it had been kicked up from their pacing, but she knew better. Something mystical in the earth was responding to the dwarf's vehemence. The rich scent of overturned earth reached Fig's nose.

The faraway look in the dwarf's eyes made Fig's heart ache for them. Though she had no desire to live beneath a mountain for the Bard's sake, it was their ancestral home. Like the Gold Wood was for her.

"And now the silverswords have the Sword of Morin. A deep blow to an already festering wound."

Dev bowed his head. "So what do you want us to do, get this sword back for you in exchange for your support for my return to the throne?"

The spell was broken; the dust cloud dissipated as Firth began pacing again.

Firth threw their arms up. "Gods no," they guffawed. "We want our mountain back."

"Are you sure we shouldn't have just let them take Emrah and call it a day?" Dev whispered to Fig as they bid the dwarves goodbye the following morning.

Dev, Fig, Mairead, and Vaelor had piled into the long Virenish boat, along with a little smoked meat from last night wrapped in some leaves to eat later. Silva had even begrudgingly parted with a waterskin at Firth's request. Mairead had filled it from a small stream near their campfire; it wouldn't last the four of them long in the salt swamps, but it was better than nothing. The red sister had also found some silversap growing by the stream, which Vaelor, Fig and the dwarves used to cover their burns. No one wanted to show weakness in front of the others, but Fig thought Mairead's designation as a healer lessened the embarrassment a little.

Emrah settled in to nap on Mairead's pack in the prow. The little dragonet hadn't slept all night, after insisting on keeping an eye on the dwarves so the others could sleep. They had reached an uneasy truce, but Fig still hadn't been keen on sleeping near Firth and his axe without some kind of guard.

She shook her head. "What, and received nothing in return?"

Dev said, "They're not exactly marching on Rayva in my name, though, are they?"

The three dwarves now stood at the edge of the trees, watching their departure. Fig hadn't asked where they were going.

"A promise for a promise is the best you can do right now, I think," Fig said. Dev had promised the Mountain, and the dwarves had promised their assistance in reclaiming the throne. As for the sword? The dwarves had decided they would take on that issue...for now. But it was a problem they all needed solved. The silverswords being in possession of a bloodril sword would have dire consequences for the country, both for dwarven politics, and the danger of whoever the enclave let Weld to the sword.

Fig went on with a sigh, "Having the dwarves—a prominent clan, anyway—on your side could tip the scales. You never know."

Dev turned to look at her, a slow smile forming. "I knew there was a reason I sought you out—you're becoming a most wise advisor, Fairaleigh Veil."

She rolled her eyes, and watched Vaelor's back as he rowed them away from shore. He looked smaller without his armor, though not by much. Just more vulnerable. Recovered from his near-death experience yesterday, his strength had returned, and he had turned down Dev's perfunctory offer to help row.

The dwarves disappeared into the trees, and Fig stared after them with apprehension long after they were gone.

It was a clear morning, the skies showing a thin blanket of clouds that allowed plenty of sunshine through. Clear enough that, if the dwarves ran off to the nearest silversword post, Fig and the others could easily be discovered in a matter of hours on the open water.

Fig shook her head. No. The dwarves were not beholden to the silverswords. Firth and their people knew better than anyone not to trust them. She would have to hope that a promise for a promise was enough to keep them all alive.

"How long do you think until we reach the lowlands?" Dev asked Vaelor an hour later. The rolling hills and massive moss-draped oaks of the Virenish highlands had been a wondrous sight from their vantage point at the edge of the sea, though Fig wouldn't have minded trading their boat for some horses and experiencing the landscape firsthand. It was a beautiful country, despite what ruinous turmoil the silverswords had set into motion in the recent years.

The problem was that they were far more likely to run into roving patrols of silverswords in the recently conquered country, than they were by sea. And once they entered the lowlands, there was almost no chance of being discovered.

"It's there," Vaelor grunted, nodding. "On the horizon."

Fig searched the horizon, thinking she spied a dense green canopy where the land met the sea.

"And we're *sure* we need to go through the lowlands?" Mairead chimed in, picking at the end of her red sleeve.

"Is anyone ever sure they need to enter the lowlands?" Dev muttered.

Fig frowned at the girl, but in a kindly way. "You know, we would have understood if you wanted to go with the dwarves to the next village or something. We seem to be nothing but trouble."

Mairead shook her head, sending her red hair cascading over her shoulders. "I wouldn't go with them! Not after what Firth did to your stomach! And..." She lowered her voice. "I don't think Nova Istra will ever be safe for me again. Possibly any of Tytan, in fact." She sighed, then remained silent, keeping her eyes on the horizon.

"Well," Fig began, "I don't think even Vaelor can row all the way across the Hollow Sea, so south to the Notch is unfortunately the only way out of Tytan for all of us. And we've got our papers—even one for you Mairead. We can cross the isthmus and make our way by land to Tirnalore to get on a ship there. At least we'll be out of Tytan."

"But what about the tagors?" Mairead asked quietly, not looking at anyone.

A low rumbling came from Vaelor, and Fig realized he was chuckling. "I'll handle them, and I'm sure Emrah wouldn't mind another crack."

Everyone was silent for a moment, then—

"I *knew* that was tagor meat!" Dev cawed.

"What?" Fig and Mairead said in unison.

Even Emrah flinched awake from his cozy position on Mairead's pack. *What's going on?* he murmured sleepily.

Nothing, Fig told him. *Go back to sleep. You might have more tagors to slay later.*

A snort of smoke came from his nostrils, and he curled back up.

"But it *did* taste like vorse eagle," Mairead was saying to Dev.

Fig stared at Vaelor, making light work of the rowing. It really was strange to see him out of his armor.

"It was only a small one," he said.

"Have you ever seen one, though?" Mairead asked as their boat drifted under the canopy of trees in the salt swamps early in the afternoon. A curtain of Andisia moss hung from the branches of the waterlogged cypress trees, welcoming them inside.

Vaelor's oars stilled for a moment as they glided by a patch of cypress knees, the range of wooden protuberances poking out of the water. With the dwarves gone, they could get by with just one rower, particularly one of Vaelor's strength. He seemed at ease navigating through the waterways in the long Virenish craft; Fig was thankful the dwarves had let them take it.

She admired the grandiose cypress and oaks towering over them, as well as the smaller and more exotic viragrove trees, all draped in curling Andisia moss, which hung from any surface it could find. The moss shifted in an invisible breeze, as if the very salt swamps were breathing: a humid, verdant exhale.

They had exhausted the topic of charting their course around the outskirts of the lowlands territory, but it had become clear they should go *through* it to get to the Notch. Vaelor had assured them that the edge of the salt swamps were far more dangerous. With the unpredictable tides of the sea at its narrowest part, they were likely to get smashed or caught up within the cage-like roots of the Viragrove trees and cypress knees there, a fine catch for any roving tagors.

The beasts, however, were also likely to be wading through the calmer waters they had chosen.

"I saw an eight-span tagor at an exhibition on Virenish history and gods," Dev replied to Mairead. "But that's probably nothing compared to what Vaelor's seen..." He trailed off. Emrah twitched on Fig's shoulder, silently watching the swamp.

Vaelor shrugged, oars still. "I've seen many while visiting my *grimazir's* house." He nodded vaguely inland—if you could call the random patches of soggy islands land.

"Gree-mah...?" Fig began.

"*Grimazir*," Vaelor said. "Er...grandmother."

"She lives in the salt swamps?" Fig asked, shoulders creeping slowly up to her ears as they drifted deeper into the green-hued darkness cast by the cypress trees.

"Near enough," he replied.

Tired of glancing over her shoulder, Fig angled herself toward the back of the boat, so she could easily spot anything behind them. With Dev and Mairead watching the front and sides, they should see anything that approached.

I wish you could keep an eye out from above, Fig told Emrah.

He shifted on his claws. *You think I like sitting on your shoulder like a trained parrot? You could use a bath, you know.*

Fig exhaled in amusement. *Sorry. No bath to be had here—and the Bard knows, I wouldn't be caught dead getting in these waters.*

Dead is right, Emrah said, his mental words somehow quiet. *Same reason I'm staying out of the air. I know the tagor keep to the water, but still...*

"Well, what's the biggest one you've seen, then?" Dev asked Vaelor, peering around at the shapes lurking in the water. So far none of them had proved menacing. All the lumps Fig had spied turned out to be clumps of mud or sunken patches of moss.

Vaelor dipped the oar in the water, propelling them gently around a small, waterlogged island. "You...probably don't want to know," he hedged.

"Well, now I do," Dev urged.

The silversword hesitated for a moment. Fig glanced back at him, and he said quietly, "Twelve-span." He gave the oar another pull.

Fig's mouth popped open. She quickly closed it and returned to her post, vigilantly watching the water. She swallowed hard, trying not to imagine a beast that size.

Really wish we'd all gotten on that ship before the dwarves showed up, Fig said to Emrah.

He chittered. *And gotten blown up inside it? At least we have all our limbs.*

Ah, gods, you're right, Fig said. *They blew up the pallet of firejack without our help. Well, maybe if we hadn't sent in Vaelor…*

And if wishes were crowns, fools would be kings, Emrah said.

Yes, yes, she acquiesced. *We'll have no fools here. There's no going back now.*

Vaelor continued to paddle at a snail's pace, carefully guiding their little boat through the winding water trails. They sometimes heard rustling overhead, but Fig never saw anything besides birds and the occasional tree frog. Despite the ever-present fear of what lurked in the murky water, she was in awe of the beauty of this place.

She trained her gaze on a lump just above the water's surface, twenty-span to the left side of aft. Was that…?

Two eyes emerged from the water, reptilian lids blinking slowly as the creature surveyed their craft. She knew beneath the water lurked a maw of sharp triangular teeth, and a long scaly body that could crush a man with its tail and claws.

"Th-there's one back there," Fig whispered.

"Holy mother, save us," Mairead hissed, turning to look at it. "Where?"

"Keep watching the front," Vaelor told her. "That one's no bother to us. I saw it before we passed it."

"You knew it was there?" Fig demanded, not taking her gaze from it, though, indeed, it did seem disinterested. She had expected it to swiftly surge through the water toward them the moment she spotted it.

"As long as we remain calm," Vaelor said, his voice low. "And no swift movements. Then they won't bother us."

"They?" Fig whispered, but she wasn't sure it came out loud enough for anyone to hear.

"Are we really sure this is the only course to the Notch?" Mairead squeaked.

"Regretting coming with us so soon?" Dev jested.

"Well, honestly—"

"Where did it go?" Fig said.

The tagor's eyes, and what little they could see of the beast, had slipped beneath the water and out of sight.

FENRA

Fenra curled her willowy fingers around the cypress limb, her own leaves rustling as she pulled herself up onto another gargantuan branch. Finally, she could *breathe* again. She soaked in the humid air, the exhilarating rush of energy exiting through the leaves cascading from her head. She was about to be in heaps of trouble, but she could take a second to breathe. Finally.

Home again...but for how long? Her elders were not going to be pleased. The last time Fenra had come home, her mother had nearly uprooted herself. Then the younger saplings had tripped over grandfather's knees helping mother back onto her ledge.

Like all the other dryads her age, Fenra was supposed to be out living an uprooted life, a "pilgrimage," a *voixage*—her journey out of the *solanse* for fifty years of travel and life before putting down roots. But what did she have need of *employment* for? She had no use for coin, and therefore, couldn't possibly stump the miserable way of life.

She scoffed, a creaking sound emanating from her wooden chest. The elders had assured her it was *only* for a half a century, waxing prolific about their various years abroad. She had heard no less than a hundred times about Elder Elizareth's trip to the islands east of Tysaine;

the dryad never stopped talking about it. Before Fenra left, Elder Eliza had encouraged her to gain employment, so Fenra could use the money to travel, something Fenra had absolutely *no* desire to do.

She had everything she needed here in the *solanse*. Clean air, family and friends, and of course, Vilvan. Her throat swelled, and she clutched the tagor tooth necklace she wore. He was supposed to be on his *voixage* right now, just like her.

Would anyone notice if Fenra just rooted on the outskirts of the *solanse* for the next forty years?

She shook her head, leaves rattling. If she did that, she might never see her family again. Putting down roots was no small thing.

The cypress she had climbed felt like home. Not like that gods-forsaken livery in Thoan she'd worked at for the last two years. Though the employers at this particular establishment had been less harsh than others she had endured—no one asked her awkward questions about her leaves, or tried to snap off her twigs, anyway—things that had occurred at several other occupations. The only place she wanted to be was home. Here. In the *solanse*.

Here where she could breathe and her bark didn't absorb the scents of horse manure or, even worse, deadwood smoke.

She inhaled again, glancing southward with a frown. She was in no hurry to return to her family's ledge, but since she had deserted her post at the livery in a fit of pique—thereby destroying any ideas the elders might have of her returning there—she really didn't have anywhere else to go at the moment.

So, she balanced on the cypress limb, walking down its length until it grew too thin for even her willowy feet to balance on. With a great leap, she flung herself toward the next branch. She had miscalculated, though, and only just caught the branch with her hand, her fingers extending a few inches to grasp it.

Strengthening her fingers as best she could, she swung her body like a pendulum until she could hurl herself upward. She landed on her bare wooden feet with a huff of air. "Well, that wasn't so bad." Her woven satchel jangled at her side as she landed, and she checked that the clasp was secure. Though *she* had no use for her earnings, she planned to give her money to the younger saplings for their pilgrimages—those who wanted to travel, anyway.

Carrying on this way for several trees, skirting around great wide trunks and using her nimble fingers to grasp handholds in the bark, she made her way in the direction of the family's ledge, where her elders had stood for close to a millennia. She had never liked plodding through the wet mud, her steps sluggish. This way was much more effective.

She knew the elders thought the half-century abroad a mere tick of the clock—and to them, it really was. They would tell Fenra to weather it like anything else. She felt she had weathered enough already. Why did the dryads have to keep up this pointless tradition?

She paused at the end of a branch, her light frame barely weighing down its tip. The next branch would require a great leap, and she debated climbing down the tree's trunk to cross by way of the islands. The sun had begun to descend into the swamps to the west, making the waters shine as red as human blood. She shrugged and backed up, getting ready to leap.

It wasn't like she would drown in the waters or get eaten by a tagor if she fell. Snap a few twigs maybe.

Vilvan had been bitten by a tagor once. The thing promptly let go, but not before burying some of its teeth in Vilvan's trunk. He had let Fenra feel the marks left by the tagor's teeth, up by his shoulders. She shivered at the memory, leaves rustling. One of those teeth now hung around her neck, strung on a twine of viragrove fibers Vilvan had woven for her before he left on his *voixage*.

When would he return to the *solanse*? The passage of years sometimes went in great spurts or strenuous slogs, and she had already lost track. Her own *voixage* felt as if it were taking a *century*. But her brother El would know. El was a master at tracking the movements of the sun and stars, and he could be trusted to know the exact date of anything. Often wouldn't shut up about it, in fact—spouting off a steady stream of facts and dates to anyone willing (or unfortunate enough) to begin a conversation with him. She wasn't sure where in his rings he stored all the information.

Fenra nodded, deciding. Before she confronted the elders, she would find El, and figure out just how much longer Vilvan would be away. Though she had absolutely no desire to follow him across the Hollow Sea, where she knew he was working in some human library as big as a city, it might make her own *voixage* a little more bearable knowing when he would be back in the *solanse*. And then her "employment" would also be a little more bearable.

Gathering air, she sprinted for the edge of the branch, fingers elongating in preparation to grip the next branch. She leapt, pinwheeling her legs and arms to give her just a little more momentum, with a burst of air to assist. Soaring, fingers outstretched—she snatched, willing her fingers just a *bit* longer—and saw something completely out of place.

A small boat with four humans and a green and gold dragonet sitting bravely on the prow.

She was soon grasping at empty air. She tried to let out a burst of air, willing it to propel her forward again, but it wasn't enough. Resignedly, she fell.

She crashed into the murky waters, which splashed about her and soaked her leaves. She promptly righted herself. Sucking in air from all directions, she let it out through her trunk to dry her leaves and moss. Checking that she still had her coins—which she should just give to El—she glanced up to see the boat that had so disastrously distracted her.

The occupants of the boat stared at her in horror.

Fenra scowled. Had they never seen a dryad before? "What?"

A girl draped in all red raised a pale white finger. The large man at the center of the boat quickly took up the oars as Fenra turned around to look.

A gargantuan tagor was rising from the water. Fenra wheezed a sigh. *Of course.*

Its black vestigial wings—scaly and reptilian—beat backward, lifting the creature's gaping maw from the murky waters. A jagged row of triangular teeth leered open at them.

The elders weren't going to be pleased if she came home with bite marks.

Splashing came from behind her, and she whirled to see the large man coming through the waist-high water toward her, sword unsheathed.

"No," Fenra said. "You stay back. It's my fault—"

Vaelor, get back here! the dragonet spoke, its words emanating through Fenra's mind. She hadn't seen a dragonet in decades.

With a great surge of water, the tagor lunged toward Fenra.

She elongated her fingers to sharp tips, hoping to pierce its rough hide if she could. Its small wings raised it out of the water enough to be intimidating, but it couldn't fly. No, not like its distant kin the dragonet that now circled above their heads, sparks drifting down from it.

"Damnit, Emrah, you too!" a woman shouted from the boat. She and the other two had gathered in the center of the boat, too horrified to row away as they rightfully should. The man who got out must have a death wish. But Fenra recognized a strange magic about him and his silver-ringed eyes.

The tagor lunged again, slick wings propelling the beast.

She darted to the side, annoyed at how the water weighed down her movements. Aiming a slash at its belly, she tripped on a cypress knee hidden in the muck and fell sideways into the water. The tagor straightened its wings and flopped back into the water with a horrific splash, somehow pinning her foot.

Jaws snapping, dead-looking eyes locked onto her, she slashed again and again.

It did nothing. Perhaps there was more to fear than snapped twigs.

Suddenly, her head was underwater, and she didn't know how. Muck and claws and teeth and...boots. Boots?

The large human had planted his feet between her and the tagor. She couldn't see much else. She tried in vain to raise her head above water—though she didn't need much air, she couldn't see anything through the murk. She was no good with water—that was El's specialty.

Finally, the tagor shifted, and she scrambled to the side, her feet dragging in mud and her limbs weighed down by the salty waters. She dragged in some air as the man slashed a great sword at the abdomen of the tagor, which had risen up again.

The man threw himself out of the way as the beast came crashing down, and Fenra followed suit, launching herself toward the humans' boat.

The tagor thrashed in the water, its beastly eyes filled with murderous reptilian rage. Its wings began flapping again, and its jaw snapped, preventing the swordsman from getting any closer.

The mage—Fenra could smell the ancient Svoran blood—grabbed at Fenra's arm, dragging her closer to the craft. Fenra let her. She stood beside the boat, twigs shaking.

If the tagor got any closer, she could push the boat to safety. She had brought this beast upon them, after all. Everyone in the *solanse* knew not to wake sleeping tagors.

Vaelor, get back! the dragonet called, darting toward the tagor.

"Emrah!" the mage cried.

Fenra's chest constricted as she watched the tiny creature confront its much larger cousin. Though her elders said the two species were distantly related, Fenra was immensely glad the tagors couldn't breathe fire.

As though summoning the sensation, Fenra felt a sudden heat. She turned to the mage beside her, who had gathered fire at her hands. Fenra hastily lunged to the side. "Hey, watch it!" she snapped.

"Sorry! Sorry!" the mage blurted, extinguishing the flames.

The man with the sword, Vaelor, and the dragonet were both doing their best to tire out the tagor, which had a wound on its stomach and a few slashes near its neck, though nothing seemed to be slowing it down.

The dragonet swooped in, a burst of flames headed for the tagor's face, but the beast surged back in a sweep of its wings, rearing up again. The swordsman readied to strike as if this were choreographed, and this time, the blade struck true, sinking deep into its belly.

But the ancient beast wasn't going to give up so easily. Jaws snapping, it thrashed, its wings flapping wildly while its claws reached out blindly.

"Out of the boat!" Vaelor called. *"Out of the boat!"*

"Out of the—?" the red priestess cried.

After one more thrash of the tagor's tail, Fenra knew the swordsman was right. The tagor was writhing ungainly in their direction, spurting murky water everywhere. The tail—

She yanked on the mage's arm, pulling the woman out of the boat. The mage in turn grabbed the other man with her. The priestess leapt out of the prow with a yelp, her robes turning the color of dried blood in the water.

The tail crashed down on the boat just as Vaelor delivered a deathblow to the creature's skull, blade sinking in through the top of its head and coming out through its fleshy neck.

Everything stopped.

Out of all of them, only the *solanse* breathed.

Broken planks lay floating on the surface of the water, and Fenra couldn't help but picture herself shattered to pieces, splintered and left to soak up the salty swamp water as her limbs drifted apart for eternity.

Finally, Fenra drew in some air and let it out through her leaves in a shaky burst.

The shorter man gave an uneasy chuckle. "What was that one, Vaelor? Ten-span?"

Fig inhaled the scent of tagor meat, her mouth reluctantly watering.

The creature lay dead only twenty-span off, not nearly distant enough in her opinion. The stench wasn't noticeable from here, thank the Bard, as if the salt swamp's humidity made the scent hang in place where it was.

The dryad sat twenty steps in the other direction, though she had watched curiously over Vaelor's shoulder as he slaughtered the tagor with the small knife he had pulled from his boot.

Clutching her knees to her chest, Fig gazed into the fire, the tagor meat roasting on a spit Vaelor and Mairead had rigged up. Her stomach hurt, but she knew without a doubt it was from hunger and thirst. They had already run out of fresh water in their one precious waterskin.

Emrah lay sleeping on the ground next to her, curled in a little ball. Fig felt a surge of pride at the creature; if she were his size, she wasn't so sure she would have faced down that tagor.

Together, he and Vaelor had slain the swamp beast. Hearing about them was one thing—but seeing them rear up on their wings and surge out of the water... She shuddered, glancing back toward the dead animal. She really hoped they wouldn't see another one up that close.

What Fig wouldn't give to be back at Green's Tavern sipping ale right about now. Or back in the Gold Wood, in Emrah's tower, safe and surrounded by delicious magic. Dev had dried them all off with a burst of amethyst air, but Fig's tunic and pants were stiff with salt and reeked of swamp water.

"It's almost ready," Mairead said, turning the meat on the spit once more.

Fig glanced at the dryad. "You can join us, if you want."

The dryad met her gaze then glanced at the fire. "My kind doesn't eat meat."

"I know, but you could still join us."

"I'd rather not."

"I can keep the fire under control," Fig said, "if sparks go astray or anything."

The dryad clutched her arms about herself, glanced up at the sky as if praying to the gods, then trudged over on her bare wooden feet.

"I could do with a bit of drying out," she admitted quietly as she approached. Her face seemed to brighten as she reached the circle of heat coming from the fire. Moss covered parts of her torso, and twigs stuck out from her trunk in a V-shape on her upper chest. More twigs came from Fenra's wrists, almost in the fashion of bracelets. Leaves fell in a cascade halfway down her back, willowy and green. Even now, her bright green eyes blazed in the darkening night.

Dev, lounging against the cypress tree that took up much of their little island, said, "So, care to tell us why you fell out of the sky and sicced a tagor on us?"

The dryad's leaves curled up, and she clutched herself tighter. "Look, I said I was sorry! You startled me! What are you people doing out in the middle of the *solanse*, anyway?"

Fig shot Dev a look to shut up. "What's your name?" she asked the dryad.

"Fenra of the de Wald gathering."

"Well, Fenra of the de Wald gathering," Fig said, "you're looking at the king of the Rayvan throne, Devryn Verrence, and his assorted..."

"Council," Dev offered with a nod.

"I was going to say ruffians," Fig japed.

"Hey," Mairead piped up, "I'm no ruffian. And I don't think I ever agreed to be on any kind of council, either."

"Look, if you don't want to associate with me—" Dev began.

"And I'm Fig," she continued, speaking over him. Fenra didn't seem amused by their jesting and was still standing woodenly on the edges of the firelight. "Fairaleigh Veil, that is. But everyone calls me Fig."

Dev whistled and said, "She doesn't often admit to being named Fairaleigh. You should feel special."

"I'm sorry," Fenra said, "but did you say you were the *king*?" Her tone was unmistakably stern.

That shut Dev up. He crossed his arms, watching Mairead take the skewered tagor meat off the fire.

"It's complicated," Fig said. Something popped in the fire, and she caught the resultant projectile with her magic, tossing it back in with a flick of her fingers.

"Thanks," Fenra murmured.

"Are you drying out at least?" Fig said.

"A little."

Silence descended upon them, growing more awkward by the minute.

"Look, I'm sorry for dropping out of the trees like that," Fenra admitted. "I was heading back to my family ledge, and I got distracted when I saw your boat, and—"

Fig glanced at him out of the corner of her eyes with a smirk.

Fenra crossed her willowy arms over her chest. "But aren't you k—"

"King? Yes, well..." Dev said, accepting a piece of meat from Vaelor. He sucked his teeth. "A few days ago, my *father* was king. Now he's dead, and his killer sits on my throne. And despite securing two good companions to aid in my escape from Tytan, not *one* but *two* boats upon which I was supposed to flee on have been destroyed."

"Oh," Fenra said, voice growing quiet. "Well, my trouble isn't so bad as that."

"Dev likes to be dramatic," Fig explained. "But I am a little concerned about the whole destroyed boat thing myself. How are we going to get to the Notch?" *Or out of here alive?* Not that she would voice that aloud.

"We have to go inland, right?" Mairead said, hopeful.

Vaelor nodded. "Yes, if we make our way to Verindas, we can charter another boat. Or a carriage, if we decide to take the roads."

"I vote carriage," Mairead blurted out.

"It'll be slower," Vaelor added. "The lowlands roads aren't very straightforward. And we'll have a greater risk of running into the silversword patrols."

"I'll take slower over more tagors myself," Fig muttered. "How far is it to Verindas?"

Vaelor glanced around, and Fig was again struck by how different he looked without his armor. She wondered if he had always been so muscular, or if the transformation to a silversword had something to do with it. Perhaps the weight of all that armor had prompted it. Her eyes lingered on his for a second longer than necessary. She glanced down at the meat skewer Mairead had given her and dug in.

"A day's walk, perhaps. It's slow without a boat. That's obvious, I suppose."

Fig gave him a half smile. "Well, there's no way out but through," she said bracingly.

Fenra grimaced. "How very true," she said, almost to herself. "I'll escort you wherever you're going. It's the least I can do."

"Are you sure?" Fig asked.

The dryad looked away from the fire, examining her woody fingers as she flexed them. "I'm really in no hurry to get where I'm going, and it's my fault the tagor attacked you."

Relief sank into Fig's bones. Though Vaelor said he was familiar with the salt swamps, the dryads lived here—they were a part of it. The elder generations rooted themselves in ancestral gatherings and stayed there for eternity.

"I'm certainly not going to turn down your offer," Dev said. "And you're welcome to come with us to the Notch and even beyond, if your—er—troubles are something that you need to get away from."

Fenra shuddered, her leaves shaking in a charming way. "No, no. I'd rather stay in the *solanse*. But I can guide you to Verindas, I've been dozens of times with El, my brother. Besides, I can get you there in half a day."

"Even better," Fig said with a grin.

Then the firemoths came out, their green bodies glowing in the canopy above them as they flitted about. It was reminiscent of the glittering glow of the Gold Wood, and Fig clutched her arms around herself. The *solanse* did have a deep magic to it, albeit a different one than the Gold Wood.

She could do without the tagors, though.

Dev's laughter rang out as he chatted with Mairead, and Fig turned to give him a dirty look as they picked their way through the wetlands. "Keep that up and you'll draw the tagors," Fig called over her shoulder.

Fenra led them along the dryest route she could, but they had already waded through the swamp waters a few times when there wasn't another choice. The dryad didn't seem to like getting wet either and bemoaned the waterlogging of her feet every time they had to enter the water.

Dev waved off Fig's chastising and kept up his banter with Mairead, though admittedly a little quieter. Fig smiled at the sight of him looking happy. The red sister didn't look happy, but for once, she looked less miserable. Fig supposed the woman had a lot on her mind since getting ousted from the sisterhood.

Looking good still, Emrah reported to everyone, now on alert from above. Fenra had assured them that Emrah was in no danger flying through the salt swamps, as long as he didn't fly near the water. The tagors couldn't see too far above the surface.

Thank you, Fig replied to him, meaning it.

"We'll have to cross here, I'm afraid," Fenra said, standing on a short ledge of land, the cage-like roots of a viragrove tree descending into the swamp water. "But the good news is we're close to Verindas!"

Fig's dry mouth rejoiced. The first thing on her agenda was to get a hold of some fresh water, then they could worry about getting out of here. She had learned her lesson in Nova Istra—health first, escape second. And Fenra had found them some dark purple berries which had wetted their mouths as they continued their damp trek.

Fenra easily slipped down into the water with a grimace on her wooden face and trudged on. Vaelor paused at the edge and offered Fig his hand.

"Thanks," she said, accepting it and lowering herself regrettably into the water once more. She quickly followed Fenra, not wanting to be a lone target in the waist-high water. Oh, how she looked forward to a nice long bath. She hardly dared to get her hopes up about having enough time in Verindas. And then to be fully dry after...

"Is that it?" she said, squinting into the distance.

"Verindas?" Vaelor said, sloshing through the water right behind her, his hand on his sword hilt. "Oh, aye, that's it."

A series of boardwalks broke up the swamp, their horizontal lines sticking out like a sore toe amid the trees. Emrah flitted down to land on her shoulder.

"Thank the Bard," Fig breathed. "I can't wait to get out of these clothes."

A snort came from Emrah. Fig dragged her sopping wet feet from the water and onto the next soggy island.

"That's it, is it?" Dev said, coming up behind her, Mairead clutching his arm.

Fig nodded. "Let's find a tavern first—and get water. Then we can deal with a carriage."

"Agreed," Dev said. "I'm wetter than I've ever been in my life. Bard strike those silverswords, I'm sure they can't have gotten this far south yet—if they even saw us."

As Verindas came into view, Fenra guided them toward one of the boardwalk openings by a dock, a rotten set of stairs leading out of the muck. Fig sighed when her feet touched the steps. It felt good to finally be on what passed for dry land. The boardwalks all led inland; they were out of the swamp.

Fig gasped, freezing on the steps. "I think the silverswords outside

Nova Istra saw us." Four silverswords stood at attention at the next dock; another two strode down the boardwalk, inspecting some of the shops and run-down inns. The place was crawling with them.

Fig pulled away. "Fenra," she hissed, "we can't go up there. Emrah, tell her."

As Emrah's words no doubt filtered to the dryad's mind, Fenra fell back as well, and they all retreated quietly down the stairs, hearts racing, back into the muck.

"Did they see you?" Fig whispered to Fenra, drawing her behind a set of cypress trees. The rest followed, hastily glancing over their shoulders.

"N-no, I don't think so," the dryad said.

Emrah flitted off Fig's shoulder and scrambled onto the tree so he could peer around it. *They're just standing there,* he reported.

"Bloody Bard!" Dev said.

They had been so close.

"Vaelor," Fig said. She reached out to touch his forearm, but he turned at the sound of his name. "Are there normally half a dozen 'swords at just one corner of Verindas?"

He frowned, his silver-ringed eyes shadowed in anger. "Rhivven will have sent them. He's had time, so he's probably got them in all the ports, even one such as this."

Bloody Bard, Emrah repeated. *We'll never get out of here.*

"What are you complaining about?" Dev griped. "Your feet aren't even wet! I've got salt water in places I don't even—"

"Dev, calm down," Fig said. "Vaelor, didn't you say your *grimazir* lived near here? Would she be able to help us?"

Vaelor crossed his arms and looked away. "I...perhaps. But let's just move away from here, aye?"

Fig nodded, letting Fenra lead the way, while making sure to keep plenty of trees between them and the boardwalks. It felt like they were losing ground, going back north to skirt around Verindas. Her mouth was suddenly a hundred times drier. Oh, and how she had been looking forward to bathing. She would never take clean clothes for granted again.

She caught up to Vaelor, who was hacking away at some vines with unwarranted violence. Emrah flew up ahead with Fenra, keeping an eye out from above.

"So your *grimazir*..." she began. "She's around here?"

Vaelor nodded, slicing through the vines with a final slash.

"Careful where you're swinging that thing, eh?" she said.

He gave her a look. "*Mir desz*," he muttered to himself in Virenish.

"So..." she prompted. "We've got nowhere else to go."

"Actually, the Ebenze market is a few days south of Verindas. I doubt Rhivven would send any silverswords there, and we could get a carriage."

She gawked at him. "A few *days*? Of walking through the swamp?" She was exhausted after spending one morning without a boat. "We're all out of water!" she hissed.

Maybe we go back and steal a boat, Emrah chimed in to Fig, sparks sifting down from where he flew up ahead.

Are you eavesdropping up there? she asked him.

Why? he replied. *Are you having a private conversation with the swordsman?*

Her face warmed, and she chose not to respond.

"Your *grimazir* not like you or something?" Fig asked quietly.

Vaelor gave a reluctant chuckle, emanating from deep within his chest. "The opposite, actually. But I haven't seen her in two years."

"And...?"

"Not since I was turned silversword."

"Oh." Fig paused, thinking. "Oh! She doesn't know?"

"She knows," he said darkly.

The sun chose that moment to slant its rays directly into Fig's eyes, and she stumbled on the muddy bank. She reached for something—and found herself clinging to Vaelor's outstretched arm.

"Thanks," she muttered with a glance into his silver-ringed eyes. Something etched into his face made her decide to stop her interrogation. She knew what that pain looked like. They would just have to find another way.

To her surprise, though, only a few minutes later, Vaelor spoke again. They were waist-deep in the swamps, the gold-orange rays of the sun blinding them every so often through gaps in the foliage, as it began its descent toward the horizon.

"My *grimazir* was there when the silverswords came to House Resbrok, during the Slaughter. I thought she would be safe there, her and Perrin. But as each of the other Houses fell, including House Ashbrok—our last defense—we were done for." His voice shook, and he gazed at the path ahead.

Fig remained quiet; she had only ever seen the aftermath of the Slaughter: the fires.

Vaelor cleared his throat. "In the end," he said, "they gave me two choices—die by my own sword or take up the silver. The only way I would know my family and people would be safe is if I weren't dead."

"I see," Fig said quietly.

"But I didn't think my *grimazir* would want to see me as a changed *thing*."

She gasped, mind reeling. "You're not a *thing*, Vaelor! Is that why you don't want to see your *grimazir*? You think she...won't want to see you?"

"I know she won't."

"Well, I think you're wrong," she said with a huff. "You did this to protect them. You...what, went to Rayva after the Slaughter to work under the king?"

"Yes," he grunted. "I wasn't the only one, either. A few from the other Houses crossed over too. Though I know at least two who didn't quite survive the rite."

"I was wondering how a Viren became a silversword so close to the prince," she muttered.

A chuckle burst forth from him. "Oh, aye? What else have you been wondering, goldfire?"

Her cheeks warmed, and she let out her own chuckle. "If you're always this grumpy, or if it's just because you got stuck following Dev around?"

They were walking side by side now, and he rolled his silver-ringed eyes, then let his gaze settle on her. "Very well," he said, changing the subject. "We'll go to my *grimazir's*."

"Are we sure we should be so close to the boardwalks?" Mairead asked an hour later.

Vaelor had left Fig's side to lead with Fenra, and they were charting a course parallel to a series of boardwalks that Fig was certain led back to Verindas. It was as if her longing to be in a nice dry inn was only a few steps away.

Emrah snarled in an affronted sort of way. *I'll tell you if I see any 'swords.*

"It's unlikely they'd be patrolling all the way out here," Vaelor said.

"Yes, but isn't it also unlikely there would be *that many* 'swords in Verindas?" Dev asked.

"I suspect if they had really spotted you in Nova Istra, there would have been a whole army here."

Nodding, Fig said, "There *were* a Bard-forsaken amount of them in Nova Istra."

"Are you sure it's safe to go to your *grimazir*'s?" Mairead asked. "Won't the 'swords know to look for you there?"

Fig's stomach plummeted and she stopped in her tracks. "Bard's quill," she muttered. "You're right. We can't put Vaelor's family in danger."

Vaelor exchanged glances with Dev as everyone drew to a halt. "It will be safe," Vaelor said cryptically.

Fig furrowed her eyebrows, and Dev changed the subject. "Does this boardwalk lead to your *grimazir*'s?" Dev asked. "Can we just follow it?"

"It does," Vaelor said, leading the way again, "but I think that would be like asking a tagor 'round for tea."

Dev slapped his leg, descending into a fit of chuckles. "Vaelor! I don't think I've ever heard you so much as make a play on words before! Where is this coming from?"

"I think I have you to blame, Your Majesty."

Fig glanced between the two men, a smile dancing on her face. Despite Vaelor's nervousness at meeting his *grimazir* again, he seemed to be in a better mood than usual. She supposed they all were—the swamps were getting shallower the further they went, leaving the waters far less likely to be hosting any lurking creature. Up ahead was the promise of dry land and fresh water...

She licked her lips, searching for a house in the distance.

An arrow landed at her feet with a wet *thunk*.

She threw herself behind a cypress, yanking Dev with her. Vaelor halted in his tracks, unsheathing his sword.

Clutching the bark, Fig leaned out from the tree. Should she use her flames? But Fenra stood her ground beside Vaelor, and Fig didn't want to threaten her with flames.

Another arrow *snicked* through the air, right at Vaelor. He knocked it aside with his wide blade, and called, "Knock it off, Perrin!"

A mangled yelp came from somewhere in the near distance, and Fig heard someone land in the muck, cursing.

"*Vaelor?* No! By the Bard!"

A dark-skinned boy of about eleven approached them, a bow slung across his back, his cheeks flushed. "It *is* you!" he called. "*V'rai! Ver dan Vaelor!*"

The boy headed straight for Vaelor and wrapped his skinny arms about the silversword as best he could. Vaelor patted his back once, then stepped away, his eyes downcast.

Dev took a step forward and said, "Who's this, then?"

Vaelor cleared his throat. "King Devryn," he began, "This is Perrin Resbrok. Perrin, this is King Devryn Verrence."

Perrin's already wide eyes threatened to leave their sockets. "King? King Devryn? *Bard's quills!*" Then he smacked his hand across his eyes. "I just shot at the king!" he bemoaned. "*I shot at the king!*"

Fig glanced at Dev with her mouth quirked up in half a smile.

Oh, give the boy a break, won't you, Emrah said to them all, winging above.

Despite the emergence of a dragonet in his midst, Perrin still stood in shock, one hand covering his mouth in horror. Dev schooled his expression into a properly kingly one and approached the boy. Perrin immediately dropped to his knees, looking—if it were possible—even more mortified for not offering the correct obeisance.

"Perrin, is it?" Dev said. "Please stand. I'm no king here. Well, technically—"

"Get on with it," Fig hissed. The poor boy was shaking.

"All is forgiven," Dev said. "Stand, please. You were merely protecting your property, I assume?"

Perrin scrambled to his feet, nodding. "Yes, sir. Your Majesty. Sir."

Dev gave him a regal nod. "Completely understandable."

"How come you're out here?" Vaelor asked. "Is everything well with—"

"They're fine," Perrin said, "but the Agnars' goats have been going missing far too often. *Mazir* asked me to keep an eye out."

Vaelor nodded absently. "Oh, aye. I can help you look for a territorial tagor later, if you think that's the cause, but these folks and I could do with some solid ground and clean water first."

"Of course," Perrin blurted out. "Of course! I'm sorry. Let's go!" He turned tail and headed back the way he'd come.

Fig fell into step with Mairead, whose red robes had seen better days. "Will you try to launder them?" Fig wondered aloud, waggling her fingers to indicate the ex-priestess's robes.

Mairead's gaze went first to her hand, where the red sisters had burned that brand into her skin. "I suppose I should just get rid of them," she said.

"You sound surprisingly accepting."

A long sigh came from the ex-priestess. "First of all, they're disgusting, so I wouldn't mind throwing them into the nearest fire once I have another set of clothes to change into. And second"—she lifted her branded palm to catch the sunlight—"I'm no longer fit to wear them."

Fig stared at her. "Aren't you, though? You can still heal with the holy water."

Mairead's eyes flashed in annoyance. "What does it matter, anyway?"

Fig's mouth popped open. At that moment she caught sight of a Virenish manor through the trees, but she couldn't make out much. "Look, I'm sorry, I was just—"

"Don't worry about it," Mairead said in a calmer tone. "What's done is done."

Glancing at the flask of holy water hanging from Mairead's belt, Fig shut her mouth, and opened her mind to Emrah. *I don't understand. Mairead can still heal. What good is the word from the holy city, if the goddess they all worship still allows Mairead to use the powers bestowed upon her?*

Sparks sifted down from Emrah where he drifted a lazy path above them through the oaks. *Bard only knows,* was his only reply.

She watched Emrah's progress through the trees, and they soon found themselves walking down a sandy path bordered by great oaks draped in Andisia moss like they were drowning in it. At the end of the lane stood the great manor Fig had spotted through the trees. As they approached, she could make out a finely detailed veranda wrapping around the entire first floor of the house, with spindly rails and masterfully carved brackets at the corners. The front door was bolstered by two columns and a gabled roof. The house itself was three stories, with one large tower emerging from the southern corner, all of it done up in gleaming whitewash—or as gleaming as a wooden building in the salt swamps could possibly be.

Fig caught up to Vaelor, hurrying to match his pace. It wasn't easy with his immeasurably longer strides. "This is Resbrok manor?" she asked.

His only answer was a grunt. He kept glancing up at the house and then away, as if afraid to look too long. As if it might be taken from him if he enjoyed it too much. She had seen that look on his face before.

"The house appears in good shape," Fig said. Clearly it hadn't suffered from the fires during the Slaughter.

After earning another grunt, she sighed and turned to Perrin instead. "So, Perrin, are you Vaelor's nephew, or...?"

The boy let out a chuckle, and Fig thought she saw Vaelor's shoulders relax at the sound. "No, no," Perrin said. "I'm Mistress Zula's son."

"Oh," Fig said, glancing between Vaelor and Perrin. Wouldn't that make him...

"Adopted son," Vaelor clarified.

"And therefore, Vaelor's uncle," Perrin said with a wild grin.

Vaelor shook his head. "As you love to remind me." He tousled his uncle's tightly coiled black hair.

Perrin fixed Fig with a look. "Mistress Zula adopted me when I was only a few years old. Vaelor was still living at Resbrok manor at the time."

They had come close enough that Fig could make out the vorse eagles carved into the columns framing the front door. Some Andisia moss had drifted onto the veranda and hung from the spindles lining the top of the wooden porch as well. The moss swayed in the gentle breeze like the breath of the salt swamps.

"I love this moss," Fig said, pointing it out. Dev and Mairead had drawn closer, while Fenra had drifted to the back of the group, unsurprisingly wary of human dwellings.

"Oh great," Perrin said, eyeing the moss. "Maybe you can help me clear it off the rafters while you're here. It's powerfully invasive. The slightest breeze and it starts spreading to a new place."

"Oh, um..." Fig hedged. "Sure."

Perrin let out a peal of laughter, mischief dancing in his eyes as he raced up the front steps. He pulled on one side of the double doors, his whole back going into the effort to get the heavy door open with a creak. "*Mazir*, I'm back!" he called as he waved the others ahead of him.

Fig fell in line behind Vaelor as they entered the darkened manor. He had sheathed his claymore on his back.

The damp scent of the salt swamps seemed to fade away as her senses swam in the aromas of fresh flowers, roast meat, and vegetables. Her mouth watered, but a more pressing need urged her to put her hand on Vaelor's back.

"Fresh water?" she whispered.

He nodded. "I know, goldfire," he said in a low voice. She swallowed, the nickname making her cheeks warm.

Perrin led them on an unspoken trek through the house, which Fig barely paid attention to until they reached a brightly-lit sitting room decorated in pink and gold. Cream-colored curtains lined with frilly lace bordered all the windows along one wall, the rest of the walls so thickly covered in paintings that it was hard to make out the gold and pink paper underneath. Austere portraits framed with gold-painted wood dominated the artwork with a few Virenish landscapes mixed in. Amid spindly tables, cushioned chairs, and an unlit fireplace, an old woman sat in the most-cushioned chair of all, her feet propped on a pink and gold footstool.

They all hung back as Vaelor approached his grandmother. Fenra hadn't even accompanied them into the house, which wasn't surprising to Fig. She also wouldn't be surprised if Fenra disappeared entirely, having brought them this far into safety. A dryad had worked in the Carriage House during Fig's residence there, briefly teaching them the history of Viren before moving on somewhere else, so she knew a little of what to expect of them.

Fig smiled when she spotted Fenra through one of the windows. The dryad stood stoically beside the veranda, as still as a tree. Fig licked her parched lips as Vaelor came to a halt three paces from his *grimazir*.

"*Ida moz'n, grimazir*," he said.

What's he saying? Fig asked Emrah who had swept into the room and landed on her shoulder. *Do you speak Virenish?*

I'm here, grandmother, Emrah translated. *You know, I had some friends from Viren once.*

Dragonet friends? Fig asked.

Wouldn't you like to know.

Though it was strange communicating with Emrah in her head, it felt natural somehow. She almost wished she could communicate with the others that way too. *Almost.* Because there was no way she wanted Dev talking back in her head. He sidled up to her just then, but remained silent, as though sensing the importance of this meeting between Vaelor and his *grimazir*.

The old woman lifted her chin. Her eyes were gray, and though heavily framed by wrinkles, she pierced Vaelor with a look that was in no way clouded by her age.

"Vaelor," she said. She worked to clear her throat. "*Visat* you?"

"*Va*, it's me."

Somehow, the large man looked small in that moment, his head bowed before his miniscule-in-comparison grandmother. His face was shielded by a curtain of his hair, and Fig thought she saw one of the beaded braids shaking. Without thinking, she took a step closer to him. Once she was there, she restrained herself—had she really almost just put her hand on him again? What in the Bard's name was she thinking? Too much time spent with an admittedly handsome silversword had clouded her senses.

"These are my friends, *grimazir*,"Vaelor said. "Fairaleigh, Mairead, Emrah, and"—he stopped himself and glanced at Dev, who nodded—"King Devryn Verrence."

"Oh, *mo desz*," she said, "Perrin! Help me stand!" She snapped her fingers, reaching for the boy's hand. He hadn't gotten far.

Dev, however, strode forward, saying, "No, please. Mistress Zula, is it?"

Vaelor made room for him and bumped into Fig, who was nearly knocked off balance by the simple maneuver. "Sorry," Vaelor said to her, grabbing Fig by the shoulders and easily righting her.

"It is," the old woman said, still reaching for Perrin's hand.

"Please, do not trouble yourself," Dev implored. "This is your home, and really, I'm no king here, I don't think."

"Well, of course you are," Zula all but growled.

"*Mazir*," Perrin warned quietly.

Zula cleared her throat. "Very well, *mo* king, but please know that I welcome you most graciously into my home. Everything is at your disposal. We have heard of the coup already, what with the silverswords flooding into Verindas. I do not fear them or that *briigard* Rhivven."

Vaelor's shoulders tightened.

We shouldn't stay long, Fig told Emrah. *Just get water, get clean, and get going.* Emrah chirped in agreement, and Zula's gaze found him tucked on Fig's shoulder.

"*Mo desz*, I thought I saw you there a moment ago, but then I believed my old eyes were playing tricks on me! Where did you find such a creature?" she asked. Then, in an undertone, she added, "Perrin, tea service for everyone, please."

We could all do with some water, actually, Emrah said. *The salt swamps were not kind to us.*

"Of course, of course!" Zula bowed her head, "Plenty of water," she instructed Perrin's retreating back. "And tea and sandwiches. Have Marlow help you bring the trays."

Fig watched Perrin go. Her mouth would have watered if it could; the promise of fresh water and something to eat other than roasted tagor meat and berries was all that was keeping her standing at the moment.

"And who are you, again, *mo der*?"

It took Fig a second to realize Zula had addressed *her*. "Oh, um, Fairaleigh Veil, I'm—"

"My closest advisor," Dev offered.

Zula raised her thin white eyebrows and gave Fig another appraising look. Fig's face warmed at Dev's explanation. Was she really?

"*Grimazir*—" Vaelor began, but she spoke over him.

"Once Perrin comes back and you've all had your fill, we can get you washed and clothed. *Desz*, the swamps are not kind to many." Her gaze lingered on Mairead's robes, which had mostly dried, save for the bottom hem which was completely caked in mud. "But then I do expect to hear the *full* tale of how five of you came to be together—*and* with the dryad besides."

Fig grimaced at the way Zula was ignoring Vaelor. Of course, the appearance of Dev at her estate, amid such a ragtag crew was curious, but this woman hadn't seen her grandson in years. Not since the Slaughter. Vaelor, however, took it in stride, and remained silent, his worst fears perhaps coming true. Fig, who had no family left herself, felt heat rise in her chest. How could Zula ignore him like this? Yes, he was now a silversword, but he was still the same person—wasn't he?

They didn't have long to wait before Perrin came bustling back into the room with an older dwarf, each carrying a large silver tray filled with food, jugs of water, and pots of tea. Fig had to restrain herself until they'd laid it all out on the sideboard and Perrin put out the plates. She was just about drooling while she let Dev go first; it seemed like the right thing to do.

Emrah had no such qualms and swooped in to grab a sandwich before Dev could make his own plate. Everyone laughed as the dragonet took his pilfered sandwich to the top of a nearby bookcase to pick it apart.

At least Zula likes you, Fig told him.

A snort of sparks came as the reply. *Everyone likes me.*

Fig chuckled again as she loaded up her plate with everything she saw. *I could name a few dwarves who beg to differ*, she replied. Her plate was loaded with cheese sandwiches, potato croquettes, and cold roast vegetables. She didn't think she could stomach any more tagor meat, which she suspected played a big part in the lowlands diet, based on the other sandwiches and the meat pasties she spotted.

Perrin poured large mugs of water for everyone, and Fig accepted hers before finding a seat. In the bustle of filling their plates, Zula had left the room, for which Fig was grateful.

Perrin was easier company. He filled his own plate alongside a cup of strong-smelling tea. Fig leaned over to the boy and nodded at his cup. "What is that? It smells vaguely familiar."

Perrin swallowed a huge gulp of his croquette. "Viragrove leaf tea. We pick the leaves ourselves in the spring."

"Ah," she said, "Must have smelled it in the salt swamps. I don't think I've ever had it before."

"What *were* you all doing in the salt swamps, anyway?"

"Perrin," Vaelor intoned.

"What?"

"It's the king's business, that's what."

"Oh," Perrin said, ducking his head and hiding his embarrassment in another bite of his croquette.

Fig picked up her own croquette with a smile. "I don't think Dev minds. Do you, Dev?"

Dev, who hadn't uttered a word since sitting down and attacking the food on his plate, waved his hand in a *go on with it* sort of motion.

Sparks sifted down from Emrah. *Eh, no point in keeping secrets when the svorcat's already out of the bag about who you are.*

Mairead shifted in her seat, evidently disagreeing. She hadn't exactly been in *such* big trouble when she joined up with them, but she certainly was now. Fig had lost her concern for her own reputation somewhere between getting blown up in the port of Nova Istra and nearly being snapped in half by the massive tagor in the swamps. All she cared about now was getting herself and her friends out of Tytan alive.

She finished off her food and sighed, turning back to Perrin. "It's a really, *really* long story. Right now, I think we could all do with a bath and clean clothes."

"Oh, right! Of course. *Mazir* said I should—"

"Where did she go, anyway?" Fig asked.

Perrin shrugged and glanced at Marlow. The dwarf had returned at some point and stood by the open doorway. Fig noticed a plate of cookies had appeared on the sideboard and leapt to her feet to snag a few. She also helped herself to a cup of tea and found herself edging closer to Vaelor.

He was perched on the edge of a chair in the corner of the room, as if afraid he might sully it by sitting in it fully. As if he didn't deserve the hospitality of his home.

"Can I get you anything?" Fig found herself asking.

When he looked up at her, the silver rings in his eyes looked shattered. She lifted her plate of cookies weakly. He shook his head and glanced back down.

For some reason, the memory of their sopping wet embrace at Nova Istra popped into her head—the way he had clung to her, he had felt breakable then. Maybe silverswords weren't as invincible as they seemed to be. She set her plate down on a side table and took a sip of her tea to cover the awkward moment—

Coughing, spluttering, and trying not to snort it out her nose, she tried to swallow the offending stuff. "What—eugh—" she blurted out as the taste and smell of the salt swamps invaded her senses.

Perrin snorted into his own teacup, covering a laugh.

Vaelor turned, half-rising, then stopped as he realized what was going on. "Ah," he said. "I should have warned you about the Viragrove tea. It's...an acquired taste."

Fig let out a final cough and quickly swapped her tea for the mug of water. After the cool water slid down her throat, she said, "Thanks, you two." She glanced at Perrin, whom she suspected could have told her about the strong flavor when he explained the tea.

Vaelor glared at Perrin with a brotherly look, then shook his head. "Perrin, why don't you show King Devryn to the bath?"

To everyone's surprise, Dev shook his head. "No, I'll let someone else go first—Mairead?"

The ex-priestess leapt to her feet, but just as quickly, her pale cheeks turned red. "You should really go, Your Majesty..."

"No, no, I insist. I feel terribly responsible for dragging you down with us."

Fig shared a look with Vaelor, and her heart inexplicably began pounding faster as their eyes met. Something had changed between her and the hulking silversword, but she wasn't sure what. Ever since Nova Istra. Or was it before that? Maybe when she'd almost died of the stomach wound? She swallowed, her chest tight with confusion.

Silverswords had been a constant thorn in her side ever since she'd left the Carriage House. The silver-ringed eyes spelled trouble. They were ruthless and violent, secure in the knowledge that they were stronger and better. Some said the crossover made them crave spilled blood.

But Vaelor wasn't the typical silversword. She eyed his sword hilt warily, wondering if she was imagining the faint scent of copper that had wafted to her nose. He wasn't a mage, like her; he was also no longer as human as the day he was born. She shook her head to clear it, not sure how her thoughts had meandered down this path. "Mairead, just go ahead, then we can all have a turn."

A grin spread across the girl's face, and she hitched up her filthy robes to follow Perrin from the room. Before they could leave, Marlow stepped in front of Perrin.

"Mistress Zula says you're to head straight for your lessons," the dwarf told him. "Master Taskor has been waiting in the schoolroom."

Perrin gaped at him in disbelief. "What? *Now?* But I have to—"

"You don't *have to* do anything," Marlow said gently. "Besides attend your lessons, as expected."

The boy turned and sought each of their eyes in turn, as if hoping one of them would step in and tell him he could stay and hear all about their adventures. Perrin's mouth twitched into a smile when he looked up at Emrah, who was dozing on top of the bookcase, light snores now reaching their ears.

Vaelor gave Perrin a sad shake of his head. "Perhaps you can show Mairead to the bath, and then go straight to your lesson. Would that be all right, Marlow?"

The dwarf grunted in assent. Perrin set his shoulders back. "Very well," he forced out. "This way."

Marlow disappeared after the two of them, no doubt making sure Perrin headed in the correct direction afterward.

Dev snickered after they had gone. "Poor kid. Fig, do you want to go after Mairead?"

"No, you should go. Kings need to be presentable, you know," she said, settling herself on the chair next to Dev. She didn't want to settle in too much, and she understood why Vaelor had perched so precariously on the edge of his chair. She was filthy, and every cushion in this room was soft and pristine. Instantly, she regretted turning down the offer to bathe next, feeling ten times as filthy.

When she opened her mouth to change her mind, Mistress Zula stepped back into the room. "Your Majesty," she said, bobbing her head to Dev. "Once you are settled in, I would love to take dinner with you this evening and hear more about your plight."

"Of course, of course," Dev said, glancing once at Vaelor.

"That is, unless my grandson would deign to speak with this old woman first," she finished.

CHAPTER 18

Fig's jaw dropped, and she raised her empty water mug to her mouth to cover the motion. Dev, to his credit, didn't flinch; he merely focused his attention on Vaelor as if giving him a turn to speak in polite conversation.

Vaelor looked at Zula and just as quickly turned away, as if not wanting to meet her eyes with his silver-ringed ones. "I...*grimazir*..." He huffed. "Yes, let us speak."

In unison, Fig and Dev leapt from their seats as if the chairs had suddenly turned to flames. "We'll leave you to it," Dev said. Fig barely had time to set her mug down on a side table before they both fled the room and the family conflict.

Since there was no door to the sitting room, they hastily made their way down the hall, back toward the front door. Fig didn't know where else to go but did *not* want to overhear the private conversation.

They closed the front door behind them, safely out of hearing on the front porch.

Fig frowned. "I hope Vaelor's not in trouble," she whispered. "His *grimazir* sounded more upset that he hadn't spoken to her, than about the whole..." She waved her hand.

"Silversword thing," Dev offered.

Nodding, Fig pushed herself away from the door, heading over to lean on the porch railing. "Oh, we forgot Emrah."

"He could use the sleep," Dev said. "As long as Vaelor and his grandmother don't wake him."

Raised voices now reached their ears, and Fig nodded to the steps. "Shall we?"

Dev leapt down the stairs. Fig followed. "Fancy having a look around?"

"Sure," Fig said. "But let's try to stay out of sight, eh? Telling Vaelor's grandmother you're here is one thing, but if there's anyone else about…"

"I knew you would be a wise advisor," Dev said, leading the way around the north side of the manor. Andisia moss clung to some trellises along the house, meant for the decorative flowering vines planted there. Fig liked it, even if the moss was invasive. It was as if they had been transported to another continent entirely. The lowlands were indeed a special place. It was a pity the silverswords had conquered them for the glory of the Tytan empire.

"I wonder where Fenra got off to?" Fig mused as they spotted an out-building. The scent of horses confirmed its purpose, and Fig decided to lead Dev in the other direction.

"Well, I guess we won't find out if she's in the barn," Dev said.

Fig rolled her eyes. "Marlow said Perrin's tutor was here. You really want him or any stablehands finding out you're here too? I'm starting to wonder if we should get you a disguise."

A mischievous grin danced across his face. "Oh, I like that idea."

"I'm serious." Fig flicked annoyed sparks from the fingers of her right hand. "How long do you think Vaelor and his *grimazir* will be having their *talk?*"

The sound of splashing water met Fig's ears, and as they turned a corner of the house, they spotted Mairead emerging from an enclosure abutting the manor. The wooden door of the enclosure slammed, and Mairead jumped, hitching the towel on her head back up. She was dressed in a simple black dress cinched at a modest height across her chest. The structure she had emerged from looked like a newer addition built onto the original house.

Though no longer dressed in her signature color, Mairead's face flamed red to make up for it. "Oh, hello," she said. "I guess you found the bath yourselves. Perrin gave me some clothes…" she trailed off, sounding unsure.

"You look great," Fig said, meaning it.

"I'm not sure my robes are salvageable," Mairead added.

Fig looked at Dev, but he seemed even more unsure of what to say than Mairead had. So Fig soldiered on. "Well…if they're not, maybe we can…er…get you some more…if that's what you want?"

Apparently the vagueness of Fig's response was just what Mairead needed to hear. Her head perked up, and she expertly caught the towel as it fell from her locks. Shaking out her long red hair, she ran her free hand through it, attempting to untangle the mess.

"Ugh," she said. "Do you think they would let me borrow a comb?"

Fig grinned, eyeing the bathhouse behind Mairead with envy. "Probably. Now, Dev, are you going next or what?"

***

You should come down here, Emrah's voice came into Fig's head.

Fig jolted up from where she lay curled up in a large, cushioned chair in the room she was sharing with Mairead. It was dim; dusky blue light filtered through the semi-translucent curtains that hung from floor to ceiling over the windows.

Had she fallen asleep? She had specifically sat in the chair and not on the bed so she would stay awake. Shaking her head ruefully, she rose and stretched, her body stiff from the position she had put it in for the last hour or so.

After her outdoor bath—which had been quite pleasant despite Dev chatting away through the wooden walls of the structure as he waited his turn—she had selected a dress from the pile of clothes Perrin left for them. She had schooled her hair into a quick braid and waited while Dev bathed, not wanting to leave him alone either.

The silverswords at Verindas had brought a sobering edge to their arrival into the lowlands, which they had all hoped would be a quiet escape. Once anyone realized who Dev's guards were, surely they would come calling at Resbrok. They needed to leave fast before they endangered Zula and Perrin.

Why, what's going on down there? Fig asked Emrah as she shut the door to the room quietly. Mairead had had no such compunctions about not sleeping at this time of day and had promptly fallen into the bed the moment she saw it.

You'll want to see for yourself, Emrah said, much to her irritation.

She quickly descended the stairs in her borrowed shoes, which fit perfectly, but weren't her normal style. Her boots were so waterlogged, they had probably been thrown into the stove that was used to heat the outdoor bath.

No candles were lit in the sitting room, so she wandered toward the sound of voices coming from farther down the hall. Perhaps later she would ask Perrin to give her a tour. She had a feeling the boy would love to show her and the others around.

In a great long dining room, she found the source of the voices. Vaelor sat at the head of the dining table, wearing a magnificent turquoise tunic embroidered in silk runes and designs. His hair had been washed, and he wore a few more tiny braids. The top half of his hair was swept back and framed in braids lining his scalp, the sides of his head freshly shaven. His sword was at his hip, a less aggressive position than the hilt sticking out from his back—though his *grimazir* was eyeing his posture and the sword which caused him to sit forward warily. But everyone knew you couldn't part a silversword from their Welded weapon.

Zula hitched up her smile when she spotted Fig loitering in the doorway. "Ah, join us. Marlow is about to serve supper. Who are we still missing?" She looked around.

Perrin was situated between Vaelor and Dev, clearly pleased about his placement. Fig felt obligated to sit next to Zula, who sat at the other side of the table alone.

"Mairead's asleep," Fig said. "Should I wake her?" she asked the room at large.

Dev shook his head. "I wouldn't bother. I wouldn't begrudge anyone their sleep at the moment."

"And what about the dryad?" Perrin piped up. "Where'd she go?"

Fig glanced at Vaelor, and they both shrugged. A few new beads had been woven into his braids, matching his tunic. Her eyes lingered on his a second longer than necessary, before she turned her attention to Perrin. "I think she's more comfortable outside. Though I wouldn't be surprised if she left without saying goodbye. She only came with us this far as a favor."

"Oh?" Perrin said, eyes wide.

Fig grinned as Marlow entered the room pushing a wheeled cart piled with a feast. To anyone else, this was probably a normal meal, but even after their afternoon tea, Fig was famished. As everyone loaded their plates, she and Dev began their tale.

By the time they were finished, Perrin was asleep at the table, his head of dark curls resting on his arms. Zula sat quietly, her face an unreadable mask. Fig and Dev did most of the storytelling, while Vaelor sedately ate his food. Fig wondered how his talk with his grandmother had gone; she couldn't read anything between the two of them. Maybe it was the Virenish way.

Emrah, too, had fallen asleep in one of the chairs; his little dragonet snores coming from halfway down the candlelit table were adorable— though Fig would never tell him that. He seemed to be catching up on sleep today, something that Fig longed to do, but she felt they owed Mistress Zula an explanation for showing up at her manor, and possibly putting them into danger.

"Well," Zula said, wiping her mouth with a pristine napkin seemingly in pretense. The woman was the neatest eater Fig had ever seen. "What can I do for you, Your Majesty? You've been through quite a lot, it seems."

Dev opened his mouth then paused, for once, out of words.

"Thank you, *grimazir*," Vaelor said, "for sheltering us. I believe King Devryn would like the use of a carriage to get to the Notch and perhaps a day to recover."

Dev nodded. There were deep circles under his eyes. "Yes, thank you, Vaelor. I'm all out of sorts, as you can imagine, Mistress Zula."

"I can. The silverswords are capable of setting terrible things into motion."

No one spoke, and Fig tried to glance at Vaelor from the corner of her eye. Warmth built in her chest, and she fought to find words that would sound polite, but Zula went on.

"I'm just glad Vaelor found his way back after all these years." Her voice was heavy with emotion, and she reached out to take her grandson's hand.

He clutched it back gratefully, and the bubble in Fig's chest burst. Her eyes stung a bit, and she smiled at him.

"I didn't think you wanted me here," Vaelor mumbled.

Zula cleared her throat. "I know you had to leave, Vae, and I am grateful for why you did it, but you should have known better than to not keep in touch." She sniffed indignantly. "It's the greatest dishonor in Viren, to cut off communication with your elders for no good reason," she said to Dev.

A light chuckle came from Vaelor, and he squeezed Zula's hand once more. "Only you would say that, *Grimazir*. Not everyone in Viren thinks so."

She straightened in her chair—though Fig thought the old woman had already been sitting pin-straight—and gave an airy laugh. "Go talk to the dryads then! And the people of my generation."

Belly full and a smile on her face, Fig was ready to fall asleep in her chair herself. Just as she thought about saving a plate for Mairead, Zula spoke again.

"I can get you a carriage and horses, Your Majesty," she said. "But it might take a few days. We haven't one of our own, and to acquire one without a lot of questions..."

"That's quite all right," Dev said. "I wouldn't mind with a less strenuous diversion for as long as you feel comfortable hosting us here. We don't want to put you in danger, though."

"Excellent," she said. "Because I do have a diversion in mind."

Vaelor shifted, dropping his grandmother's hand. "What is that?"

"The lowland nobles are restless, Your Majesty, what's left of them, anyway," she told Dev. "Probably another reason you saw so many silverswords in Verindas. Though the silverswords took our country for the might of Tytan, they did allow the nobles who didn't fight to keep their titles, as empty as they may feel. It's my hope that Your Majesty could meet with some of them, especially now that Vaelor is home and can return to his title."

CHAPTER

19

"How is meeting with the local nobles a safe diversion?" Fig grumbled to Emrah as they wandered the woods around the manor the next morning. "And how—*how* could Vaelor possibly return to his title?"

Emrah chirped and flitted to another tree branch above her. *Can we really say no to her?*

"I don't know, but I feel like Dev should." She shook her head, gazing around at the trees. "Where *is* she?"

Mairead hadn't been at breakfast, and no one could find her anywhere in the house, so Fig and Emrah had volunteered to go searching. The poor girl hadn't eaten dinner last night either.

I wouldn't be at all surprised if she left, Emrah said, flitting to another branch.

"Really?"

Would you?

Her borrowed shoes squelched a little in the damp ground, and she focused on her path through the trees. They were far from the deep pools of the salt swamps, though not as far as she would like. They passed an occasional pool here and there, and Fig had made Emrah promise to keep an eye out for tagors roaming this way.

"I guess not," Fig replied. "She did kind of get roped into our odd little troupe by accident. And she's in far more danger with us than when she only had her original troubles, I think."

Sparks sifted down seemingly in agreement, glinting in the verdant sunlight filtering through the mossy branches.

Suddenly a small branch on the nearest tree reached out and smacked Fig across the chest.

"Wh—" she began.

"Quiet," the tree said.

"Oh, Fenra—"

"Shh!"

Fig glanced up at Emrah in confusion. He sailed down to land on Fig's shoulder. Annoyed, Fig asked him, *What's going on?*

Mairead's over there. Looks like she's praying or something.

Oh, Fig replied. She took a quiet step away from Fenra, who was standing close to a young tree, peering around at it to watch Mairead.

"What's she doing?" Fig whispered. "And what are *you* doing?"

"She's worshiping," Fenra said, not answering the second question.

"Ah," Fig said.

Mairead knelt beside a large pool of water with her eyes closed, her palms hovering just over the surface. Fig shuddered, hoping Mairead had at least checked the water first for any lurking creatures. It was large enough to hide a small tagor.

"We should leave her in peace then," Fig said. "Come on." She tugged on Fenra's arm, the dryad's skin as hard and textured as a real branch.

Fenra didn't object, and followed willingly, not at all abashed that she had been spying on Mairead in the first place. Her leaves rustled as she spun around and headed back toward the manor.

I think I'll stay behind and keep an eye out, Emrah told them.

Good idea, Fig replied. She had no idea why Mairead wasn't terrified of tagors sneaking up on her as she sat there with her eyes closed, the perfect oblivious meal.

When they were a good distance away, Fig said, "I'm surprised you're still here. Did you spend the night in the swamp?"

"I did," Fenra said from where she strode in front. Fig could hear the smile in the dryad's voice, making Fig's mouth curl up as well.

They walked on in silence, and Fig didn't press with any more questions. She knew it wasn't any of her business, but she was curious. Weren't dryads Fenra's age supposed to be out of the swamps? She shook her head. She didn't know much about dryad customs; she had only ever been around the one who worked at the Carriage House.

When the manor came into sight, Fenra spun around, causing Fig to stop in her tracks. A waft of the freshest air came over her.

"Do you think the mistress of this house is in need of any *employees*?" She said the last word as if it were a disgusting swear, making Fig chuckle.

"I have no idea," she replied. "But we can ask her?"

Fenra's emerald eyes darted a panicked look toward the manor.

"*I* can ask her," Fig clarified.

Another waft of fresh air came over her, and Fenra blurted out, "That would be perfect! Thank you so much, Fairaleigh!" The dryad flung willowy arms around her, enveloping Fig in a cloud of pure air. Fig breathed it in like the intoxicating scent of magic. It was almost like being back in the Gold Wood, except with a cleaner, saltier smell.

After Fenra let go, her emerald eyes expectant, Fig said, "I'll ask her this morning, then, shall I? And please, just call me Fig."

They resumed walking, and curiosity getting the better of her, Fig asked, "What trouble were you running from in the swamps, anyway?"

Twisting her wooden fingers, Fenra replied, "I fled my place of employment in Thoan. I wanted to return home, but I'm not done with my *voixage* yet."

"Really? How come?"

Fenra threw her hands down. "I hate it. I just want to live in the *solanse*. And my elders are going to be enraged that I left another job."

"*Solanse*?"

The dryad gestured all around. "The *solanse*. The...salt swamps."

"Ah. Is that Virenish?"

Emerald eyes squinted in confusion.

"Never mind. Let's go talk to Zula."

Fig let herself into Resbrok, holding the door out for Fenra, but finding only empty air. The dryad had run off. Fig snorted, glancing around the expanse of moss-covered trees in front of the manor. Fenra was nowhere to be seen. She let the large door swing closed and turned to look for Mistress Zula when she ran straight into a wall of muscled chest.

Hands grabbed her biceps and kept her from falling over. "Sorry, goldfire," Vaelor said, his hands grazing her skin before stepping out of the way.

"It's all right, *Vae*," she jested.

He dropped his chin, color flooding his cheeks for once. "I guess it was too much to ask that no one heard my *grimazir* call me that."

"Much too much," Fig replied. "Where is your *grimazir*, anyway?"

"Out at Verindas with Marlow," Vaelor said, looking relieved at the change of subject. "She said she would inquire about the carriage, but I think she's also meeting with some of the lords."

"Where's Dev?"

"For once, being prudent and staying in his room."

"Oh, thank the Bard," Fig said, slumping against the wall. "I really don't think it's a good idea for him to meet any of the lords."

"I agree. The lords are capricious, even if having them as allies might strengthen his position."

Fig bit the inside of her lip, staring absently at a painting on the wall along the stairway. It was a landscape of the salt swamps, done in turquoise and gold. "Some advisor I am," she muttered. "I know he needs allies, but... At this point, I think we should just focus on getting him out of the country."

"We're in agreement there," Vaelor said, glancing at the painting that had caught her attention. A slight smile tugged at his lips. "That was always one of my favorites. It's called *Twilight Solanse*."

"It's beautiful," Fig said, staring at the yellow and gold twinkling lights scattered throughout the moss-draped trees. Again, the place reminded her of the Gold Wood. "Did someone in your family..."

Shaking his head, Vaelor said, "No, no. *Grimazir* has always been a patron of the arts. She commissioned this from a local painter, just like all the other artwork."

"Ah."

"The frames, though, those my father made."

Fig stepped on the first stair so she was just below the painting. The frame was simple but exquisitely carved, painted gold. "It's beautiful."

"He built most of this house, actually."

"Really?" Fig stepped back down, finding that Vaelor had come closer to examine the painting too. She bumped into his chest. "Oh, sorry." Sparks of surprise flickered at her fingertips.

He stepped back several paces, his expression closed.

"I'm so sorry," Fig gushed, her face flaming. Normally, her control was much better than that. "Did I burn you?"

"No, no," he said from across the entry hall, his posture stiff. "Did you find Mairead?"

Cold rushed into her fingers as she examined him. *Did* she burn him? His face looked closed off, as if *he'd* done something he shouldn't have. She huffed. "Yes, she was praying in the salt swamps, I guess. Emrah is watching over her now."

"Ah," Vaelor said. "I had hoped he could help me look for Perrin."

"He's gone missing now too?"

Vaelor shrugged. "Missing or hiding from his tutor more likely. Master Taskor should be here shortly."

"Well, I can help you look," Fig said brightly, wanting to help smooth over whatever had passed between them on the stairs.

He rumbled a throaty hum of assent and indicated they should head outside.

"You think he's in the salt swamps?" Fig asked, following his tall silhouette out the door.

"Not really, but if he's hiding in the house, he can probably hear us."

Fig snorted out a laugh, and she hopped down the front steps after the Viren, glancing once toward the swamp and wondering just how long Mairead would pray this morning. *Everyone all right out there?* Fig sent the words to Emrah, wondering if their distance would allow communication. She still wasn't really sure how this worked.

Fine, he replied immediately, soothing Fig's conscience. *She's opened her eyes, at least, but is still praying by the pool, so I'm doing some hunting. I think she's making up for lost days of praying or something.*

Have fun then, Fig replied. *Maybe when you're done you can help me and Vaelor look for Perrin. I guess he's trying to skive off his lessons again.*

A sort of laugh filtered in her brain, and she grinned at the feeling. She liked having this connection with Emrah, though she often wondered why the others couldn't talk back to the dragonet. Perhaps it was a mage thing. But then, why couldn't Dev do it?

Golden yellow light filtered through the tall oaks surrounding the manor, and Fig followed Vaelor through the various outbuildings, even taking a peek into the bathing area behind the house—after thoroughly knocking and checking through the bottom slats for signs of anyone's feet—but they didn't have any luck.

Fig began to wonder if she had imagined the awkward moment on the stairs. Once again, Vaelor was his normal quiet self, save for the occasional comment about Perrin or the property.

"Do you want to check inside again? Catch him unawares?" Fig suggested after they checked the small stables, which were void of any horses, though the smell of animals still lingered. Could you *ever* fully really get rid of the scent of horse manure? Fig wondered briefly with a sharp exhale through her nose.

"Yes, lets," Vaelor agreed. But as they began the short walk up the sandy cart road from the stables to the house, they heard the sound of horse hooves.

"Your *grimazir*?" Fig asked, her gut inexplicably flooding with apprehension. What if the woman had brought some of the lords back with her? She wasn't ready to introduce Dev to the locals.

"No," Vaelor groaned. "Taskor."

"Ah, Bard's broken quills. Want me to run in and look for Perrin real quick? Maybe I can convince him to come out?"

"*Va*, yes," he said. "Thanks, goldfire."

As she turned and headed for the front door, she felt her cheeks warming. She glanced back to see Vaelor standing stiff-backed beside the cart road, waiting for Taskor's carriage to come to a halt.

The front door shut with a bang. "Perrin? I know you're in here!" Fig called out. She stalked through the entry hall, poking her head into the sitting room. "Your tutor is here, and I don't think Vaelor should have to offer excuses for you!"

Voices raised outside, and she turned. Just as she was about to leave the pink perfection of the sitting room, she heard furniture scraping aside.

"Perrin?"

"Hi Fig," the boy said sullenly, coming out from behind Zula's chair. He turned his back to cover up the hidden panel in the wall, but Fig had already seen past him into the dark opening.

"Your tutor is here," Fig intoned, cocking a hand on her hip.

"I know," Perrin said.

Fig's ears perked up again at the raised voices outside. Should she go and intercede? It wasn't as if Perrin was even late yet, right? She had never heard Vaelor raise his voice before, but his baritone definitely contributed to the shouting.

Deciding to stay out of it, she asked Perrin, "How come you don't like your lessons?"

He rolled his eyes, then shrugged. "It's...they're fine. I would just rather be doing other things."

"Like sneaking around in hidden hidey-holes?"

A mischievous grin lit up his face, and he glanced at the wall panel, beckoning her closer. "It's not just a hidey-hole," he divulged, "it leads to—"

The front door slammed open, and he jumped. Fig turned to catch sight of Taskor striding stiff-backed down the hallway, a black cloak fluttering in his wake.

She shared a startled look with Perrin, whose face had emptied of all mischief. Fig reached out and awkwardly patted him on the shoulder.

"Hey," she said, "How about when your lessons are over, I'll take you outside, and Emrah and I can show you our fire magic."

His deep brown eyes lit up, and she grinned back at him. And with that, he skipped off, leaving Fig alone.

She wasn't alone for long, however. After she spotted the teapot sitting on an iron trivet over a lit candle, she crossed the room, and heard someone enter the room behind her.

"What were you and the tutor shouting about?" Fig asked, lifting the teapot and pouring some into one of the clean cups on a tray. It didn't smell like viragrove tea, for which she was thankful.

It wasn't Vaelor who answered, but Zula. "What's going on with Vaelor and Taskor?" the old woman asked sharply.

Fig's mouth formed a little *o* of surprise as she realized. The front door boomed shut again. This time, it really was Vaelor who strode into the room. Fig moved back to her position by the teapot.

"What's this I hear about shouting at Taskor?" Zula inquired. Vaelor lingered in the shadows of the doorway, and Fig thought she saw a deeper shadow around one of Vaelor's eyes. Zula went on, "Perrin wasn't late again, was he? Pour me a cup while you're there, *der*, won't you?"

Fig did as she was asked. She caught Vaelor's eye, but he shook his head *no*, so she settled down into a plump chair with her own steaming cup.

"No, Perrin was on time," he said. "Taskor just wanted to have words with me."

Zula pressed her lips into a thin line, and she peered closer at what looked like a bruise forming on Vaelor's face. He turned his face away, as if he were considering a cup of tea from the sideboard.

Teacup clattering onto her saucer, Fig thought a change of subject was in order, and blurted out, "Mistress Zula, the dryad who accompanied us here, Fenra, wanted me to ask you something."

"*Va?*" Zula said, taking a sip of her tea and turning toward Fig. "And what's that?"

Leaning back into her chair, her cup positioned on her thigh, Fig went on, "I think she needs employment, for her pilgrimage, you know? I'm not sure what she's fit for, but are you...in need of anyone?"

Zula frowned in thought. "*Ida*... Perhaps. I'd like to speak to the dryad, of course. And her elders, *meve*."

"*Grimazir*," Vaelor said in astonishment. "You can't go out into the—"

A wily grin stretched across Zula's face. "*Mo der* Vaelor, I am capable of a great many things and have been since your departure."

He hung his head. Fig was certain that was a bruise around his left eye. Had Taskor punched him? What in the Bard's inky fingers had they been arguing over, anyway?

"*Ida moz'n* now, *grimazir*. I'm here now. You know I cannot begin to—"

"I do not fault you for it," Zula said. "As I told you the other night. I understand why you did it. You and I both know the 'swords slaughtered the families of anyone who chose death over the sword. I don't care what you are now, only that you're *here*. And Perrin and I are only alive because you chose the sword."

"But if I *hadn't* fought in the war, like Lord Onalde, or—" Vaelor began as if bringing up a point from earlier.

"Well, he was too old." Zula swatted her hand. "And if you hadn't fought, you would not have guaranteed our safety or helped Viren stand just a little longer. You did the right thing."

Fig tried to shrink further into her chair, much like Vaelor was trying to blend into the shadows of the doorframe. She shouldn't be here for this. Shouldn't be picturing Vaelor being taken from the manor, leaving Perrin and Zula behind, clinging to one another on the front steps.

Shouldn't picture the silverswords dragging Vaelor away and performing the mysterious arcane ritual that had transformed him into the fastest, strongest version of himself, imbuing his sword with the power that flowed through man and weapon. His strength in his sword.

Had they done it somewhere in the salt swamps? Or taken him out of the lowlands first?

Fig toyed with her upper lip, vowing never to voice those questions aloud. It wasn't her place. But she couldn't stop staring at Vaelor and wondering. Before, he had just been a slab of muscle and armor, handsome, and good at protecting Dev. Now, she saw a depth to him she hadn't expected.

Zula resumed speaking. "Anyway, *der* Vaelor, I will save you the anguish and not venture into the *solanse* to meet the dryad's elders. A conversation with the girl herself will do."

"Thank you," Fig said after clearing her throat. "I gathered she would like to finish her pilgrimage near the *solanse*."

"And who wouldn't?" Zula replied. "Now, Fairaleigh, would you be so kind as to retrieve our king from his room? I need to arrange something with him."

With her teacup deposited on the sideboard and a polite nod at Zula, Fig left the sitting room heaving a sigh of relief.

It wasn't until she heard footsteps on the stairs behind her that her chest tightened again. She knew it was Vaelor this time.

She whirled around at the top of the stairs, clutching the dark wooden baluster. "What happened to your eye?" she demanded.

Vaelor opened his mouth, then closed it. "I..."

"Taskor hit you?"

He said nothing, all but confirming her suspicion.

"Not going to tell me what that was about, huh?" she asked, crossing her arms over her chest.

"It's not important."

"It better not be," she said, relenting. "Perrin's safe, right?"

He grunted, "Of course. This is between Taskor and I."

She narrowed her eyes, but who would want to hurt that sweet kid, anyway? "What do you think your *grimazir* wants Dev for?"

He shook his head slightly and leaned closer to whisper, "Morgha only knows. Meeting with the lords, probably."

"And we're sure we want to let him do this?" Her fingertips tingled, and she reigned in the sparks she longed to summon out of nervousness.

Vaelor shook his head slowly. "I don't know if he'll listen to me."

"It's not like he'll listen to me, either."

"But he sought you out," Vaelor said. "He told me you were the best thing that happened to him at the Carriage House."

"Really?" Fig's chest constricted, and her eyes suddenly burned. She hung her head. "And I left him. I left him there alone when I ran away."

Vaelor was silent. "I know how you feel," he admitted. His voice was so soft she had to lean closer to hear him. "When I left Resbrok. I broke ties with my family and became the one thing we all hated. It's like I don't deserve..." He trailed off, clearing his throat suddenly and looking away.

Fig's hand slid along the banister, her fingertips getting closer to his by the second. Her heart racing, she lifted her fingers—

He pulled his hand away, his expression one she'd seen a few times before. Like he didn't deserve happiness.

"We'll have to speak with him," Vaelor said, gesturing with his retracted hand toward Dev's door.

Fig swallowed, nodding. What had she been thinking? Her hands balled into fists, attempting to restrain the sparks that longed to burst forth.

"Right," she said. "Also, how long can we stay here? Won't the 'swords know that you might come here?"

Vaelor crossed his arms over his chest. "The 'swords know I was his protector, of course. I've been his protector since crossing over. But that is where we have some security."

"What do you mean?" she hissed.

"I took an oath," he said. "When I crossed over. I swore to serve House Verrence."

She narrowed her eyes. "Don't silverswords normally swear to serve the enclave?"

He lowered his head in a nod. "That is the usual way. But as the last fighting House in Viren to fall, I used that to my advantage. My oath is to the Verrences, not to the crown or the enclave."

"Oh," Fig said. "So if they come looking..."

"I've done nothing illegal, nothing punishable. Many saw my oath or heard of it. It's not often Virenish lords cross over. They'll know."

"But they'll probably still think Dev is with you," Fig said.

"That's—"

A door down the hallway creaked slightly, and Fig thought she saw a glint of purple in the air. She huffed out through her nose, and jerked her head to tell Vaelor to follow as she strode toward the door.

Stiff-arming it open, she caught a faint "Ow!" as she headed into Dev's room.

He was standing behind the door, rubbing his nose.

"Not very *kingly* of you, Dev, to be eavesdropping on us," Fig said loftily. "Nor very subtle."

The king in question rolled his eyes and sauntered over to his bed, where he flopped onto it in a *very* unkingly way, then sat upright, surveying the two of them.

"Not very *advisorly* of you two to be whispering secrets at the top of the stairs, is it?"

"We were strategizing!"

Dev scoffed. "Strategizing?"

Throwing her chin out, Fig said, "Yes, that's what advisors do, isn't it?"

A smirk etched into his features, Dev leaned back onto his pillows. "Very well, advisors. Advise me. I've got a meeting with a Virenish lord that Zula's setting up. What do you think I should angle for?"

Fig shared a worried look with Vaelor. Her stomach swooped as their eyes met. "Dev," she began. "Do you really think it's wise to let anyone know you're in the lowlands? I mean, the silverswords at Verindas might not have known you were here, but if word gets out, they'll definitely..."

"I think it's wise," Dev said carefully. "We might as well not squander away our time here, and the more allies we can draw, the better. Besides, this one knows something about who's ruling in the Hollow Isles."

Drawing nearer the bed and leaning against the wooden bedpost, Fig stared at him. His hair was perfect as ever, and he had donned a black tunic and dark gray pants, which laced up at the calves. He had on a gaudy purple necklace; he must have hidden it under his clothes, since Fig hadn't noticed it before. But the black tunic had a deep *V* at the neck, revealing it.

"Isn't that..." Her breath caught, remembering twining her fingers around that very necklace, while her other hand wove through his perfect hair... She shivered, reining in the tingling in her fingers. *Stop it,* she told herself. *That was a long time ago.* But something about her conversation with Vaelor at the top of the stairs had shifted something in her.

"My mother's, yes," he said, his hand straying toward the purple, black, and gold trinket. "Amethyst from Nithe, remember?"

"What a coincidence," Fig deadpanned. "Exactly where we're headed. And you think this lord knows something about who's ruling there?"

He nodded, dropping the gem back against his chest. "Quite sure. And since Zula said the carriage wouldn't arrive for another two days—"

"That long?" Fig cried out.

"Not many to rent out here," Vaelor explained. "And they don't have the money for—you know, with the upkeep of horses and everything..."

Fig frowned. "Couldn't we just, I don't know, borrow someone else's?"

"Like Taskor's?" Vaelor asked sardonically.

Scoffing, Fig said, "Fair point. Maybe you'll tell *the king* why Perrin's tutor punched you in the face?" Victory surged in her chest as she pulled the ruling marstone on Vaelor.

Dev bolted up straighter, examining the silversword's eye. "I thought I saw something there! Well?"

Shooting Fig a dirty look, Vaelor clasped his hands behind him in a military fashion. "Your Majesty—"

"Don't you *Your Majesty* me," Dev interrupted. "I think after everything, and the salt swamps—"

"Your Majesty," Vaelor repeated, and Fig thought she saw a

mischievous glint in his eye. "Aidienne Taskor was known to my father before his passing, and the man simply felt..." His shoulders shifted as he searched for the right words. "He felt he needed to get some things off his chest."

Dev eyed Vaelor. "Very well, Vaelor. So did he get it all? Off his chest, I mean."

"Aye, I think he did," Vaelor replied, ducking his head a little. "And he's a fine tutor for Perrin, otherwise."

"He better be," Fig said.

"Right," said Dev. "Well, try not to provoke the man, Vaelor. If young Perrin is to become Master of Resbrok, then he'll need that fine tutor. Although I do remember Zula mentioning something about you taking that title back up...?" Dev pried.

Vaelor looked as if he were chewing the inside of his mouth, then he quite obviously shifted the conversation. "About the carriage. We're going to take it into Tysaine with us, right? So we'll need—"

"To wait," Dev said. "And in the meantime..." He turned to Fig like a child eyeing a table of sweets and seeking permission.

"Fiiiine." Fig drew out the word. A hint of pride coursed through her. "But I'm going to be at the meeting."

"Of course," Dev said. "I think you'll want to see him yourself, anyway."

An hour later, Fig found herself walking down the boardwalks to Verindas, Vaelor by her side. *Advising.*

Fenra walked ahead of them, alone, her leaves rustling down the back of her head, and her willowy feet somehow quiet on the weathered planks of the boardwalk. Behind them trailed Mairead, thoughtful and wide-eyed.

Fenra had wanted to set out for her elders right away; she had spoken briefly with Zula and come to some agreement about employment. And when they had found Mairead sitting on a bench in one of the overgrown gardens reading a book, she'd jumped at the idea of going to Verindas—now that they didn't look like a group of travelers fleeing the king's justice.

They left Dev back in his room of course, with Emrah for company—and protection. When Fig had left the manor, she spotted Marlow delivering a tray of food to the room. Dev was in good hands. Probably deserved a bit of pampering and relaxation after the horrible week he'd had.

"Do you know where this is?" Fig elbowed Vaelor, holding the scrap of paper with an address Zula had given her.

"Oh, aye," Vaelor replied easily. He wore a moss-colored cloak, common among the locals, its hood helping to cast his tell-tale silvery eyes into shadow. So far, they hadn't seen any silverswords, and the lightly increasing traffic on the boardwalks indicated they were close to the city.

Humidity stuck to her skin, and she was grateful for her borrowed tunic and leggings, both of which were made from a material that didn't chafe her skin, nor bake her in this climate.

Verindas grew closer with each step; more locals joined the boardwalk from various smaller ones leading from other places in the lowlands, she presumed, like many smaller streams joining a great river.

The cypress and oak seemed even older in this part of the swamp, towering over them, and forming a mossy ceiling with crisscrossed branches and a leafy canopy. Under this roof lay Verindas, a network of boardwalks lined with shops, food vendors, and all manner of people. The sun hung heavy in the sky, dripping its orange hues over the swamp and its inhabitants.

Fenra turned back just long enough to grin and wave goodbye to her human companions before disappearing into the crowds, hardly even looking at the things she passed. Caring nothing for what drew the humans to Verindas, the dryad only wanted the fastest route to her elders. The way Fenra's face had lit up when she spoke to Zula had filled Fig with delight. The poor dryad girl just wanted to stay in the swamps. Not everyone wanted to up and leave when adventure came calling. If only Fig had that choice.

She had tried to say no, anyway, but here she was, running an errand for Dev, with a silversword by her side.

"Do we have time to try some of that?" Mairead asked, pointing over Fig's shoulder.

That was some kind of confection on a stick, a sticky ball skewered at the end, dozens of which lined the vendor's table to their right.

"Possibly," Fig said, eyeing the sticky treats. Something did smell good. She spied a cobbler on the next corner. Her borrowed shoes were functional, but she missed her boots.

Most of the stalls were piled high with produce from the highlands, fruits and vegetables that couldn't be grown here. One vendor had a sign that boasted the Softest Wool This Side of the Notch. Another read Chocolates From Tysaine.

Fig's mouth began to water. "Possibly," she repeated, turning to grin at Mairead. "But first, we need to find..." She glanced at the paper again.

"It's this way," Vaelor said, nudging her shoulder to turn left down the next boardwalk.

"Didn't Mistress Zula already come down here this morning?" Mairead said. "I saw her leave when I went out to say my prayers."

"Yes, well," Fig said, "she must have been gauging interest first. We're arranging the meeting now."

"I imagine," Vaelor said, "she probably came earlier to set down the roots and decide if they were rotten or not."

Fig frowned in thought at Vaelor's surprisingly poetic words. She turned to Mairead, and asked, "Do you always pray like that?"

The ex-priestess shook her head. "No, but it's been a few days since I've performed my morning prayers, and a lot has happened since then."

Vaelor gave a grunt of amusement at that.

"Think that's funny, do you?" Mairead said.

"Not at all. She's my goddess too."

That made the ex-priestess go quiet for a second. "Yes, that's right. Do your...*folk* even pray?"

Fig eyed him with curiosity. Of course, everyone knew Morgha had two aspects: the healer and the dealer of death. The giver of life could also take. Just as the silverswords took life and the sisters gave it.

Vaelor shrugged. "We pray," he said simply, "just not the way you do." Mairead opened her mouth to ask another question, but Vaelor held up his hand. "We're here." He pointed to a nondescript door, one which led to the second floor above a produce stall.

"And they know we're coming, right?" Mairead asked as Vaelor opened the door, revealing a set of stairs.

"Yes," Vaelor said, leading them up.

"And it's someone we trust?" Mairead hesitated at the bottom of the stairs.

"Mairead," Fig said.

"Sorry, sorry," the ex-priestess mumbled, slipping into the staircase and quietly shutting the door behind them.

Vaelor knocked quietly at the top of the stairs; the click of a lock sounded, followed by the creak of the door. An old man stood there, face framed by long gray hair and a short beard in the identical shade.

Fig came up short behind Vaelor, almost bumping into him. The man standing in the doorway was so familiar. It couldn't be...could it?

"Master Afrith?"

"Fairaleigh Veil?" He blinked at her. "Not from the Carriage House?"

"What are you doing all the way down here?" Fig asked when her former instructor invited them inside his flat.

It was airy and soaked in the orange haze of the dying sun from a large front window, which gave all of his potted plants a warm glow. The floors were made from the same wooden planks as everything else in Verindas: the boardwalks, the buildings, everything.

"I could ask you the same thing," Afrith said, sitting delicately on a settee by the front window. He brushed imaginary dust off his tan and maroon kaftan robe. The settee and surrounding tables were mostly of Tysainian design, with intricately carved wood and splashes of color and gold in their framework. Tapestries and paintings lined the walls, making the small flat look like it could be part of the boardwalk market—a traveler's collection from all over the continent.

Fig gave him an enigmatic smile, not quite ready to divulge exactly what she was doing in the lowlands, despite their reason for meeting Afrith this afternoon.

"Can I get you and your friends some *kafye*? It's imported directly from Tysaine."

"Um, sure," Fig agreed, glancing between Mairead and Vaelor, who were clearly deferring to her.

Suddenly wishing Emrah were here, if only for the snarky comments inside her head to make the situation less odd, she found a seat on an upholstered hassock beside a plant stand and made herself comfortable. Vaelor stood by the door, not looking the slightest bit inconspicuous in his military stance. Mairead glanced around with a panicked look in her eyes before settling awkwardly into a cushioned rocking chair and promptly sneezing.

They sat in silence while Afrith busied himself with a kettle and *kafye*-making contraptions. "Now, really, Fig, to what do I owe the pleasure of your visit? I heard you left the Carriage House some years ago."

He bustled over, a silver tray with decorative glass *kafye* cups in a circle around a matching tall pot. Then he poured the cups and offered them around.

Fig's mouth stretched into a smile as the aroma hit her. "I remember drinking this with you at the Carriage House."

"Of course," he said with a warm smile as he sat down with his own cup. He inhaled the steam first, a look of pure joy on his face, and took a sip. "I never go anywhere without it."

"Are you from Tysaine originally?" Mairead asked, clutching a cup she had yet to sample.

"I've traveled so much over the years, one could reasonably say I'm from anywhere," he said. "I have spent quite a lot of time on the other side of the Notch, however."

"Didn't you go to Tirnalore after you left the Carriage House?" Fig had been devastated when her favorite teacher had left.

"Ah yes," he said. "I was intrigued by their theories on the magic of the Gold Wood and taught at the Tirnalore Academy. I still teach there some seasons. I've got an office whenever I return."

"I'd heard they were studying the Gold Wood," Fig said. "Have you—"

Vaelor cleared his throat.

"Ah," Fig said, "um, actually, we're here for a different reason, Master Afrith."

"Not Master anymore," he said, *tsking*. "Or not at the moment anyway. Who knows, next month I may find myself taking up the podium again."

Fig said, "We're actually here on behalf of Mistress Zula?"

Enlightenment dawned in his hazel eyes, and he stroked his beard, nodding. "She came to see me this morning, about a delicate sort of meeting?"

"But I thought she was approaching the local lords...?" Mairead blurted out.

A light chuckle came from Afrith, and he set down his empty *kafye* cup on the silver tray. "Yes, that would be me. I hail from Viren originally—though I was raised in Tysaine in my youth. And then I was abroad during the Slaughter, but since I didn't engage with the silverswords, I am one of the few left with a title. Lord of Senaka, as it were."

"Oh," Mairead said, gazing at him in wonder.

"And you are?" he asked the ex-priestess politely.

"Oh!" Mairead repeated. "I'm Mairead Joiros, sir."

"A Sister of Morgha, I presume?" Afrith nodded at the tattoos on the back of her hand.

Mairead's hand froze. Fig assumed she was trying to keep the brand on her palm hidden. The ex-priestess gave Afrith a tight smile and nodded once.

"And this is Vaelor," Fig said, nodding at him. She didn't want Mairead to have to explain, and Afrith might draw the story from her. He had a way of doing that—his wonder at viewing the world, she supposed.

"Resbrok, I assume?" Afrith said, steepling his fingers together in his lap.

"The very same," Fig said. "Hence why we are here on Mistress Zula's behalf. She didn't want to make the trip from the manor twice, so she asked us to come."

"Understandable. She inferred a political meeting of some sort was in order."

So Zula hadn't told Afrith exactly *who* he would be meeting. Afrith had taught Dev at the Carriage House, too, but Fig was glad that Zula hadn't been throwing his name about.

"Right," Fig said. "Well, it's settled now. Resbrok manor, tomorrow night. You have a way of contacting the others?" She narrowed her eyes. Though she trusted Afrith and was relieved that *he* was the lord Zula had met with, she was unsure about this part of the plan. The rest of the lords could have loose lips and easily alert any of the silversword patrols.

Afrith nodded. "In deepest confidence, of course. I understand the nature of the meeting completely, Fig. Viren has suffered much. Though I haven't spent much of my life in the lowlands, my roots are here. My beginning. That's how the Bard starts all his tales, *va?*"

Her shoulders eased away from her ears where they had crept up against her knowledge. She glanced at Vaelor and nodded. That was it, then.

She went to take another sip of her *kafye*, but the drink had turned bitter with cold. She must have made a face, because Afrith said, "May I?"

Taking her cup, he circled it with one hand in a spherical motion, and when he pulled his hand away, steam rose from the cup once more. A glint of green sparkled in the air around it before winking away.

He handed the cup back to her. "It's best drunk fast. These cups don't hold much heat, though they're nice to look at."

Fig accepted it with a grin, sipping the newly warmed beverage. "How do you do that? Without flames, I mean?"

He sighed, settling himself into the cushions of the settee as if readying for a lecture. "Fire is not always about flames, Fig. Consider the embers of a fire—"

Something furry brushed Fig's leg, and she jumped.

Chuckling, Afrith said, "That's just Elfie." He snapped his fingers, enticing the svorcat closer to him. Elfie purred as he stroked her golden fur, and the svorcat pushed her head into his palm.

Mairead leapt to her feet with a small gasp. "I'm sorry, I—I'm allergic to svorcats."

Afrith stood as Mairead backed away from the svorcat. "My apologies, I should have mentioned—"

"It's all right. It's not your fault," Mairead said, edging closer to the door. "I just shouldn't touch anything really, or my eyes…" She trailed off. Her eyes did look a bit red.

Fig stood, though she longed to spend the afternoon sipping *kafye*, discussing fire magic theory, and soaking in all she could learn about Afrith's travels. It wasn't often that she encountered another fire mage. "Maybe we can find some time to talk more tomorrow night," she told him with a sad smile.

Nodding, he said, "Perhaps. Now you better get going before your friend…"

Mairead was bouncing on her heels beside the door.

"Sorry, Mairead," Fig said, "Go ahead, I'll be right behind you."

Vaelor followed Mairead down the stairs while Fig turned back to Afrith.

"Thank you," she said. "I'm so glad to see you. We're leaving town soon after the meeting, but I hope we can talk more tomorrow night."

"And I as well. You and I aren't meant to stay in one place forever, are we?" he said with a charming smile.

Her chest swelled, and she nodded. "I think you're right about that." For once, that idea didn't hurt as much as usual. She thought back to her cottage with Bruna; it was somewhere to sleep, a friend, and a roof over her head. But that wasn't all she needed, was it?

Back down on the boardwalk, suddenly feeling ages lighter, Fig looked around for Mairead and Vaelor, who seemed to have disappeared. Trying not to worry, she strolled to the right, keeping an eye out for them. It wasn't long until she spotted Vaelor at one of the last places Fig would have suspected—a chapel of Morgha.

She headed toward the red lantern. It shone brightly in the ever-darkening afternoon, the sun having sunk down into the depths of the swamps while they were in Afrith's flat. Fig still couldn't believe her former teacher was part of all this. The luck of the Bard must be with her; she might even get to peruse Afrith's thoughts about fire magic, if they had time. Her confidence in her magic had been slipping of late. Ever since her jaunt into the Gold Wood, it had seemed more unpredictable.

Vaelor loitered outside the chapel, his bulky form unmistakable even under the moss-colored cloak.

Fig strode up to him, nodding at the lantern. "I've always loved the different patterns on these, you know?"

He nodded with a low *hmm* of agreement. The paper lantern that hung from the wooden sign arm was decorated with a series of dots and swirls and a few prominent abstract shapes Fig couldn't decipher. They were melded together in a contrasting display of black on red. Perhaps that shape was...it couldn't be...a tagor?

Vaelor chuckled, the rumble in his chest surprising Fig. "I always wondered how it is that every Sister of Morgha excels at painting. Perhaps I should ask Mairead."

"A requirement for joining?" Fig joked.

"Perhaps," he agreed, a rare smile turning up the corners of his mouth. When their eyes met, Fig's stomach jolted. Vaelor looked away first, casting his silver-ringed eyes down toward the boardwalk.

When Mairead came out five minutes later, her face was set in a scowl and her eyes puffy. Vaelor and Fig shared a look; it wasn't the right time to ask the ex-priestess anything.

"Let's go back," Mairead said, striding past the food stalls and other vendors.

Fig frowned, but followed, with Vaelor silently guarding from behind.

"*V'rai!*" Perrin exclaimed. "Can you do that again?"

The boy's wide eyes turned to Fig, and she smiled, letting the fire dance across her knuckles.

They sat at a bench near the dock behind Resbrok. The water wasn't that deep, though she had flat out refused to sit at the edge and dangle her feet off it like Perrin was doing when she came to find him. Though the sun had set, its light still lingered thanks to the long summer nights, giving the salt swamps a golden glow. It was almost like that painting Fig had spotted inside the house.

Marlow had already lit the outside lamps, two at the docks, and several along the porch that wrapped around the house. Fig wasn't sure she wanted to stay outside much longer. Though she could see around the dock and the water, the water itself was a black mirror. Anything could be lurking in there—despite Perrin's assurance it wasn't that deep.

"Wow," he said. She could see the light dancing in his deep brown eyes, and she lifted her other hand, both fists out. The fire leapt from one hand to the other, flickering across her knuckles in a writhing dance.

He drew closer, and she pulled back, snuffing out the flames.

"Sorry, kid," she said. "It's still fire—it'll burn you, even if it doesn't burn me."

"But didn't you get burned when Emrah cauterized your stomach wound?"

Her mouth popped open. "Who told you about that? We didn't tell you that part!"

He ducked his head and resurfaced with a sheepish grin. "King Dev did," he admitted. "I brought him his lunch today while you were out, and he asked me to keep him company."

At the words *King Dev*, Fig grinned. From the way Perrin said it, it sounded less regal, and more like *Uncle Dev*. She couldn't wait to poke fun at Dev for bonding with the kid. Though it was hard not to.

"Yes, fine," Fig admitted. "Emrah burned me—and saved my life doing it."

"But you didn't get burned at Nova Istra." It wasn't a question, but he seemed to expect an answer.

She snapped her fingers, pulling sparks to the tips, and letting them crackle there. "True. Well, not badly burned. Fire magic is...complicated. If I focus, I don't get burned. It's like I have to reach out and connect with the fires to make them obey me. But sometimes, the flames are too much. Too wild. Too hot. And I get burned."

She put a hand on her stomach. "And when Emrah—" The word *cauterized* was suddenly too much to say. "I was out of my mind in pain. So I couldn't ask the fires not to burn me, as I like to think of it."

"*V'rai*," he whispered.

Dropping her hands, Fig crossed them amicably across her lap. "What does that word mean?"

A low chuckle sounded behind them, and Fig and Perrin turned.

"Looking to learn Virenish, are you, goldfire?" Vaelor asked, approaching.

Fig was glad for the vague darkness as her face warmed at the nickname. "*Va*," she said tartly.

Perrin bounced up. "Good one, Fig!"

"*Yes* was easy enough to figure out," she said with a shrug.

"*V'rai* is like a..." Perrin started eagerly, then frowned. "Well, maybe, there isn't a direct word for it—"

Vaelor tilted his head. "No, there isn't. It's something you say, when you're amused, or—"

"Incredibly impressed," Perrin added, beaming.

She looked at her hands, and said with feeling, "Thanks, Perrin."

"Do you need to get cleaned up for dinner?" Vaelor asked the boy.

Perrin shook his head, clearly not wanting to miss out on any more of Fig's fiery display. They didn't have much time left at Resbrok between the meeting tomorrow night and their carriage coming soon after. She indulged him and snapped her fingers again, producing one continuous flame.

"It's like a candle," Perrin said.

"It can be quite useful," Fig agreed.

"Was it hard to learn how to do?" he asked, waving his hands to encompass the entirety of her fire magic.

She tilted her head from side to side. "Yes, but..." she pursed her lips and sighed. "I left the Carriage House before I finished my training. I've been teaching myself ever since. There aren't many mages who live outside the Carriage House, but I wanted to be on my own. The Carriage House... It just wasn't for me."

Fig's chest warmed at the look of amazement on Perrin's face, as he continued to stare at the flame.

"*V'rai*," Vaelor said quietly.

"I don't like my lessons either," Perrin said to the surprise of no one. "But now that Vaelor's home, I really shouldn't—"

"You still need them," Vaelor said sharply.

Perrin huffed. "But if you're home, I don't have to be lord of Resbrok."

A strange sensation rolled through Fig, like she'd missed a step when going down the stairs. The flame on her fingertip doubled in size. She stood, backing quietly away as she extinguished it. Zula had said that Vaelor should return to his title now. *Is he really going to stay? Leave me and Dev?* Her insides burned, and she almost didn't want to look at him.

"I—" Vaelor began.

"You're staying, aren't you?" Perrin asked, fists clenched by his sides. "That's what *Mazir* said."

A wet gurgle came from the swamp water behind Fig. She whirled around to look. But as she turned, her hands grew hot, and a sudden brightness caught her eye.

No—

Vaelor pulled Perrin out of the way just in time, and Fig threw the rogue flames into the swamp. Thankfully, even in her haste, she'd avoided the canoe tied to the dock. *What in the Bard's name...*

She stared into the dark swamp in disbelief. She had almost burned Perrin. She had lost control so easily.

"Perrin, I'm so sorry!" She took a step toward the boy, but froze, thinking better of it.

"Are you all right?" Perrin asked.

"Are *you?*" she responded, heart racing.

"*Va,* I'm fine," he said, gently pulling himself out of Vaelor's clutches. "I'm fine. Did you see something?"

"I...I heard something," she admitted. Which was true, but no excuse for her fiery outburst.

Vaelor went to the end of the dock and took up the lantern hanging from the post, scanning the water in silence.

"I'm so sorry," Fig told Perrin again. "I shouldn't have—"

"I'm fine, Fig," he said. "Really."

But *she* wasn't.

"I'm going to go get cleaned up for dinner then," she said in a hollow voice, leaving the two of them at the darkened dock and blindly stumbling toward the house.

DEV

Dev looked up from his book when a knock came at his door. With a glance at the darkened windows, he realized it must be time for dinner. "Excellent," he announced.

It's Fig, Emrah told him. The dragonet was perched on the top of his four-poster bed like a bird, preening his scales.

"How do you know?" Dev asked, setting his open book upside down on the armrest of the chair as he hopped to his feet.

Emrah's reply came as a snort of sparks, and Dev opened the dark wooden door with a flourish.

Fig strode past him, her hair a bit disheveled, and he shut the door behind her. He shared a curious look with Emrah.

"Thought you came to summon me for dinner," Dev said. "Taskor's gone, isn't he?"

"It's dinnertime, yes," Fig said blankly, "but I'm not going."

Dev studied her face for a moment. "What happened?"

Fig paced the room, then *tsked* in disgust, pointing to the book on the chair. "You know that's really not good for the book, right?"

Dev chose to ignore her comment and simply cocked his head to the side. "What's wrong?" he enunciated. He could *always* tell with her.

She picked up the book and snapped it shut, throwing herself into his chair with the book in her lap. One of her fingers looked distinctly red.

Dev ambled toward the door and opened it a quarter. "Emrah? Why don't you go ask Marlow if he doesn't mind bringing Fig's and my dinner up here?" A quiet dinner would be a nice respite before tomorrow's meeting with the lords.

The dragonet was airborne instantly. Fig's eyes flicked to Emrah as the dragonet left the room like they were having a private conversation. "How do you do that?" Dev asked in earnest as he snapped the door shut. "Talk back to him?"

Fig shook her head as if she had just awoken from sleep, and let her eyes focus on him. "I don't know, honestly. One time I tried it, and it just *worked*. Emrah says it hasn't happened before. I thought it could be a mage thing, but..."

Dev had wondered the same thing, but he had already tried on several occasions to no avail. Must not be a mage thing. "Maybe it's a fire mage thing?" He perched on the edge of his bed and crossed his arms over his chest, waiting for her to divulge whatever had gotten her so bothered.

"What?" Fig grumbled after a minute.

Rolling his eyes to the ceiling and back, Dev gave her a knowing look.

She let out a great sigh. "I almost burned Perrin just now."

"What? Really?"

Betrayal flitted across her face before she shot back with, "Yes, really."

He raised his palms. "I'm sorry. I was just surprised."

"You and me both," she said. He eyed her reddened finger in a different light.

When Marlow came with two trays instead of his usual one, they moved to sit on the floor, using the trunk at the end of the bed as a table. Emrah hadn't returned. He was probably bored of watching over Dev like a trapped svorcat and relished the opportunity for more attention in the dining room. Perrin was proving to be excellent company; he often came up to help Dev pass the time with a game of marstones. Dev would miss the boy when they headed to the Notch.

Fig looked slightly less angry, but still morose. Dev knew not to press her any further, and they began to eat in silence. Marlow had brought grilled fish and spicy Virenish rice, along with a few covered pots and dishes they hadn't yet explored.

Though Dev had been trapped in his room all day, he found the quiet meal with Fig a welcome diversion. He hadn't been alone with her much since the night he picked her up outside the Gold Wood. That had been a strange enough reunion. And it had been Bard-forsaken chaos ever since.

Come to think of it, their entire stay in the lowlands had been a welcome diversion since his life had been torn to shreds by the coup.

"Nice to not have to talk politics with Mistress Zula over dinner," Dev remarked a few minutes later as he lifted the lid on a small ceramic pitcher and peered inside. "Oh!" he said, sniffing it. "Virenish wine?"

A sad smile hitched itself up on Fig's face, and she held up her cup. "You're right," she said, as he filled her cup. "I like Zula, but she's a schemer, isn't she?"

"She's Vaelor's grandmother. What else are we going to do?" Dev said, pouring the wine into his own cup.

Fig frowned, raising her eyebrows as she lifted the cup to her lips. "To King Devryn," she said. Hearing those words come from her lips made his heart pound. King... The title still belonged to his father. But Haemond—his *father*—was no longer. And the silverswords sent to kill Dev had embedded a horrible mental image in his brain of his father's last moments...lying in a pool of his own blood.

He cleared his throat, hitching up his usual smile. Fig already seemed troubled. He wouldn't burden her with his own. "I can't very well toast to myself, no matter how conceited people might think me. Ah...to meeting with old mage teachers," he added with a sly grin.

She pulled the cup away from her mouth after choking out a laugh. "You knew? Why didn't you tell me it was Master Afrith!"

Diversion accomplished. He went back to picking at the grilled fish on his plate with a purposeful pout. "I thought you might like the surprise."

Rolling her eyes, she shook her head. "It *was* a nice surprise," she relented. "He doesn't seem to settle down on the continent, does he? Last I heard, he was teaching in Intervale. I had no idea he held a title in Viren."

"Ah, but the Virenish titles are a bit of a problem, are they not? The Slaughter turned the meaning of local politics, and subsequently the lord's titles, into barely more than ink on paper. They have some influence left, but not much. And with so few of them...they're rightfully afraid to act against the crown. Hence why they jumped at the chance to meet with me. Well, 'someone who could have continental influence,' as Zula put it."

Fig nodded, swallowing. "I'm glad she wasn't spreading word it was *you* here. I didn't even say so to Afrith, though I wonder if he's guessed."

"It's a sad state we're in, Fig," he admitted, letting the wine slide down his throat to bolster him. "Hiding out in the lowlands with a silversword, an ex-priestess, and an occasionally troublesome dragonet. I just want to get to Nithe, talk to whoever's ruling there, and hope to Morgha I can convince them to help me. The Hollow Isles have been wronged by the silverswords just as much as I was—they've got to be able to assist me."

Her hand was suddenly on his knee, and she looked up at him, those gold and brown eyes melting his thoughts like honey, even after all these years.

He swallowed. "What's really bothering you, Fig?" he asked her quietly.

She yanked her hand away. "I...sorry. I don't know why you wanted me to come with you. I'm not a fully-trained fire mage. I can barely control myself."

He lifted his chin. "Fig, you've been through a lot in the last week. I mean, we all have. I had that *one* attempted murder. And Vaelor almost drowned with you. But that's just one apiece for us. You've got us all beat on the *almost-dying* front. That's enough reasoning in my book. You're a brilliant fire mage."

She barely even twitched her mouth up in a ghost of a smile at his jesting. No longer meeting his eyes, she said, "You don't know that."

"You're a fire mage," he said, "and you're brilliant. That makes you a brilliant fire mage in my opinion. And, well, I'm the king. So my word is more valid than yours."

As she emitted a laughing sigh, she finally met his eyes. "Bard's quill, Dev. I'm—I'm glad I'm here with you. Really." She leaned into him, her small shoulder warm on his arm.

He gave her a sad smile, and grasped her shoulders, moving her away with a parting pat on her back. She didn't seem offended at his rebuff. Sure, he would probably always love Fig in some way, but their time had come and gone. She looked terribly tired.

"I'm glad you're here too," he said. "There's no one else I'd rather trek through the muck of the lowlands with as I flee my country. Speaking of the muck, are you ready to get into that carriage in two mornings? I'm quite done with boats."

She nodded, chuckling. "We can't seem to get on one or keep one."

"Are you ready to say goodbye to Vaelor?"

Color drained from her face, and she pressed her lips together and didn't answer.

"I think Vaelor is staying," Dev said gently, eyeing her. "When I talked to her earlier, Zula was going on about Vaelor's oath at his crossover..."

"He told me," she admitted. "Why didn't you say anything? That was your foolproof reason for trusting him, right? Why didn't you just tell me?"

He nodded. "Vaelor has always liked to keep the oath to himself. It was unusual at the time, but he didn't want to be a pawn of the crown, as he put it. He wanted his master to be a person with a name and not an entity."

"Yes, I know the feeling," she said darkly.

"You know, it was a conversation like this that caused you to leave the Carriage House, right?" *To leave me.* He bit the inside of his mouth. *I shouldn't have said anything.*

Instead of hanging her head like he'd expected, she looked him right in the eye and said, "I'm not going anywhere now. I...I don't regret leaving the Carriage House, but I regret leaving you the way I did."

"Ah, well, it was my fault, wasn't it?"

She shook her head, curls falling over her shoulders. "If you hadn't told me, I would have realized it eventually. How could I not?"

"The crown shouldn't own mages," Dev said, clenching his fist. "I know that more than anyone. "For decades, we've promised a beautiful life in the Gold Wood for mages, but the price is too high. Your freedom is worth more."

"Why *did* you tell me?" Fig asked.

He laughed uneasily. "That your home at the Carriage House was more prison than academy?" Shaking his head, he looked down at his hands as he spoke. "I don't know. I've thought about it a lot for the last two years, trust me. But in truth? I was angry. I'd just come from a trip to the palace, as I think you knew. It had been a few months, and my father was still too busy to see me." His fists clenched as he remembered. The embarrassment. The rage.

Fig opened her mouth to speak, but he continued. "I know he was just busy, and it really wasn't his fault. He was the *king*. But the 'swords in the castle made sure to explain that the king didn't have time for mages. 'Swords were his priority, they said. I think there was an altercation going on near the Virenish border at the time. They laughed me out of the castle and told me to go back to my prison.

"And it was then that I realized, how could I not have seen it? Mages never left the Carriage House for good. And if they did, they never came back and were practically shunned."

"I know."

"I know you know," Dev said, this throat burning. "That's not what I'm—At the time, I felt like a prize idiot. I'd been shunted to the Carriage House when my brother Shadryn—" His voice cracked, and he swallowed, his thoughts sinking to the depths as they always did. He dashed the backs of his hands across his eyes as tears sprung up.

"Dev," she said quietly.

He cleared his throat, which now felt swollen. "It's all right," he soldiered on. "After Shadryn's crossover...failed, and we all realized my mother had Svoran blood, they took away my training sword and sent me to the Carriage House in the middle of the night. I thought it was for my own safety, with all the riots that had happened after, but..."

Memories of Shadryn blackened his vision. The royal death that rocked Tytan—everyone had thought Shadryn would be turned silversword, but he ended up dead due to the mage blood no one knew about. The blockade of the Hollow Isles came soon after, as revenge for the perceived slight from his mother's side of the family. Tytan ran ships for a few years to scare off the other countries, punishing the Hollow Isles. After being deprived of trade for so many years, Dev wasn't sure the current state of the islands, but they were his only hope.

He searched for Fig's golden eyes and forced a smile. "And then I met you and ruined your life. Probably."

A weak chuckle escaped her. "Not at all."

Shaking his head, he added without thinking, "But my father never looked down on me when my magic finally manifested. The Carriage House always seemed the logical place for mages. I shouldn't have said anything to you. It was your home before I ever came there."

"No," she said. "You were right to tell me the truth. I just... Maybe I overreacted. I might have blamed you a little, as the prince. But you know what? When you're king, you can change the rules, Dev. A mage on the throne will be good for Tytan. Those silverswords can go straight to Morgha."

He seized his cup and downed the dregs of his wine, willing away his dark thoughts. "Bard knows it. Though, I don't know how helpful meeting with the Viren nobles'll be. I'm just hoping Afrith has some information on the Hollow Isles."

"I bet he does," Fig said, her eyes brightening. "He's traveled everywhere, he must have picked up *something*."

"Hey, why don't you talk to Afrith if you're worried about your magic? See if he has any ideas. I know there aren't a lot of fire mages out there to learn from—"

"Yes," Fig interrupted, seizing the new subject with vigor, "I should. We didn't get as much time to talk today as I wanted. As it turns out, Mairead is allergic to svorcats..."

They discussed Fig's meeting with Afrith to its fullest, mused over what they might encounter when they finally landed in Nithe, and when they had exhausted that topic, reminisced about the good years at the Carriage House. Their lessons with Afrith, of course, and their excursions outside the luxurious estate with the other mages to test their magnified powers—not always sanctioned by their teachers.

What Dev didn't voice about his time at the Carriage House was the surprising feeling of *belonging somewhere* after being ripped so violently from his promised future as a silversword. Not having to act like a prince around Fig. Gazing into the depths of her eyes at the special place they liked to hide out in the Gold Wood. It felt like an age had passed since those short years.

It felt like an age had passed since the day he'd gone to Black End, a single silversword at his side.

Fig was yawning, and Dev was glancing longingly at his surprisingly luscious blankets by the time they ran out of things to say. He stood and helped her to her feet, smiling sadly when she leaned into his shoulder.

After seeing her safely to her room, he lay awake long into the night, not willing to let the memories of the past enter his dreams.

At least when he was awake, he could control them, choosing to only relive the good ones.

And not let the dark ones haunt him.

"Are you sure you're not going to be late for lessons?" Fig asked Perrin for the tenth time that morning. It was their last full day at Resbrok, the meeting was tonight, and a carriage had been promised early the next morning, but Fig wasn't sure if she was ready.

The boy nodded, dipping his oar into the water again. Emrah flitted through the trees above them, a silent flicker of gold and green through the moss-draped trees.

"I can't believe I let you convince me to come out here again," she groaned, gazing into the depths of the salt swamp pool they paddled through.

Perrin chuckled. "You didn't *have* to come," he teased.

She had arrived late for breakfast due to the late-night reminiscing with Dev but had managed to find Perrin and apologize again for her loss of control yesterday. He said he wasn't bothered by it, but when he asked if Fig wanted to accompany him as he foraged in the swamp, she was glad to keep the boy company. As the time of their departure grew closer, he had become less and less cheerful.

"Look!" Perrin said, pointing. "More ilderberries. I think we have time."

Fig glanced up at Emrah as Perrin changed the canoe's direction.

Do we?

Plenty, the dragonet told her.

Good, she said. *I really don't want to be responsible for anyone else arguing with Taskor.*

Sparks sifted down from Emrah as he circled the small island onto which Perrin was now dragging the canoe. Fig remained in her seat as previously instructed, keeping an eye out for tagors. Perrin began to fill a sack with the purple berries. She put a hand on the gunwale, admiring the woodwork, then she narrowed her eyes. "Wasn't Vaelor's father a woodworker?"

"Oh, aye," Perrin replied. "This was his canoe. Well, he made it for Vaelor when he was born, *Mazir* said."

She stared at it in awe. "Really?"

Perrin shrugged as if it were nothing to make a canoe that would withstand use in the salt swamps for several decades. "That's amazing," Fig said, running her hand down the gunwale in new appreciation. Her thoughts drifted back to Vaelor, and her stomach sank. Was he really staying at Resbrok? Or coming with them? His oath proved he wasn't guilty of any wrongdoing. And yet that oath was to serve Dev...

She shook her head and sighed.

Something wrong? Emrah asked, winging down toward the canoe and swooping onto her shoulder.

Nothing, she told him, enjoying the warm weight of him on her shoulder. *Just...thinking about something Dev told me last night,* she told him vaguely.

Oh yes, Emrah said. *Everyone was curious about why you and he were having dinner alone in his room—*

"What?" she burst aloud.

Perrin glanced back from the ilderberry bush, eyebrows raised.

"Sorry," she told him. Her cheeks grew warm. "I was talking to Emrah."

He turned back to picking, his lips now dyed purple. "Dev said you could talk back to Emrah in your head. Wish I could do that."

Wish I didn't have an extra person talking in my head, Emrah told both of them with a snort.

Fig pretended to swat at him, and he flapped his wings. "Oh, sure. You're allowed to talk in *our* heads, though, eh?"

He settled back down, claws kneading her gently. *It's different.*

A light giggle escaped her, and she scanned their surroundings again. The only creatures she saw were an obscenely bright green frog clinging to a cypress tree and a few birds scattering in the distance. "I hope Fenra comes back today," she said idly. "We'll miss her if she doesn't."

Securing the flap on the sack of berries, Perrin returned to the canoe. With a practiced motion, he kicked them off while getting into the boat. "*Va.* I can't wait for her to work at Resbrok. *Mazir* didn't tell me what she'd be doing, but at least she'll be—"

"Perrin, what's that?" Fig demanded quietly, pointing ahead.

"Just a log, Fig." He chuckled.

She stared at it suspiciously, but as they passed it, she confirmed it was only rotting wood.

They were back at the manor in no time, Perrin a master at navigating through all the narrow waterways and pools. And with the exception of one small tagor sighting at a distance, it was a rather uneventful trip. She grinned as he held his hand out to help her from the boat. She would be glad to leave the salt swamps behind and travel by carriage to the Notch. After that tagor attack, she'd had enough of the salt swamps for a lifetime.

The humidity was already playing tricks on her hair, not to mention giving her skin an ever-present coating of sweat. "I need another bath," she said, helping Perrin bring the sacks of foraged leaves and berries up to the house. "I should be presentable for the meeting tonight. And after that, we'll be getting ready to leave."

Perrin smiled sadly at her. "I'm going to miss you, Fig."

"And I, you," she said, bumping shoulders with the kid, since both their hands were full.

"You'll come back and visit Vaelor and me?"

Her jaw clenched. "And your *Mazir*, of course," she added.

They deposited the sacks in the pantry just off the kitchen, before Perrin went to get cleaned up for his lessons. Fig went to gather some fresh clothes from the room she shared with Mairead. She desperately needed to wash the damp sweat from her skin.

The ex-priestess wasn't in their room, but Fig knew where she likely was. Mairead favored a particular pool of water for her morning prayers. They could all use as many prayers as possible at the moment. She wondered whether Mairead might like to stay behind too; with Verindas nearby, surely settling somewhere out here would be better than tramping across Tysaine on some quest the girl had nothing to do with. Fig frowned. Would it just be her, Dev, and Emrah now?

She hurried to the outdoor bath area, clothes piled in her arms. She almost ran directly into Dev as he turned the corner of the house.

His hair was clean but fully dry, surely thanks to a little magic. She would have a head of damp hair all day after cleaning hers, unless she asked for his help. He, too, clutched a pile of clothes to his chest. Her eyes softened at the sight. It was so normal, so not like the king that he now was. The king he was supposed to be.

"Hey, Dev," she said, a bit sheepishly. She thought back to last night, and the warm closeness she couldn't help feeling, especially after her accidental outburst of flames at Perrin. But Dev, as he should have, kept her at a respectable distance. She hoped she hadn't made things awkward. Of course, she still loved him, but that love had changed.

Thoughts rattling, she clutched her clothes tighter to her chest.

"*Vir dan*, Fig," he said, bowing his head slightly.

"Oh, good one," she said. "What's that again?"

"Perrin's been teaching me. It's 'hello' or something close to it."

She raised her eyebrows. "I'll have to remember that one. I wish we could stay a bit longer, just for the kid's sake, but... Hey, listen," she started, glancing down at the ground. "I think last night I was a little—"

"It's nothing, Fig," Dev said, trying to catch her eye. "I mean, I know you're still madly in love with me, but—"

"Hey!" she called, staring at him. "I'm being serious, Dev. I'm...really sorry I hurt you when I left the Carriage House. I just couldn't stay there any longer. Not as a pawn in the king...the kingdom's game."

His face turned serious, and he nodded. "I know. But the kingdom is mine—or it will be—and I don't think mages should be forced wholesale into the service of the crown. Gods, mages should be allowed to live in the Gold Wood if we so choose."

Fig nodded sadly. "You're going to make a great king, Dev. Maybe we should try to infiltrate the Carriage House first, once we have your army from the Hollow Isles. Convince all the mages to—"

The sound of horse hooves on the dirt road caused them to turn.

"That's not our carriage, is it?" Dev asked eagerly.

Fig's heart pounded. "No, that's Taskor. You'd better head back into the house, eh?"

Without answering, Dev headed for the door.

Fig spent her entire bath wondering if Taskor had seen him.

Surely, she was worrying needlessly. This man was Zula's trusted tutor for Perrin. Even if Taskor had seen him, the tutor wouldn't even recognize Dev; he looked nothing like the stately portraits that hung in Rayva and across all of Tytan. But Dev was the son of a long line of silverswords, and the entirety of Viren either despised or feared them since the Slaughter.

She sighed and sunk underwater, letting the tepid water cover her head and soak through her curls to her scalp. A small shadow crossed her face, flickering over her closed eyelids.

Surging up out of the water, she wiped her eyes and blinked, only to see Emrah circling above her. The surface of the water was covered in soap suds, so she froze and pinned the dragonet with her stare. "What in the Bard's quills are you doing?"

A chirp came from him as he perched on the wooden fence surrounding the bathing area. *Mairead's crying,* he said. *I thought you should know.*

***

"Isn't this nice?" Fig asked Mairead. The ex-priestess smiled back at her, holding a confection on a stick.

Fig's stomach clenched as she spotted a group of silverswords standing at attention down the next boardwalk, and she casually steered Mairead in a different direction.

More 'swords in Verindas, she reported to Emrah, who had stayed back at Resbrok. He had wanted to come with them, but with the impending visit of the lords tonight, Dev, Vaelor, and Zula were on edge, and Fig insisted he stay behind to keep an eye on the manor. Besides, being able to communicate at a distance was advantageous.

Before they left, Fig had seen Vaelor in the study with Perrin, their heads bowed over some papers on a desk, but she left them to it.

Mairead's prayers had evidently brought up dark thoughts about the sisterhood, and the idea of leaving it all behind, including her red robes, had tipped her emotions over the edge. So Fig thought a cheerful diversion was in order; luckily, they had time.

"I'm so glad we got to come back," Mairead said. "My eyes were just so itchy yesterday..."

"Yeah, I'm sorry about that. I had no idea," Fig said, toying with her own stick, though the confection was long since devoured. Mairead was savoring hers, much like her gaze savored the sights around them. The twinkling lights strung across the store selling crystals from Chamol, the different shafra wools on display at the weaver's stalls.

"Is this your first time outside of Nova Istra?" Fig asked.

A light chuckle escaped Mairead, as she said, "No, I grew up in Thoan, but I went to Mar Nevan when I was seven, and less than a year ago was sent to Nova Istra. I haven't been around the rest of Tytan much."

Fig twisted her mouth, not wanting to pry about the girl's situation with the red sisters.

The ex-priestess sighed and shook her head. "I keep thinking maybe the sisters would take me back. I could go to the holy mother and explain. But this"—she held up her hand, the brand on her palm just as red as the day they met—"is permanent. Just like the other ones."

Fig had seen marks like those on the back of the ex-priestess's hands all her life; they were on the hands of all the healers. They contained the magic that gave any Sister of Morgha the power to heal with holy water. Dwarf, mage, human—anyone could heal if inducted into the sisterhood.

"But it doesn't stop you from healing people," Fig said, not quite a question.

"Right," Mairead said, popping the last bit of the sticky confection in her mouth. "I wonder... Maybe the brand is just a brand, to scare me off, but the blessing of Morgha is permanent and can't be taken back. Much like when a silversword—" She cut herself off. "I shouldn't really be speaking of such things." A light blush graced her cheeks, and she laughed. "Part of why they kicked me out, I dare say. Curiosity killed the svorcat and all that."

Fig furrowed her brows. "At the Carriage House, we were always encouraged to ask questions. My problem was when I realized that they didn't always tell the truth."

She perked her head up when they neared Afrith's flat. She really wanted to go and speak to him about her magic, but she couldn't very well bring Mairead with her, and she wasn't about to let the girl wander around the boardwalks on her own—not with so many silverswords patrolling about.

"I can't wait to get out of Tytan," Fig muttered to herself.

They poked their heads in a few more stalls in amicable silence. Finally, dragonets fluttering in her stomach, Fig asked, "So, Mairead...are you coming with us to the Notch?"

Mairead put down the red *kafye* cup she was inspecting and reached for another with a different azure blue pattern.

"I've thought about it a lot since we got to Resbrok," she said slowly. "I have to say, I much prefer sleeping in a bed and having food brought to me at a splendid table among company—it's been better than my time in Nova Istra, I dare say—but I can't stay at Resbrok. And Verindas...has its charm, but I don't think I want to be in Tytan at the moment. There aren't silverswords in Tysaine, right?"

Fig picked up a *kafye* cup matching the one Mairead inspected with a smile. "Not a one. Coveted secrets of Tytan, I know that much. Are there Sisters of Morgha there?"

"Yes, I know—"

Glass shattered on the floor.

A gauntleted hand clenched around Mairead's wrist. Fig took a step back from the broken cup and the silversword who had grabbed Mairead.

"Here she is," the silversword said, a woman in her early thirties with blonde hair and a sword by her side. Her companion was a sour-faced man a little older. Both had silver-ringed eyes.

"What? I haven't done any—" Mairead began.

The blonde silversword yanked Mairead away from the broken glass on the floor, and Fig followed uneasily, setting down her cup on the nearest shelf without a backward glance at the vendor. The 'swords didn't seem interested in Fig, at least.

"Heard suspicions yesterday about a red sister who might've fled the convent," the man said in a nasally voice, thumbing a dagger at his side. Fig glanced at the weapon in surprise, sure the man must have received plenty of ribbing about his Welded weapon choice. But daggers could be fast, stealthy, and silent.

And the weapon imbued its powers into the Welded.

Mairead's panicked eyes looked Fig's way, and heat surged to Fig's hands. She tamped it down as fast as she could, not wanting to add "fleeing fire mage" to the silverswords' suspicions.

"You have no reason to take her," Fig said, shoving her hands in her tunic pockets and hoping she wasn't about to scorch her borrowed clothes with any stray sparks of anger.

"It's none of your business." The woman was now dragging Mairead down the boardwalk.

Fig glanced about in panic. She wished she had brought Vaelor with her, but that would have caused more trouble. One look under his cloak hood, and his eyes would damn him.

If she called to Emrah, he would tell Vaelor, but it would take too long for him to arrive, and his appearance would just make things worse. It was up to her.

"Stop," she called in as authoritative a voice as she could muster. "Wait, please!"

"I like *please*," the woman said with an appraising glance back Fig's way as she slowed. "Seems nobody knows the word anymore, eh,

Vinniel?"

"Please," Fig said again. "Can you just wait?"

The woman halted, armor clanking, and faced Fig. "This girl's got the tattoos of a red sister," she said with a sigh. "And she was seen in the chapel yesterday, but she doesn't wear the cloak. The chapel sister had no idea who she was. Mighty strange. We're sending her back to Mar Nevan for the holy mother to deal with."

Fig swallowed. At least they hadn't seen Mairead's brand.

Mairead's eyes bulged. "No, I..."

The silversword gave Fig a look, as if to say, *See? Guilty.*

"She's not on the run," Fig said, her thoughts whirring. "She's...she's—"

Bard strike it, why couldn't she think of a proper excuse? What was an innocent reason for Mairead to leave her post?

"Come on, Ziggrune," the man said. "Let's bring her to the chapel and talk to the sister."

Without waiting for Fig's weak excuse—which was sure to bubble to her lips any second now—the two silverswords resumed their march.

"Wait," Fig hissed, following them as she dodged other market-goers. Too soon, they stood in front of the red chapel near Afrith's flat, where Mairead had gone to wash off the svorcat fur only yesterday.

The two 'swords were having a heated discussion with the elderly sister there, who was pointing to the back of Mairead's hands. What would happen when they saw the brand on her palm? Mairead was doing her best to keep it hidden.

Fig rushed over, opened her mouth, then caught sight of a miracle. "Afrith!" she called in relief. The 'swords didn't care for her, which she should have been grateful for, but admittedly Fig wasn't much of a threat. Just an idiot who couldn't string two words together to save her friend. A sour thought wormed its way into her head; without her flames, was she completely useless? No. It was time to be the wise advisor Dev believed her to be.

"Afrith," she called again, darting after the man nearing his own flat door. "I need your help," she said, breathless. He turned in surprise and opened his mouth in question.

In answer, she pointed to the scene outside the chapel. "Mairead's in trouble with the 'swords and the sister. Is there anything you can do to help?"

Afrith pressed his lips together, glancing between Fig and the chapel and thinking. He nodded once. "What has your friend done?" he asked quietly.

"Be in the wrong place at the wrong time?" Fig answered. "She's been cast out of the sisters, and the 'swords want to take her away for being on the run or something. But she really hasn't done anything wrong."

A sound of surprise escaped him, and he strode up to the elderly sister, Fig in tow. The sister had her arms crossed as the 'swords spoke to her.

"Look, Sister," Ziggrune was saying tiredly. "*I* don't want to travel all the way to Mar Nevan. Don't you have any way of contacting—"

Afrith cleared his throat and caught the eye of the sister. He shook his head ever so slightly.

The sister threw her hands up in the air. "Fine, Ziggrune, leave the girl here with me, and I'll alert the sisters. You've done enough."

Fig wasn't sure whether the last line was sarcasm or not, but the 'swords didn't seem to care. They glanced between the sister and Mairead, then departed. Vinniel slipped into the crowd and disappeared in the blink of an eye. A chill went up Fig's spine. Perhaps she was right about the qualities of daggers. Ziggrune's departure was far more obvious, as she lingered slowly on the boardwalk before turning a corner, keeping her eyes on them the whole time. Fig pulled Mairead to her side, slipping her arm around the girl's elbow. "They could still be watching," she whispered in her ear.

Mairead nodded mutely, sneaking glances at the elderly red sister who had reported her. Afrith exchanged a few quiet words with the woman, then headed out onto the boardwalk.

The tight heat in Fig's chest eased, and she followed Afrith through the afternoon crowd, thankful for the lack of silverswords down in this direction—ones they could see, anyway.

They reached a clear space in the boardwalk, which overlooked a large green pool, probably wider than the lawns of Resbrok. Swaths of watergrass around the edges swayed almost imperceptibly, once again giving Fig the impression that the salt swamps were breathing.

"Should be out of their sight by now," Afrith said, nodding.

"Thank you so much, Afrith," Fig gushed. "They grabbed her, and I didn't know what to do, and you were there—" She stopped babbling at the appearance of his smile.

"I'm glad I was there and could help. It's the Bard's luck that I've known Sister Sterinwaith for years." He leaned his elbows on the railing, gazing out at the pool.

Fig did the same, happy they were safe, but still rattled. Her fingertips hurt as she forced unbidden sparks from appearing. What was wrong with her? Was it nerves?

"Afrith," she began, "I really need to speak with you about my fire magic. It's been...strange lately."

He picked up the hand that was nearest him and inspected her fingertips.

She suspected that to anyone else they would be hot to the touch, but Afrith could probably sense the sparks beneath. He frowned in thought.

"Control is a tight line to walk when you're dealing with fire." He picked up her other hand, so each of hers was in one of his own. "On the one hand," he gestured, "there's what we expect. Our control. And then there's what actually happens," he said, lifting the other hand. "Out of our control."

"Things have been pretty out of control lately," she said.

"And yet you've been honing your magic since you were a child. Perhaps we should—"

"Would you come back to Resbrok so we can talk?" She glanced up at him hopefully.

He frowned, thinking. "I could, but I can't stay all afternoon. I've still got to touch base with one of my contacts before the meeting."

"Of course," she said. "That would be such a relief. I don't think we'll have any time after the meeting..."

She took a deep breath to try to soothe her inner sparks as she stared out at the swamp. She wasn't at all surprised to see a small group of tagors lurking at the far end of the pool, but they seemed to be minding their own business. One of them flapped its wings in a stretch, startling a nearby bird. Perhaps she was getting used to them—when they were at a safe distance, anyway.

"Now, about Mairead," Afrith said quietly. The ex-priestess glanced over from where she was leaning against the railing on the other side of Fig.

"Sterinwaith just thought you were up to something unsavory," he told her. "No red cloak. And you didn't even introduce yourself to her."

Mairead still had that panicked look in her eye. "Right," she said.

"She did have some advice for you, though, after I spoke to her," Afrith said. "She said it might be more prudent to hide in plain sight."

Mairead furrowed her brows at him.

"Don the red again," he said.

CHAPTER 24

Deeming the dock the safest place for discussing fire magic, Fig sat with Afrith on the wooden planks, keeping a sharp eye out for lurking tagors. A faint hint of *kafye* reached her nostrils as he sat down cross-legged in front of her.

Afrith had escorted them back to Resbrok, catching up with Fig about superficial things like his recent trip to Intervale and her life at the cottage with Bruna. Fig was thrilled her nearly disastrous trip to Verindas had turned into something actually helpful. The last thing she had expected when they had entered the salt swamps was to encounter her old fire magic mentor.

She knew he didn't have much time, so she got right down to it.

"My control has been terrible lately. Last night I got startled and almost burned someone. I haven't had that happen in a long time. The *solanse* doesn't have ambient magic like the Gold Wood, right?"

Afrith steepled his fingers together, reminiscent of all the times he'd taught her lessons. "That's a good question, Fig. Some say it does—the dryads would be the first to tell you that—but I think it's a different kind of magic. The Gold Wood is a special place for mages; the aurans practically speak to our blood, don't they? The magic here...it doesn't speak to me in the same way, but I don't know everything."

"You definitely know more than I do," Fig said with a self-deprecating smile.

"That comes with age, Fig, and you don't want to rush that. Once you have it, you can never give it back," he added with a shadow of a wink. "I can't give you several years of fire magic training in an hour, but we can talk control. Control...is an illusion."

Her heart sank, but she kept listening.

"And fire is one of the hardest elements to control. Once it gets a foothold, say, in a forest fire, it takes incredible effort to halt its progress. But think on this: a fire cannot burn until you give it life. It takes effort to start a fire, does it not?"

She nodded.

"Granted, it doesn't take much effort at your stage in training to start a fire, I know. But when you give the flames boundaries, directives, then it can flicker and flame all it wants...*within* those boundaries. A person can start a campfire on dry ground without a circle of stones and get burned when it leaps from the starter logs. Or a person can set the proper guards: a circle of stones, clearing the ground of leaves, and keeping a watchful eye on it."

She pressed her lips together, thinking. "That makes sense," she said. Ever since Dev had found her, everything in her life was out of control. The place she would start her fire—her own mental space—was in shambles. No wonder her fires were in chaos. "Things haven't been very calm for me lately."

He eyed her curiously but didn't pry. She remained tight-lipped about Dev. The explanation would come later when all their contacts gathered tonight.

"I can't imagine it's easy for you living outside the Carriage House," he said.

"It's not," she admitted. "But you seem to be doing well for yourself here."

He chuckled. "That's because I'm not here, not often anyway. Tysaine doesn't hold as many stigmas against mages, probably because they don't have many of them. I'm not one to set down roots, so to speak."

"Ah," Fig said. "My roots were at the Carriage House, ever since my mother brought me there." If she hadn't, Fig would have probably caught the same illness that took her mother shortly after. "I guess I've been trying to establish roots ever since, but maybe I don't need to."

The sound of a carriage leaving Resbrok caused Fig's head to snap up toward the house. It must be Taskor leaving. She thought back to his possible sighting of Dev earlier and shivered.

"Maybe," he said cryptically, also watching the carriage leave. "But enough talk of roots. Let's see those flames before I have to get back."

FENRA

Fenra's elders were not pleased.

"You really shook their leaves," El said breezily as he sauntered through the *solanse* after her.

"Well, at least they agreed," she said happily. "Did they really say you could visit Verindas?"

"They didn't say I couldn't," he said as he came up beside her grinning. "Not like they're going to follow me."

"Too true." A lyrical laugh came out of her, and she breathed deeply of the *solanse*. She was home. And even if she has to deal with the occasional smelly horse at Resbrok house, she would still get to live close enough to the *solanse* that it didn't matter.

"When I'm an elder, I'm not going to make the younglings go on pilgrimages," she vowed, clenching her willowy fingers into fists.

El gave her a side-eyed glance. "You might think differently when you've been in the same spot for decades."

Fenra shrugged, tossing her leaves. As long as her roots were near Vilvan's, she didn't care. But according to El, Vilvan still had ten years before he returned to the *solanse*. Now that she could stay at Resbrok, she didn't mind. And she was close enough that El could visit her, or she him, if her new mistress allowed it.

"Where will you go when your time comes?" she asked El. A few lights of Verindas twinkled in the distance, and the two of them skirted around the edge of the large pool where a half dozen tagors lurked in the watergrass. One slipped into the water with a brief display of its wings. Fenra led El farther to the side, skirting around the tagors.

"Come on," she said. "Getting that close isn't fun," she wheezed through a laugh, her leaves rustling as the air blew out of her.

"I'd like to travel the continent," El said simply, "from the Notch to Tysaine, to the holy city of Mar Nevan. First, though, I'd like to visit Tirnalore, perhaps tailor my travels from what I learn there."

Fenra sensed a flood of information coming, and said, "Good thing I'm putting away all my gold for you, *va, brozir?*"

"And I appreciate it most sincerely." He gave a mocking imitation of a human bow, and Fenra chortled as the southernmost dock of Verindas came into view, a large deadwood staircase leading up to the elevated village.

"You'll be fine getting back on your own later?" she asked him. "I'll stay until dark, but then I should get to Resbrok. There's some people I want to say goodbye to..."

"Of course," El said easily. A little too easily.

"How often do you come out here?" she asked him with narrowed eyes.

He shrugged, the short twigs protruding from the tops of his shoulders coming up by his ears. "There isn't much to do at the ledge besides soak up the sun." He ran a hand through the small number of leaves on his head. They found the footpath that led to the side of the dock and gazed curiously at the boats and canoes tethered there. "I can't wait for my *voixage*," he said with a sigh.

"*Iil*, only twenty more years, and you'll get to travel the world."

"I know," he said, emerald eyes lighting up. "Which is why I've been coming into Verindas, to plan."

They lurched up the deadwood staircase, becoming enveloped in all the smells and sights of the boardwalk. "Oh, so you *have* been coming here a lot," she said with a grin.

Drawing only a few looks as they browsed the vendors, Fenra found her face aching from smiling so much. El knew all the shops, and all the merchants, and tried to show her every one of them. But she insisted she didn't need a full tour and only poked her head into the ones that interested her. She wondered how often she might get sent here on errands for Resbrok and found she didn't mind the idea at all.

"I think it was lucky I fell out of that tree," she said, as night began to draw nearer, and they both drifted toward one of the docks. "And landed my best employment yet."

"I'm happy for you," El said.

They hastened down the deadwood planks, Fenra eager to get back to Resbrok, but as soon as they reached the bottom of the stairs and she turned to say goodbye to El, a heavy clank sounded above their heads. They both froze.

"Tonight?" a surly voice said. Fenra swore it sounded like steel. She clenched the railing where she had put her hand, her fingers gripping the deadwood tightly. She gave a warning glance to El, but he already stood as still as a sapling.

"At Resbrok," a lighter voice said. No steel in this one.

The steel voice replied, "And you're sure it's him?"

"Certain."

El's face twisted as Fenra pulled in some grounding air. Resbrok? What—

"Then we'll be there," another steel voice replied, this one with no emotion at all, just steel. *What was it about them?* Fenra wondered. Then she remembered. That swordsman Vaelor sounded like that, an unnatural ringing under his voice that reminded her of sliding metal. Violence. Blades. The same silver ring around his pupils. A scar on his chest that she had never seen but could sense as if it were burning silver light straight through his clothes.

She and El stood still until one of the people began to descend the stairs.

Her panicked emerald eyes met El's, and Fenra glanced around.

What would the swordsmen do to them if they found them listening?

Trying—and failing—not to think of an axe lodged in her core, she gathered as much air in herself as she could, and turned her attention to the few stalls she could see on the boardwalk above her.

The breeze she let out rattled the nearest stalls, and whoever was at the stairs paused long enough for Fenra and El to slip away beneath the stairs, beneath the deadwood boardwalk.

Ankles soaking in the salt water, they drew away as quietly as they could. They heard boots thumping overhead, covering up any splashes they made, and saw a figure ease himself into one of the boats. A human man, that was all she could make out.

Fenra silently motioned El toward a footpath they could use to get out from under the boardwalk that headed in a different direction than the boat. The *solanse* glowed with life, a pulsing green energy she need only ask to tap into whenever she needed it. She mostly borrowed its breath, which proved useful quite often. When they came out into the *solanse* proper, the firemoths were just starting to come out.

"I need to get to Resbrok," she said, flexing her fingers. "Those swordsman can't be planning anything good."

"Silverswords," El corrected.

"Oh, *va*. Well—"

El crossed his arms. "I'm coming with you."

"Definitely not," she said. "You weren't even supposed to be at Verindas. It's even farther to Resbrok!"

"What if you need help?"

"I'll be fine."

"Like you were fine when that tagor attacked?"

She crossed her arms, her twigs crowding together on her chest. She didn't have time for this. "Fine. Let's go."

Fenra reached for the nearest cedar and started to climb it, her hands warm on the living tree. Her fingers easily fit into the grooves in the bark, like she asked it.

"Fenra," El said, grimacing at her.

"What?" She glanced down at him. He was still standing firmly in the moss.

"We need to hurry and warn them!" she insisted. "If you're coming, then keep up. I'm going this way."

"It's not any faster," El groaned, rolling his emerald green eyes.

"You know I hate tromping through all that water. It *does* slow you down."

"Wanna bet?" El said, still standing firm.

She grunted and reached the first branch. "Sure."

She shouldn't be having fun.

She really shouldn't.

The others were in danger from those silver people, not to mention the family who owned the house she would soon be working in. She needed to warn them.

She launched herself off the branch, fingers elongating to reach for the next one. She and El cast their customary dim jade glow, much like the light she could see emanating from everything else.

To his credit, El was quite fast on foot. He dodged many of the small pools with great leaps like hers, asking vines to steady him upon landing. He had a knack with plants and water. It was no wonder he didn't mind splashing and slogging around in the shallower pools.

The idea that she might be out of a job before she even got the chance to savor the sanctioned living in the *solanse* drove all gaiety from her stride. She landed on the next branch, clinging expertly to it; warmth flowed from the air around the tree as she touched it.

She could see the top of El's head, though he was a little ahead of her. She hugged the tree and climbed a few feet to the next viable branch, elongating her fingers so they would fit in the bark better.

Then she spotted El, crashing headlong into a patch of cypress knees with a horrible *snap*. He collapsed to the ground with a scream and a moan.

Fenra shouted, the airy sound bursting from the air around her head. With an all too short glance at the dark pools beneath her, she hurled herself off the tree limb.

As she sank through the air, wind whipping her leaves, she thought, *at least it's on purpose this time.*

Their meager belongings were packed into a small sack and stored in the barn, ready to be placed directly into the carriage the next morning. Marlow had a fantastic meal planned, the scents wafting from the kitchen making Fig's mouth water. And Fig wore a new gold-colored Virenish tunic embroidered with black thread that Zula had gifted her; it fit her perfectly.

After consulting with Zula, they discovered that Mairead's red robes had not been put in the refuse bin or burned after all. The two girls set to scrubbing them as soon as Fig finished her all-too-short lesson with Afrith.

While Mairead finished cleaning herself up for dinner, Fig slung the wet robes over her arm and went to ask Dev to dry them, but he wasn't in his room. She shut his door with a snap and headed down the hall and toward the stairs.

Emrah? Any idea where Dev is? she called to the dragonet—wherever he was.

We're by the dock with Perrin, Emrah replied immediately. *Oh, and Zula just got word that the carriage will be delivered promptly before sunrise.*

Perfect, she told him. Dev would meet with the lords and perhaps forge some tenuous alliances for his return to the throne. Come sunrise, they would be on their way to the Notch and out of this Morgha-forsaken country.

There was just one last thing...

Her mouth twisted wryly when she walked out the front door and spotted Vaelor sitting on the front porch. The sun had fallen low in the sky, and Marlow was out on the docks lighting the lamps.

"Ah, *vir dan*," she said to Vaelor, shifting the damp robes in her arms.

He looked up from the leather pouch he was mending with a half smile. "Very good. Perrin been teaching you?"

"Oddly enough, Dev taught me that one."

Silence fell between them as thick and dark as molasses. She hadn't spoken to Vaelor since the near-burning incident with Perrin, and she wondered if the surly look he was giving the leather string was really directed at her.

"Perrin and I went out foraging this morning," she began, her voice sounding oddly higher than usual. "I told him I was sorry again for last night."

A low rumble of acknowledgement came from his chest.

Fig huffed. "I talked to my old teacher, too, actually. About losing control," she blurted out.

He looked up, startled, perhaps at her change of tone. "That's...good, I suppose. Perrin wasn't hurt, and he wasn't scared—though not much puts fear into that boy—so it's water under the boardwalk, I'd say."

"Oh," Fig said. Tension rippled through her. Why did she still feel like something was wrong between them? "Hey, so—"

"Fig!" someone called in a panic.

She whipped around to see Dev sprinting toward the house. He ran up the steps two at a time, Perrin on his heels.

"They're coming!" Dev hissed. He was pointing toward the swamp, where the lantern was bobbing gently toward them, the shadow of the boat barely visible.

"The lords?" she asked, her eyes bulging. She grabbed Dev's elbow, leading him inside. She cast a glance Vaelor's way, but he was now staring out into the swamp pensively.

Fig shook her head and turned to Dev as they paused inside the entryway. "You need to get in place, *Your Majesty*, not be outside playing on the docks," she jested.

"Too right," he agreed, sending a burst of amethyst air to brush his clothes off. Then he glanced at the damp robes in Fig's arms. "Need help with those? I think we have time."

At her nod, he took care of them in under a minute, amethyst glittering all around the robes as the others watched enraptured. Vaelor entered silently to stand by Perrin, who waited closest to the door, ready to usher the lords inside.

Dev finished and handed the dry robes back to Fig, giving her a nod and heading toward the drawing room just as Zula hobbled down the hallway. It was really happening. She could hear voices on the lawn. She adjusted her own tunic, though it was perfectly free of wrinkles.

The stairs creaked, and Fig looked up to see Mairead coming down, her right hand closed into a fist. "Here, catch," Fig said, tossing Mairead her robes when she got closer.

The ex-priestess seemed to steal herself before slipping them over her clothes. When the robes were settled, she didn't even look down at them; they just seemed right. She lifted her chin ever so slightly, and she raised her hood as was customary. A slow smile graced her face as she gazed down at Fig.

"You look great," Fig said, taking Mairead's hand and leading her down the rest of the way.

They followed Vaelor into the sitting room to wait. He wore a pale white tunic with black lacing at the front, and his hair looked freshly braided; the few braids on each side had silver clasps woven into them.

The lord of Resbrok.

Why was Fig so disappointed he was staying? They barely knew each other. Besides, he was a silversword.

But that excuse is growing old, a voice whispered in the back of her mind. Yes, he was a silversword. But he was Virenish first. Loyal to his family, loyal to Dev. *Particularly* loyal to Dev with that oath. He had to come with them, right? But what if he wanted to fulfill his role here?

A knock came at the front door, and they all heard Perrin answer it. Fig quickly found a seat near Mairead. They were only there to watch and would let Dev and Zula do the talking, since Zula knew everyone and the plights of Viren best.

Footsteps sounded down the hall, and Perrin's face appeared in the doorway, two people behind him, dressed in Virenish finery. The woman wore a cream silk tunic with a heavy black leather belt about her waist that Fig suspected normally held a large sword. She looked about fifty, and her originally blonde hair was so fine it had turned an ethereal white color. The man wasn't nearly as polished, and wore his weapons openly; two daggers, one at his waist, and one hidden just inside his boot, Fig noted.

"*Vir dan,*" the woman in cream said, bowing her head to those assembled. They all stood to greet the guests and return the bow.

"*Vir dan,*" Zula echoed back. "And welcome, Lady Atricia of House Griveen. Lord Onalde of House Weirbrok. We are delighted to have your company this evening. It is my honor to introduce you to the rightful heir of the Rayvan throne, King Devryn Verrence."

Dev inclined his chin in acknowledgement.

"It is indeed an honor," Lady Atricia said, offering what looked like a cross between a bow and a curtsy.

"The honor is mine," Dev replied, "to make your acquaintance."

He'd readied his whole life to be king. Who knew he'd be holding his first audience wearing borrowed clothes in a manor on the outskirts of the salt swamps?

"*Vir dan,*" Lord Onalde said, the words as gruff as his beard. He, too, showed surprise at Dev's appearance.

Perrin led the two of them to their predetermined seats, his posture and manners nearly as regal as Dev's. Perhaps Taskor *was* a good tutor after all.

Lady Atricia was placed beside Fig, and Lord Onalde by Zula. Zula had said something about wanting to keep Onalde's grim comments to a minimum. Now they were just missing Afrith and Lord Eleste.

"Thank you both again for coming," Dev said, "and for your

discretion. As you might have heard—"

A bang resounded at the door just as Marlow was wheeling in the tea cart.

"That doesn't sound like our other guests," Zula said quietly, the wrinkles around her eyes deepening.

Two more bangs, like someone was knocking with a heavy fist. Or a gauntlet. Fig leapt to her feet as Vaelor and Dev did the same.

The scent of blood—copper—filled her nose. Silverswords.

Emrah? Emrah? Fig demanded, flexing her fingertips. He was supposed to be watching the outside of the house.

He didn't respond. What could have happened to him? Had the silverswords found him first? She didn't think it would be easy to catch a dragonet, but...

Perrin had already leapt to his feet but dashed beside Zula's chair instead of heading to the door. "Quick!" he hissed, gesturing at his *mazir* with one hand, and Dev and Fig with the other.

Then Fig remembered something. She grabbed Dev's elbow and rushed him toward Zula's chair. Behind it was the hidey-hole in which she had found Perrin the previous day. Vaelor gave his *grimazir* a hand, helping her rise, and Perrin and Dev picked up the chair to move it soundlessly.

Lady Atricia stared at the scene with wide eyes. Lord Onalde's face hadn't changed one tick.

The bang at the door came again. Fig could hear other voices at the back of the house.

"*Va, va,* coming!" Zula shouted, treading toward the sitting room door, and then pausing with her hand on the threshold.

Perrin got the panel free, and an empty passage gaped before them.

"Open up!" a voice outside called.

Lord Onalde wrinkled his face and muttered, "What in the Bard's name is—I knew I shouldn't have come here. *Silversword politics.*" He spat the last like a swear, his Virenish accent heavy.

Fig all but pushed Dev into the passage, then glanced around. Should she go with him? Her gaze landed on Mairead, and she motioned her forward first.

"Get in," she told the ex-priestess. "If it's the same silverswords as earlier..." She trailed off.

Mairead nodded, and accepted Dev's helping hand into the passage. They both had to crouch since it didn't fit their full height, but it looked deep enough.

"You too, Fig," Dev said, holding out his hand. "I need you with me."

Fig glanced back at Vaelor and Zula, standing side by side at the door to the sitting room.

"Go," Vaelor said, meeting her eyes. "We might not be able to explain your presence, goldfire."

Her breath hitched. She slipped in.

Perrin hastily replaced the panel, covering the three of them in darkness. A quiet *thump* told Fig the chair had been replaced in front of their hiding place. Someone's footsteps grew fainter, heading for the front door. Who had gone to meet the silverswords?

Fig attempted a steadying breath. It came out shakily. In the dark, she found Mairead's hand, and then Dev's. She squeezed both.

Emrah? she tried calling again.

Still no answer.

Her eyes stung. What had happened to him? She didn't think for one second he had fallen asleep, the only other explanation for him not answering. What had the silverswords done to him? The tears quickly escaped and rolled down her cheeks, her hands still clutching those of her friends.

How had the 'swords known they were here?

They hadn't disclosed Dev's name to anyone. They had even hidden Dev in his room...

Most of the time. Except this afternoon when Taskor's carriage drove by.

Taskor, who had been fighting with Vaelor just the other day, who must know Vaelor served the Verrences and had returned to Resbrok with a ragtag crew fleeing south.

Heavy footfalls entered the house a second later. How many sets? Five? Six? She gave Dev's hand an extra squeeze.

"Might I ask what it is you're doing here, Captain Felras?" Zula asked, her voice coming from her favored seat. Just one Virenish grandmother, sitting between them and half a dozen silverswords.

Fig's respect for the woman multiplied by a thousand.

"You've got guests," one of the silverswords said, his voice void of emotion. "Are we interrupting something? A gathering, I wonder?"

"Tea among friends," Zula said. "May I offer you anything?"

"And what is it you're here to discuss?"

Fig couldn't help but picture Lord Onalde and Lady Atricia in their chairs, having just sat down with the ousted king, but not even beginning to hear Dev's tale or what he could offer them. Lady Atricia, polished but surprised. Lord Onalde, notoriously rancorous and bitter, now thrown into silversword politics because of Dev. Fig closed her eyes, even though it was pitch dark. It helped somehow. That, and the two hands steadying her own as they crouched there on their knees.

This time, Lady Atricia's voice answered. "Oh, trivial matters, sir," she said, and Fig could picture her swatting her hand. "The calving at the Weirbrok estate. The increase in tagor sightings this season, far from the deep pools. The price of shafra wool."

"And what are *you* doing here?" the voice growled. It didn't seem to be in response to Lady Atricia.

Fig's heart turned to ice when Vaelor answered. "Meeting with my family," he said simply.

A shifting of metal, armor clanking, and the silversword's voice grew quieter, but all the more deadly. "What are you doing here?" the man repeated.

We really should have pulled Vaelor in here with us, Fig thought belatedly, her heart racing. But she knew without a doubt he wouldn't leave his *grimazir* and Perrin to the mercy of the 'swords.

"He's come to settle the estate," Perrin said. Fig pressed her lips together tightly. She had hoped Perrin would stay out of this mess, hidden against a wall, tried to be invisible. But what was it that Vaelor had said earlier? *Nothing puts fear into that boy.* Apparently not even half a dozen bloodthirsty silverswords.

"Settle the estate?" the silversword echoed.

A shifting of metal. Backing off?

"*Iil*, Vaelor was supposed to be lord of Resbrok," Perrin said, "as you probably know." Fig couldn't help but smile worriedly at his brave tone addressing these deadly fighters. "But I'm Mistress Zula's son—adopted, of course, hence my age—and technically, by the laws of Viren, I should inherit. Vaelor just needed to sign the deed in order to make it offi—"

A strange noise escaped Zula, something between an outburst and a cough. What in the Bard's name was going on?

"Oh aye," the aggressive silversword drawled suspiciously. "I'll need to see this deed. *Now*, if you please. And the rest of you," he ordered, "search every room. Go."

Cold dread seeped into Fig's stomach, but as she thought about her room with Mairead, she realized they had already packed their belongings; everything was in an out-of-the-way corner of the barn. They hadn't been sure how far into the night this meeting might go, so they had prepared everything. Dev's room had been tidy when she'd peeked her head in. But what if they found something out of place? The clothes the Resbroks had lent them or an inordinate number of cups in the washing basin... She twitched her fingers, unbidden warmth gathering there. She pulled her hands away from the others'.

No, no, not now.

She crammed her eyes shut again and tried to breathe. Dev grabbed her hand back, and though she tried to pull it away, she didn't want to make a commotion. *Fine, but if he gets burned, he'll be sorry.*

But as she listened to the heavy footfalls traversing the manor, no shouts of discovery came, and no steel rang out. Fig's pounding heart slowed to a more normal cadence, and no more sparks attempted to escape without her permission.

"What is this Perrin says, *mo der*?" Zula was saying. Evidently, she too thought the silverswords were nearing the end of their hopefully fruitless search.

"*Va*," growled Lord Onalde. "Giving away titles, are we?"

"I think it's fitting," Lady Atricia said airily.

"Why? Because Vaelor's got that silver ring around his eye?" Lord

Onalde grumbled. "And the sword chained to his soul?"

"Onalde!" Lady Atricia admonished.

"Enough," Zula snapped. "That is Resbrok business. *You* were invited here to speak of the price of wool and nothing more, Lord Onalde."

The lord remained quiet as Zula went on, and Fig pictured the man shrinking into his scruffy wool jerkin.

"Vaelor, this is your title," Zula said with finality. "You were born first, and it is in your name."

"*Grimazir*," Vaelor began. "It should be Perrin's by right as your son."

"*Iil*, Perrin—"

"I don't want it." Perrin's voice.

The empty silence was replaced with boots tromping down the stairs. Dev and Fig squeezed each other's hands tightly. The pain of Dev's grasp had made all thoughts of fire flee from her fingertips. The boots had stopped roaming about the house. Fig could feel that everyone in the manor was gathered in or just outside the sitting room. She waited for their judgment, biting her lip to shreds.

"Very well, madam," the first, emotionless silversword said. "But I'll be back tomorrow with the Verindas notary to inspect that deed further. Enjoy your talk of...wool."

It felt like all the breath Fig held in her lungs had turned to the most delicious, gold-sparkling air. They were leaving. The boots tramped to the front door, across the porch, and down the creaky salt-air-worn stairs.

Gone.

A breath shuddered out of Dev. Fig barely dared breathe. Was it safe? Had they really gotten away with it?

Then she remembered something.

Emrah? Emrah? Are you all right?

A strange itchy feeling came across her mind, along with Emrah's voice saying, *Fig? Run.*

"Emrah's in trouble," Fig said as soon as the panel door was removed. She was blinded by the flickering lights of the sitting room but shielded her eyes and scrambled from the hidey-hole. Vaelor was holding the panel, and everyone in the room stared at her as she emerged. Dev helped Mairead out behind Fig.

"What?" Mairead asked. "What's happened?"

"I don't know," Fig said, the haunting words replaying in her mind as she explained it to them. Emrah hadn't answered since. They waited until they were sure the silverswords wouldn't return.

"Can we even..." Dev began, glancing at the windows which looked out onto the front porch. They were dark, becoming mirrors to reflect their terrified faces. "Is it safe to go outside, do you think?"

"Not for you," Vaelor said, at the same time as Fig said, "You get back in there!" She pointed to the hiding place.

"If the 'swords are gone, they're gone," Dev said, but Fig crossed her arms over her chest.

"They could very easily be lurking in the woods, or—"

"Where's Perrin?" Mairead asked.

Zula looked around, but it was Lady Atricia who spoke next. "Will our meeting be resuming? I do have some concerns about the...price of wool…" She trailed off as she glanced at Dev, as if unsure how to address him.

His face transformed as if only just realizing his political duties might still be upon him.

"Lady Atricia, I'd love to stay and discuss the matters of Viren, more than the Bard loves a good tale, but I think we still have a problem on our hands. Emrah, our dragonet friend, implied there's still trouble afoot."

"It's not the silverswords," Perrin said from the doorway, breathless.

"Perrin!" Zula admonished. "Where were you?"

"I followed them," he said with a shrug. "They took the footpaths— every last one of them. I guess they really did believe you. But I found plenty of tracks around the house. They must have searched outside before they came in."

Fig's chest deflated. "Then what—"

Vaelor interrupted her, "But how did they *know*?" he asked in a growl to no one in particular.

"'Twasn't me," Lord Onalde grumbled, looking affronted.

"No one's saying that," Zula said automatically. "Not yet, anyway."

Speculations rose about the room, voices rising and beating against Fig's skull. While Perrin was confident the 'swords had truly left, a nonsensical part of her mind thought they might still be listening. And what had happened to Emrah?

"Where's Taskor?" she finally said.

"Task—Taskor?" Zula demanded. "What do you mean? I didn't invite him."

"He saw Dev earlier. He sold us out."

"Hmm," said Dev, stroking his chin. "Didn't he punch Vaelor?"

Vaelor looked away at the wall as if he wanted to disappear into it, then he bowed his head. "He only punched me because I tried to hit him first."

"Vaelor!" Zula said. "How could you! He's only—"

Shaking his head, Vaelor said, "I know, *grimazir*. He's only asked for your hand in marriage."

"So you knew?" Zula said, eyes twinkling with a mischief betraying her years.

At the same time, Perrin said, "What? *Taskor?*"

"We have bigger problems right now," Fig said, hysteria bubbling in her—she had to suppress a giggle at the idea of Vaelor trying to punch Taskor because the man wanted to marry Zula. She shook her head. "Emrah said to run. And nothing else."

"Maybe he was just warning us belatedly about the silverswords?" Mairead suggested.

Fig shook her head. "I don't think so.

"The carriage—" Dev began.

"Is not coming quick enough," Vaelor said. "That 'sword—Felras—said he'd be back tomorrow. That could very well be before sunrise if he chooses. *Grimazir*, you should come up with an excuse for hiring the carriage, in case they see it."

"Of course," Zula said quietly.

"And I'll get the papers in order for you," Vaelor said. "So when we're gone—"

"The *solanse*," Lord Onalde said. "You'll need to go by water."

Fig glanced at the man in surprise, knowing it was their only choice.

And here she thought she was done with the salt swamps.

She looked at Mairead, the ex-priestess's lips tight. "Well?" Fig asked.

"By boat," Dev agreed. "Can we borrow—"

"Of course," Perrin said. "I'll get it ready."

"No, Perrin, I don't want you leaving the house again," Vaelor said, reaching out and putting a firm hand on the boy's shoulder. "We still don't know what trouble has befallen Emrah."

"But—"

Shaking his head, Vaelor said, "You are lord of Resbrok, and you need to protect your *mazir*." He gestured to Fig and the others. "We'll go out the back, get the sack from the barn, and head for the boat."

"So you *are* coming with us then, Vaelor?" Dev asked, stealing the words from Fig's lips.

She found her gaze boring into the floor as she waited for his reply.

"Of course, Your Majesty. Even if my oath wasn't to you, I would still be coming."

Fig swallowed, then grabbed Mairead's hand and led her toward the door. "Let's go then."

"I'm sorry we couldn't stay," Dev said to Lord Onalde and Lady Atricia. "But we are indebted to you for your discretion. When I return to Tytan—"

"We look forward to the revolutionary day," Lady Atricia said with a pearly grin.

Dev nodded, a hint of worry in his eye. Fig wondered what they had just gotten into, admitting he was in debt to them in any way.

"Let's go," Fig said, "and hope to the Bard we find Emrah along the way."

In the hall, Fig, Dev, and Mairead waited as Vaelor said his goodbyes to his *grimazir*. Perrin came at them and flung his arms around Fig.

"You're really leaving?" he mumbled into her hair. "Now?"

She patted his back, vowing not to let go until the boy did first. This could very well be the last time she saw him. "We have to." It was all she could say. There were a dozen explanations, but she was sure Perrin already knew them all and didn't actually require an answer.

Finally, they heard Vaelor's footsteps, and Perrin let go. The boy turned to Dev and bowed. Fig's heart melted at the look on Dev's face, a twist of sadness and pain.

Dev nodded at Perrin, then reached for his hand. The boy gasped as Dev pulled him into a strangling hug. "You think you can get away with a measly bow?" Dev japed, thumping Perrin's back.

A watery chuckle burst from Perrin as he stepped back, wiping his eyes with the backs of his hands.

Perrin turned to Vaelor, and at some tug on her emotions, Fig decided to lead Dev and Mairead down the hall to the kitchen to give the two some privacy.

She watched their silhouetted forms with a sad smile. Vaelor towered over Perrin, but the boy stood tall until he was enveloped in Vaelor's muscled arms.

Then silently, the group let themselves out of the house and into the dark night.

They retrieved the sack from the barn and headed for the dock, Fig calling for Emrah all the while. Her final night in that comfortable bed, stolen from her. Dev, robbed of his meeting with what was left of the influential lords.

But if Taskor hadn't betrayed them, then who?

"I don't see Emrah anywhere," Dev said. "Should we check around the other side?"

"Perhaps he's injured," Mairead said.

The dock was in sight, but the lanterns were out. Fig searched for the shadowy silhouette of the boat as best she could, then sparks flared in her vision.

"Emrah?" she called, rushing down the last of the grassy slope and onto the wooden planks, her spirits lifting.

A silhouette much larger than a dragonet turned, green sparks coming from his hand.

"Afrith?" she said. "I'm sorry, the meeting's over, the silverswords came, and—"

Emrah lay in Afrith's other hand, unconscious and barely moving but for the smoke that curled from his nostrils as he snored.

Fig lunged forward, not thinking.

Sparks turned into flame, and Afrith's fire surged toward her.

"Af—" she began, then leapt back. Her mouth gaped open. Someone pulled her away and stepped in front of her.

"You're not impervious to flame, silversword," Afrith said. The silhouette of Vaelor stood in front of her, sword raised.

But how? Fig's mind reeled. Afrith...had betrayed them? With Emrah out cold in the man's arms, she was certain.

"You sold us out?" she asked in disgust.

"Why?" Dev demanded.

Afrith turned his gaze to Dev, the flames sitting in his hand reflecting green flames in his eyes. "Ah, the prince without a throne."

"It's King," Dev said. The flames in Afrith's hand were snuffed out by an amethyst wind.

Darkness surrounded them, and Afrith chuckled. "You're even less fireproof than the hired sword, Prince. You know how fire is drawn to air." His gaze swiveled between Fig and Dev.

Fig's hands were shaking, sparks pouring from them; she couldn't stop it. "But you—"

Afrith shook his head. "Please Fig, don't be naive. I thought you more intelligent than this. I, an errant traveler with contacts in every port city across Svora, *not* interested in locating Prince Devryn? A bloody coup, by the most bloodthirsty of men—if you can still call them that. *You* left the Carriage House after discovering it was merely a gilded prison, after all, you should know."

Fig's stomach tightened as hard as a rock. How could he betray them? Her teacher...

"Just give us back Emrah," Fig pleaded, coming up beside Vaelor. "Tell me he's not hurt."

Emrah, wake up, she said in her mind as forcefully as she could. *Wake up!*

"Emrah, you say?" Afrith said, glancing down at the dragonet for a second. "And where did you find the curious creature to make him your familiar?"

"My familiar?" she said, her voice hollow. "What are you—Just give him back, please!"

He shook his head, *tsking.* Fig caught a whiff of *kafye* that suddenly made her want to retch. Afrith stood between them and the boats. At this point, if they had to steal the one Lady Atricia and Lord Onalde had arrived in, so be it. She *had* to get Emrah back, and there was no way she would let Afrith stop them. Fig looked up at Vaelor, his sword steady in his hand.

If they attacked Afrith, he might hurt Emrah...

"What do you mean, my familiar?" Fig started over, inching closer to Vaelor. If she could get on the other side of Afrith, then maybe—

A circle of green flames burst from Afrith's palm, swirling above the gap between them. It grew, twisting and twirling, and wrapping around them all in an instant. Tendrils swirled from their ankles to their middles. Green flames shifted around them like watergrass in the swamp.

Fig could feel heat coming off the swirling vortex, and the others must too. She had no doubt in her mind that Afrith was a better fire mage than her. How could she protect herself against his flames, let alone anyone else?

"Perhaps you should have stayed to learn at the Carriage House," Afrith said. "Though I only stayed a short while there myself. I gleaned what I could from the court missives, which came from the palace every day, to keep the prince updated."

"How dare—" Dev began.

But the flames circling them tightened, sickly green and hot. Purple wove angrily between the green swirls, as Dev tried to snuff out the flames. But they merely undulated and multiplied, fueled by the air, so Dev backed off.

"Of course, it was unheard of: a Verrence having Svoran blood. The Carriage House had no protocols for having a prince in residence. So it was that I became the one to deliver his messages to him personally."

Dev growled. Vaelor held him back with one arm. There wasn't much room in the circle, particularly with Dev fighting to lunge through it. He threw another burst of amethyst wind at the circle, but it didn't fare any better than his previous attempt.

"Yes, well. Raised like a silversword, weren't you?" Afrith said, looking down his nose at him.

"What are you, some kind of spy?" Fig demanded. "Whose side are you on?"

Afrith smiled enigmatically, and Fig wanted to punch him right in his well-groomed face.

"Were you even helping me with my magic?" she blurted with ire.

A crease formed between his eyebrows as he frowned. "Of course. But my assumptions were correct about the guest you and Mistress Zula hinted at. Truly, who else would it be? After disappearing from the botched assassination, burning down the nearest port city—where else could you head but the *solanse*?" he said to Dev.

"And after only a little digging, to find that Prince Devryn's closest protector was the oldest male heir to the Resbrok clan? Well," he shrugged, a pitying look on his face, "perhaps you should have chosen better advisors, Devryn."

"That's King Verrence to you," Dev spat.

"Oh ho, no," Afrith said. "That title, in fact, belongs to your brother."

"Shad?" Dev whispered. An unfathomably deep pain crossed in front of his eyes.

"How dare you," Fig hissed at Afrith. "Do not speak of such things, especially to him."

Fig's chest hurt as if she were holding back all the flames she longed to throw at Afrith, but she didn't know if it would hurt Emrah—she herself was susceptible to flame when asleep or out of her mind. She couldn't risk it.

The swirling fire circle had resumed its slow creep toward them, ever tightening. Vaelor grabbed her shoulders to steady himself and she suddenly found him pressed up against her. Mairead squealed, clinging to Dev.

This had to end. The others would burn.

And Afrith was mad.

Her old teacher rolled his eyes and let his attention drift to the boats behind him for a second. Fig thought of taking advantage of his momentary inattention, but the flames tightened even closer. Everyone shifted together. Mairead was whimpering. Had she been burned?

"As delightful as this is," Afrith said, "we really must be going. I didn't expect the 'swords to take you, merely smoke you out, but if we linger much longer, they could return. Captain Felras was quite taken with the story, as I thought he would be. Why, he hadn't even known that the eldest Resbrok was in residence."

The breath that exploded from Fig felt like flames themselves, and she was astounded it was merely air. She stared at Emrah, still cradled in Afrith's arms. The crazy briigard. The green in Emrah's scales appeared brighter in the reflection of the flames.

The flames.

Her problem, as Afrith had said, was expecting control. Control was an illusion...or something like that. Could she attempt to best him?

She had to try.

The ring of flames began to move, dragging the whole lot of them forward. Mairead shrieked from the back, then hastily tramped forward with the others, crying in earnest. Dev hissed sharply when the circle moved, indicating he'd been burned too.

"You don't hurt them," she growled.

Fig inhaled and thought back to the magic of the Gold Wood. The *solanse* also contained magic. But even if it didn't, she willed herself to believe it; she *could* best Afrith. She took a deep breath. She would set her fire from a controlled environment, and then let it rage. She flung her hands wide, gold flames bursting from each palm. She dashed forward.

Gaze locked on Emrah and that light curl of smoke rising from his nostrils, she shoved her fear aside and surged forward through the wall of green flame. Immense heat passed over her, along with a brief flare of pain, but she willed her own gold flames over the green ones. The gold burst through in bright flares, protecting her.

She slammed into Afrith, coal-like palms against his chest.

He staggered backward.

Panting, Fig barely registered the rest of the pain which hit her seconds later, as if it had waited until she drew breath to make itself known. But she had made it out of the circle. To Afrith's credit, the damn thing still held.

He withdrew, pulling Emrah out of her reach.

"I don't need you anyway, Fig," he said with a sneer, "but I will take your dragonet. Perhaps he'll bond with *me* when he's far enough away from you."

"No!" She lunged forward. *Emrah!* Her hand lashed out as more flames spewed from Afrith's free hand. She didn't care. Emrah was no one's to take.

Afrith jerked in surprise as Emrah flinched in his arms. Seizing her opportunity, Fig grabbed for the dragonet with both hands.

Emrah, wake up! she called, stumbling back a few paces. *What has he done to you?*

In a fluid motion, she shifted Emrah to one arm and brought up the other, fire burning in a wall of flame before her. "Don't you touch him again."

From what she could see through the flames, Afrith merely looked annoyed. "Very well. Like I said, I won't be taking you, Fig, just Prince Devryn here. His brother wants to see him."

Her mouth dropped open, and she dared a look at Dev. Luckily, since she was no longer in the fire circle, they weren't in immediate danger of burning, but that wouldn't last long with Afrith's apparent zeal.

"My brother is *dead*," Dev croaked.

"I don't believe they like that term," Afrith said in a stage-whisper, eyeing Vaelor purposefully.

"S-silverswords? What are you playing at?" Dev demanded. "He died! I saw it! Svoran blood is incompatible with the crossover!"

Afrith shook his head, as if he were about to dispute a point in a lecture. "Well then, come with me to Nithe and see for yourself."

"That's who's on the throne in the Hollow Isles?" Dev asked in a monotone. "My dead brother? You really have lost your mind."

The fire tightened, adding new tendrils to the swirling trap. She needed to do something, but what? Could she protect the others with her flames too? But to keep them from getting burned, she'd need definitive control.

Control. The swirling green vortex looked *quite* under control, contrary to Afrith's assertions that control was an illusion. Perhaps that was all a ploy to make her doubt her already tenuous connection with her magic.

She couldn't trust a word this man had said since inviting them into his flat for *kafye*.

Emrah? Can you hear me? After his first twitch in Afrith's arms and a brief wiggle upon settling into Fig's, he hadn't shown any other signs of consciousness. What had Afrith done to him? Knocked him out? Drugged him?

Please, please wake up.

"You'll see for yourself when you arrive at the Hollow Isles," Afrith told Dev.

"He's not going," Fig shouted.

"If you think we're going to let you just take him—" Vaelor began.

A tendril of flame whipped from the swirling circle and wrapped itself about Vaelor's sword. Vaelor slumped, and a cry wrenched from his throat.

"I'd be careful with that if I were you," Afrith warned, gazing at the fire-wrapped sword.

The ring of silver in Vaelor's eyes tightened, and Fig seized her moment.

Cradling Emrah as gently and securely as possible, she gathered all her remaining energy and hurled it at Afrith in an enormous blast. To the Bard's inkpot with *control*.

The fireball lit up the night with crackling overhead as some Andisia moss burned up and went out.

The man emerged from the flames, laughing and unscathed. "Oh, Fig. You'll have to do better than that."

She glared at him, her insides churning and her face hot.

Another swirl of green sparks sprung from thin air, twisting like the vines of the *solanse* and swirling right over her head. The flames wrapped around her before she could even flinch. A stray rope of green whipped free.

"Ah!" she cried, her hand going to her cheek, surprised at the burn.

A faint splash in the distance sent fear down her spine. There weren't tagors over here, were there?

She caught some commotion over by Vaelor as she tried to focus on the fiery tornado Afrith had trapped her in, its tendrils multiplying around her.

She would not let fire be the cause of her death.

Fire *was* chaos. And control was an illusion, like Afrith had said. Push it in the right direction, give it the best conditions, and you'll get that perfect campfire—a safe lantern to light you through the dark of night, without burning down your house.

You simply had to give the chaos rules. Boundaries. Then the chaos could burn as much as it wanted.

With barely any room to maneuver in the ever-tightening vortex, she cradled Emrah to her chest like a precious scaly baby and focused her thoughts on protecting her friends.

She raised a fist and summoned a ribbon of gold flames, which wove around the whirlwind that trapped her. She let her ribbon get pulled into it, mixing with the sparking green. She couldn't tell what was going on with the others; all she could do was feed the flames.

A slip of amethyst wove into the whirlwind then, making it billow and bend. Had Dev broken free of the other vortex? Shouting reached her ears, but she couldn't see past the green and gold.

She let her chaotic and bound gold get sucked into the whirlwind. Shouting came from beyond the wall of flame. The vortex had doubled in size.

Half green, half gold. Its boundaries stretched past their limits.

She snuffed out her own flames and held her breath.

Chaos needed boundaries—or at least, that's what she was counting on.

The green flames, loose and limp, flickered out, sparks winking out all around her. The vortex had grown accustomed to the gold flames as they grew, their boundaries growing, and found themselves unable to hold up in their absence. Warm relief flooded her, and she clutched Emrah harder.

When the flames dropped like a stage curtain, a scene of chaos was revealed.

Mairead lay collapsed in a heap in the grass just off the dock, but from the slight keening sound, Fig was fairly certain she was alive.

Vaelor and Dev were locked in a battle with Afrith.

It was no small thing to fight a silversword. Vaelor's might rang out as steel crashed against flaming wards thrown up in seconds. He lunged again and again.

And though a sword would normally cut through fire like air, even Fig had felt the strange solidity of the vortex vines like the one that whipped her on the cheek. He had bound the flames to serve him, and serve him, they did. The flames were solid enough to battle silversword steel.

Fig raised her free fist and sent a wave of controlled flames—no, bound flames—toward Afrith. She knew she didn't possess nearly enough mastery to create something like his vortexes, but flames burned no matter what form they took. Quick and dirty, her mother always used to say. As long as it worked.

Though her flames were not solid, Afrith had been in the middle of blocking one of Vaelor's attacks and it threw him off guard. He teetered near the edge of the dock, and Fig pushed her fist higher into the air. Ribbons of flame wove toward him, twisting in the air like a dancer's silks on Morgha's Day. She gave them the freedom to move but bound their direction. It seemed to work, lashing in front of his face as a distraction from Vaelor's attacks at the very least.

Dev held his hands in front of him, an amethyst sphere of air forming near his middle. Before Fig could cry out, Dev threw the ball, just as Fig's flames whipped toward Afrith.

The flames sucked in the air like it was their first lungful after nearly drowning. Lifegiving, powerful air. The ribbon turned into an undulating wave, and Fig saw Vaelor go down on one knee, shielding his face with an arm.

Fig rushed to his side and focused on shielding them both from burning. Since they were her flames, it was easy. And they had been heading for Afrith—had she...had he...?

But after the last wisps of flames flickered out and she looked up, she saw something even worse than the dead body she'd feared: Afrith holding his hand at Dev's throat. Though no flames were visible, Dev's neck was scorched red as if Afrith's hand held coals.

"Let him go!" she screamed. She dared not lunge for him, not knowing what Afrith might do. The man seemed out of his mind. And all those claims about Dev's brother Shadryn? What had all that been about?

Still crouched beside Vaelor, with Emrah in the crook of her arm, she let Vaelor help her up. Her feet were unsteady. Her hands were shaking, and she had more than a few burns across her body. The gold tunic Zula had given her was ruined.

A low groaning came from somewhere deep in the salt swamps, and Fig shivered. Afrith backed away from them, guiding Dev to the nearest boat—the one Lord Onalde and Lady Atricia had arrived in. Fig spotted Lady Atricia's sword in its sheath, sitting in the prow. Could she...?

Dev didn't speak, and his eyes watered, presumably from the pain. Fig watched him acquiesce to Afrith's wordless demands with tears burning her eyes.

At the edge of the dock, fiery shackles formed midair, and Dev's face drained of all color.

"Oh, don't worry, Your Highness, this won't hurt. Unless you resist, of course."

A disgusted terror seized Fig's middle as Afrith slipped Dev's hands into them. At least he had been telling the truth—after a brief hiss of pain from Dev, anyway. How had Afrith done it? The man could make heat without flames and solid flames without heat. He was more of a master than she had.

Afrith pushed Dev into the boat and leapt in after him, his burning hands raised in warning. Dev lunged for the sword in the prow, but Afrith was faster. The fiery cuffs flared, and Dev went down on his knees, making no further attempts to fight back. Silhouetted in green flames, Dev grimaced in pain while Afrith reached past him for the sword and tucked it safely behind himself.

"We could use another mage," Afrith said to Fig. "A revolution has begun, with our kind at the head. You're welcome to join us, Fig— if you can handle it."

Her gaze went immediately to Vaelor's silver-ringed eyes, then back to Dev.

If she went with Afrith, could she keep Dev safe? Or maybe, even though he was a conniving briigard, she could learn something from Afrith...enough to help Dev escape.

Her old teacher summoned another set of manacles, green flames spinning slowly in the air before him, as he gestured to her. Dev pleaded at her with his eyes. *No,* they said.

No.

She couldn't leave him behind. Not again.

She thrust Emrah at Vaelor, and the silversword scrambled to hold him. Slamming her fists together across her middle, a burst of sparks built to flaming swaths that trailed her arms.

"No," she said aloud. "You're not taking him!"

The flames flew through her veins and out her fingertips, the ribbons aimed at the back of the boat, rather than Afrith.

But Afrith was faster, throwing a burst of fire at the explosion, and redirecting it back toward her. She threw herself down onto the dock, and Vaelor managed to curl Emrah between them as he huddled over her. Green and gold fire enveloped them. Fig reached out to protect them as best she could.

Doubt ran through her mind; what if she couldn't? Could he pervert her own flames against her? But the gold dispersed, though her eyes still stung from the heat. Next, she focused on containing the heat from the savage green flames so it wouldn't hurt her, Vaelor, or Emrah.

But it was too late for the dock. The green flames persisted, not having mingled with the gold flames long enough to be dependent on them for anything. The green fire corroded the salty wood planks, raging all around them.

Fig could do nothing to snuff it out. She flung her hands out, calling to it. Why wouldn't it listen to her?

"Ahh!" she cried, as a tendril of green flame came too close. Then she saw the boat floating into the salt swamps, Dev, still bound at the wrists.

"No!" she screamed, her throat hoarse. "Dev!" She reached for him—*stupid!* She yanked her hand back, yet another burn marring her skin. "*Dev,*" she sobbed.

Vaelor yanked on her arm. "Come on, goldfire. We better get off this. We can—"

"The other boat," she said. "Quickly!"

But the rope tying up the canoe was engulfed in green flames. Fig and Vaelor were on the last shrinking bit of dock that wasn't burning. They had to get off. And they had to go after Dev.

Vaelor used his sword to lift what was left of the rope off the pillar. The rope fell into the water with a hiss, freeing the boat and saving it from the same fate as the dock had suffered.

How far away had Afrith gotten? Fig could barely see a glint of light in the distance—was that them or firemoths bobbing far-off? She panted, staring into the swamp as if it would bring Dev back to her.

It was impossible to tell with the trees and plant life blocking her way. She glanced down at the canoe, which drifted idly away. "But now we—" Fig began.

A great roar made her raise her head. An immense wall of water rose from the swamp, glowing faintly green and surging straight toward them.

They had no time to move before it crashed over the still-flaming dock. Vaelor covered Emrah's face with his enormous hand, shielding the dragonet's nose and ears.

The crackling of flames was gone. The dock hissed like a thousand snakes as hot coals fought against what was left of the water and a dripping sound pounded in Fig's ears. Hair clinging to her head and neck, Fig wiped the water from her eyes.

It was pitch black, save for a few firemoths amid the scorched Andisia moss above. Then, a light green glow approached them. Fig's heart was thumping so wildly she didn't care if it was the goddess Morgha herself come to take her in her arms of death.

But the glow split into two and solidified into the forms of two dryads.

"We've got to go after them," Fig mumbled. It was the third time she had said it.

The canoe had been retrieved from its listless floating—either by Vaelor or Fenra; Fig had barely been paying attention. Emrah was still unconscious in her lap.

It all seemed useless now. How could they possibly track anyone down in the salt swamps at night? She had utterly and completely failed Dev. Failed to see the danger. Failed to protect him.

Fig sat on the grass next to Mairead, who had revived sometime around when Fenra and her brother dumped all that water on the dock. The ex-priestess seemed understandably shaken and burned in more than a few places. Her newly cleaned robes were singed. Vaelor stood silent at the edge of the grass. If the dock had been safe, she imagined he would have gone to the very end, to stare pensively into the *solanse*.

Fenra paced back and forth, her brother sitting in the grass clutching a moss-patched injury on his trunk.

"We tried to get here sooner," Fenra was saying, "but El got his foot stuck amid the cedar knees, and there were a couple of tagors nearby—"

"It's not your fault," Fig said in a dead voice.

Mairead hesitantly cleared her throat. "Why don't we all go inside?"

Fig couldn't even bring herself to answer. Go inside and tell Zula and Perrin how they had let Afrith—of all people—kidnap Dev? See the looks on Lady Atricia and Lord Onalde's faces, if the nobles were still there. Though, Afrith had stolen their boat, so...

She hauled herself to her feet.

"Fine, let's go in. But I don't want to talk to the nobles."

At the very least, she needed to figure out what was wrong with Emrah, and they all had some burns that needed to be looked at. Fig's cheek stung something fierce. Why couldn't she fight Afrith's flames?

Heat flooded her face. Those green flames, so menacing and deadly and precise. His earlier words felt all the more condescending as he lectured her on control. Compared to his magic, she was a child throwing a fistful of sand, instead of a carefully crafted weapon delivering a precise blow. Her magic was big and flashy, and got the job done—normally.

Fire itself was enough to intimidate most people.

But wasn't that all they taught her at the Carriage House, anyway? Wracking her brain as they trudged their way up the lawn, she tried to remember anything else about the precise control and strange methods Afrith had used—the other fire mages who had taught her had done nothing like it. Nothing. Even the way Afrith heated the *kafye* without flames. How the manacles of his fire became solid, with minimal heat. And the painful precision of the vortexes.

Fenra followed behind them, her brother steadying himself on her arm. The two were murmuring to each other, and Fig was glad for their presence, even thought they hadn't been able to warn them in time. That hadn't been the dryads' fault. Fig should have seen this coming. Afrith with his worldly connections. Her accidental hints that Dev was here at Resbrok. They should have realized when Afrith didn't show up to the meeting.

Cold gripped her fingers as she cradled Emrah to her chest with both hands. He was still breathing, at least, the occasional wisp of smoke rising from his tiny snout. What had Afrith said about him being her familiar? Her brow furrowed. How could she trust a single word out of that despicable man's mouth?

Her pace slowed as they drew nearer to the porch steps. Resbrok towered above them, warmly inviting from its aging wood and candles twinkling from the windows at the lower floors. The lamps were still lit on either side of the front door, but Fig hesitated.

Vaelor turned to them all, holding his left arm awkwardly away from his body. "I'll go in and tell them everything," he said quietly. "And then we can all dry off."

Warm relief filled Fig's chest, and she nodded. After everything that had happened, she had no strength left to deal with Lady Atricia's calculating looks, or Lord Onalde's gruff inquiries, and particularly, not Zula's judgment.

Vaelor opened the large front door with a creak. Fig and the other three shuffled toward the kitchen as Vaelor paused at the entrance to the sitting room, where hushed voices were arguing. The voices stopped abruptly, to be replaced by Vaelor's baritone.

Fig and the others settled into the kitchen to lick their wounds. Or so it felt. Mairead quickly found some towels and handed several to Fig, who started on her hair to stop it from sticking to her neck. Feeling suddenly colder, she placed Emrah gently on the table, tucking his tail around him. She dried herself off as best she could, then sank into a hard wooden chair at the equally hard wooden table, well-worn from use. This was her first time sitting here. All the meals had been served in the dining room...or to Dev's room.

"Could you look at him?" she asked Mairead, looking up at the girl.

Mairead frowned, her hands flying to her waist where she kept a pouch of the holy water on her at all times, as if to check that it was still there. The flask was secure, but Fig knew they had to ration its contents. Mairead could only heal using Morgha's waters from the holy pool at Mar Nevan.

The healer pressed her lips together, studying the little dragonet.

"Perhaps I can look," Fenra offered in a breezy whisper. Mairead hastily stepped back and let the dryad come closer to the table.

El lowered himself into a chair at the table, after a covert glance at Fig, as if to study how she was sitting. After checking his moss-patched wound, he ran a hand back and forth along the grain of the table.

Fenra placed a hand on Emrah's back, her wooden fingers curling around him and elongating to encompass his tiny form. As she did so, Fig caught sight of the dim green glow that seemed to emanate from her on occasion.

"Hmm," Fenra said. "He is only asleep. Though I sense something that doesn't belong...perhaps a compound he should not have digested."

"Poison?" Fig said in a hush.

"Not as you might think." Fenra spoke slowly and ponderously. "It could be foli-leaf. That isn't harmful to humans, but it is to animals."

Fig twisted her mouth. Was Emrah technically an animal? No, of course not. He would shoot sparks at her for even thinking such things. "So essentially poison to him," she said gruffly.

Had Afrith known about Emrah before coming tonight? She tried to wrack her brain about the now-despised training session this afternoon. Had she mentioned Emrah at all? She didn't think so. But Afrith had discovered plenty that she had tried to keep hidden.

"Will he wake up?" Fig whispered.

"Yes," Fenra said, "and with a mighty aching in the stomach and head." She gave his scales a final stroke and stepped back near her brother.

Fig's eyes closed, and she reached for Emrah's head as Fenra pulled away. She scratched his ears and ran a hand along his little snout.

"Could be etru," El suggested, still running his fingers up and down the wood grain.

They all looked at him, but he didn't seem interested in meeting any of their eyes.

"It's not native to the *solanse*," he went on. "But in Tysaine, it's a mild sedative they sell in the street markets."

"That could very well be it," Fig said darkly. "Afrith is no stranger to Tysaine. He's probably got *kafye* vendors all over Tysaine who distribute to him. What's a few more herbs?"

The front door shut, and they all looked at the doorway leading down the hall. None of them had bothered to light any candles in the kitchen, and they could only see by the fire so safely contained in the heavy iron stove across the room. Somehow the darkness enveloping them was comforting.

Fig's eyebrows rose when she saw Zula coming toward them, then a stone dropped in her stomach.

"Vaelor and Perrin have gone to escort Lord Onalde and Lady Atricia home," she said, heading straight for the iron stove. The weight in Fig's stomach grew heavier. She didn't want them out there, not with the silverswords knowing Vaelor was here in the lowlands. And she hoped to the Bard none of the 'swords came back while they were gone. She was so exhausted, she'd probably burn down the house trying to defend them.

Mairead *tsked*. "I wanted to look at Vaelor's burns," she said. "I could tell he had a bad one on his side."

"*Va, iil,*" Zula began, "He was eager to see them go, just as I was."

"Did you see what happened?" Mairead asked the matron in a whisper.

Zula shook her head. "We could hear the commotion down by the dock, but I forbade Perrin from leaving the sitting room—we would only do more harm than good. I thought maybe the silverswords, but Vaelor explained..." She didn't need to finish the thought.

Suddenly a cup of tea was placed in front of Fig. She hadn't even seen Zula make it, but now her eyes registered the steaming kettle and the open tin of tea. She hung her head and breathed in the steam. It wasn't viragrove leaf tea, thank the Bard.

After a while, Fenra drifted outside with a muttered excuse that she wanted to inspect the outbuildings and woods. Fig could sense her discomfort at being indoors, but her brother El was another story. It was difficult to tell ages in dryads, but from his wide eyes and the fact that he was still in the *solanse*, she suspected he was the younger of the two.

Fig's cup of tea was nearly cold before she remembered to take a sip. She had been staring into the depths of the iron stove's flames. The tea had the faintest warmth left and tasted of simple floral notes. She stared morosely into the cup, wishing she had tried it sooner. The thought of being able to warm it—like Afrith could—only made her grit her teeth.

With a huff, Zula stood, and came back over with the kettle to top off her cup with hot water.

"Thank you," Fig mumbled. Sighing in appreciation, she drank the rest in silence. Mairead was slumped in the chair beside Fig, and El had moved on from studying the wood grain to seemingly cataloging everything in the room with his gaze. Emrah slept on, his tail curled around him like a svorcat's.

Hours passed with only the crackling of flames in the stove and the raising and setting down of teacups to fill the silence. An emptiness Fig hadn't felt in a long time, gouged a deep hole in her chest. But instead of thinking about it, she stared into the wood stove, watching the flames dance. No one suggested they retire to bed. Fig couldn't possibly go back upstairs to the room she had so recently said goodbye to, with Dev's doorway just down the hall. Not to mention she was still damp from swamp water.

No one brought up the silverswords again either. Fig didn't care if a dozen of them came in the morning.

The faint rosy glow of dawn had begun to peek through the trees by the time Vaelor and Perrin returned. The back door eased open, and everyone holding vigil at the table turned at once.

Something eased in Fig's chest, and she gave them a sad smile. At least the two Resbroks were safe.

"They're both settled back at home," Perrin reported, breaking the spell of silence that had settled over them. "Though Lady Atricia says we owe her a sword—and Lord Onalde a boat."

Zula straightened, somehow betraying no stiff muscles from her night's watch at the kitchen table. "I can't see why we would be responsible. We all know who took it."

Fig unfocused her gaze, sensing Zula had skirted around Afrith's name.

"We also ran into Lord Eleste right after we left here," Perrin said. "His wife had kept him—but as soon as we told him about the 'swords—"

"He wants nothing to do with it," Vaelor added.

Vaelor joined them at the table, but when he sat, Zula got to her feet. "Breakfast," she said. "I'll call Marlow down to help. You'll need to get on the road soon before those silverswords return."

"What?" Mairead asked.

"The road?" Fig said. "But..." She paused, unsure why she was objecting. That was the original plan, after all.

Vaelor looked thoughtful as Zula set a cup of a stronger tea in front of him. More cups were handed out to the rest. The time for soothing flowery teas was over. Vaelor stood to offer his *grimazir* a hand, but she waved him away. A minute later, Marlow came in and took over the production at the stove, handling the frying pans, fish and eggs, and boiling water.

"Where do we go?" Fig finally asked, her mind moving slowly.

"The Hollow Isles," Vaelor said.

"You really believe all of that?" Fig said. "That Afrith is taking him to his brother?"

"Afrith did sound..." Mairead trailed off.

"Out of his mind?" Fig supplied. "None of that makes any sense. Shadryn died when he tried to cross over. That's why Dev was sent to the Carriage House, and why Tytan ran a blockade, and scared everyone off from trading with the Hollow Isles. How could Shadryn even be alive? Dev said—" Her breath hitched, and her throat started to close up.

Vaelor shook his head, running a hand over the stubble that had gathered on his chin. El watched the two of them like a rather interesting marstone game was taking place in front of him. Perrin tried to pretend he wasn't watching anyone, but he was.

Fig shook her head with a tired laugh. "Fine. You're probably right. Even if Afrith is delusional, that does seem to be where he was taking Dev. Maybe someone *is* there, impersonating Shadryn."

"Well, what if Prince Shadryn *is* alive?" Perrin said. "He could help Dev get—"

"The throne back?" Fig said. "*Shadryn* would technically be next in line. But this is all still a rumor from a madman." She shook her head. "Fine. We'll go to Nithe. We can book passage directly from Tirnalore after we get through the Notch."

Vaelor was nodding. Fig looked up at Mairead, and said, "Are you sure—"

"If you ask me one more time if I'm sure I'm coming, I'm going to put a spider in your bed."

An ungainly snort came out of Fig, and she covered her mouth. "I'm sorry," she said, eyes watering. "I won't ask again."

Looking pleased with herself, Mairead picked up her fork and dug into the plate of food Marlow had just set in front of her. Fig did the same. It didn't take long before the plates were wiped clean, runny eggs and bits of grilled fish sopped up with slices of bread. One by one, the three of them excused themselves to the bathhouse to wipe off as much of the dried stickiness of the swamp water as they could and to change their clothes. Fig almost cried when she placed the burned golden tunic on the sad pile in the corner of the bathhouse. It could be mended, but the embroidery would be hard to repair.

Mairead came back last, clutching her robes in her hands. There were a few burned patches and a rip along one of the sleeves. Zula leapt up once more to leave the kitchen. She came back with a small box clutched to her chest, which she handed to Perrin.

He got to work mending some of the burned patches, though Mairead insisted it didn't have to be perfect—most of it wouldn't be noticeable in the folds of the garment. Fig watched Perrin with a smile, his deft stitches and cuts with the sharp scissors expertly done. She wondered if Zula had taught him, or if he'd learned this from his lessons with Taskor. Well, Taskor was about to become a part of the Resbrok household himself, she mused.

It wasn't long before they heard carriage wheels on the drive.

What happened next was a blur: repeated goodbyes, packages of food and skins of water pressed into hands, more hugs from Perrin. Zula provided a basket for Fig to scoop Emrah into.

Fig unfocused her eyes and let Vaelor lead her into the carriage with Mairead. The pack secured, Emrah's basket held tightly on Fig's lap, Vaelor drove the horses back down the drive, leaving the carriage delivery driver to head back on his extra horse.

Out the carriage window, Fig watched the lusciously green edges of the *solanse* disappear into the distance, not sure whether she would ever see them again. Because when she found Afrith, she was going to kill him—or die trying.

She pulled the curtain shut and closed her eyes.

TYSAINE

ZIGGY

Ziggy Ashbrok stared down the road in boredom as yet another carriage approached the new gatepost at the Notch.

She rolled her shoulders, adjusting her armor. How in the name of the Bard did she get assigned here? Word was she had missed out on some raid last night too. She must have really pissed off Liess when she didn't show enough respect.

Of all the silversword assignments in the lowlands, this had to be the worst. Mostly because it involved talking to people. Intimidate the local troublemakers? Right up her alley. Track 'em down when they went and did the illegal and stupid things she had just warned them not to do? Even better. Swing her sword when they really deserved it? The best.

Normally, travelers passing through the Notch went through the Tysaine gate, which was farther down the isthmus. But King Rhivven had ordered them to immediately slap this gatepost together and check the papers of everyone passing through the Notch. A bit redundant, that. But Ziggy knew the 'swords were still looking for the missing prince. They had traded one bloody sword for another.

What did she care?

The view was nice, though. If she faced the Hollow Sea, the salt swamps stretched to her left, and the coast of Tysaine far in the mist to her right. The isthmus was narrow, merely a thread tying the two nations together, though it was rumored they had once been a united continent, instead of split down the middle like a pair of lungs. But she was no historian.

"Papers," she grunted at the two scholarly-looking kids inside the coach.

The one closest to her raised a tentative hand, the papers shaking a little. She rolled her eyes under her helm, then ran a cursory glance over the papers.

Her gaze was drawn to the dates stamped inside the inky black circle, no doubt the reason the kid's hand was shaking. "This Tysainian stamp is two weeks overdue," she said in a monotone. "What delayed you to stay so long?"

"Well, ma'am, we—" he began in a shaky voice.

"What is going on here, Ziggrune?" Liess sidled up to her, the axe at her belt singing for blood, as always.

Ziggy could hear a distinct ringing from Liess's weapon—a bloodthirsty tune Ziggy had gotten to know all too well over the last couple of years. Ever since Ziggy had crossed over, she had heard the same, albeit faint frequency coming from her own Welded sword, Mystic. The name was stupid, but it was a family sword, and there was no changing it now.

At the end of the war, when blood streamed in rivers through the fields of the highlands, it had come down to Ziggy laying down her life or crossing over. She had taken one glance at her little sisters' eyes and taken up the sword in duty to the throne—the throne that had put Viren under its silvery boot.

But she couldn't keep her mother and sisters safe if she was buried in the dirt. She was lucky they had let her take a post in the lowlands, where she could keep an eye on things. It helped that she knew everything about the country and its geography, something the other silverswords stationed there struggled with.

Ziggy tried to ignore the blood-song coming from Liess's axe. The woman was insatiable.

"Scholars heading back to Tirnalore, Commander Astor," Ziggy said.

"Let me see," Liess demanded, yanking the papers from Ziggy's hand with a leer toward the carriage.

The boy's face paled. Ziggy averted her gaze. She had planned on letting them go, after threatening them a bit. What did she care if two students came to visit some family in the lowlands? Family stuff got complicated. So what if they were late?

But that wouldn't sail with Liess. "Out of the carriage," she demanded. Ziggy resisted rolling her eyes. Did she seriously think these two kids were hiding the former prince?

She had seen him once. At the end of the war. On the battlefield with his father, the silversword. The prince, though, was fated to never cross over like his father. Not with that mage blood of his. Not after the disastrous fate of his brother.

Ziggy spied another carriage coming up the road and went to greet it. It was a welcome distraction. She didn't really want to see what Liess had planned for the schoolboys. As she passed the boys' carriage, Liess and other two 'swords were already tearing apart its interior. Ziggy put her hand on Mystic.

The newcomer's carriage came to a stop, the two horses stomping their feet in the dirt. Ziggy halted in her tracks. She would recognize the man driving it anywhere. Her eyes bulged. What in Morgha's bloodstained cloak was Vaelor Resbrok doing here of all places?

He had a mossy lowlands cloak drawn over his head, but she had known him well before he donned his silversword armor. Seen him fight and kill with that sword before it became Welded to him.

Her steps wooden, she approached him, and held out her hand for papers. "You idiot," she hissed. "What do you think you're doing here? Didn't you hear they set up a checkpoint?"

Vaelor looked at her, and she could see his silver-ringed eyes easily under the cloak's hood. He handed a stack of three papers to her but didn't reply. Was he mad?

"If Liess wouldn't notice your carriage turning around, I'd tell you to get out of here," Ziggy said. "They're saying you helped Prince Devryn escape. He's—he's not...?" She tried to peer through the cracks in the curtains, but only glimpsed a woman with golden-brown eyes before they were pulled shut.

"No," Vaelor said. "He's not."

A whisper came from inside the carriage. "Liess?" It was quiet, but not quiet enough to escape Ziggy's enhanced hearing. "Liess Astor?"

"May Morgha be merciful," came another whisper.

Ziggy glanced over her shoulder at the scholar's carriage. Liess was still going over it, looking for the missing prince. And here was the 'sword who had helped Prince Devryn escape his death. A death that King Rhivven still craved even though he was already sitting on the Rayvan throne. But somehow...somehow Vaelor had kept Dev alive through the coup.

Probably the only reason Vaelor wasn't dead yet was because he hadn't broken his oath. She had watched him swear it on that blood-soaked battlefield at the edge of the highlands.

To serve House Verrence until the end of his days.

Even if the prince wasn't with him, Liess would never let him pass. She would take him straight to Rhivven.

She shoved the papers back in Vaelor's hands, glancing briefly at the fake names. They were forged well enough that Vaelor and his friends should make it through the Tysainian gate. "Go. Go now, get past that carriage and you might get past Liess."

Vaelor wasted no time, flicking the reins to spur the horses on. She had no idea who those women in the carriage were, or where they were heading, but Vaelor needed to get out of Tytan. Now.

Ziggy sent a quick prayer to Morgha as she walked around the other side of the scholar's wagon. Her boots scuffed the dirt on her way to the gatehouse.

Liess looked up as Vaelor's carriage rolled by.

A ringing began in Ziggy's ears, in her heart, in her sword. Her blood-song.

She put a hand on Mystic and trudged toward Liess instead of the relative safety of the gatehouse. She owed it to Vaelor.

The two scholars were on their knees in the dirt road. Their papers had been thrown on the floor of the carriage and trampled a few times by searching boots. A pathetic flaunting of the woman's might.

"Where's that carriage going?" Liess said, striding over to catch up. "Halt!" she cried.

"Their papers were fine, Commander Astor," Ziggy called after her, crossing her arms over her armored chest. "What, are we hand-inspecting every carriage now? They don't have the ex-prince under their cloaks and books."

Stupid. That was stupid. The Bard would laugh when he scribed this part in her life's story.

Liess didn't take the bait. She continued striding toward Vaelor's carriage. He was moving at a pace that wouldn't mark him as guilty, but Ziggy wished he would hurry up. *Just go,* Ziggy thought at him. *Get out of Tytan!*

"Liess!" Ziggy called. "Their papers were fine."

But Liess had gotten in front of the carriage, momentarily becoming a blur as she ran to catch up properly. The horses pranced nervously in such proximity to the woman's bared axe.

"I'll deal with your insubordination later," Liess promised without looking at Ziggy.

The blood-song was ringing in her ears now, begging for her to pull the sword.

Insubordination. Did this haughty 'sword even know who Ziggy was before becoming bound to her blade? Eldest child of House Ashbrok, the oldest in Viren, yet Ziggy was expected to lick the boots of every other silversword from the Notch to Mar Nevan. She spit in the dirt.

But it wasn't just about Ziggy.

As soon as Liess got a good look under Vaelor's cloak, he'd be sent directly to Morgha's arms. There was nothing else for it—

"What, calling you Liess, you mean?" Ziggy goaded.

"You little kirich," Liess hissed, finally turning. "You'll taste my axe for that. When I slice through your mouth—"

She didn't finish her threat before Vaelor came flying from the carriage, his sword down in a double-handed grip. With similar speed, Ziggy unsheathed Mystic, her blood-song rising to a glorious crescendo in her ears. She could slice, she could cut. She could kill.

And Liess had it coming.

Liess sensed Vaelor, though, and whirled around, her movements so fast she became a blur. But Vaelor had been endowed with great strength when he crossed over, and he met her axe with a great *clang* of steel.

Ziggy finally reached them and joined the fight, bringing her sword to Vaelor's side. It was too late for Ziggy's reputation now. But this man had killed for her before. And then there was that time Ziggy had almost killed him on the battlefield in a pique of misunderstanding. She owed him.

Liess scored a hit on Vaelor, and the tang of blood filled the air. A current of electricity ran from Mystic and up her arm, jolting through her nerves like she held a bolt of lightning. Deadly. A force of nature.

Ziggy timed a blow with Liess's movements. Vaelor didn't have his armor, and though his strength was enhanced, he could still bleed. Ziggy's strike landed hard at Liess's shoulder, but it didn't slow her down.

Vaelor's hood had come off when he jumped from the carriage.

"You!" Liess shouted. She lunged at him again, her axe's blood-song nearly deafening Ziggy.

Ziggy had no idea if Vaelor had spoken the truth, and the prince wasn't in the carriage—but there was no way Liess would let Vaelor pass, prince or no.

Vaelor grunted at the force of the strike and pushed her back.

Two more silverswords rushed from the gatehouse, their weapons singing a song probably only Ziggy could hear. She hadn't bothered to learn their names. All the 'swords not from the lowlands treated her like a pile of manure, so she returned the favor. One of them, his armor highly polished like a mirror—probably so he could stare at himself in it when he got bored of making suggestive comments to anyone who walked by—held his blade up as he charged Ziggy.

She whirled toward him, practically knowing his movements

before he did. She managed to shove him off for a second while the other man went for Vaelor. Ziggy stuck her leg out to trip him, but he latched on and pulled her down in a tangle. His short sword went flying wildly. Ziggy kicked him in the gut and lurched to her feet.

Now Liess was heading straight for her, the axe aimed at Ziggy's head. "You traitorous kirich!" Liess shouted.

No matter how much faith Ziggy put in her dwarf-crafted armor, she knew the force from Liess would cave it in along with her skull.

Ducking at the last second, Ziggy heard the axe slice through empty air as if cutting the very fabric of reality.

Vaelor lunged in. He managed to snake Liess's legs out from under her, but not before Liess threw her axe straight for Ziggy's chest.

Just as she had predicted, it caved in the steel with a sound like a dying vorse eagle.

She heard Mystic singing to her as she collapsed. A symphony of blood.

"Oh Bard, we are so dead," Fig groaned. She cradled the blonde woman's head in her lap, while the carriage rumbled beneath her. Blood. There was blood everywhere. All over their hands, Fig's clothes, and Mairead's robes. They awkwardly held the woman's torso across their laps as Vaelor spurred the horses on past the silversword checkpoint. Discarded armor rattled on the floor; the two of them had wrenched it from the woman's chest.

"Don't we know this woman?" Fig asked, her bare hand pressed to the woman's wound as Mairead readied to heal her. "She was the 'sword at Verindas who wanted to arrest you. So why was she helping us?"

Mairead wasn't listening. Her bloody hands reached for the flask of sacred water at her belt.

Fig hadn't seen what had happened after Vaelor leapt from the carriage. Not wanting to attract the attention of Liess Astor, they'd kept the curtain shut, and Fig and Mairead clung to each other, listening to the awful clangs of swords on armor. Strike after strike. Not knowing who would prevail.

Finally, Vaelor had ripped open the carriage door and practically thrown this woman inside with the words, "Keep her alive."

Fig focused again on the woman's face; there was nothing else she could do at the moment. Her hands were sticky, and she didn't want to think about that.

And she certainly didn't want to think about Liess Astor. The silversword was relentless; if she'd survived the fight, there was no doubt she was still in pursuit.

When had the silverswords set up a checkpoint at the Notch, anyway?

Mairead let out a low whine, holding her flask of sacred water in one hand and the regular water in another. Fig immediately realized her predicament. The sacred water could—and should—be diluted, so it could be used for more healings. But with the unsteady rumbling of the carriage, Mairead was bound to spill half the precious water just opening the damn thing. And it wasn't like they could easily get more.

"Um..." Fig began, thinking, then her gaze landed on their pack. "Anything we can use as a bandage in there? At least until we get somewhere you can heal her safely?"

Shifting the woman's armored legs out of the way, Mairead reached for the pack; her fingers groped inside for a moment. She yanked out a man's tunic, and without a second thought, pressed it hard on the wound. Then she motioned for Fig's hand.

"Here," Mairead said. "You take over. I need to talk to Vaelor. She won't last long like this."

"Ask if the gate's in sight yet," Fig called as she got up. "There's no way we'll get through like this!"

Mairead stood at a crouch and leaned over the front seat to pull aside the little wooden slat that opened out to the driver's seat. It was hard to hear what either of them was shouting over the rushing air, pounding hooves, and rattling armor.

The white tunic quickly became splotched with red, and the blood seeped under Fig's fingernails.

Was this Dev's shirt? She stared at it without seeing. Afrith could be anywhere with him by now. Had he gone through the Notch too? That seemed too dangerous with the silverswords on high alert and the new checkpoint. Or did he have a more direct route to the Hollow Isles? It wasn't like any ships were sailing out of Nova Istra right now.

Fig realized she was practically panting in anxiety and tried to take some deep breaths. The first few came out shaky.

Ashes. Is Drakioryn rising? What is this gods-awful racket?

The voice in her head had never been so welcome.

"Emrah!" Fig cried, her eyes stinging with tears. "You're awake! Wait, you *are* awake, right?"

Hand glued to the woman's chest as she pressed on the wound, Fig tried to lean over to look into Emrah's basket, which she had tucked into a ledge on the floor. He was standing on all four legs in the basket, looking at Fig as if she had murdered his entire family.

*What in the—*he began, sparks flying. *What could have possessed you to put me in a* basket? *What do you think I am, some sort of fluffy pet svorcat?*

Despite the seriousness of the situation and his expression, Fig burst out laughing.

He snarled good-naturedly and hopped out of the basket, quickly winging to a better position on the front seat.

Mairead finally turned around. She spared a relieved smile for Emrah, then returned to her patient. "Here, let me," she told Fig. "Vaelor said we have time. He's going to find a place to pull over."

Fig eagerly traded places with Mairead, letting the red sister take the bloody cloth. Fig threw herself onto the front seat; Emrah fluttered down into her lap. The dragonet found a spot free of blood and made himself comfortable, kneading her legs with his clawed feet before sitting down. She couldn't help but smile slyly at his earlier remark about the svorcat.

I assume you escaped that briigard Afrith, then? he asked her. *Or is that what we're doing now?*

Her grin faded faster than it had come. *No,* she replied, not wishing to voice it aloud. *He...he took Dev.*

After several minutes which felt like an eternity in the darkest pits of Malhela, Fig recounted the events of the night and morning for Emrah. The little dragonet was understandably outraged at Afrith's betrayal, and they worked out that Emrah had been poisoned—though not how he had done it.

The carriage finally began to slow. "Thank the mother," Mairead said.

Fig yanked aside the curtain to reveal a swath of lowlands forest. The trees looked the same as those they had just left in Viren, but it was significantly less swampy here—no waterways or pools filled with murky water, just moss-draped oaks and cedars on the edges of the Hollow Sea.

Fig hoped the tagors didn't come over here, but the creatures were known to swim in the narrowest part of the Hollow Sea, and she probably shouldn't get her hopes up.

The carriage door jerked open, and Mairead let out a little scream. "Vaelor! What in the love of Morgha are you doing? I just opened my flask—you scared the life out of me!"

Vaelor ducked his head and mumbled an apology.

"Where are we?" Fig asked him.

"Out of sight of the road," he said. "I only just spotted the highest turret of the gatehouse—they didn't see us. As long as Liess and the others don't pursue us...but I don't think they will."

Fig wasn't sure whether that was because they were all dead or because the 'swords didn't want to tangle with the Tysainian soldiers. She shook her head and looked past Vaelor's shoulders at the surrounding trees, then asked Emrah, "I don't suppose you'd be up for scouting about? Unless you're still not feeling well..."

The dragonet chirped and darted out the carriage door. Fig smiled after him.

Mairead was already at work, diluting the sacred waters with the mundane and muttering some holy words over it. Fig thought she saw the red tattoos on the back of Mairead's hand glow briefly as she did so.

The healing waters were ready. Mairead pulled away the now-crimson tunic.

The woman was barely breathing, the axe wound on her chest only slightly moving up and down with each breath. Vaelor eased further into the carriage, though it was already quite crowded with Fig, Mairead, and the woman. He held the woman's arm, helping to steady her. Fig met his eyes for a brief second before they both looked down.

Mairead poured the water over the wound and pressed her hand to it, murmuring her prayer. The tattoos again glowed dimly.

She repeated the process over and over. Fig had seen red sisters heal people plenty of times, but her own recent disastrous injury brought even more respect for the magic.

"How do you know this woman?" Fig asked Vaelor under her breath. His face was inches from hers as they both leaned in to watch.

"She's Virenish," he said.

"And, what? You know every person in Viren?"

"No. But Ziggy and I, well, we fought together in the war. Had seen each other at gatherings since we were kids. Didn't know her that well until the war, though."

"Oh," Fig said, staring at Mairead's hands; they were dripping with bloody water.

Mairead poured more water over the wound, which was closed up now. The scar was still red and angry, and the woman, Ziggy, apparently, was still breathing weakly.

"And she was turned at the end of the war too?" Fig guessed quietly.

Vaelor nodded. They didn't say anymore until Mairead's motions halted. Ziggy's breathing gradually became more and more regular. The wound now looked like a year-old scar.

Blinking at her, Fig said, "Well done. See? Worth pulling over for, huh, Vaelor?"

He didn't reply.

"What is it?" Fig asked. "Do you think the 'swords will follow us into Tysaine?"

"A line on the map will not stop Liess. She knows of my oath to Dev, whether they think he's with us or not. If I didn't kill them, they will pursue us."

"*Did* you kill them?" Mairead asked.

He sighed. "I couldn't tell. Between getting Ziggy into the carriage and—"

"It's all right," Fig said. "You got us through, and we're all alive thanks to the two of you."

He cleared his throat. "Now that she's healed, let's go."

"Wait. Emrah?" Fig called. "How's it looking out there?"

There's a brook. Lots of trees. One in particular that you'd be interested in.

Really? Fig replied in her mind.

But maybe now's not the time.

Fig nodded. "Emrah said there's a brook. We should clean up. Can't go through the gate covered in blood."

A gasp rent the air, and Ziggy rose from her bench like she was rising from the dead—which, really, she was. Her wild eyes met each of theirs until landing on Vaelor.

"N-no. No, no, no, no. What am I doing here—"

"We had to take you," Vaelor replied. "Liess Astor was going to kill you. What did you go and provoke her for, anyway?"

"To keep you alive. I have to go back," Ziggy insisted, trying to push her way through Vaelor—no small feat in such a crowded space. "I can't desert my post. You know very well what they could do to my family."

Fig's jaw clenched. The two of them, bested in the war and forced into servitude as silverswords. And she had thought life at the Carriage House was bad.

"What do we—" Fig began, glancing between Vaelor and Ziggy.

"*I have to go back,*" Ziggy said, shoving Vaelor.

Vaelor caught her forearm. "Stop. You can't," he insisted. "Liess will rip your throat out."

Ziggy tried to wrench herself from his grip and slip around him. He pushed her back toward the bench. She sneered, "I don't care what Liess does to me. I care what she'll do to *them.*"

"If any of the soldiers at the gate are alive, you won't make it back through the Notch."

She groaned in frustration and fell back into her seat with a loud *thump.* "Why did you have to pick the day *I'm* assigned to the Notch to come through here?"

To Fig's surprise, Vaelor rolled his eyes and turned away from the door. "Hands of fate, I guess."

Ziggy sighed. "Hands of fate? Well, let a woman stretch her legs, will you?"

"Fine, but we shouldn't stay long. The sooner we're through the gate and in Tysaine, the safer we'll be." He let Ziggy pass. Fig followed, needing some air after the crush of so many people.

Mairead came too. "Did you say Emrah found a brook?"

The brook turned out to be smaller than Fig had imagined, though it probably seemed quite large to the dragonet. Still, they were able to wash off the blood and fill their skins and flasks. It was a glorious reprieve after the last half hour of blood and swords, although Fig was in dire need of a real bath after only sponging off the swamp water from last night. The clouds provided reprieve from the early afternoon sun, which was growing warmer in the humid air.

After unceremoniously splashing herself down with water, Ziggy stretched her legs along the mossy bank. Mairead meticulously cleaned the blood from under her nails. Vaelor disappeared upstream.

Feeling reasonably better, Fig found Emrah sunning on a rock and said, "What was that about a tree I might like to see?"

He flitted up into the air, green sparks falling from his wings. *Oh, let me show you!*

A smile pushed its way onto her face, and she followed the trail of sparks through the trees. She threw a worried glance over her shoulder at the others, but Mairead was with Ziggy, whom Vaelor seemed to trust, and Vaelor could protect himself. Still, she was anxious to reach Tirnalore and follow the long path of getting Dev back.

The last thing she expected to see in this corner of woods was an auran tree.

A faint shimmer of gold rained from the leaves, and she walked toward it slowly—as if it were an animal she might frighten away. "What is this doing here?"

Emrah chirped in a way that Fig interpreted as *I don't know.* Golden leaves gently fluttering above, Fig placed her hand on the gilt trunk, the thin golden bark peeling a little. A pleasant warmth of magic seeped into her, as if filling her veins with the sweetest golden honey.

A sigh heaved through her chest. Could they just stay here a while?

In the isthmus between the two countries, with this little golden ray of magic? She longed for even a brief moment of peace.

"Hey, Emrah?" she asked after a while.

A pleased chirp was his response from high in the auran leaves.

"Do you know anything about mage's familiars?"

Can't say that I do, he told her.

Fig bit her lip. She should keep quiet until she knew more about them. They were headed to the city with the biggest library in the entire world. She was bound to find answers there.

But little sparks sifting down from above made her sigh. "Afrith said something about them. That you were my familiar." She cringed, like it was her fault. "But I don't know if we can trust anything he said," she added in a rush.

Emrah was silent for a few minutes, then he finally said, *Could be why you can speak back to me in your head, when I've never had that happen before. I haven't noticed anything different other than that.*

A sigh of relief burst from her. "That could be it. But how did it happen? It's like something from one of the Bard's legends."

The golden leaves rustled as Emrah sailed down to hover in front of her face. *You're all right for a Svoran,* he said. *If we're connected somehow, I'm all right with that.*

She smiled and raised a finger to him. He bumped it with his nose. "We'll figure it out. In Tirnalore, I'm sure they'll have some book about it."

Splashing water drew their attention, and Fig looked over at what they could see of the stream in the distance.

Vaelor was there, holding his sword purposefully out in front of him. He was standing in the water, then he got down on one knee.

What is he doing? she asked Emrah.

I don't know. Emrah settled on her shoulder, his warm weight as comforting as the golden magic sifting down from the tree. Her hand clenched the bark, and she shrunk closer to the tree, feeling like they were intruding on something.

Vaelor raised his sword, his lips moving with quiet words, and he carefully laid it in the water.

A minute dragged on. Finally, he lifted the sword with both hands, and carefully dried it with a cloth he'd withdrawn from a pocket.

Fig remained frozen until he walked away.

Do you think we should get back? Emrah said to her. *We should probably get moving.*

She stroked the trunk of the auran once more and took a deep lungful of air. *Right. Let's go.*

When Fig returned to the stream a few minutes later, after giving Vaelor an ample lead, no one was there.

Panic surged through her, and Emrah darted overhead in the direction of the carriage. Fig was sweating as she jogged back, following silver sparks sifting down from Emrah.

Before she saw anyone, she heard Ziggy and Vaelor shouting. Her pace slowed. A shouting match wasn't a good idea, but she guessed they wouldn't be doing that if they were in trouble.

She burst into the clearing where the carriage was parked and spotted Vaelor and Ziggy at each other's throats.

Mairead was standing awkwardly to the side, so Fig approached her. "What's going on?"

The ex-priestess crossed her arms over her chest. "Ziggy threatened to tie me up. She wants to head back to the Notch. But when Vaelor came back, he went after her..."

Fig's mouth opened in an understanding *o*. "I'm sorry I left you there. Emrah showed me to an auran tree, right in the middle of—" She caught Mairead's dark expression and stopped talking.

"You can't stop me!" Ziggy was shouting. "I'm healed up and can get myself through. I need to get them out."

"Ziggrune—" Vaelor began.

Her fist sailed straight for his face, but he caught it in his palm.

Sparks dripped from Fig's fingers, and for once, she didn't feel out of sorts about it. It was her flame; she could use it. Amplifying the sparks, she pointed her fists down by her sides in two bursts of fire. "Stop it! Both of you!"

Two sets of silver-ringed eyes turned her way, and cold seeped into her chest. She cleared her throat. "We need to get moving to the Tysaine gate. Ziggrune, I'm sorry about your family, but—" Her gaze landed on Emrah, who had perched in an oak at the edge of the clearing. She sent a quick thought to him, conferring first.

Fig went on, "What if we sent someone to warn your family? You said you needed to get them out, right?

"Wh-why would you?"

"Well, you helped us get through the checkpoint."

Ziggy's gaze went up and down Fig's form as if assessing every flaw and flame. "But who?" she demanded. "If Vaelor insists, I won't make it, no offense, but I'm not sure either you or the red sister—"

Emrah fluttered over with a snort of sparks and landed on Fig's shoulder. *She's talking about me, 'sword.*

Ziggy's eyes bulged and she took a half-step back. "A *drixia*? I thought those were tales from Old Svora. W-where—" She shook her head. "He can talk?"

Fig grinned. "Talk. Fly. Warn your family. He can go faster than any of us. If that works for you."

Ziggy glanced at Vaelor, eyes still wide. He nodded once.

"Y-yes, that should be fine. They've been prepared since the day I crossed over, really. And my little sisters can protect Mother just as well as I can if they have to go into hiding."

"Very well then," Fig said. "But promise you won't threaten one of us again." She nodded at Mairead.

Ziggy raised her chin and said, "As long as you don't deserve it, I promise."

Fig narrowed her eyes, trying to read the woman's expression, but she seemed genuine enough. Emrah chirped, then hovered in front of

Ziggy to get directions. It didn't sound like it would take him long, and it was the least they could do for Ziggy. The woman had chosen to act out against Liess Astor and the others, just to help them get through the checkpoint.

But a few minutes later, when it was time for Emrah to depart, Fig was wringing her hands. She and Mairead were in the driver's seat of the carriage, having agreed they might look less suspicious than Vaelor with his cloak draped over his face to hide his eyes. Fig wondered more than once how the silversword checkpoint would have gone if they hadn't let Vaelor sit up front... No, the 'swords were searching all the carriages. There was no way they could have gotten through that checkpoint safely. Not without Ziggy's sacrifice and Vaelor's strength.

Be careful, Fig told Emrah.

I'm sure I'll be more careful than you will be, he said, bumping the side of her head with his.

She chuckled, then frowned as he took wing.

Don't worry, he called from the air high above the clearing. *I'll fly fast.*

Still watching, she said, *And you'll be able to find us?*

Svoran, I can hear you in my head. I think we'll be able to find each other.

And with that, he turned about, soaring west toward the Notch in a fluttering of gold and green.

She bit the inside of her mouth, then turned to the others. "Well?"

"To the gate," Vaelor said, handing the stack of forged papers to Fig. "Ziggy'll just have to claim the identity of Abenforth instead of Dev."

Ziggy, who had been watching the empty sky since Emrah left, hitched up a grin, saying, "I think I could pass for an Abenforth." She drew her hair back into a ponytail, then snorted. "Armor on or off though? We're obviously not trying to pass as silverswords."

"Off," Fig said, and Ziggy began taking the plate off her legs and stowing it in the compartment under the seat.

"What happened to yours, Vael?" Ziggy asked, undoing the last piece. 'Thought you'd be proud of that prince-issued metal."

"It's at the bottom of the Nova Istra Bay," he said. They were all silent for a moment. "It's a long story."

Fig nudged Mairead with her elbow. "You ready?"

"I think so," Mairead said. She patted her flask of holy water.

"Oh, and uh, I'm sorry I tried to arrest you," Ziggy told Mairead. "Thank you...for healing me. I'd probably be dead now if that sister hadn't taken you off our hands, eh?"

Mairead blanched, turning paler—if that was even possible. She mumbled a thank you, and exchanged an unsure look with Fig, who shrugged.

Hooves thundering beneath them, Fig held the reins securely as they barreled down the dirt road toward the Tysainian gate. Barely a moment after they'd gotten back on the road, the gate came into view. It loomed countless spans above them, two towers bordered by a stretch of wall, all made of ancient stone. How the ancients of Svora had built such a structure and why the silverswords of Tytan hadn't battled Tysaine for it by now was a mystery to Fig. Tytan seemed to take whatever else it wanted, but treaded lightly when it came to Tysaine. Perhaps they were two sides of the same coin, struck from the same ore. Or perhaps Tysaine carried more might than anyone realized.

Fig's stomach roiled with uncertainty. She and Emrah had talked before they left the clearing; he was fine. She had gotten so used to his presence in the last week that it felt strange with him gone. But she had felt obligated to help Ziggy; it was pretty much their fault she had gotten involved in the first place. Ziggy had gone up against Liess for them.

We're pulling up to the gate now, she told Emrah.

A weak ringing filled her ears, and she heard no response as she pulled the horses to a halt.

Emrah?

The ringing grew louder.

The soldier at the gate strode up to her. She reached a hand for their papers, working hard to keep from shaking. The man took the papers, and Fig carefully folded her hands in her lap. To her relief, her fire magic lay dormant—as it should. No stray sparks for once. Maybe she had finally figured out something about control. All the good Afrith had done her.

Emrah? she called again. The soldier slipped his glasses on to read the documents. Outfitted in lightweight black metal armor, the Tysainian soldiers were as well-equipped as the silverswords; only they were simply human with the exception of a few dwarfs.

The silverswords wouldn't dare storm this gate unless they wanted to start a war with Tysaine. Surely even Rhivven's desire to track down Dev wouldn't extend to that. Fig and the others would be safe...as long as they got through. From what Vaelor had said, she wasn't entirely sure any of the 'swords at the checkpoint were still alive. A grim prospect but one that would assure their safety.

The man was taking forever to peruse the documents. Fig's stomach roiled, her thoughts whirring. Was something wrong? No, no. Bruna was a master paper mage. She was always perfect.

But what if these hadn't been complete? What if the spell was directed at other people? Fig wasn't quite sure how the paper magic worked. She cursed herself for never asking Bruna more about her life.

The only thing keeping Fig together at the moment was her knowledge that despite all her inner turmoil, her fire magic was still under control. For the past few days, it had been so sporadic. She took a deep breath, making sure to school her face into one of polite patience. It didn't help that her incessant calling of Emrah was only answered with ringing in her ears.

"Step out of the carriage," the man said to the two inside, banging on the door.

Fig's heart began to pound, but when Vaelor and Ziggy came out, both with their hoods over their heads, the soldier only glanced perfunctorily at each of them.

The soldier nodded, picked up a stamp from the small podium beside the gatehouse, and slammed it down into a pad of red ink before stamping all four of their papers. "Welcome to Tysaine."

Fig nodded politely to the soldier, who was already putting away his reading glasses as she flicked the reins. About a dozen other soldiers in black armor were stationed at the gate, standing at attention at various points along the wall and the gate opening.

The movement of the carriage beneath her felt good. As soon as they passed under the shadow of the gate, a weight lifted from her shoulders. They had made it. They were in Tysaine.

Too bad they were escaping without the one person who most needed this escape.

As she led the horses down the well-kept dirt road, her mind ran through their confrontation with Afrith at the dock. She couldn't help it. Dev should *be here*.

They passed trees draped in Andisia moss, leaving the wetlands farther behind with every hour that passed; still she replayed Afrith's betrayal in her mind, trying to figure out just what in the Bard's inky quill they were supposed to do.

The green flames danced in her mind's eye, and a horrible sickly feeling squirmed into her gut as she thought over the parts of Afrith's story that truly unsettled her:

Dev's brother Shadryn.

The Hollow Isles.

Come with me to Nithe and see for yourself.

Fig had never been gladder to see a roadside tavern. It wasn't the first one they had passed.

She and Mairead had driven the carriage all the way from the Notch; they had agreed that if the 'swords somehow came looking for them, then the first tavern they came across would be the stupidest place to stop. So they continued north until they had passed a few more villages.

As soon as Fig brought the carriage to a halt and tried to climb down, she realized all of her limbs had been turned into jelly from the constant shaking. Her head, too, was a jumbled mess.

Steadying herself, she forced her way down, desperately needing to stretch and get her rear off that wooden seat.

The first thing she did when her feet found the ground was look into the sky. The cloudy late afternoon sky was bereft of flying gold and green specks, and her mind was empty of any words apart from her own. Emrah had not returned, and she still couldn't hear him.

Ziggy's blonde head bobbed out of the carriage and Fig shot her a look. Why in the Bard's name had Fig sent Emrah back into Tytan? She barely even knew Ziggy.

Of course, Emrah was his own being; he had agreed to go. But he was closer than any friend Fig had had in the years since leaving the Carriage House. And then there was the possibility that they had some other, more uncertain connection.

She resisted reaching out to him again as the four of them headed for the tavern, the Cloaked Shafra, the carriage safely parked at their stables. Scents of good food, ashbar smoke, and stale ale assailed them as they walked in, only to be greeted by the presence of a handful of patrons and one surly barkeep. The patrons—mostly human with the exception of a dwarf in the corner with his ale and a dryad behind the bar clearing up glasses—ignored them.

Fig strode up to the long wooden bar and rapped her knuckles on it. The barkeep looked up from the boxes he was digging in behind the counter and jerked his chin at her. "Aye?"

"Have any rooms?"

"Aye."

Fig glanced at her companions, furrowing her brow. "Um, two rooms?" she guessed. She didn't know how much money they were going to have to spend—they had all of Tysaine to get through on their way to Nithe, or a lengthy sea voyage to pay for. And Dev had been carrying most of their money.

Ziggy swaggered over. "That'll be three, actually," she said. "I'll take my own room, if you please. What, you thought I would bunk with Vaelor?"

Fig's face grew hot, not knowing *what* she'd been thinking. "Well, I don't know, you both fought togeth—"

"Yeah, fighting on the same side doesn't mean I want to hear him snore all night. If he snores. I wouldn't know."

Vaelor didn't respond but flashed a look at Ziggy.

"Oh, of course not," Ziggy said loftily. "How could I even suggest it?"

"Well, you can pay for your own then." Fig turned back to the barkeep. "Three," she said firmly. The man had resumed digging through boxes behind the counter and was now ignoring them completely.

"It'll be three rooms, please," Fig repeated louder.

"Oh, aye," the man said, straightening up and digging in his pockets for the keys.

Once that was settled, Fig would have been happy to collapse in a chair and order a pint and a meal, but Ziggy had other plans. She led them to the top of the stairs.

"Vaelor filled me in on what's happened with the prince," she told them. "We can't stay here long—just tonight, and then on to Tirnalore. So get your rest, and we'll be off bright and early tomorrow."

Fig scowled in the silversword's direction as she found the room she and Mairead would share. Two doors shut down the hallway, and Fig closed their own, only gleaning a small amount of relief at the comfort.

"What about Emrah?" she grumbled aloud as Mairead inspected the small beds for...bugs? She peered under the covers and looked through the pillow stuffing.

"I'm sure he'll turn up," Mairead offered. "We don't know how long it will take him to fly to Ashbrok and back. These look surprisingly clean," she said, tossing the pillow back onto the bed she had picked. "I'm glad we chose this tavern."

"Yes," Fig hedged, wringing her hands. "Well, I'm just a little worried we're further into Tysaine than Emrah might expect."

"He knows we're going to Tirnalore. I'm sure he'll know to go there if he can't find us."

Fig let out a huff. "I know," she said, displeased it sounded so much like whining.

For no reason other than needing to occupy herself, she dumped her pack onto her bed and went through the contents, arranging them again. The three of them had rustled about in it several times since leaving Resbrok, and the food, clothes, and supplies had gotten all out of sorts. Mairead helped her clean up the biscuit crumbs that fell onto the bed when she dumped it out, and they sorted the food into what needed to be eaten right away, and what might keep for the rest of the journey.

When that was done, Fig used the washbasin to clean herself, already missing the glorious outdoor bath at Resbrok. A deep ache settled in her chest as she thought of the place and the people there. Dev's face swam into her mind more than once—that last day she had run into him outside the bath, devilishly handsome and with that glint of hope in his eyes. He had been so looking forward to the meeting with the nobles; the one light in the dark path he had been descending since his flight from Tytan began. And now that path had become even darker.

Rivulets of water ran tracks down her arm as she paused and studied herself in the small looking-glass on the wall. Her hair hung in lank curls, and she had shadows under her eyes that hadn't been there before.

She knew she should rest, but it could barely be called evening, let alone late afternoon, so she convinced Mairead to accompany her down into the tavern for a bite to eat. Though her last tavern meal hadn't ended very pleasantly, she hardly expected the same disaster to strike again; for one reason, she wasn't wounded, and for another, Mairead was with her.

A fire crackled in the hearth downstairs. They ordered food and drink from the barkeep, once they got his attention. The two women barely spoke, for which Fig was grateful. Not only had the trek from Resbrok been trying, but the entire time she'd known Mairead, it had been under unreasonably frightful circumstances.

It was nice to just sit.

Fig finally broke the pleasant silence after they'd begun their meal. "Never thought I'd miss the Virenish lowlands," she said around a mouthful of peas and mash.

Mairead chuckled. Ever proper, she wiped her mouth with a napkin. "Yes. I'll miss Fenra too. And Perrin, of course."

Smiling sadly, Fig agreed. "I didn't spend much time with Fenra. She was an interesting dryad, and she sure knew what she wanted—to stay in the *solanse*."

"Right," Mairead said, nodding. "But at least you were able to get her a job at Resbrok…" She trailed off quietly, her gaze drawn to something behind Fig.

Footsteps sounded on the stairs leading up to the rooms, and Fig felt a prickling sensation ripple over her neck.

She wasn't surprised when Ziggy came over to them, launching herself into the empty seat. "Was wondering where you two went," she said.

Fig gave what she hoped was a smile, but it couldn't have been more forced. The 'sword signaled the bartender with some vague hand gestures, which he apparently interpreted, because a few awkward minutes later, he brought out a meal and drink for Ziggy. She dug in with haste, knife and fork working industriously.

Mairead gave Fig a look from under her hood. Fig suddenly found herself wishing she could talk to people in her mind, like she could with Emrah. A stabbing pain in her heart made Fig's gaze turn down to her plate, and she toyed with the remains until she'd cleared it. The last thing she wanted was to talk to Ziggy, who was the entire reason Emrah was gone. Being unable to talk to him made their separation so much worse. What if he had been killed and that was why she couldn't hear him?

"Traveling to the cathedral?" a gruff voice called over to them.

Startled, Mairead turned to the dwarf in the corner, who had been sitting there since their arrival at the tavern. "Oh, we've—er—quite a few destinations, yes," she said vaguely.

"Magnificent architecture," the dwarf went on easily. "I haven't visited the Narndian in a shafra's age, I'll tell ya that. Make sure you admire the stained glass for me, aye, Sister? Dwarven made, it is."

Mairead bobbed her head, her cheeks reddening. "Of course," she mumbled, looking pleased. With that, the dwarf set down his last tankard amid a forest of them, belched, and walked straight-backed out of the tavern.

Ziggy wasted no time in telling Mairead, "We won't have time for sight-seeing."

"We might," Fig said. "We were already planning on stopping in Tirnalore."

Ziggy slung her booted foot across her knee, tipping back in her chair. She still looked imposing even without her armor, and of course her sword was strapped to her side. "Your...*friend* is in danger. We don't have time to stop to look at books and windows."

Flames danced across Fig's knuckles, although her hand rested on the table. She was tired of Ziggy telling her what to do. "I think we might," was all she said. She had to look up familiars. And Afrith had an office at Tirnalore Academy; she wanted to find out anything more about him or what he thought was going on in Nithe.

Ziggy let her chair fall forward with a *smack*. "I think we don't."

Fig turned so forcefully that the chair legs scraped across the floor toward Ziggy. "And just who put *you* in charge? I know you fought with Vaelor in the war, but that doesn't give you the right—"

"The war gave me a lot of things," Ziggy said through gritted teeth. Her voice got quieter and quieter. "Half of which would give you nightmares for the rest of your life. You want to spend a couple weeks lazing around Tirnalore on some kind of holiday while a psychopathic mage drags your friend across the country? Fine," she said in a voice so quiet Fig could barely hear her. "But Vaelor for one can't give up on that *friend* of yours."

Opening her mouth in disgust, Fig shot back, "You think *I'm* giving up on him? You don't know a gods-damned thing about me and him!"

Ziggy crossed her arms, looking down her nose at Fig. "Vaelor certainly seemed to know a lot about it. And with his oath, he doesn't have much choice about continuing to protect him, does he?"

Fig brushed her fingertips with her thumb, sending sparks onto the floor. "It's not as if I said we were going to lounge about Tirnalore." She spat the words out. "I have specific things we need to research before leaving the city, is all. Mairead may yet have time to look at some pretty windows while we're doing that, all right?"

The red sister in question had turned to watch the fire as intently as if she'd been assigned the task at sword point. She made no comment about windows, pretty or otherwise.

Fig shook her head. She didn't care what Ziggy thought. She flicked the last of the sparks off her fingers like annoying pieces of dust. "You don't know any of us or where we came from to get here. If you don't like it, just leave."

Ziggy slapped the table. "And you think I want to be here? Vaelor literally threw me in your carriage and into this bloody mess!"

Something snapped in Fig's chest. "I sent Emrah to help your family, and now he could be dead, thanks to you! I can't hear him at all!" She slammed her fist down on the table, flames erupting from it.

The silver ring around Ziggy's eyes narrowed, and Fig only had a second's warning before the woman swung a fist in her direction.

Fig leapt backward, toppling over her chair, but she evaded Ziggy's punch. Part of her thought Ziggy must not have been trying. She kicked the chair in Ziggy's direction, scrambling back and out of the silversword's reach. Fig summoned another burst of flame into her palm—not intending to throw it but hoping to intimidate Ziggy.

A scrambling noise from behind the bar drew Fig's attention, though, and she turned to see the barkeeper disappearing out the front door. Then she remembered seeing the black armored soldiers stationed nearby, as foreboding as a patrol of silverswords.

"Bard's ink!" Fig cursed, extinguishing her flames, her cheeks suddenly warm. What was she thinking, summoning flames in the middle of a tavern? "I bet he's gone to get soldiers. Stop it, *stop*—"

Ziggy crashed into her and grabbed her leg, pulling her along the floor. Fig yanked at another chair to no avail. Someone's beer spilled nearby, the yeasty smell pervading her nostrils. Ziggy's grip was like a vice on her ankle.

"You spoiled little mage," Ziggy hissed, pulling Fig up with a fistful of her tunic. She reeled her fist back.

But the fist stopped. Vaelor had appeared, though Fig hadn't even seen him on the stairs. He looked questioningly at her. "The barkeep's gone to get soldiers, we need to—"

She didn't have to say any more. Vaelor sent Ziggy to get everyone's belongings. The 'sword went without a word, moving at an unnatural speed up the stairs, her face a mask of anger.

Fig was all too glad to let Vaelor usher them out the back door of the tavern to the stables, her head reeling. *We should just leave Ziggy behind*, she thought.

And Fig would have done just that if not for her pack being upstairs, their carriage already being unhitched from the horses, and soldiers storming into the tavern behind them.

"*Merda*," Vaelor swore at the sound of boots tramping into the tavern.

Fig grabbed Mairead's arm, her heart racing as fear of being sent back to Tytan surged through her. She didn't even want to ponder what the silverswords and Rhivven would do to them.

But their horses were now enjoying hay in separate stalls, thanks to the quick work of the tavern's stable hand. The carriage wasn't happening anytime soon.

"We've no time to hitch them back up," Vaelor said, shoving a massive crate in front of the door, although that would probably only buy them a few minutes. He stalked across the barn to convince the horses to abandon their hay. "Come on!" he called to Fig and Mairead.

They followed, rushing to untie the horse's halters.

Vaelor started backing one of the horses out. A loud *bang* resounded on the door leading in from the tavern. But with the crate there, it didn't budge.

"They'll go around next!" Fig said. They were really in deep. Why did Ziggy have to go and start that fight? Who did she think she was, bossing Fig around out of nowhere?

Too soon, the front door of the stables began to roll open. The red remnants of sunset blazed in, outlining a dark figure.

Fig brought fire to her hands. Vaelor drew his sword, and Fig caught a faint tang of copper in the air. His movements seemed to change as he held his sword, even more powerful, careful, calculated. He stalked forward.

But the figure that emerged from the doorway was a swordswoman carrying two leather satchels.

The scent of copper grew stronger as Ziggy walked forward.

"You didn't kill them, did you?" Fig said in horror. She didn't banish her fire. Not yet.

"Course not," Ziggy said easily. A little too easily.

"Ziggrune," Vaelor intoned.

"I really didn't!" she said, holding her palms up. "I didn't want to go down the stairs and start a fight, so I jumped from the window. I'm not that *stupid*." She spoke the last word toward Fig, who glared back at her.

"This is your fault," Fig hissed, flames blazing from her hands.

Ziggy surged forward. "You sure about that, fire*starter*?"

Vaelor's hand shot between her and Ziggy. "Enough. You can fight about it later."

Fig doused the flames at her hands and turned away, her cheeks flaming. Fig hadn't started the fight. It was Ziggy, she was sure of it. That cocky woman who'd almost gotten Mairead in trouble in Verindas and was the whole reason Emrah was missing. So why were her insides churning in guilt at the look on Vaelor's face?

Vaelor went on. "We need the horses or another way out of here. The soldiers will come around this way next."

"I wouldn't count on that," Ziggy said.

"Wait, I thought you said you didn't—" Fig began.

Ziggy ignored her and spoke to Vaelor. "I blocked the front from the outside, but that place was full of doors and hatches, there's probably other ways out."

Mairead had gotten the other horse free from his stall and now stood with both lead ropes.

"We can't all ride," Fig said.

"Can't even steal any," Ziggy said, glancing at the empty stalls.

A series of bangs came from the tavern, making Fig jump. She and Mairead could fit on one horse and Vaelor on another. Ziggy seemed perfectly capable of fending for herself.

Thoughts of hastily hitching the horses to the carriage flitted through her mind too—ending in a fantasy of them bursting through the doors just as the soldiers came to stop them.

But then a strange gust of air sailed through the stables, yanking her out of her fantasy into cold reality. Fig's heart nearly broke when her first thought was of Dev summoning the air. She closed her eyes in pain.

No. It couldn't be. He was probably halfway across Tysaine by now. Plus, there was no amethyst glow to it. More like...yellow?

Curious, Fig lurched around the far corner where the gust seemed to be blowing from.

Standing there, arms crossed and looking slightly bemused, was a dryad. His leaves were short, and he had a collection of twigs jutting out from the tips of his shoulders, moss covering parts of his trunk. He wore a familiar-looking tagor tooth necklace.

"Come on," he said, waving a willowy hand. His eyes had a faint yellow glow about them. "This way."

Fig threw a cautious glance back at the others. Vaelor had come up right behind her. Fig suspected he was keeping himself between her and Ziggy.

"But—" Fig said, gaping back at the dryad.

"Wait, you're not Vilvan, are you?" Mairead called from behind.

A loud bang sounded from the tavern, and the dryad grabbed Fig's hand without further explanation. She accepted it and went, the others trailing swiftly behind her.

"But what about the horses—" Fig began.

"No time," the dryad said, flinging open a door. "This alleyway leads straight to the Fienn—you can follow it north. The bleaks'll be on you in seconds. Let's go!"

"The who?" Fig muttered, skirting around a barrel behind the tavern. She didn't expect an answer. The dryad led them at a clip around a few buildings, then through what looked like a shafra field, judging by the fences they hopped over. It was overgrown, though, with no woolly creatures in residence.

Shouts came from the direction of the tavern, but no one seemed to be searching in their direction.

So much for the night in a reasonably clean tavern.

The dryad headed toward thick woods, made of briars and thickets that looked completely impassible, then he crashed right into the underbrush. Bushes and tangly vines that should have slowed him down parted neatly to let him pass. Delighted that she wouldn't be thrashed by the twigs and vines, Fig lunged in after him.

The thickly settled woods cast an even dimmer glow in the wake of the sunset. Fig was glad she could follow Vilvan's faint yellow glow through the dense woods. And the Tysainian soldiers would be unable to follow them here.

After ten more minutes of maneuvering through the woods, Fig thought she spotted moving water ahead. "Is that the River Fienn?" she asked.

"*Va*," the dryad said. "You can follow it north. That's where you're headed, right?"

Fig's steps slowed. "How do you know that?"

"Oh, I—"

"Do you know Fenra?" Mairead pressed.

The dryad bobbed his head, short leaves rustling as he glanced back to address Mairead. "*Va. Belon de solanse*, she—"

"I knew it!" Mairead said triumphantly. "You're Vilvan."

"Aye." He kept his eyes on the river ahead. "But how do you folk happen to know her? That's the reason I came to get you. I heard you talking about her in *de* tavern earlier."

"*Ohh*," Fig said, finally realizing that the necklace he wore was a twin to the one about Fenra's neck.

Mairead moved closer, following the path in the brush Vilvan was sweeping aside with his magic. "But I thought you worked in the Tirnalore Library?"

"Yes, well..." He came to a stop and made a sweeping gesture with his hand. "Here's the river, anyway. Don't walk too close, because sometimes—though not often—we get tagors this far inland. Walk upriver and you'll reach Tirnalore *vit* no trouble. I have to get back to work at the tavern, though."

The four of them stood staring at the river, the calm waters flowing in the early evening light, which was only growing dimmer. A wave of exhaustion flooded Fig; so much for getting a good rest in a clean bed. And the bath... She nearly cried at the thought.

"But—" Mairead began, keen to get answers to her questions.

Fig had some of her own. She narrowed her eyes at Vilvan. "Won't they know you've helped us? Why *did* you help us?"

He shrugged, his twigs rising and falling. "Like I said, you know Fenra. *Solanse* doesn't leave you when you leave the *solanse*, you know?"

A corner of Fig's mouth twitched into the beginnings of a smile, but then Ziggy swaggered forward. "And who are you again?"

"Vilvan of *de* Lokin gathering," he said, with a little nod of his head.

"And why, Vilvan of the Lokin gathering, do you think this is a safe escape? A clean shot straight from the tavern to the river? Paths carved in the field and brush pointing in our direction?"

Vilvan threw her a yellow look, his eyes glowing a little. "Because I've used it plenty of times myself. And besides..." He looked pointedly at the path they had taken.

The branches and vines had returned to their natural state. Without snapped twigs and misplaced branches, the soldiers would be hard-pressed to argue that their fugitives went this way.

Fig shrugged. "Why not?"

"Because we were *supposed* to be traveling as quickly as we could to find your prince," Ziggy said, "and now we're treading up a footpath without a proper night's rest."

"I suppose you think that's my fault, then?" Fig shot back.

Vaelor took a step closer and grabbed both of their shirt collars, "Enough, you two. If I have to treat you both like children, I will. I say we take Vilvan's advice and travel upriver. We won't need the carriage in Tirnalore, anyway, since we'll be getting directly on a ship. We've still some dregs of light left—let's use it. Mairead," he said pointedly, "what do you think?"

"M-me?" Mairead squeaked. "I mean, yes, that seems like our only option at present. But won't you come with us, Vilvan? We're heading for Tirnalore. Fenra spoke so highly of you."

He shrugged awkwardly, glanced at the horizon, and said, "I can walk with you for a little while, but I do have to get back soon. Perhaps you can fill me in on Fenra's *voixage*. Last I heard, she was working for a livery in Thoan."

"Oh, no, she hated that," Mairead said, launching into Fenra's story as they walked.

Fig walked up front with Vilvan and Mairead. He bent back shrubbery for them, which sprung back where it belonged after everyone had passed. It was nice having him as their guide, even if he couldn't escort them all the way to Tirnalore. Now that she thought about it, she had heard Fenra mention her friend Vilvan working in the library there. Perhaps something had happened that he didn't want to talk about.

She could hear Vaelor and Ziggy walking behind them, far enough behind that Fig couldn't hear their conversation. Cold rage burbled in her chest when she thought of the punch Ziggy had thrown at her in the tavern—the whole reason they'd had to flee for their lives.

If they were caught in wrongdoing by Tysaine, they'd have their papers inspected again. And anyone paying close attention to Vaelor and Ziggy for longer than ten seconds would realize what they were.

Which would mean more silverswords. And the Tysainian guards would hand them right over.

Night had fallen, but the lights from the village across the water provided some ambient glow for them to mark their way by.

"At least we weren't followed," Fig said to Mairead. "I just have *no* idea how Emrah is going to find us now."

"There's still Tirnalore," Mairead said reassuringly. "You can't speak to him at all?"

She shook her head. "No. Still nothing."

"Maybe he's too far away for such a thing? I've been wondering about that."

Fig sighed. "Maybe we'll have to add dragonet lore to our Tirnalore Library research list. After admiring the windows in the Narndian, obviously."

When her joke fell flat, Fig glanced at Mairead. "What?"

Mairead paused a moment, the silence heavy. "Well, seeing the windows—or anything in Tirnalore—isn't really that important. You know that, Fig. Not worth starting that fight over—"

"You think *I* started it?" Fig hissed. "She's the one who put herself in charge like she was the queen of Tytan! As if *I* don't want to rescue Dev!"

"Of course you do," Mairead said soothingly. "I know that. And Vaelor knows that. But Ziggy—"

"Can go ask the Bard for a quill for all I care," Fig grumbled.

So Mairead also thought it was her fault they got kicked out of the tavern. That was just great.

She stomped ahead, tramping through the night, her thoughts a painful jumble.

What she wouldn't give to talk to Emrah or Dev right now.

CHAPTER
34

Darkness had fallen when Vilvan told them he would leave them on their own. Fig was grateful he had stayed this long; the tavernkeeper must not keep a very good eye on his employees.

Ziggy and Vaelor drew up close as they all came to a halt.

Mairead turned to Vilvan. "Do you want us to pass a message along to Fenra when we see her again?"

Vilvan's yellow gaze settled on the dark waters of the river where something had made a soft splash in the distance. Then he smiled, touching his tagor tooth necklace briefly. "I'd love for you to tell her *vir dan*, and—"

"Vilvan? Is that you?" A hoarse whisper came from ahead.

Vilvan turned, a gust of yellow wind twirling around him. "Fang, what are you—"

"There's no run tonight," the newcomer said. "What are you doing out on the Fienn? And who—"

There was a sudden, swift movement. Mairead let out a yelp. Something growled nearby.

Fig glanced around before summoning a small ball of flame to see by, despite knowing it might be a beacon to their location. She didn't care; she needed to see.

Someone was holding a dagger to Mairead's throat.

A tall copper-skinned man stood behind Mairead, holding her as a target toward Vilvan. The man's dog was growling at all of them, teeth bared and black ears pointed forward.

Steel rang out behind Fig as Vaelor and Ziggy both drew their weapons but held their ground.

Vilvan held up his palms toward the newcomer and took an experimental step forward, his wood-like fingers shrinking in placation. "Easy, Fang," he said. "Just put the dagger down, and we can talk—"

"Who. Are. These. People." Fang ground out each word. His dog looked ready to lunge but kept its intimidating stance.

"They're just some friends, Fang, I promise. They're not going to—"

"You showed them our paths? Our hideout? You know what that means, Vilvan. In order to keep the secrets of the Fienn-Da."

"No, Fang, really," Vilvan pleaded. He looked as if he wanted to take another step forward but thought better of it. "Trust me, please. How long have you known me, eh? They're my friends. They were just passing through."

Fang sneered. "Passing through with no loyalties and an easy excuse to run to the bleaks with word of our run lines?" He made to adjust the dagger at Mairead's throat.

"No, please!" Fig cried. "We know nothing of—whatever it is you are speaking of! Vilvan only saved our skins from the soldiers. We got into a bit of a tavern brawl, and—well..." She paused. "Just let go of Mairead, please. She's a Sister of Morgha. You can see her cloak, right? She's no spy or what have you."

Fang thought for a moment, but from the shadows cast over his face, Fig couldn't see his expression or what thoughts passed over it. After a minute that seemed like an entire painful day, he lowered the dagger. An almost inaudible whistle, and the dog backed down and went closer to its owner's side, its ears still pointing forward at them.

Mairead hastily came forward, grabbing Fig's outstretched hand. With her other hand, she threw her ball of flame into the air to hover

over the group. The two of them twined their arms together, Mairead shaking a little.

But Fang wasn't done. He lunged at Vilvan, the dagger a little less of a threat to the dryad than a human. "Tell that fire mage to stop signaling our location, and maybe I'll spare your life, too, traitor."

Vilvan cut his yellow gaze at Fig, who snuffed it out at once, throwing them all back into darkness. She felt someone move nearby, but it was only Vaelor, stepping in front of her and Mairead. She still felt Ziggy at her back, and she wasn't sure whether that made her feel more or *less* safe.

"What is going on here, Vilvan?" Vaelor demanded. The steel rang out in his voice just as sure as his sword.

A cloud shifted, drawing a miniscule amount of moonlight, and Fig could see their vague shapes again. Fang still wielded his dagger, but Vilvan had taken a few steps back from the group.

"Vilvan?" Mairead demanded quietly.

The dryad backed up another step, mouth opening and closing. Too fast for anyone to see or intervene, Ziggy dashed to him, her sword reeled back over her shoulder so she could use it like an axe.

"Ziggy!" Vaelor warned.

"What is going on here?" Ziggy demanded.

Vilvan glanced at Fang who still held out his dagger. It drooped a little as he considered the situation. "It's, well—"

"You *really* don't work for the Tirnalore Library, do you?" Mairead piped up.

Fang let out a snort. "That stuffy place? Of course he doesn't—"

Vilvan cleared his throat. "Shut it, Fang. No, I don't. I work for the tavern, and for—Fang, stand down for the mother's sake—and for the Fienn-Da."

The faint hum of insects and the burbling of water were the only sounds in the clearing. Fig ran her thumb over her fingertips but kept her sparks at bay. "And what in the name of the Bard is Fienn-Da?" she demanded quietly.

"They...we deliver goods...and services...throughout Tysaine."

"Ah," Fig said. "I see."

"I don't," Mairead muttered.

"Smugglers and such," Fig leaned in to whisper.

"Not such as you think," Vilvan said defensively. Fig shouldn't have been surprised he could hear so well.

"Yes, yes," Fang said. Now a safe distance from the silverswords, he held his dagger with renewed confidence. He put a hand on the head of his dog, whose tongue was lolling out. "But you're in our territory, and I can't have you running to the bleaks with all our information."

"The bleaks?" Ziggy asked, annoyed.

"The blackguard," Vilvan clarified. "Soldiers with their armor all shined with blacking?"

"Oh, please," Ziggy said, silver-ringed eyes flashing, "I've seen them in action, they're not much of a threat."

"They are to us," Fang said. "And I don't know exactly what they'd do with two traitorous silverswords and whatever else is going on here, if they came across you lot. If Evandahl finds out you blabbed our operations to Tytanians, Vilvan, you're done."

"Sod it, Fang!" Vilvan said. "I was just helping them out. They're friends of Fenra's, and—"

"Ahhhh," Fang said, lowering the dagger saucily. "I should have known *love* was behind this. You're usually so reliable."

Vilvan scoffed, wordless. He shook his head. "I don't—You don't—Look. They're heading to Tirnalore. They could very well have discovered this path on their own. Just let them pass."

"Oh, and they just pushed their way through Ifhurst Woods to get here, did they? Right, right. I'm sure. Although, if you're heading to Tirnalore..."

Fang grinned and scratched his dog's ears. "I've got a job for you. And it pays in your freedom to pass through Tysaine. There's a certain item from the Tirnalore Library that the Fienn-Da need."

"Look, we get to sleep in a bed tonight, after all, eh, Fig?" Ziggy said.

Fig said nothing. The silver-eyed woman set their packs down on the earthen floor as they made themselves comfortable inside the Fienn-Da's one-room cache-house somewhere just off the river. With Fang and his dog standing guard at the door, Fig actually felt a little safer.

But payment for the protection of the Fienn-Da wasn't going to be cheap. No, that would come tomorrow, when they were thrust into a venture they had nothing to do with *and* no time for.

The word "bed" was also generous. Blankets were strewn on the floor with a few rolled up to use as pillows.

"Not as clean as the Cloaked Shafra, I'm afraid," Fig said apologetically to Mairead.

The red sister shrugged resignedly, fluffing up the blankets Vilvan had found for them among the crates. Fig didn't look closely at the crates; she didn't want to know whatever it was the Fienn-Da had stored in their cache-house, this hidden building tucked in the side of a hill.

Woodwork secured the earthen walls and ceiling, but the place was dry and seemed somehow clean for packed dirt. Fig had seen worse hideouts. Had stayed in worse while doing the odd job here and there in Tytan. Those ambivalent enough to hire a lone mage weren't usually the affluent type. But she had scraped by. And then she'd met Bruna and gotten some local contacts near Thoan who would pay for her services.

All that was now thrown in the fire, though. And here she was in some dirt hole in Tysaine, roped into yet another scheme.

Vilvan sat on a crate across from them, Fig and Mairead settling onto blankets next to each other. Ziggy sat propped up against a wall, shunning the blankets entirely. Vaelor hadn't even sat down, and stood silently by the entrance, looming over Fang's shoulder.

"Well? Can it be done?" Fig asked Vilvan. "This job you want us to do?"

The dryad rested his head on one propped up fist thoughtfully. "I don't think Evandahl would take it on if he didn't think it couldn't be done."

"What does that even mean?" she asked, lounging back on an elbow. Gods, she was tired.

"It can be done," Vilvan said with forced confidence.

Fang chimed in. "The Androzigma Collection is well-protected, much like the rest of the library, but Evandahl's a master at this."

"You shouldn't worry," Vilvan added. "I trust him."

"I don't," Ziggy offered loudly. Apparently, she could hear them all the way across the cache-house. "Who is this Evandahl, anyway? And why does he need some moldy old tome so badly?"

"Careful," Fang growled. "You're lounging under Evandahl's roof, 'sword."

"Don't need a roof that bad," Ziggy said. "So tell me, why should we trust him? If he'd so much as kill us for walking on your footpath?"

Fang and Vilvan exchanged a look. Finally, Vilvan said, "The Fienn-Da aren't some dark-market smugglers, like you think. We...help people."

"Oh, sure you do," Ziggy said. "Help them right out of their money for whatever you get for them, right?"

Vilvan shook his head. "It's not like that. You wouldn't understand."

"I bet," Ziggy said, rolling her silver-ringed eyes.

"Tysaine isn't as peaceful as they make it out to be," Vilvan said, "and Tirnalore isn't some magnificent city of books and intelligent people. Its streets and morals are just as filthy as anywhere else—filthier even." He flicked a piece of dirt from his wood-like knee. "The blackguard are everywhere, 'keeping the peace,' according to King Artaxis. But the trouble is, this 'peace' is a series of rules set down centuries ago, and they don't work."

Ziggy shrugged. "Sounds like literally everywhere I know."

Fig couldn't help agreeing with her, but she wasn't about to say it out loud.

"So Evandahl developed a network to help people," Vilvan went on. "*Va*, sometimes it's smuggling, I'll admit. But the rest...I have to believe it's more helpful than joining the blackguard."

"Yes, but why aren't you working in Tirnalore Library?" Mairead pressed, laying on her stomach, her head propped in her hands.

Vilvan grimaced good-naturedly.

But it was Fang who answered. "Couldn't get the job, could he? Didn't have the training, they said, those snooty fusspots." He spoke in a mocking voice as he scratched his dog's head.

The dryad dipped his head, cheeks glowing faintly yellow. "I wanted to. It was my dream to work among the famous stacks of Tirnalore for the decades that I planned my *voixage*. And that's where I set out for. But when they wouldn't have me, and I didn't have any more money to live in Tirnalore without a job, I fell on some...less desirable employment. Evandahl saved me from the maw of the local undesirables."

"And now you work for him, while maintaining a job at that tavern?" Fig clarified.

Vilvan nodded. "It gives me legitimate employment to show the blackguard tax collectors when they come 'round and a way to make connections with people the Fienn-Da need to contact."

"And are you going to tell Fenra all of this?" Mairead pried.

Fig shot her a look and Mairead's face flushed. "What?" Mairead demanded quietly. Fig shook her head, bemused.

But Vilvan answered anyway. "Eventually," he hedged. "But I've got decades still on my *voixage*—not that I'm ready to go back to the *solanse* just yet." Fig couldn't help but smile at the dichotomy between the star-crossed dryads, with Fenra's deep hatred of leaving the *solanse*.

"Couldn't you spend some of that time getting the training you need to work in the library?" Mairead pressed.

Vilvan shrugged but didn't say anything.

"I really don't think the library's important right now," Ziggy said.

"Except it is," Fig said. "If we're to do this job for the Fienn-Da."

"Aren't you supposed to be tracking down a certain prince?"

"Back off, Ziggy," Fig said wearily. "Of course I want to find him, but it doesn't seem like we have much of a choice about this."

Fig glanced at Fang, who tapped the side of his nose in agreement. *On the nose.*

"So we're doing it then?" Ziggy said. "Robbing the library so these fools will 'let us live'?" Her tone clearly indicated that Ziggy needed no such permission from anyone.

"Well," Fig said, glancing at Vaelor. He hadn't said a word during the entire discussion. "I think there's something the Fienn-Da can do for us too. Passage to Nithe when the job is done won't be too hard to arrange, will it?"

And so it was that Fig found herself walking beside the River Fienn the next morning, looking to steal from the largest establishment on the Svoran continent.

"How did we get into this mess?" she muttered to herself.

Vaelor, walking next to her, grunted in amusement. "I was just thinking the same thing."

She turned to catch his eye in the pre-dawn light. "We're doing the right thing, though, aren't we? This'll get us to Dev, eventually."

He nodded, "*Va*, especially if they secure us passage to Nithe like they said they would; it was clever of you to ask for such."

Fig ducked her head, feeling anything but clever. It felt like her fault they were out of a carriage and fleeing the soldiers in the first place. She had summoned flames for a tavern brawl like a Bard-forsaken idiot.

Vaelor continued. "We could have easily taken Fangalore, but I didn't want to put Mairead in that situation, nor Vilvan when he was only trying to help us. And then there's the rest of this Fienn-Da. Who knows how far their network stretches or what they would have done to retaliate."

"Right," Fig said.

They walked on in amicable silence for a minute, then Vaelor said,

"Still no word from Emrah?"

Fig's shoulders slumped. "None. You don't think... He wouldn't have just left, right? I mean, he had a home and everything in the Gold Wood, and was square with the Feijowa..."

A hand grabbed her elbow, and startled, she looked up at him. "I'm sure he's going to come back. I think you mean more to him than that."

"Me?" she scoffed, reaching up to pull a spiderweb strand she'd just walked through away from her face. "But I'm not..." She trailed off. What was she to Emrah? She hadn't mentioned the idea that he could be her familiar to Vaelor or Mairead yet. There hadn't been time.

"I don't know," she said firmly, "but if that's not it, I'm afraid something's happened to him."

"Ziggy's family isn't much farther than Resbrok, and Emrah's familiar with the area. Perhaps he stopped to check on Perrin," he said with a smile in his voice.

The thought made Fig's heart ache a little. "That would be nice," she admitted. "Do you think Ziggy's family will be all right?"

He nodded, giving an "mm-hmm" of agreement. "She's trained her sisters well, particularly after... *Iil*, in the beginning of the war, her older brother was killed."

"Ahh," Fig said, her eyes on the footpath as she lowered her voice. "I feel worse that she got involved in this, that they might go after her family."

He lifted one shoulder in half a shrug. "She had a choice at the checkpoint when we arrived. She could have stood by and let Liess search us."

Fang's dog circled over to Fig and Vaelor at that moment and shoved its nose into Fig's hand.

"Oy, Ursa, leave her alone, will ya?" Fang called. "Nobody wants a wet nose in their hand this early in the day." He had donned a low shafra wool cap. He was dressed quite smartly for someone Fig had only recently thought of as a ruffian, with gray wool trousers matching his coat and dark coppery skin glowing faintly as the sun came up.

Fig chuckled and allowed Ursa to sniff her, then the dog returned to her owner, tail wagging. She was covered in long tan fur except for her ears, paws, and tail as though her extremities had been dipped in ink.

"Blessed by the Bard, that one," Fig said to Vaelor.

"Oh?"

"Her paws and tail," she said, pointing vaguely. "She looks like she's been dipped in ink."

He let out an amused breath from his nose and shook his head. "You speak a lot of the Bard," he observed.

"He's not as prevalent in Viren, I take it," Fig said.

Vaelor shrugged. "*Iil*, it's not to say I don't believe in him. If he did actually see the gods when they lived a mortal life on this plane, I don't doubt that he would have followed them and recorded their exploits."

"But, what?" Fig mused. "You don't think they made him a god to record everyone's story when they die too?"

Another shrug.

"That's the best part," Fig said with a smile. "Knowing that someone will acknowledge what you've done, your deeds, and..." They both lapsed into silence as Fig pondered on the recent parts of her life she wouldn't want recounted to her.

"I don't think I'll want to hear this part recounted myself," Ziggy said, coming up next to Vaelor.

Fig gave her a look. She was coming to realize Ziggy had ungodly good hearing. Must be one of her silversword enhancements. "Yeah, I'd rather the whole stealing part was left out of mine too," Fig admitted, hoping Ziggy hadn't listened to their *entire* conversation.

"No, I meant this whole trip into Tysaine," Ziggy said. "At least the stealing bit is going to be exciting."

Fig let out a quiet sigh, steeling herself. "I'm sorry you got roped into this. And I'm sorry about yesterday."

Ziggy whistled appreciatively. "*V'rai*, a mage who apologizes. We've got a good one here, eh, Vaelor?"

Fig narrowed her eyes, unsure if she should take that as a complement or not.

"If you're looking for an apology from me, though," Ziggy said a minute later, "you're not getting one. I didn't ask to get thrown in your carriage, and I didn't ask you to send your dragonet. I *do* feel bad he hasn't returned yet, though."

Jaw clenching, Fig nodded.

"Now," Ziggy went on, "we just need to steal this whatsit, and then we'll be on our way to Nithe, right?"

"Right," Fig said, glad for the change of subject. In the distance, they could see the tall towers of Tirnalore high above the trees of the Ifhurst Wood.

It was there that she had pinned all her hopes of finding Emrah.

And then there was Dev. Would Afrith need to take him through Tirnalore first to get a ship? Or did he have some other means of whisking Dev out of Tytan?

"What is it again that the Fienn-Da want?" Ziggy was asking. "The tall one said it wasn't a book, right?"

Fig gave a reluctant snort, glancing at Fang's back. He was up front with Vilvan, leading the path. The Fienn on their left and the dense wood on their right, they watched the rising sun throw its light on the towers of Tirnalore as they headed for it.

"Some artifact, yes," Fig said. "Fang said it was an ancient Svoran relic—a chalice of some kind?"

"Mm-hmm," Vaelor agreed. "Something like that. I'd like to go over the plans again before we get inside the city."

"Me too," Fig said.

"We'll have time once we're in Tirnalore," Fang shot back, evidently overhearing. "There's a flat near the library where we'll meet up with the rest of the crew."

Ziggy groaned quietly. "I don't know if I can deal with anyone else," she complained under her breath.

Fig silently agreed.

Despite Vilvan's opinion of Tirnalore, Fig found herself slack-jawed in awe at the sight. Even from the entrance to the city, they could see the library looming up at them. It took up an entire district, its towers soaring above everything else and its high bridges and passages connecting building to building.

They passed by the Narndian Cathedral and glimpsed the stained glass windows from the outside. Mairead grabbed Fig's arm, grinning. The pain in Fig's chest eased. They passed by all manner of shops and houses, hearing music and early morning laughter and shouts. Fig found herself wondering what the trip to Tirnalore would have been like if things hadn't gone awry every step of the way. She and Dev could be filling up on pastries and *kafye* before glancing through the stacks in the library...

Except their original plan had been to go to Nithe, a place that now filled her with dread and confusion. What would they find when they got there?

Fang led them to the flat owned by the Fienn-Da and unlocked the rooms on the ground floor. Ursa dashed inside before anyone else.

Vague ideas of a proper bath or bed or even just a chair to sit her bones in were dashed when Fig realized someone was already inside the almost empty flat.

"Ah, Quinnetra, you're early!" Fang exclaimed, holding his arms out high.

The woman, perched on a cushioned chair, inclined her head in greeting. Her posture was as perfect as her appearance. Her straight black hair was twisted into a bun, streaked with gray from one temple. She wore a red dress with tasteful yellow and gold details, and heavy matching earrings weighed down her earlobes, amber set in gold. She looked like she had gone missing from a high society tea. Fig eyed her warily.

"Of course, Fangalore," the woman said, leaning back a few inches in her chair as Ursa came to greet her. "I'm not in the habit of doing a run by the seat of my pants like some people."

Fang let out a deep chuckle, and Quinnetra joined his laughter, smirking. Once she shifted her dress out of the reach of Ursa's paws, she reached out a friendly hand to scratch the dog's ears.

"To each their own," Fang said, shrugging. He strode over to one side of the parlor and grabbed a chair that had been pushed up to the wall, flipped it backward, and sat facing them.

"And who do we have here?" Quinnetra said.

Vilvan stood to the side of the door and ushered the others forward. Fang gave them a mischievous look and said, "I'll let them introduce themselves."

Fig glanced at the others but found them staring at her; she was standing closest to Quinnetra. "Oh. I'm Fig." She pursed her lips, leaving it at that.

The others were similarly tight-lipped, but when it came to Mairead, Quinnetra gazed with interest at her tattoos—her branded palm carefully pressed to her leg. "Have you been to the Narndian, my dear? Even for us unholy folk, it's a sight to see."

"Not yet," Mairead admitted.

"I'm not sure we'll have time," Fig heard herself saying.

Behind her, Ziggy snickered.

Fig closed her eyes. *Now I've turned into Ziggy. The Bard will laugh at that one.*

Fang clapped his hands once. "All right then. You lot get cleaned up. The rest of the crew'll be here soon."

Alarm pulsed through Fig's nerves. This was really happening. She flicked a few sparks from her fingertips where they fizzled to nothing on the black and white tile floor.

Vilvan exchanged quiet words with Fang, then exited through the front door a minute later.

As had become her recent habit, she tried calling for Emrah, but she heard nothing back other than ringing silence. Of course, she had no idea what his "range" might be, even if he were in Tirnalore.

She clenched her fist and followed the others to find a washing room.

"You know," Ziggy said as the four of them wandered down the hall, "I don't remember volunteering to be the pack mule." She shucked off one of the bags and pushed it into Vaelor's hands.

He took it without comment. When he offered to let Fig bathe first, she immediately agreed.

The bath Fig took was one of the most glorious experiences of her life. The Fienn-Da's flat was equipped with a large copper basin for bathing, which went right over her head when she sunk down deep into the soapy water.

As the grime of what felt like a thousand years rinsed off of her, she had a hard time tearing herself away. *This is definitely better than the Cloaked Shafra,* she thought to herself, finally pulling herself, dripping, out of the water.

Then she looked over at the chair where she'd discarded her clothes and grimaced. She had nothing else to put on.

They took turns bathing; while Mairead washed, Fig sat outside the door—at her friend's request—and then the two of them hung about in the empty room across the hallway as they waited for the silverswords to finish. Finally, Fang reappeared, sauntering down the hallway.

"You lot look like you've been living in a ditch. Come on, there's clothes this way now that you're clean. Can't step into the library looking like that."

Fig peered into the other empty rooms as they passed. "Does anyone live here? What is this place?"

Fang sucked his teeth and merely said, "Just one of our places. You're lucky Evandahl agreed to let you in."

"And how did he know we were involved?" Ziggy inquired.

"Good question," Fig muttered. Ziggy shot her a gloating look.

"Oh, I let him know last night. He had me recruiting for the job. It was the Bard's luck you lot crossed my path."

"Crossed your path?" Ziggy said. "Yes, not like you coerced us or anything."

Fig narrowed her eyes at Fang. Between the hard-packed earth and the weight of all her troubles, she hadn't slept much. She didn't think she'd fallen asleep long enough for either Vilvan or Fang to go and alert anyone about them.

"Here we are," Fang said cheerfully, holding his arm out to the next bedroom.

It contained only a wardrobe and a closet beyond. No bed or other furnishings filled the space. Fig was surprised they didn't even keep beds in their hideout, but perhaps they didn't need them inside the city.

They crossed the empty room and inspected the clothes in both the wardrobe and closet. There were a variety of fashions, from high society Tysainian like Quinnetra wore, to the mundane hose and tunics Fig normally preferred. They even found a set of red robes, though Mairead kept hers, despite the blood and patches signifying all she'd been through.

Fig turned around with her selection to see a swath of bare skin. "Ziggy!" she cried. "What are you—"

"Oh, leave off, fire mage," Ziggy said, her back turned. "I'm almost done, anyway. There." She dropped the brown tunic over her head and turned around, tugging on the laces at the front of the neck. "What?"

Fig rolled her eyes. "I'm going to find somewhere to change."

"I'll come with you," Mairead said. "I don't need anything."

"Of course. *You* didn't get soaked by swamp water," Fig muttered. Lips pressed into a smile, Fig led them to another empty room, leaving Vaelor to whatever clothing he decided on.

"Thanks," Fig told Mairead as they headed into the next room. Mairead turned her back and stood by the closed door.

"Not at all. I don't really—Ziggy is a little..."

"Yes, she's...interesting," Fig said as she slipped thankfully out of her dirty clothes. She almost wanted to take another bath after having to put on the filthy clothes again. "I...can't believe I'm saying this, but I think she's actually growing on me."

Fig thought she heard a sound from the next room, then Ziggy's faint voice called, "I knew you liked me!"

"By the Bard," Fig groaned. "Would you leave me alone?" She shook her head. "That woman has the best hearing on the continent."

An amused snort came from Mairead. Fig hurriedly fastened the belt on her new turquoise tunic, thrilled it contained multiple pockets. It was more flowy than she was used to, and she rather liked it.

When they emerged back into the hallway, voices from the parlor reached their ears. Ziggy and Vaelor were heading their way, and Fig said, "Can you hear what that's about, then?"

"Of course," Ziggy said. She had donned a maroon coat over her tunic, and the collar came up under her short locks.

Vaelor had chosen a gray and black ensemble, though from what Fig had seen, there didn't seem to be much selection for someone of his height and build.

"Well?" Fig asked.

"There's some new people here. One of 'em's a mage," Ziggy reported.

Fig raised her eyebrows. Mages weren't common in Tysaine for some reason, and they often came to train at the Carriage House since Tysaine didn't have much in the way of magic training, even with the Tirnalore Academy.

When they emerged back into the parlor, someone had arranged more chairs in the center of the room, where Quinnetra, Fang, and two others sat talking quietly. Vilvan had returned and stood at attention by the front door. Ursa lounged on the floor beneath Fang's chair; she raised her head as Fig and the others came in and gave them a soft woof of greeting. The discussion stopped as Fig and the others entered.

Fig sat a few chairs away from Quinnetra with Mairead on her other side. One of the newcomers was a girl who looked no more than eighteen or nineteen, with dark skin and short tightly curled hair, she perched on her chair with both legs folded under her. The other was a refined older gentleman with a short black beard grizzled with gray. He wore a low cap similar to Fang's and a dark coat and trousers.

Vaelor and Ziggy positioned themselves behind Fig and Mairead. Fig didn't blame them; the chairs were grouped tightly together, and with their swords, it would be a tight fit.

"Hi," the new girl said. "I'm Kerafina."

Fig nodded and gave her name, as did the others. The gentleman waited until they were done and straightened in his chair.

"It's not often we trust outsiders with such a job," he said, eyeing each of them, "but from what I know about you four, I think you'll do. King's own handpicked advisors, am I right?"

Fig's chest tightened. "And how exactly do you know who we are?" she asked.

He drummed his fingers on his knee, once, twice. Then he said, "A fire mage and a silversword on the run. Though you seem to have picked up a second one, I see. Oh, and a priestess of Morgha. Quite the unforgettable crew."

They were silent for a moment. Fig felt Vaelor shift behind her.

"I don't mean you any harm," the man said quietly, "if that's what you're thinking. Just know that your reputations precede you."

Fig glared at the man, wondering just how much of her "reputation" he knew about. "And who might you be?"

"Oh," he said, putting a hand to his heart. "Thomat Evandahl."

"Ah," she said, half-glancing at the others and wondering when she had become their spokesperson. Although she'd rather it was her than Ziggy... "It's nice to meet you," she said reflexively.

"Vilvan's told me all about your troubles at the Cloaked Shafra and how you unwisely stumbled upon the Fienn-Da's private paths. I'm glad we could work something out to make us even."

Fig nodded tightly, holding her tongue.

"Though I think we will be *more* than even once we provide you passage to Nithe. To rescue a certain king, I hear?"

How in the Bard's name did he know about Dev too? She didn't think they had mentioned him at all in front of Fang and Vilvan.

"I'm not sure what measure you use to account for evenness," Fig said, "but I think it's pretty even."

"You trespassed on Fienn-Da land," Evandahl said in a cold voice.

Fig's gaze flitted to Vilvan. She didn't want to throw him into Morgha's arms, so she said, "And you've asked us to commit a much larger trespass. I think boat passage will tip the scales back to center."

A slow smile formed on Evandahl's face, and he smoothed his beard. "Very well. I will arrange for your passage to Nithe, but only if you succeed in retrieving the chalice from the library's collection. I've followed it for quite some time now, but only recently learned it would be moved here, where we have a much higher chance of acquiring it."

Fig didn't understand why he was so interested in this chalice, but that wasn't for her to know or care about. As long as she didn't have to kill anyone, she'd do the job. It would probably be easier than trying to book passage to Nithe themselves. They had barely scraped through the checkpoints at the Notch, and they needed to get to the Hollow Isles more urgently than ever.

Evandahl went on, turning to the others. "But we have a problem. The Androzigma Collection's been delayed in delivery, so we'll need to push the job back another day. The bleaks in Chamol took an interest for once and delayed the paperwork. When it arrives, we'll be ready for it. In the meantime, I want you all to focus on the plan and what you'll need to do to gain access."

"We've done it before," Kerafina said. "It's not exactly hard."

Quinnetra cleared her throat. "Yes, but this will be a secure collection—not one open to the public. They don't let just anyone handle ancient Svoran artifacts."

Kerafina clucked and leaned back in her chair.

"Quinn's right," Fang said.

Evandahl stood, clutching a cane Fig hadn't noticed before. "Our new friends will need to be briefed on the library's security and weak points—Quinnetra, I'll leave that to you. Kerafina and Fang, you'll take care of diversions, as usual."

Fig nodded, trying to follow along. She sincerely hoped Evandahl was going to share the stack of papers in his hand that he kept consulting. She did much better with written instructions; long and detailed oral instructions tended to go in one ear and out the other.

"I'll be back tomorrow, with an update on the collection," Evandahl said to the group. He handed the sheets of paper to Quinnetra. "Stay alert 'til then. If there's movement on the collection, you'll need to be ready."

He shared a simple handshake with the Fienn-Da crew, though Fig thought she caught a sleight of hand gesture at the end.

Fig and Mairead stood too. Evandahl pulled Fig aside as she was preparing to put her chair back against the wall like the others.

"Fairaleigh Veil," he said quietly. "A word."

She stiffened and turned to face him. She couldn't bring herself to correct him while those cold eyes stared back at her. He led her to the small foyer by the front door, leaning on his wooden cane as he walked. A mixture of dread and defiance filled her stomach.

"Following a fleeing king across the continent," he said, when they stood there in front of the door. "That's either a very brave or very stupid thing to do."

Clasping her hands behind her back, she kept her mouth shut. She had met this kind of man before. Though she longed to burst some sparks at her fingers, she wasn't keen on provoking him.

"I'll have to see which way the scales tip for myself, then, shall I?" he said.

"I suppose you shall."

"And where is your king? Nithe, I suppose?"

She pressed her lips together, not sure how much Evandahl knew. He certainly seemed as if he'd borrowed the Bard's scrolls and gained some insight into Fig and her friends.

"I don't rightfully know," she admitted, "but we're hoping to check there."

He frowned in thought, assessing her. "I see. A loyal advisor he has in you, then. I'll admit, I had been quite looking forward to seeing a mage on the Rayvan throne. I still am.

"If you and your crew help pull off this job, I'll consider aiding your king in his attempt to reclaim the throne. If you find him, that is."

Fig clenched her fingers together, her stomach in knots. "That is...very generous of you to offer."

"But know this," he said, leaning close to her ear, "if you fail, or betray the Fienn-Da, there will be consequences."

VAELOR

Vaelor watched Evandahl leave as the rest of the Fienn-Da began dissecting the plans he'd left. Fig came back from her conversation at the door looking a little shaken, but seemed to recover once she rejoined the rest of the crew.

He wondered what Evandahl had said to Fig that had made her react the way she did. Vaelor hadn't been able to see Evandahl's face, wreathed in shadow though it was, but he was certain he had threatened her. That wasn't something Vaelor was going to allow.

Quinnetra took the lead in going over their plans—with interjections from Fang about certain people in the library to avoid or passageways to never find yourself in, lest you get completely locked in with no escape. Speaking from experience, it sounded like.

"Very well then," Quinnetra said finally. "We'll leave you four here in the flat. Fang will keep you company and get you anything you need. Any questions?"

"How many times have you stolen from the library?" Fig asked.

Kerafina pursed her lips. "Oh, only two—no, three times. There was that time we retrieved a book on ancient dwarven rituals for—" She cut herself off, then shrugged. "Only a few times."

"Why do you even need to steal from the library?" Mairead asked. "It's a library. Can't anyone see what's inside it?"

"Not the private collections," Fang said. "And besides, there's plenty of items in the artifact halls that don't belong there in the first place."

"What's this chalice we're after?" Ziggy inquired from where she lounged against the wall.

Vaelor looked back at Quinnetra with interest. So far the Fienn-Da had been tight-lipped about the actual item. Their only clues were what Fang and Vilvan had let slip last night. Vilvan, of course, had returned to his mundane job at the tavern, but Vaelor suspected that job was more than it seemed.

"An ancient Svoran artifact," Quinnetra said.

"Right," Ziggy said. "But please tell me it's more than just some old cup."

Quinnetra's eyes flashed in Ziggy's direction, but then visibly forced down her ire. "It's more than just some old cup."

That quieted Ziggy. The others left one by one, leaving only Fang and his dog. It was obvious they'd stayed to guard them, but out of all the Fienn-Da who could have been assigned the job, Vaelor found Fang tolerable.

Except for when he'd threatened Mairead and turned them in to Evandahl, that is.

Vaelor eyed the man from across the room. Fang didn't seem bothered by his stare and kicked his feet up on the chair across from him. Vaelor let out a quiet sigh and turned to Fig and Mairead, who were quietly discussing what they wanted to do while they waited for word about the job.

"Do you think they'll let me?" Mairead was saying.

"I don't see why not," Fig said. "We just need to be here when it's time to go. Tomorrow's the earliest, Evandahl said."

Mairead nodded. "I'll ask him."

"Ask him what?" Vaelor said, crossing his arms.

"If I can go to the cathedral," Mairead said, nodding in Fang's direction.

Vaelor frowned. "I'm not sure you should go alone, Mairead."

"Oh, well, Fig's coming with me, aren't you?" she said, turning to Fig.

Fig brushed strands of hair from her face, looked down at the floor, and said, "I was actually thinking I'd stay here. Remember how much trouble I caused at the tavern? But you should go and enjoy the cathedral—Vaelor, would you go with her?"

"Of course," he replied automatically, though he wasn't too keen on the idea of leaving Fig behind. "I wouldn't mind seeing the Narndian myself." Perrin would berate him to no end if he found out Vaelor had turned down the opportunity. Besides, it was only a few streets over.

Mairead went over to ask Fang if they were allowed to explore Tirnalore, and Vaelor's gaze landed on Fig's face. She met his eyes, sending a jolt into his stomach; his gaze lingered a moment too long. He cleared his throat and hastened over to Ziggy. She was still lounging against the far wall, hand on her sword hilt.

"What do you reckon?" he asked her.

She blew out a breath. "Whatever it is, this item's a big deal. And Evandahl seems like a cold briigard, but I admire a man with his own rules."

"You just admire a man with gray hair," he ribbed quietly.

She scoffed. "So what if I do?"

He let out an amused breath and shook his head. "Looks like Fang gave permission to visit the cathedral," he said, nodding. Mairead was beaming, her freckled cheeks pinched in a smile that lit her whole face. "I'll be going with her; but I want you to keep an eye on Fig here."

"Will do, m'lord," Ziggy quipped.

He kept himself from rolling his eyes. "And don't antagonize her."

"Wouldn't dream of it. Actually, I might dream of it—I was planning on taking a nap."

"Just keep an eye out, will you? I'm surprised she didn't want to go into the city with Mairead."

Ziggy shrugged. Fig left for the back rooms, and that was that. He adjusted his sword and headed over toward Mairead. He held out an arm toward the door with a rare smile. He'd never seen Mairead so happy. Outside, he gave the flat one last glance before starting toward the cathedral. He just hoped Ziggy would keep her word and watch over Fig. The last time he'd left Fig alone they'd had to hasten away from the tavern and the pursuing blackguard.

He and Mairead found their way to the cathedral with ease; its finials and flying buttresses soared high above the small buildings nearby making it impossible to miss. Early afternoon sunlight peered at them from behind spires, and glinted off the high windows.

"I'm a little surprised Evandahl didn't give orders to keep us in the house," she remarked as they reached the cathedral steps. She stood there smiling for a moment, then hastily stuffed her branded hand into her pocket and began the ascent.

"*Va, iil*, they know we need passage to Nithe, so we're less likely to cut and run on them, of course."

"Oh, right," she said. She looked up at the architecture once more in amazement and sighed. "It's even more beautiful than Mar Nevan, and I spent most of my life thinking that was the most peaceful and beautiful place on the continent. I wish I could remember this moment forever. It's just so...perfect."

"Mm-hmm," Vaelor agreed.

Mairead chuckled. "Come on, let's go inside."

He smiled behind her back, inspecting the architecture as they went. It was beautiful and perfect, but Vaelor admired the craftsmanship even more. How many people had it taken to build those flying buttresses? He tried to picture the stone masons high on their ladders and scaffolds, measuring those angles just *so*, and hauling stones to fit exactly *there*.

Inside was no less magnificent. The heady scent of incense wafted over them as soon as they stepped into the vestibule. The smell seemed to be a fixed element in this place that would linger in his hair long after he'd left. Candles were lit in braziers on columns running the length of the central nave, but at this time of day, most of the light in the main part of the cavernous building came from the stained glass windows.

Below the vaulted ceilings down each side of the nave, tall windows told stories in colored glass. The back of the cathedral was significantly darker, and the stories told of Morgha as the goddess of death. Mairead surged forward to explore, and Vaelor wandered wordlessly behind her.

They explored as much as they could without trespassing; Mairead offered up the occasional anecdote about her time in Mar Nevan. But she kept her branded hand stuffed tightly in her pocket the entire time, and a bittersweet sadness settled across her expression.

Finally, they stopped at the bank of candles near the front. Vaelor put two silver coins in the coin box before he lit two fresh candles to place in the sconces there.

For once, Mairead didn't ask any questions. She focused on lighting her own candle at the other end of the rack.

Vaelor bowed his head, staring at the flames he'd ignited for both his parents. They had passed before the war—before death ruled his life the way it did now. Death stalked him, strapped into his scabbard as his constant companion.

Ever since he'd crossed over and felt Morgha's arms reaching for him only to be ripped away—saved by the strength of his very sword— well, it made sense that death ruled his life now.

And then when death had come for King Haemond and Vaelor's life was once again ruled by death, his oath to the Verrence family wasn't something he could break—an oath the enclave surely regretted letting him take but one that had saved his grandmother and Perrin's lives.

He had lost much since his parents had passed. The flames flickered in the rack, and his eyes stung. Gone were the days when anyone would hold his hand and tell him everything would be all right. Gone was his true humanity, ever since he'd crossed over and become bound to his sword. He didn't regret it. Nor did he regret his parents not seeing him become this way. He was thankful they hadn't seen the war at all. And he was thankful his *grimazir* didn't look upon him differently than she had before his eyes were ringed in silver.

But gone were the days of peace in Viren.

And gone was his title to Resbrok. He never thought he'd mourn it—it was a mantle he hadn't always been keen to assume—but signing those papers had broken something inside him. His title had been a rope, mooring him to home. Would he ever return?

At least he and Perrin had been able to draw up the papers in time; he suspected the excuse was one of the only things that kept that silversword patrol from slaughtering them all where they stood.

He pressed his eyelids shut and felt moisture trickle down. Wiping it with the backs of his hands, he straightened, only to find that Mairead had wandered away.

"*Merda*," he said under his breath. With one last look at the candles, he went on the hunt for Mairead, approaching the first red sister he came across, an old dwarf woman with thick gray hair divided into two braids.

"Excuse me," he said. "You haven't seen a visiting priestess, have you? Red hair and freckles?" He pointed at his own face vaguely.

"Oh, yes," she said. "Sister Fringa is showing her the hospital. Would you like me to take you to her?"

He nodded, and she led him through a series of stone doorways, small rooms. and corridors that connected the cathedral to the hospital next door. He had heard that people came from all over Tysaine to be treated here; the Sisters of Morgha had fewer chapels in the country, whereas every respectable village or town in Tytan boasted at least one.

The smell of blood knifed through his enhanced senses. Old blood and new. Death.

Eventually they found Mairead in a ward of patients, watching another sister perform a healing. There was quite a lot of blood from a deep leg wound. A third sister had a sharp knife in her hand and was explaining, "Sometimes when there's a foreign object, you have to retrieve it yourself."

"Oh," Mairead said. "I've never had to do that before." She turned to Vaelor, blood on her hands from helping hold down the patient, and grinned. "Ah, Vaelor! Sorry. I didn't think you'd mind if I looked around a bit more, and Sister Fringa said—"

"It's fine," he said. "But do you want to—"

"Oh, yes, I'd love to stay," she said. "Sister Soros was going to show me the disease ward after we're done here."

Vaelor nodded tightly. He had been about to say, *Do you want to head back*, but he couldn't bring himself to puncture her happiness.

At least Mairead still had her calling.

CHAPTER 37

"You're new to Tirnalore?" the young scholar asked Fig.

She adjusted the scarf over her hair and nodded. "Yes. And I thank you for showing me around the academy. I have some schooling, but nothing like what's offered here."

The young boy stuck out his chin and led her along the stone corridor of Tirnalore Academy, where, she had falsely told him at the front offices, she was hoping to enroll.

Fig walked sedately by his side, as if she hadn't a care in the world and was in no rush to return to the flat before anyone noticed she was gone. Ziggy had fallen asleep on a sofa, and Fang didn't seem to care that Fig wanted to go out, only giving her a warning smile as she left, but she had answers to find.

"It's a long application process," the boy—she thought his name was Stenoh—told her. "And the entry exams—well, I hope you're prepared."

"Of course," she said confidently. "Now, what can you tell me about the courses on magic studies? I've heard there's a small department on the subject...?"

"Sure, I'll take you there," Stenoh said, navigating down another hallway, all of them lined with aging stone vaulted ceilings.

Of course, she could have started at the library, and that would be her next stop if she had time, but first she needed to know what Afrith knew about Nithe. And about Shadryn, if that part of his story wasn't a complete fabrication.

And for that she needed...

"Here it is," Stenoh announced. "It's a small department, but it does have this." He gestured needlessly to the center of the courtyard on their left.

Fig gasped and stepped out from under the corridor, closer to the single auran tree glinting in the center of the gray courtyard. Moss lined the stones, and a few faint gold sparkles drifted down to land at her feet.

"It's a transplant," Stenoh told her proudly. "I heard it was grown in Tysaine."

"I see." She inhaled the faintest scent of honey, that golden glow reaching right into her core—faint, but still there. She didn't think Stenoh was a mage—it was unlikely he would be studying *birds* of all things if he were—but you didn't need Svoran blood to admire an auran tree.

Part of her wondered whether she should say something about the one Emrah had found in the wild on the Notch. She knew they could—and did—grow anywhere on the continent; they just seemed to prefer to grow together. She always wondered why mages were so affected by aurans.

Were there fewer mages in Tysaine because there were fewer auran trees? Or were there fewer trees because there were fewer mages? Did the trees and mages even have anything to do with each other?

Questions she would have been happy to discuss with Afrith before his treachery, the slimy briigard. And speaking of...

"This is wonderful, Stenoh," she said. "And you know what, I think I do need that application after all. Would it be possible for you to get me one? I could fill it out here, couldn't I?"

He took another look at the tree and gave her a knowing smile. "Of course. I'll head back to the registrar's office. Would you like to wait here by the tree?"

"I would love that," she said, settling herself on a little stone bench.

As soon as Stenoh was gone, Fig was back on her feet and heading down the corridor in the other direction where she suspected Afrith's study might be. She knew he had a standing position at the academy; he had mentioned he still had offices here. She had little worry that he would actually be in residence—even he was too smart to bring Dev somewhere so public as the academy. With the delay in the heist slowing them down, Afrith was probably long gone from Tirnalore already...if he'd come here at all.

A familiar scent drew her to one office in particular. Its door was shut, but the scent was strong: *kafye* and—now she knew what it was— svorcat fur.

Of course, any professor might have a penchant for coffee and own a svorcat, but she took a chance and put her hand on the handle. It was unlocked. Letting herself in, she briefly debated whether to shut the door or keep it open—the latter choice she might be able to better explain away should someone come upon her. She decided to close it, anyway. She lost no time in diving into Afrith's things, making no effort to hide the fact that it had been searched.

If she had her way, Afrith would never make it back to his office ever again.

She rifled through books, sheafs of parchment, random scraps of paper stuffed untidily in drawers, careful not to knock over the various *kafye* cups stored throughout the room lest she make a noise. On one of the bookshelves, she came across a small, battered book on fire magic, which she pocketed. It looked like something Afrith had studied more than once, so it must be good.

Letters, journals, notebooks. All absent of valuable information on Nithe, Shadryn, or anything about familiars. Frantically, she kept searching, thinking she would find something in the next one...and the next one...

A small sound in the hallway drew her to her senses, and she stopped at once. The office had been thoroughly turned over, and it looked it. A sudden dread settled over her; what was she thinking? Of course, Afrith wouldn't leave valuable, kingdom-shattering information just lying about in an unlocked office when he wasn't here for months at a time. And it was stupid to think he would have anything on familiars; she could check the Tirnalore Library for that.

She gave the office one last look—there wasn't any point in attempting to tidy up—and left.

When she shut the door behind her with the smallest sound she could make, she saw another scholar leaning against the wall only a few feet away, eating an apple. A satchel of books lay on the floor at his feet.

"Oh, hello," Fig said breathlessly. "Just, uh—looking for something for Master Afrith. He sent a letter." Something she'd learned from a few years of trying to fake her way out of dangerous situations, was that too much information in a cover story was always suspicious. It was better to be vague.

He took another bite of the apple and crunched away, then said, "Interesting. Did'ja find it?"

"No," she said, annoyed.

"Shame," he said, then lowered his voice. "You know, I've had a letter from Afrith too."

A chill went down her back, but she swallowed and went on. "Oh?"

"He sends his regards."

A knife went straight for her middle. She reached out and grabbed his knuckles with a coal-hot hand, shoving his hand to the side. He dropped the knife with a clatter, but he wasn't done yet.

The knife reappeared in his hand as if it had never left. An ugly smile graced his face, half hidden behind his greasy chin-length hair.

Fig forced more heat to her hands, reaching out for the knife again, but he evaded her grasp.

"You know," he said, his voice grating on her ears, "I can make this knife appear anywhere, not just in my hand."

Picturing it sticking out of her ribcage, Fig summoned a ball of flame to send right toward him. What kind of mage was he? She'd seen metal mages before, but this was different.

The flames, however, bloomed three times the size she'd meant them to. The mage leapt out of the way, dashing across the hallway toward the courtyard. *What in the...*

Just then a small figure swooped in from the courtyard.

"*Emrah!*" Fig cried, glancing around in confusion. Where did he go? Had she imagined him?

The knife had disappeared from the mage's hand, and in a moment of terror, Fig wondered if she was going to look down and find it in her gut. She glanced down, hands moving intuitively to her stomach. It was fine. Her heart raced, images of axe-wounds and cauterization filling her mind.

The knife clattered to the floor at her feet, courtesy of Emrah, who swooped by. "It *is* you!" she exclaimed as he perched on her shoulder.

"Now!" he told her.

She summoned another burst of flame; this time she had a second set of flames on her side. The mage staggered backward to avoid the brunt of it and, in his haste, slammed his head right into the stone column at the side of the corridor.

He dropped to the ground with a *thump*. Fig picked up the knife with two fingers, not wanting to touch the thing, but deciding to take it with her.

"We should hide him," she said. Then she remembered who she was talking to. "Oh, *Emrah, where were you?* We were so worried!" She reached a hand up to pat the top of his head, and he pushed his head into her palm.

Enough of that now. Someone's coming.

Right, she told him, shaking her head and grabbing the man's ankles.

So Afrith had known she might come to Tirnalore and try to look into his things. What had he been worried she would find? Or did he simply not want her following him?

Lifting his feet, she dragged the man across the hallway and into Afrith's office, dropping his feet without care as soon as she got him through the doorway, then shut the door as quietly as she could. Had someone heard the commotion? She knew it was probably Stenoh returning with her application, but she stood frozen for a few minutes, listening with her ear against the door, as her heart raced. Finally, she asked Emrah, *Can you hear anything?*

No, I think they're gone.

Good, I didn't think they would look in here. Gods, I can't believe you're back! What took you so long? Why didn't you answer me?

A low snort came from Emrah as he hovered before her. *Why didn't I answer? Why didn't you? Ziggy's family wanted me to pass a message to her, and then you never even checked in!*

She shut her eyes for a second. *I guess we just couldn't hear each other. The distance, maybe? I thought you'd died or something!*

He dropped a few hand-spans before recovering himself. *I suppose I've never needed to speak to anyone so far away. I'm sorry you were worried.*

"You shouldn't have to be sorry," she mumbled aloud. "I'm just glad you're all right." Hastily, she dashed tears from her eyes with the backs of her hands.

Then she found Emrah's scaly head bumping into her hand. She gave him a watery smile.

We better get out of here, Emrah said, *while the corridor is empty, and before this briigard wakes up.*

Yes, let's go, she replied, *I've got a lot to catch you up on.*

"Fig?" someone called from behind her just as she knocked on the front door of the flat.

She whirled around to see Vaelor and Mairead heading toward her, and her face flushed. Mairead called, "Is that *Emrah?*"

Seizing the happy subject, Fig grinned and waited on the front step for Mairead to rush over and greet Emrah. His green and gold scales flashed in the early afternoon sunlight. Even Vaelor looked relieved to see the dragonet perched on Fig's shoulder.

"How was the cathedral?" Fig asked as the door swung open to reveal a bored-looking Fang. Ursa nosed her way over to greet them, her tail wagging. But when Ursa caught sight and smell of Emrah, her excitement turned to a mix of nerves and fear. The dog danced about unhappily, crashing into everyone with little barks of warning.

Between calming Ursa down, getting through the doorway, and the excitement over Emrah's return, Fig hoped her excursion from the flat would go unnoticed.

They managed to get to the back halls before Mairead asked, "Where did you find him, Fig? Where'd you go?"

Fig grimaced where no one could see her at the head of the line. They entered one of the bedrooms, where Ziggy was lounging on a couch.

Emrah beat her to answering. *The Academy,* he told them as they stepped through the threshold. *Some goon of Afrith's caught her stealing from his office.*

Fig's jaw fell open. She had somehow neglected to mention to Emrah that her little trip to the academy had been an entirely private venture. She shut her mouth.

"*What?*" Ziggy demanded, sitting upright.

"I—" Fig began.

"What were you thinking?" Vaelor demanded, whirling around to face her. His gaze swept up and down her, as if making certain nothing was missing.

A great huff exploded from her chest. "I wasn't. I wasn't thinking."

"Afrith's office?" Mairead asked quietly. "What did you think you'd find there?"

She shook her head and began pacing. "I don't know. Something that might give us a clue about where he's headed with Dev. Or what we might find when we get to Nithe, if that's really where they're going."

They stared at her, and she wished to the Bard someone would say something. The disapproving silence became intolerable, and she burst, "Look, Afrith betrayed us—betrayed Dev. He was one of our teachers at the Carriage House for the Bard's sake! And he's got people here in Tirnalore keeping watch for us, for some reason."

"Gods, I wonder why," Ziggy drawled.

"I'm sorry," Fig said again, the words ripping from her throat. "But with Dev gone, I needed to do something."

"Well, did you find anything?" Mairead asked.

She shook her head, not meeting their eyes. She felt like she was on a stage like some kind of performer. Except her performance was in flames, and she was a terrible player.

"I was also looking for something on"—she glanced up at Emrah, who'd perched on the mantel—"familiars. Afrith said Emrah was my familiar, and I'm not sure if I should believe him. But the fact that I can speak to Emrah with my mind, and...wait a minute—" Sparks gathered at her fingertips. She flicked them away.

She turned to face Emrah fully. "You showed up right when my flames bloomed like crazy. It was like I was back in the Gold Wood—my magic was amplified. There was that auran sapling, but it didn't have any effect on me since it was so little until you showed up... Is that why..."

After standing with her lips partially open for a second, she voiced her realization. "If Emrah and I are bonded somehow and he's my familiar, it might explain why I haven't been able to control my magic as well. Like when I almost burned Perrin." She looked up at Vaelor.

He crossed his arms over his wide chest. "You still should have told us you wanted to go to the academy. I would have gone with you."

Fig bit her lip and nodded, her stomach doing a flip at the surge of protectiveness in his gaze. "I know. And I'm sorry. I—" She glanced over at Ziggy self-consciously, but the woman was watching Emrah—"I didn't know what to do. My magic's all I've got. And facing up against Afrith? It feels like I have *nothing* compared to him."

Vaelor put a hand on his sword hilt, not in aggression, but out of habit. "If you wanted to go, we should have—"

"I know, I should have asked for help. I'm sorry." She met each of their eyes, even Ziggy's.

"That was stupid," Ziggy said.

"I know."

"And selfish."

"Yes, I—"

"And I probably would have done the same thing."

Fig didn't know how to respond to that, so she kept her mouth shut. Emrah snorted in amusement from the mantle.

"Well, I did find this." She held up the book she had swiped. "Fire magic."

"Looks well-read," Mairead observed, taking a step closer.

"Do you think it has anything on familiars?"

Fig looked up from the book, surprised that Vaelor had asked the question.

"I don't know," she said, glancing over at Emrah. "I guess we'll have to see. But I can't see why it would—they're probably just a myth. Has there been any word from the Fienn-Da?" she asked Ziggy.

Ziggy stretched her legs out on the couch again and frowned. "Not a chirp. Guess that's good though."

"Maybe we won't have to do it after all," Mairead said brightly.

"But then we won't get a boat either," Ziggy said.

Mairead visibly shrunk in on herself. Then she huffed and went over to the closet, poking around and muttering about bedding.

"I could do with a nap, myself," Fig said. "I wonder why they've got no beds here if this is one of their hideouts."

"It's storage," Ziggy said. "Floors are all scuffed from crates, and I found a bunch of boxes in one of the back rooms. I doubt they have to house traveling ruffians like us too often."

Mairead came out from the closet empty-handed and left to talk to Fang. They heard Ursa whining happily from the parlor as Mairead approached.

Fig collapsed into one of the two chairs by the couch, glad her trial was over.

"It really was a stupid thing to do," Ziggy said quietly.

Fig huffed in annoyance. "You've already covered that. Mind getting off my back about it?"

Ziggy held up a finger. "One more thing, and I promise I'll drop it. Stupid will get you killed. If you want to get things done, be bold. Being bold means you can ask for help and still get on with your plans."

The front door slammed, and Fig immediately put her feet back under her.

"Relax," Ziggy said. "It's just Quinnetra."

But when no one came back to see them, Fig cracked open the book on fire magic. It had no title, or if it did, the title had long since worn off the leather cover. Deciding not to start at the beginning, she flipped through and skimmed for the word "familiar."

But when a set of high-heeled footsteps that were definitely not Mairead's came to the doorway, she looked up.

"Is it on?" Ziggy asked eagerly. "The heist? I do love that word."

"Not yet," Quinnetra said, a little appreciation showing through her glare. "Evandahl put the word out, and we actually spotted your prince—er, king. You were right. He's on a ship heading to Nithe."

Afrith turned up his collar as the stiff south wind coming from the Hollow Isles hit them aboard the ship.

Dev had no such luxury. His hands were still bound by fire magic he'd only heard of in legends and lore—flames that didn't burn. Well, they didn't burn unless he struggled against them.

There were no forged papers, no checked identities. The first mate who'd helped him onto the ship—bound hands still hidden under a vast cloak—didn't even look at his face.

Surely, *surely*, someone would recognize him.

He was Devryn Verrence, after all. The missing king of the Rayvan throne.

He didn't feel much like a king now.

Afrith made a show of getting one last glance at Tirnalore as their ship pulled away from port. "Come," he said, giving Dev's shoulder a little push.

"I doubt your friends will be joining us," he said as he guided him belowdecks. "Though, maybe one or two still will, on my terms. Tirnalore is my city. I've already seen to them."

There was still no word from the Fienn-Da the next morning. Between that and another night on the floor cushioned only by a few blankets—Ziggy had claimed the couch, and absolutely no one wanted to challenge her for it—Fig's nerves were on high alert. They ate a simple breakfast of hard-boiled eggs, gouda, and a hard sourdough that Vilvan had brought from the tavern. Fang, as usual, seemed rather bored to be watching them, but readily dug into the provided food, tearing off bits of bread for Ursa to gnaw on.

Emrah had settled on the back of Fig's chair. He and the dog had come to a sort of truce; Ursa's eyes never left Emrah, though, anytime they were in the same room together.

"How much longer 'til we hear?" Fig finally said, washing down the meal with the weak ale Vilvan had provided. "We need to leave Tirnalore. Soon. Especially since we know Dev is on a ship *right now*."

"However long it takes," Fang said, slicing off another piece of cheese and popping it into his mouth. "Can't do the job if the job isn't here yet."

Fig rolled her eyes and turned back to Mairead who was tidying up her bread crumbs with a napkin. "Want to help me go through that book on fire magic this morning, then?"

Mairead ducked her head. "I'm sorry, I actually said I'd return to the

Narndian today if we weren't busy. They really liked having me there yesterday."

"Oh," Fig said.

"Sorry," Mairead repeated, her voice filled with guilt.

"It's fine," Fig said with a wave of her hand. "I'm glad you can help out there. Do you want me to walk over with you?"

"Sure!" Mairead said, her guilt visibly melting into relief. "Although Vaelor said he would too."

"Then we'll make it a party," Fig said easily. She still felt terrible for running off on her own yesterday, only to get attacked by Afrith's mage, and was all the more eager to do her part for the group.

So the three of them plus Emrah set out shortly after breakfast to escort Mairead to the hospital. Emrah had declined Fig's offer to let him ride in her tunic hood, insisting he'd rather fly. She realized why when she saw him stalking birds on the rooftops as they turned the corner for the cathedral. She looked away; there hadn't been any meat at breakfast, and she couldn't very well expect him to live off bread and cheese like everyone else.

Mairead directed them down a wide alley to the back entrance to the hospital. Though it was early, the city had been alive for hours, with scents of *kafye* drifting out of windows, people calling to one another from the shops, and a steady stream of travelers moving along the main roads, on horse and on foot. The alley was quiet, though, tucked away on the side of the hospital.

"How long do you think you'll stay?" Fig asked Mairead, at the same time Vaelor asked, "Would you like us to stay here with you?"

Mairead smiled sheepishly at the two of them. "I'd like to stay as long as possible, actually."

"Shall we come and get you for the heist when word arrives, then?" Fig asked. "I'm kind of hoping it's today." Dev had been with Afrith long enough. Too long.

"Actually..." Mairead began, looking at the sidewalk. "I-I...don't want to do it. I don't want to do the heist."

They stood in silence for a minute, only interrupted by the faraway squawk of a bird on a rooftop.

"But..."

"It's against my vows, first of all," Mairead said, "and even if Mar Nevan won't have me, I'm still a Sister of Morgha." Her back straightened at these words, and she took her branded hand out of her pocket where she normally hid it while in public. She opened her palm to them. The circular runes were the same blood-red as the first time they saw it. "I actually... One of the sisters saw my brand yesterday."

Fig gasped. And Mairead *still* wanted to go back to the hospital?

"And they said it didn't matter," Mairead went on. "They saw that I could still heal, still use the holy waters. And they're right. It doesn't matter. Here, I can still be a Sister of Morgha."

"Oh," Fig said. She glanced at Vaelor and back to Mairead, unable to form any words. "Does... Does that mean...?"

"I'd like to stay here. In Tirnalore. At the Narndian."

Fig's eyes burned. She swallowed, suddenly forgetting how to breathe properly. "Oh," she said again. "Well, if you... But what about Dev?"

Mairead reached out to grab Fig's hand. Numb, Fig let her. "I trust you and Vaelor and Emrah to rescue him. And even Ziggy." A smile lifted her voice.

"It's just...you said you were *with us*," Fig said blankly, remembering the time she had last questioned Mairead's plans to come with them. "Is it just, now you've found a better place to stay?"

The words hurt Fig as soon as they came out, and she was sure they hurt Mairead even more. But the numb part of her wasn't sure she cared.

"I-I," Mairead stuttered. "I thought you'd be happy! They'll accept me here even with my brand! I can heal people and follow my life's calling without being on the run!"

"Right," Fig said, suddenly cold. "Right. I'll ask Emrah to stay with you today. He can keep an eye out and should still be able to speak with me from this short of a distance."

"Fig, I—"

"We'll come by to get you whenever you need, unless we're...busy." They *had* to do the heist. They had to get to Nithe and rescue Dev.

Mairead's face crumpled, and she whirled around and dashed into the side door of the hospital. Tears broke through the barrier of Fig's lashes and cascaded down her face.

She sank to a crouch, clutching her knees to her chest as she racked with sobs, regretting every word.

Why was I so mean to Mairead? she thought. *She found somewhere she belongs, even with her brand. I should be happy for her!* What *is wrong with me?*

Warm hands wrapped around her arms, lifting her up, then crushed her in an embrace. Vaelor.

She cried uncontrollably for several minutes, feeling very small in Vaelor's warm arms. Her forehead sank against his chest. She should have known Mairead would want to leave, to make a home in a place that would accept her just as she was. Despite Mairead's promise that she would stay.

The racking sobs started to slow. Fig should be used to it by now. Who was she to demand that Mairead stay? What could Fig possibly offer, besides a likely fatal excursion to save their wayward king? Mairead didn't need her; Fig had nothing to offer. Not acceptance. Not a place of belonging.

Fig couldn't give her something she could never seem to find for herself.

When her tears subsided, she pulled away from Vaelor who loosened his grip. Their eyes locked. The silver rings around his pupils framed a color between gray and blue. As she took a shaky breath, the silver rings contracted a little.

His arms suddenly felt very warm wrapped around her. She blinked and looked away, feeling pathetic. Vaelor was only here because he was bound to serve Dev. He would probably leave just like Mairead when he no longer had to fulfill his oath. But that would only be if Dev was dead; then she'd really have no one.

She pulled away from his warm arms regretfully—a bitter chill had seeped into her chest.

"Thanks," she muttered. "We should get back and see if there's been any word about the heist." Wiping the tears that had started to dry on her face, she turned away from him.

There was still no word when they returned to check in with Fang, so Fig asked him instead for a favor. She might as well focus on the one thing she had left—the one thing that would never go away—her magic. Now that she was certain what was causing the disruptions, she wanted to explore what she could do.

"Sure," Fang said. "Right this way." He whistled to Ursa, who got up from her spot under his chair, and he led her around the back halls to a door.

Vaelor, who had wordlessly walked by her side back to the flat, hovered behind her like a benevolent ghost: silent and present. Of course, it was his nature as a silversword to protect, that was all.

Fang opened the door which led down into the cellar. "Here's a place you can use. There's lamps down there, if you want to grab a torch—"

"I think I can handle lighting them," Fig said with a melancholy smile.

As Fang headed back to his post, Fig looked over at Vaelor. "I don't need protection down here," she said, "except maybe from myself."

He shrugged, looking past her into the dark cellar. "I know you don't," he said gruffly, "but there's no reason you should have to train alone."

"Fine," Fig said, secretly pleased for the company. She tried not to think about his warm, muscled arms wrapped around her as they stood outside the Narndian. But she couldn't help her sharp awareness of his nearness. Her face warmed. "Oh, I should go get that book."

A few minutes later, and now with Ziggy tagging along too—the 'sword was bored of lying around, she said—they descended into the cellar. Fig sent little balls of flame to each of the lamps on the walls, which provided a modest amount of light.

With a thought, she reached out to Emrah. *Everything all right with you?* she asked.

Just fine, he replied immediately. She smiled. At least her connection with Emrah had been restored.

Warn me if you happen to come back, she added. *I'm going to do a little fire magic training here at the house.*

Don't burn the place down, Emrah quipped.

Stay away, then, Fig replied with a smirk.

"She's doing that thing, isn't she?" Ziggy asked from across the cellar. "Talking to the dragonet?"

Vaelor chuckled and glanced at Fig. "*Va,* it certainly seems so."

"Quiet, you two," Fig said, sticking out her chin. "I'm just glad he's back."

"Oh, aye." Ziggy dusted off a crate in the corner of the cellar where the sunlight slanted in from a hatch leading outside. "And I'm glad he was able to get my mother and Ishi and Evvy out of Ashbrok. I just don't think it's fair he gets to talk in my head, but I don't get the same courtesy."

The corner of Fig's mouth twitched up. "Well, that's part of the reason I think there's some kind of familiar bond between us."

"And what does that even mean?" Ziggy said, sitting back against the wall and propping her leg up.

"I don't know," Fig admitted quietly. "That's part of why I went to the academy yesterday."

"Right," Ziggy said, never missing a word, "but couldn't we just check at the library?"

"We should," Fig said. "Maybe this afternoon." She opened the book to the first place she had marked last night when she'd skimmed through the first few chapters. After not finding anything on familiars, she had gone back to the beginning and sought out spells she thought she could pull off. Most of what she had learned at the Carriage House had been simple flames: lighting candles, throwing fireballs, or putting *out* fires—the one thing the crown preferred she did with her magic— nothing nearly as intricate as what Afrith could do.

"Should we wait for Mairead to get back before we go?" Ziggy asked.

"No," Fig said, staring at the page without seeing any of the words.

She heard Vaelor mutter a few words to Ziggy and then a hum of understanding. Fig stared harder at the words, willing them to come into focus in her suddenly blurry eyes.

Fire circle.

It wasn't quite what Afrith had summoned, from the illustrations on the page, but a simple spell that enclosed the mage in a circle of protective fire from the ground. Sure, she could light several little fires to form a circle, but the illustration indicated this would be much more effective. And depending on how well she did it, she could form a flaming wall as tall as she was to protect herself and anyone inside the circle. Her only hope was that it would protect her from malevolent flames as well.

But she wouldn't try to make it too high, not down here in the cellar. She shook her head. She was getting ahead of herself; she didn't even know if she could pull it off yet.

Holding the book in one hand, she used the toe of her boot to draw a circle around herself in the hard-packed earth of the cellar. It wasn't perfect, but that was probably all right. It was just a visual for herself, according to the book.

Closing her eyes for a second and feeling a bit stupid, she twirled on her toes while throwing down her hand, picturing her flames flying out in a ring of fire like the book said.

She opened her eyes to find the ground singed in a half-circle. As the last of the tiny embers burned away, she bit the inside of her mouth and stared back down at the page.

A sudden thought struck her harder than her initial disappointment; she probably *would* have learned this kind of thing at the Carriage House if she hadn't up and left. Most mages spent decades there, never declaring their training "done." They claimed they were always learning. Fig had thought it a lie they told themselves; the throne wanted the mages rounded up in one place and extending their training indefinitely was one way to do it.

But maybe she had been wrong. She hadn't learned everything there was to learn.

Of course, that didn't mean she agreed with what King Haemond wanted for mages. They should be allowed to live or work in the Gold Wood without being tied to the throne, whatever they chose to do. But just like the dwarves' Mountain, the kings of old had taken what they wanted and kept it for themselves.

Until Dev becomes king. He understood that mages deserved freedom, deserved the Gold Wood. And with a deal with the dwarves already in progress, things might balance out for Tytan, and not just leave the silverswords on top for once.

Fig sighed and got back to the words on the page. One thing at a time. First, she needed to get better at fire magic. Whether it was her fault for quitting her training or not, she still needed to defeat Afrith. She looked closer at the instructions and decided to sit down in her circle, crossing her legs under her.

She put a hand on the line she had drawn and closed her eyes.

The book said to draw on her inner fire and construct a barrier with the connection. She *thought* that's what she did when she used her fire magic, but maybe she needed to actually work on that part.

Connect, she told herself. It sounded gentler than how she often thought of her fire magic—being *thrown* or *surging* out of her. But to *connect* her fire to its intended purpose...

Fingers gently feeling the dirt ridge she'd created, she envisioned her inner fire—the source of her magic—and pictured a small spark of intent running through her veins and out her fingertips, skating along the circle line and leaving flames in its wake. A tingling jolt ran through her senses.

The sensation of flames forced her eyes open just in time to see the low wall of fire encircling her but already starting to go out. "Oh!" she exclaimed. Panicked, she urged more flames into it from her hand, sure they would add to the circle.

The surge of flames *whooshed* through the circle and dissipated, going out with the rest of the circle.

"Well," she said to herself, "that was a good start, I guess. But I don't think I can add to the circle like that. I think the intention needs to be stronger from the beginning."

She remembered something about her lesson with Afrith, and

though the thought made her stomach roil, she recalled him saying something about the conditions for setting the fire needing to be optimal. She had thought he was referring to her mental state; her thoughts were always jumbled when everything was in chaos. It was when she created the flames that the boundaries needed to be set. The intentions formed.

Neither Vaelor nor Ziggy said anything. Their silver-ringed eyes glinted at her from the half-shadowed corner of the cellar.

Fig got to work again. Envisioning. Connecting. *Not* throwing or surging. She needed to start strong and spend more time connecting.

It was well into the afternoon by the time Fig stood surrounded by a knee-high wall of flames that crackled merrily in a constant circle around her. After all the practice, it had taken only a few seconds to pull it up this time. Intent, strong, and connected.

She grinned at the two 'swords through her flames. "Now I just need to work on making it bigger."

At that moment, the door to the basement burst open with a *crack*. It creaked on its hinges as it swung slowly back. "You lot still alive down there? Nobody burned to a crisp?" Fang hollered down. "The job is on."

CHAPTER 40

The high spires of Tirnalore were wreathed in starlight under black velvet skies when Fig followed Quinnetra through a back door into the library.

Inside, Fig reached out a hand to stop the door from slamming, but it moved faster than she had expected, and she was too late to stop it.

It shut but made no sound at all. She furrowed her brow, her impotent hand touching the closed door.

Fang came up next to her, cap low, and a grin on his face.

"Did you just…"

He clicked his tongue at her and put a finger to his lips.

The Fienn-Da had gone over the full plan with them that afternoon, finally revealing more details. Fig remembered Fang having a role in the plans, but she didn't remember anyone saying he was a…sound mage?

Quinnetra was an air mage, she had known that. It was she who had picked the lock to the back door with a collection of metal tools and the help of her red-colored wind.

The number of mages in the Fienn-Da astounded her, especially considering Tysaine's notoriously low mage population. The fact that no one had mentioned Fang's abilities indicated that the Fienn-Da hadn't divulged everything about the heist. Clearly, they didn't yet trust Fig and the others.

The hallway had no windows, so the six of them stood in complete darkness. *Oh*, Fig thought, then snapped her fingers to summon a small flame—half of her assignment for the heist, providing light.

She hoped she wouldn't have to do the other half of her job—providing flames for defense.

In the meantime, she remained alert, ready to snuff out the flames at a second's notice as she moved to the head of the group.

Among the reports Evandahl *had* shared were thorough schedules for the night librarians, including room assignments, rotations, and break schedules. But it wasn't the night librarians they had to watch out for. With the Tirnalore Library being such a respected institution, it was given royal protection, which meant the blackguard.

"The mail chamber is up ahead," Kerafina whispered, waving them over. "Should be two bleaks in there."

Fig nodded tightly, watching Vaelor and Ziggy position themselves in front of the door, hands on their weapons. At their signal, she extinguished her light.

To the right of the door, Kerafina dropped her hand.

Vaelor opened the door, and he and Ziggy charged forward, but no one inside paid them any mind, thanks to the work of Fang and Kerafina.

Fig had been expecting this. Distractions, Evandahl said—that was Kerafina's job.

The blackguards inside remained as calm if no one was there. They were practically invisible. Fig looked down at herself and could see her body, but it glimmered with something that reminded her of a mirror. Kerafina was an illusion mage.

Feeling like a haunting spirit, Fig walked through the door with the blackguards on either side none-the-wiser. Fang was muffling any sound they made, while Kerafina cast her illusion magic. Fig's confidence in their success grew with each moment. The Fienn-Da were skilled, and they knew exactly what they were doing.

They got through the mail chamber with no incident, and Fig cast a final glance at the two bleaks standing by the door that led to the back hallway, which Fang had closed as the last one through. The two guards exchanged a bored look through their helms, probably wondering why they were guarding such an obscure door to the library.

But if the Fienn-Da had stolen from the library before, it was no wonder they had such security in place.

Quinnetra took the lead, walking swiftly ahead in a black dress that fluttered behind her as she stalked the moonlit halls. When they passed through corridors with no windows, Fig did her job of providing light, and whenever they encountered any bleaks or night librarians, Kerafina and Fang played their part.

In one of the larger halls, as they quickly crossed a bridge that soared over the fourth floor atrium, Fig's jaw dropped in wonder. She barely had time to admire the towering shelves of books, dozens and dozens in each direction as she followed the others. A pang went through her chest when she realized her training that afternoon had prevented her from coming here during the day to search for information on familiars. And now she was only here to rob the place.

They crossed to the other side, deep into the inner hallways again, searching for the private collections.

Down a dark hallway with very few doors, Fig asked Fang, "How come we entered so far from the collections?"

He tilted his head as if listening for something, then said, "Too many bleaks at the other entrances. Kerafina's illusions are great, but she can only hold them for so long." He shrugged.

"Ah," Fig said. "And you're a sound mage? How come you didn't say so?"

He shrugged again, this time grinning.

She narrowed her eyes at him. "You don't just block sounds, right? You can create and...send sounds distances?"

"Perhaps."

"And that's how you told Evandahl about us that first night."

"Might be."

Fig let out an exasperated sigh. "I'm not even mad about it anymore. You were just doing your job. But I didn't realize there were so many mages in the Fienn-Da."

"Oh, aye," he replied. "Evandahl looks out for us."

"He certainly seems to."

Quinnetra had stopped, her black dress fluttering about her, at an open arched doorway that led onto another bridge. "Last one," she said.

Fig got another glimpse of the seemingly endless stacks in the great room below before they went through another wooden arched doorway. This one led to a spiral staircase, which they took right back down to the ground level.

Keeping her thoughts away from such positive things as, *This is going really well so far,* so as not to curse the job, Fig cast her light so it hovered in the center of the stairs as they all descended, their steps unnaturally silent.

They continued down another wide hallway, this one with locked double doors on each side. Quinnetra led them to one set of doors and got to work around the keyhole with a red glow.

Doors thrown wide, Quinnetra strode inside, outlined in moonlight. Fig followed her into the chamber of the Androzigma Collection, Vaelor and Ziggy right behind her. The high mullioned windows illuminated a half-unpacked series of artifacts, with wooden crates and packing sawdust strewn about.

Some artifacts were set up on plinths, while many others were still nestled in their crates.

"They got to work fast," Kerafina said, blowing some sawdust off a plinth where a cobalt blue vase stood.

"Private collectors," Fang scoffed. "Always rushing to put their stuff where no one will see it."

"No," Quinnetra said. "I heard they're having a gala, tomorrow. So the *invited* people get to see it."

"Good thing we're here tonight, then," Fang said. "Everyone, spread out. There should be manifests here, somewhere, even if they locked them up."

Fig nodded, suddenly uneasy. Sure, it had been thrilling stalking through the library when they were only trespassing. Now the real lawbreaking began. But she knew that going into this. And in the end, what did it matter if some rich collector lost a fancy cup from his collection, when it got Fig and the others a seat on a boat to Nithe?

Even during her brief jaunt to the academy, Fig had seen the city crawling with blackguard; there was no way they'd be able to book their own passage to Nithe, not with so much scrutiny. They needed the Fienn-Da's help, and for that, they needed to snag this chalice.

Fig started rustling carefully in the nearest crate, scooping sawdust aside to unearth a large cast metal art piece in the shape of an ox head. Shaking her own head, she carefully replaced it and covered it back up, then proceeded to check the two crates underneath.

Vaelor and Ziggy stood guard near the doors, the only entrance.

Fig knew they didn't have long to search, considering the night librarians' schedule. Though they wouldn't be working in this room, they did conduct regular patrols of the halls. Another crate, then another. No cups or anything that resembled a chalice. She had sawdust all over her clothes, and some had definitely crept into her boots.

"Hasn't anyone found the damn chalice yet? Or the manifest?" Ziggy grumbled quietly.

"I heard that," Fang replied.

Fig smirked. "Finally, someone whose hearing skills rival Ziggy's."

"No," Quinnetra said. "And I checked the curator's workstation. Nothing there. Locked drawer was empty."

"Oh?" Fig said.

"It's probably nothing," Quinnetra said. "We've got about twenty more minutes free, before the night librarian comes. Which just means Kerafina will have to—"

A soft sound came from the far back corner of the room, and Fig spun around, keeping her inner fire tightly contained in her core.

"You know, we were wondering if it was the chalice you were after," a vaguely familiar voice mused.

Amid the larger crates at the back of the room, the mage Fig had encountered at the academy stepped out of the shadows. Fig didn't see his knife anywhere, but immediately her stomach went cold.

He wasn't alone. A haughty woman stood beside him, her black hair pulled back in a severe bun and dark makeup on her eyes. She had a curious necklace that initially looked like it was made of several chunks of shiny glass, but upon closer inspection, looked more like gray water frozen in place.

She took an experimental step back, toward where she thought Vaelor was, but a dagger appeared at her neck, pressing against her skin.

She froze. Out of the corner of her eye, she thought she saw Fang's lips moving. The next thing she knew, the dagger had gone from her neck to Fang's. A drop of blood ran down his neck.

"Enough," the man said. "I could open all your throats in a matter of seconds. We were just leaving, anyway, when you arrived." He hoisted a paper-wrapped object that was definitely the size and shape of the chalice they had come for.

No. Not when she was this close.

Evandahl's warning about the job notwithstanding, she *needed* to get on that boat to Nithe. And there was only one way to do that.

"Afrith pays you to steal too?" Fig called. "Or do you just do it as a favor?"

He and the woman headed for the double doors and ignored her.

"I hope you got the right fancy cup!" she said frantically.

The woman cackled and whirled around. "Oh, you dried up little ember, it's not about the chalice, but what's inside it."

"Shut it, Estill," the man said, brushing his hair out of his face. "Do you have enough to bind them or something?"

"No," Estill said, pouting as she fingered the hunks of suspended water hanging from her necklace. "But I could do—"

"Don't. That's horrible."

A chill went down Fig's spine at the disgust in the man's voice. What could the woman do that even he found so distasteful?

"Bard's quill, Allifrey, live a little."

"No, I'm in charge here," Allifrey said, pushing strands of hair out of his eyes in annoyance. "We've got the chalice. Now lock them in or something."

"That I can do," Estill said, yanking her necklace off in a practiced movement that made the hunks of water collapse into one large bubble, which she held in her hand.

"Enjoy being found by the night librarians," Allifrey said, lifting the package in salute and striding away.

Fig couldn't let that slimy mage walk out carrying her only ticket to Nithe. But what was she to do against a man who could slit her throat the instant he saw her coming?

Estill lifted the sphere of water as they got to the door, a haughty smile on her lips. But Fig wasn't worried about a lock made of ice. It was whatever else the woman could do with water that worried her.

She glanced at Vaelor, but couldn't read his expression, his silver-ringed eyes closed off as they were.

Then Allifrey walked straight into something. Fig blinked. A column had reappeared, which he hadn't seen. At his triumphant speed, he was knocked back for a second, long enough for Vaelor and Ziggy to charge him.

Allifrey was fast with his knife, but Vaelor and Ziggy were faster. Vaelor grabbed the knife with his bare hand, holding it to Allifrey's throat, but it disappeared.

Fig gasped. There were a million awful places that knife could turn up next.

But Vaelor kicked Allifrey off him, and Ziggy lunged at the same time the dagger clattered to the ground. Blood covered Ziggy's sword, dripping onto the marble floors as Allifrey's knees hit the ground. Vaelor kicked away the man's dagger, but the danger had passed. The light in Allifrey's eyes had gone.

No wonder Evandahl had been pleased to have two silverswords accompanying the crew.

Vaelor seized the package from Allifrey before he collapsed forward.

An exasperated groan came from Estill, and she flung her hands down, her gray water sphere just as quickly surging into a dozen ice shards near her palms.

"Not happening, you blood-hungry 'sword," she growled.

Fig jumped as Vaelor tossed her the package, and she deftly caught it, cradling it in both hands. She drew back to the others, where Quinnetra, Fang, and Kerafina had huddled.

Vaelor and Ziggy faced down Estill, but the woman showed no fear.

She loosed her ice shards, and the two 'swords deflected them easily with their blades.

Then a satisfied look came over Estill's face, and she twisted her hand into a fist. The blood spilled on the marble by Allifrey's body drew up in bloody icicles that Estill flung at Vaelor, who had gotten in front.

Quinnetra and Fang came out from behind Fig, a blast of wind preceding them. Fang drew his dagger, ready to fight, when Estill sneered. "You're not taking that," she called to Fig. "Hand it over."

Before the word "no" could leave her tongue, Fig's limbs were seized by a force so strong she felt her legs shuffling forward, her own body moving without...

She looked down and saw the blood shards on the floor.

Water mage. Blood.

A wordless scream ripped from her mouth, which Fang quickly stifled. Having her voice taken from her was almost as bad as some water mage controlling her blood.

Her throat raw from the silent scream, she felt her legs moving her closer and closer to Estill. She couldn't move her arms, though they were still wrapped around the package.

"Give me that," Estill said, a disgustingly satisfied smirk on her face. She swiped for the package, and Fig was unable to stop her. She felt it leave her fingertips but could do nothing about it.

Fig? a voice in her head called.

Rage boiled inside her, trapped in her own limbs. She pictured what the woman could do with her blood, turning it to shards inside her very skin.

Fig? Emrah called.

Not right now, Emrah!

"Wonderful," Estill said, turning her back to them, now that the package was in her hands. She was still ten paces from the doors, but she let Fig drop to her knees. Fig scrambled to right herself, her hands going to the ground.

The ground. It only took seconds to focus on her inner fire and form the connection. Only this time, she needed it to be much, much bigger.

She flung one hand out, envisioning her spark connecting to an imaginary circle on the ground.

One that included Estill.

The flames went up even faster than she'd expected. And they were taller than the last time she'd attempted it.

The smell of burning blood reached Fig's nostrils, and she nearly gagged. Allifrey lay just outside the circle, but the shards of blood were right in the flame circle.

Estill's eyes flashed in Fig's direction. Fig feared the worst—would the mage rupture her insides or force her to walk through her own flames?

But the circle was enough of a distraction for Estill, whose mask of haughtiness slipped for the first time. Vaelor took advantage of the distraction and came up beside her. A sword burst through the water mage, blood spurting out her mouth as she looked down at the blade now sticking out from her middle. Vaelor had reached right through the wall of flames.

Vaelor pulled back, and the package in Estill's hands was seized by a glowing red wind that carried it into Quinnetra's outstretched arms. Her etched face creased in worry, she told them, "We need to get out of here. Now."

Fig looked down at the bodies in and around her fire circle. "Well, what do we do about—"

Fig! Emrah burst through her mind again. *What in Drakioryn's flaming claws is going on?*

Emrah! I'm all right.

A small shadow crossed over the windows above, and Fig looked up. *No, wait. You're not here, are you?*

Panic seized her just as her fire circle surged, doubling in height. No!

The ceilings were high, but the heat of the fire blazed out at everything nearby, lighting the sawdust on the floor like a match to firejack.

Holy Mother Morgha. Fig slammed her hand down on the ground, willing her circle to go away. The circle itself dropped, but the resultant flames licked hungrily at the wooden crates and sawdust, oil-cloths draped over stacks of crates lighting in seconds.

"Go," Quinnetra urged, coming forward.

"But I should—"

"There's no time. The bleaks will be here any second."

Vaelor grabbed Fig's arm and dragged her toward the door. They shut it behind them, instantly drowning in the darkness of the wide hallway.

Gasps ripped from Fig's throat, and she let Vaelor lead her down the hallway. No one asked her to summon any lights.

When they heard boots tramping down the spiral staircase, they huddled together against the side wall and prayed to Morgha that Kerafina's illusion magic worked.

Night librarians and bleaks raced toward the Androzigma Collection. Distantly, Fig remembered that there were often water mages among the librarian staff. She hoped that was the case tonight.

They fled. The rest of their trek through the library was a dark blur for Fig. Betrayal on so many levels coursed through her. At her own limbs for being manipulated by her blood. And at her magic for betraying her yet again.

Finally, she remembered Emrah around the time they were heading into the mail chamber.

Emrah? I'm sorry, I-I went out of control when you showed up. We're going out the back now, by Bilbrey Street.

Got it, he replied.

She sank into the depths of her thoughts once again, and they crept down the final hallway. Fig didn't even care that she'd missed her last sight of the stacks of the great library—a library she'd probably never see again. Certainly not, if they knew what she had done.

It was well past midnight when they emerged outside into the night. Fig sucked in a gulp of air and leaned her back against the building, looking up at the stars. Had they looked so different, only a few hours ago?

"Come on, goldfire," Vaelor said, tugging on her arm.

Ire rose up in her chest and she snapped, "Stop calling me that."

Her fire. She couldn't control even that.

Of course, Afrith's voice whispered in the dark of her mind. *You can't control fire, Fairaleigh. It's not about control.*

She slammed her eyes shut, pushing out the wetness that had gathered there.

A soft chirp brought her eyes open, and a comforting weight dropped onto her shoulder. *I'm sorry*, Emrah said. *I thought something was wrong.*

It's not your fault, Fig said automatically. *Something* was *wrong. But it's over now.*

Good.

Fang led the way. Fig followed numbly, clutching her elbows. Several minutes passed before Fig realized he wasn't leading them back to the flat.

Ziggy noticed at the same time. "Where are we going?" she demanded quietly.

"The Fienn."

"What?" Fig burst, shaking off her dark malaise. "I thought—"

"Evandahl has your ship, and the docks are crawling with bleaks, so you'll be boarding from the riverbank."

"Tonight? Now?" Fig said.

"Aye," Fang said. "Especially now."

Fig's eyes bulged. "But the flat, our things—"

"Evandahl's bringing them."

"I didn't even get to say goodbye to Mairead."

Fang didn't have an answer for that one. Instead, he soldiered on through the back streets of Tirnalore, a city they didn't know well enough to navigate by themselves. A city where they had no resources or friends. A city whose darker parts were run by the Fienn-Da.

Or in some cases, mages owned by Afrith. How had they known about the chalice?

Tears streaming down her face, Fig followed blindly. They were done, weren't they? They had done the job. They could get out of Tirnalore. And Mairead wanted to stay.

He waited a few minutes to tell her, but Emrah finally mentioned that Mairead had been given a room in the hospital's priestess quarters. Fig's heart hardened, and she stopped crying. That was it, then. Mairead was gone anyway.

She clutched her arms, stumbling through another arched doorway in the hidden tunnels the Fienn-Da used to get out of the city unseen.

Then they were once again along the banks of the River Fienn, trudging through the watergrass. Tonight, Vilvan wasn't there to part the grasses for them, so the going was a little more intensive than before. But the moon was brighter, and there were enough of them keeping an eye out that Fig didn't worry about the possibility of a rogue tagor happening upon them.

She wasn't at all surprised when they stopped outside the same cache-house where they had just spent the night. And near the run-down dock across from it, a vessel was anchored on the Fienn, its sails tightly furled. It wasn't large, but it looked seaworthy, both fast and able to move enough cargo to be useful. A smuggler ship.

"Perfect," Fig mumbled.

"I'm glad you think so," a cool voice murmured. Evandahl appeared amid the tall grasses clutching his cane. As soon as they got close, he pulled a narrow sword from the cane's casing, aiming its tip right at Fig.

She froze. She had had quite enough of this tonight.

Quinnetra came around her and wordlessly showed Evandahl the package, perhaps hoping to placate him.

"Well, you've done the job, I see, but just who were those two mages in the Androzigma Collection tonight, dear Fairaleigh?" he said in his lilting voice, low and menacing.

"I don't kno—"

"Oh, but you knew them."

"How do you—"

"I have ears."

Fig glanced at Fang out of the corner of her eye, incredulous. If Evandahl knew about the other mages, he knew everything about the job. Heart racing, she said, "I only recognized one of them. He attacked me the other day at the academy. I hadn't met him before that. He works for Afrith Senaka, who teaches there—"

"Oh, I know well of that snake. But what did you think you would gain from telling his mages where to get the chalice? So they would get it before us? It seems like they almost did."

"I-I didn't, I—"

He yanked the sword away, but swiftly replaced it with his bare hand on her throat. Hot breath in her ear, he told her, "The seed is mine. I knew I was wrong to trust a runaway mage from the Carriage House."

His hand tightened, and she tried to gasp but couldn't.

Emrah chose that moment to swoop over Evandahl, fire building in his belly and scales glowing hot.

Evandahl fell back, tripping, with only the sword to catch his balance. A sweep of red wind righted him, but Quinnetra didn't lift a hand to help him. He didn't look like he would accept one.

"Ah, yes, your *drigone*," he said, rubbing his bearded chin. "You might have plenty of fire to fight with, but you'll not be getting on that ship. You've betrayed your own kind, selling out the job."

"What, mages?" Fig asked incredulously, looking around at the Fienn-Da. They *were* all mages. What were they...

"Of course, mages," Evandahl said. "The chalice contains the single most important thing that could change the way of life for mages everywhere—including your Tytan. And you sold us out to that snake, Afrith. And for what? Were you hoping to trade it to get your prince back? You know they'd still keep you in a cage even if they had this." He hefted the chalice.

"What are you..." Fig shook her head. "What are you talking about? I did *not* tell those mages any of the plans for tonight! I barely found out the details myself before we went! And—and passing over that, they *tried to kill me*. I suppose Fang told you that part, too, right?"

Fang had the courtesy to look a little guilty.

Evandahl had his head tilted down, his face in shadow, but he seemed to be listening.

"They tried to kill me," Fig hissed through her teeth, "and one of them used my blood to force me to hand over the chalice. I distracted her long enough for the others to get it back."

She was not about to elaborate on the extent of the distraction, though she was sure Fang had ratted her out.

Evandahl didn't answer. After a long moment, he began unwrapping the chalice, but kept his gaze on Fig. "Afrith Senaka tried to join the Fienn-Da six years ago, shortly after he arrived to teach at the academy," he said, peeling off the paper wrapped around the thing. "The Bard only knows how he found out about us in the first place. But I could tell he held the ideals of Tytan, despite the amount of time he spends in Tysaine and places abroad. Mages are *kept*. And he *keeps* a lot of mages around here."

"Look," said Fig, "you know he's the one who kidnapped Dev. I would *never* work with him. Why else would I be trying to chase down Dev?"

He finished peeling off the wrapping paper to reveal a dull gold chalice with a few gems studded in the rim. The words *fancy cup* floated through Fig's mind as, yet again, she wondered what was so special about it that it could change the course of history for mages. It didn't look like anything special.

But she hadn't noticed the enclosed top, a lid with a tiny hinge hiding a compartment, which Evandahl was now opening. So it wasn't just a cup, after all.

Evandahl gestured for her to peer closer, and she did so reluctantly. She saw a small seed, similar to an acorn...but with the faintest hint of glowing gold.

"An auran seed?" Fig whispered. "But the aurans don't produce seeds anymore..."

"They haven't for centuries," Evandahl agreed. "The Gold Wood is all that's left of the great auran forests of old. That's why old King Bailemor took it upon himself to claim the Gold Wood as the king's land, to 'protect it.' Only a few lone trees are left scattered across the continent. But this one was collected long ago. It was placed in this chalice by the youngest daughter of a family of explorers, the Androzigma. And it had been forgotten until some recent writing came to light.

"If what you say is true, Veil, I will have to suppose that Afrith happened upon the same writings as I did. He is, of course, a magnificent scholar and a liar."

She took it that was the closest he would come to an apology and remained quiet.

"What are you going to do with it?" asked Ziggy.

"The right thing," Evandahl said, closing the chalice and wrapping the paper back around it. "Whatever that ends up being. But getting to it first was my priority, and I was right in acting so swiftly. If Afrith was after it, others might be as well. With the news of the Tytan coup spreading, things are shifting on the continent, and not in ways that will be good for mages.

"We will keep it safe. What happens next? Well, that might be up to your king."

Fig's mouth opened in surprise. "What? You would plant it in the Gold Wood?"

"Perhaps," Evandahl allowed. "If that is the right course of action. That place does seem to have the right growing conditions. And then, since it is an older seed, perhaps it would produce *more* seeds that could be transferred to Tysaine, and Svora could be made whole again."

They were silent for a minute with only the sound of the river rushing by. Fig thought back to the sad little sapling in the Tirnalore Academy courtyard. If there were more, all across Svora... Magic would be abundant for all mages everywhere. The dream was so profound, it almost hurt.

"Very well," Evandahl said. "Quinnetra, you're on."

Quinnetra nodded, shook hands with Evandahl, and strode toward the ship. Fig and the others stood frozen in uncertainty.

"Are you lot coming?" she called back.

Fig could hardly believe it.

"May the Bard go easy on you," Evandahl said. "And if you don't find what you're looking for, Fairaleigh, you're welcome to come back to the Fienn."

Fig bit her lip and nodded. *Not likely,* she thought. Did he mean join the Fienn-Da? After he'd nearly choked her not ten minutes ago? She couldn't think of anything to say that wouldn't damage their already tenuous relationship, so she left it at the nod. The promise of the Fienn-Da's mission to better lives for mages was like dangling a feast in front of her starving mouth. But it would mean working for Evandahl, and she wasn't exactly sanguine about that idea just now.

Quinnetra stood on the small dock, and Fig hurried to catch up. Suddenly she found herself having to say goodbye to Fang, a prospect she hadn't realized would bring sadness.

She lifted her hand in farewell to Evandahl, wondering when he would cross their paths again. He held the auran seed in its package close to his side. Fig could only hope the "right thing" actually was right for everyone.

A rope ladder fell over the side of the vessel, courtesy of Vilvan, who was already aboard. Quinnetra shunned the ladder, using a red gust of wind to lift herself up and over the rail.

Fig grabbed a rung and hauled herself up as Emrah took wing.

On the deck, she gazed up at the stars, then back at the silhouettes of Tirnalore's spires in the distance. The sound of river grass rustled in the stiff breeze that would take them down the river.

CHAPTER 42

MAIREAD

Mairead smiled to herself as she lifted her new red robes over her head and settled them across her shoulders, her skin warm and soft from the bath and lotions. Her old robes had probably been burned as an offering to Morgha, covered in blood as they were.

The priestess quarters of the hospital boasted a lovely bathing room, and robes and underclothes were available for any of the sisters. It was like being back in Mar Nevan but better.

Here, her purpose was focused on other people and not on herself. Here, she could be curious and ask questions, and no one even scolded her.

She only wished she had done a better job of breaking the news to Fig. She could try to talk to her again tomorrow. Emrah had let slip that the heist was happening tonight. He had left the hospital a few hours ago, while Mairead was elbow deep in a late-night healing. Since she had been given quarters at the Narndian, she didn't expect him to return tonight.

She left the bathing room to head to her new chambers. She would ask permission from the head priestess to visit the flat in the morning.

Perhaps Fig would return to Tirnalore again someday. Her friend certainly had an eye for learning, despite leaving her own mage training early. Still, Mairead could tell that Fig respected knowledge and books and learning. She just didn't fit into the institution, a sentiment that Mairead had shared until recently. But Mairead just hadn't found the right institution until now. The Narndian would be her new home. She could worship in the cathedral, a dream almost too good to be true, and she could heal at the hospital, where people from all over Tysaine came seeking the help of the sisters. Morgha's love was alive and well in Tysaine.

And Mairead would never be asked to perform a crossover for a silversword ever again.

It was incredibly late, so the hallways in the sister's quarters were dark, but she found her way by the moonlight slanting in through the window at the end of the hallway. She glanced up at the doors she passed, trying to remember which was hers.

But as she turned her head, she thought she saw a dark shadow behind her.

Then something came down over her head, blocking her vision. As she struggled against the cloth, multiple hands secured her limbs. She fought against her captors until ropes replaced hands that dragged her, stumbling, around corners and forced her down flights of stairs. Her heart pounded furiously beneath her new robes. Then fear struck as she smelled the night air.

She fought harder. The ropes cut into her skin despite the layers her robes provided; they were laced around her so tight. Not only had they put a sack over her head, but a gag across her mouth over the sack, and her spit soaked the thing as she tried to scream for help.

If only Emrah had stayed to watch over her.

Though, he of course was leaving with the others the next day, and she was supposed to be safe at the Narndian.

Who would even notice that Mairead was missing?

Her limbs were tiring from the struggle, and her mind began to slow. The sisters might notice, but if a priestess who had only just arrived in Tirnalore disappeared, would they even care? And Fig and the others... They had their job at the library, and then they would be off on their quest to rescue Dev. Mairead had already left them.

A final attempt at kicking her captor left her exhausted in their arms. She could do no more.

PART

IV

BLACK ICE

The salty breeze did nothing to enliven Fig's senses as she stepped out onto the deck. But she came up to the deck just the same, if only to feel the sun on her face. It was the third time today she'd left her cabin, though she hadn't spoken to anyone all day...or for the past couple of days.

Vilvan was there as usual, manning the ship. And as usual, he said nothing to her; he only nodded and kept his focus. Between him and Quinnetra, the sails were always full, and the water listened to Vilvan like no one else. Vilvan, however, seemed less than pleased to be sailing the Hollow Sea, and from what Fig had gathered from the comments that passed between the dryad and Quinnetra, this was Vilvan's punishment for letting Fig and the others trespass on Fienn-Da land in the first place.

They were rounding the northernmost coast of Tysaine and would soon find the Hollow Isles in sight. Dread filled Fig's senses with every passing hour until she could barely make herself leave the cabin she shared with Ziggy. Under different circumstances, she would've shared with Mairead. But Mairead had chosen to leave and was happy at the Narndian now, an ever-present reminder that Fig's friendship had meant nothing to the girl.

Fig also had nothing to show for their stop in Tirnalore, besides the book of fire magic she'd barely learned anything from. She still knew nothing about her connection with Emrah and had only managed to learn one new spell that could possibly help her against Afrith.

She was a pathetic fire mage and a pathetic friend. She had let Dev get kidnapped and hadn't been happy for Mairead when she found her place at the Narndian. And the closer they came to the Hollow Isles, the more it seemed they were sailing toward their death. A suicide mission to save the heir to the Rayvan throne—an heir they had no way of installing on that throne.

The Hollow Isles had been Dev's last hope from the beginning—a non-existent army he wanted to enlist, his only allies from his mother's homeland. But then there were the rumors of Shadryn. Were they true or not?

When *had* the rumor of mage blood being incompatible with the silversword crossover started, anyway? Fig remembered hearing about it well before Shadryn's crossover. And the stories about the elder prince's death had all been centered around one thing: their mother Eileigh's betrayal of Haemond and the kingdom keeping her mage blood a secret. But if she had lived long enough to see her sons readying to become silverswords, she would have stopped them, right?

Heavy footsteps sounded on the deck, and Fig rolled her eyes. Speaking of silverswords. She had managed to avoid everyone until now.

Ziggy headed over to join her at the rail. "Not long now," Ziggy said, irritatingly.

Fig grunted in reply.

"You know your problem, Fig?"

The alchemy of emotions in her chest boiled to a high point, and she whirled to face the silversword. *"What?"* she hissed with venom. "I'd love to know, especially coming from *you.*"

Ziggy merely smirked. Fig would love to wipe that smile off her stupid face, but that carried the risk of burning down the *Trevena,* and she had worked hard to keep her fire magic inside since coming aboard, particularly with Emrah's proximity.

"You've had too much freedom."

Fig scoffed. "I suppose that's a problem?"

"You've tasted the unknown and seen beyond the bars and know that life could be different. You left your little mage training house and saw the world for what it could be. Do you know the first thought I had when I woke up halfway into Tysaine?"

"You hated us."

"No. *Finally. Finally I'm free.* If you know anything, you'll know I never wanted to be a silversword. Ever. Didn't want to cross over, Welded to Mystic, here. Yes, I know it's a dumb name."

"I don't think it's—"

"But even though I was worried about my family back in Viren, I realized I was free of the regime. Free of the enclave. I'd crossed a line with Liess, and there was no going back.

"Before I crossed over, there was the war. And even if Viren was victorious, I'd be the heir to Ashbrok the rest of my life since my brother had died. Never free. Chained to Ashbrok if we won or chained to my sword when we lost."

Fig knew there had been a third option, but Ziggy didn't even mention it. Laying down her life would have meant her family wouldn't have survived either.

Ziggy put her hand comfortably on her sword. "When you get past the bars, Fig, you can see a little more clearly. And in some cases, too clear. Things aren't as shiny as they looked from the other side. They're gray and ugly up close."

"Thanks for the thoroughly generic advice," Fig mumbled. "Very inspiring."

Ziggy grabbed Fig's shirtfront and forced Fig to look at her. Fig struggled a little but for some reason didn't care.

"I wasn't done," Ziggy said. "The important thing is that you made it. You're here. Whether everything shiny on the way has lost its polish or the people in your life didn't follow your expectations. You. Are. Here. You've made it this far. You can seize whatever you want and make it yours."

"Why do you care, Ziggy?"

Ziggy let go with a little push. "I care, because we're on our way to rescue your friend the king, and you've barely lifted a finger on this boat, let alone made any attempt to prepare."

"Oh, so you're worried I won't pull my weight when we get to Nithe," Fig said, returning her elbows to the railing to look out at the water.

"You lost one friend in Tirnalore, but you gained a network of allies for King Devryn. Quit moping about it and get to work."

"I'm glad we're done with the vagaries," Fig said. "It wasn't very becoming of you, the whole big sister routine."

"That's right," Ziggy said with a swagger. "I *am* the big sister, so you'd better listen to me. You and Emrah are going to work on your fire magic tonight, since that's your biggest hangup, and we're running out of time."

"What? No. With him, I'll burn down the ship."

"I already talked to him and Vilvan and Quinnetra about it."

"What about Vaelor?" Fig said.

"What about me?" Vaelor said, coming up from below with half a smile on his lips. His hair looked different; his braids had all come out, and it was swept back into a simple half-knot.

"Fig was just looking for more excuses not to practice."

"Hmm," Vaelor commented, joining them at the rail on Fig's other side.

"This doesn't feel fair, you two ganging up on me like this," Fig said, but the tension was already dissipating. "You could both literally kill me in seconds, and here you are trying to peer pressure me."

"We're not quite peers, then, are we," Ziggy mused.

Fig sighed in reluctant acceptance. She didn't have much of a choice. Afrith would be at the Hollow Isles, and she didn't think he would let them take Dev without a fight. "Fine. But I want Vilvan standing by ready to put out any fires."

He's already agreed to that, Emrah said, swooping over and tossing something into Fig's hands.

"Hey!" she said, grabbing the fire magic book. "I could have missed, and that would have gone overboard, you know?"

"Ah, the talking scaly bird's here," Ziggy said. "Pity I can't get it out of my head."

And it's a pity I can't get your smell out of my nose, 'sword, but here we are, Emrah told them all with a snort of sparks from his nose.

Fig glanced incredulously between them. When had they gotten on such chummy terms? *Probably while they were ganging up on me earlier,* she thought grumpily.

"Well, where do I start? I can't exactly do the ring of fire here." Fig gestured at the deck.

Ziggy waved her hands. "No. You've already figured that one out, anyway."

"Not really," Fig said. "It went horribly at the library."

"No," Ziggy said slowly, "it went just right. It just got...out of control when Emrah came near."

"And he's pretty near right now," Fig said in a mock whisper, "if you hadn't noticed."

"I don't think 'too much power' is going to be the problem when we get to Nithe," Ziggy said. "If you don't think you're a match for Afrith, more power seems like the answer."

"But I can't control it."

A hand clasped her arm, and Fig looked up at Vaelor, who was giving her a stern look. Those silver-ringed eyes glowered at her, as if saying, *Stop making excuses.* A light shiver ran up her spine, and she looked away.

If she were being honest with herself, her excuse rubbed her the wrong way, too, like she was petting dragonet scales backward. Control. Hadn't she realized before she just needed to set boundaries for the chaos incited by the flames?

Control was an illusion, a piece of advice that had cost her too much.

She bit her lip and sauntered out to the middle of the ship to catch Vilvan's attention. When she was satisfied he was all right with the plan and ready to throw sea water on any rogue fires, she sat down in the middle of the ship with the book and began looking for something that would help them defeat Afrith.

"Actually, I marked a few," Ziggy offered.

"Seriously?" Fig said.

Ziggy shrugged. "You've been moping about. I didn't have a lot to do besides watch the waves."

Fig's face warmed at Ziggy's apparent interest. She went to the first page Ziggy had marked by folding over the top of the page—cringing inwardly at the mistreatment of the paper—and found a spell on flaming arrows. She frowned. "I was never good at archery," she remarked.

"You don't need to be!" Ziggy said, lurching forward and kneeling nearby, pointing at the page. "It says no bow involved."

"Wow, you really did read this, didn't you?"

"I said I was bored," Ziggy sniffed. "There was nothing else to read."

Fig smiled, narrowing her eyes at Ziggy in amusement. "Fine, I'll try it." Ziggy retreated to the rail by Vaelor, wearing a purposefully patient expression.

Fig read the page thoroughly, trying not to feel everyone's eyes on her. Emrah had settled on the rail beside the others, wings tucked in tight so as not to catch any wind. When she thought she understood the spell, she put the book under some heavy coils of rope piled near the mast to keep it safe. Sometimes the gusts of wind rattling through the Hollow Sea caught her off guard.

Feeling even more stupid than when she'd practiced in the basement of the Fienn-Da's cellar, she rubbed her hands together, preparing to try the spell. She turned her back on the others, hoping to aim over the starboard side.

She kept rubbing her hands far out in front of her. She could feel the sparks beneath her skin, begging to come out. She cast out her senses, the strong scent of salty air bringing with it its own magic. She wondered idly if there was magic everywhere, not just in the Gold Wood. The *solanse*, the sea, it all held *something*. She pulled a deep breath into her lungs, and then another.

Drawing her right hand back as if pulling a bowstring, she tried to do what she had done with the fire circle and connect with her inner flame, following the connection to a spark in her veins. Flames gathered at her right hand near her chin, and she let them strengthen for a second before letting go, picturing an arrow sailing overboard.

The fire sparked and fell to the deck in front of her.

"Bard's quill!" she cursed, staring down in panic at the errant sparks. But they fizzled out and died all on their own. She stomped her boot on them just in case, but mostly just moved the black marks around on the hard wood. She refused to look at the others as she stalked back to the book for another look.

Emrah flitted over and landed on her shoulder, peering at the page.

I don't know why you need to do this fancy fire work, he said. *I've gotten by just fine without anything like that.*

Well, neither of us got by too well when we went up against Afrith in the solanse, Fig said.

Hmm, agreed. But in my defense, I was unconscious for the fight since he'd managed to poison me. What's that say there about hardening your flames?

Fig looked at him pensively. *You can read?*

He fluttered back, gray sparks sifting from his wings. *Of course I can read!*

"Well, excuse me for not knowing everything about dragonets!" Fig replied aloud.

Emrah snorted, sparks extinguished. *Well, not all of us can. I'll give you that.*

"I'm sorry, Emrah. What were you pointing out?" Fig said slowly.

Hardening your flames. It says it right there. He pointed his tail with more than a little attitude at the exact spot on the page.

"That's something Afrith can do," Fig said. "I saw it when he bound Dev's hands." Fig frowned, flipping through the pages looking for anything more about hardening flames. She saw the words in the instructions for a few other spells, then finally, on a page of its own.

"What's going on over there?" Ziggy called, after a few minutes of inaction.

"This isn't like the training you're used to, I'm sure," Fig said without looking back. "But I think I need to master 'hardening the flames' before I can try that arrow spell."

It's something that maniac Afrith could do, Emrah told the others.

"Then you need to do it too," Ziggy said.

After a few more minutes of watching Fig stare at the page, Ziggy grumbled something about her stomach being empty and went belowdecks to rummage through the supplies Evandahl had left them. Vaelor wandered over to look at Fig's book. Emrah fluttered over to watch Vilvan work at the prow.

Fig straightened her back as she sensed Vaelor's gaze on the book in her lap. "Come sit," she said, an odd thrill running through her as she patted the deck beside her and he acquiesced.

He was surprisingly light on his feet for his size as he folded his legs underneath him and joined her. Her face warmed when he saw her watching him. She looked back down at the page.

"I never even knew you *could* harden flames," she said, then sighed. She held in her complaints about quitting the Carriage House. She was sure even Vaelor had heard enough of it by now. And the last thing she wanted was another lecture like Ziggy's. But she had barely talked to Vaelor since they'd gotten on the ship, and things felt off between them somehow.

"Listen," Fig told him, "I'm sorry I snapped at you the other night after the heist. I was out of control in the Androzigma Collection. I could have hurt you, could have hurt everyone. I always thought I was good enough at fire magic. Fire is just dangerous in its most basic form, and I thought that was enough."

"It is enough," he said fervently in a quiet voice. "Fire is dangerous. I've seen it damage plenty."

"That's true," Fig acknowledged. She had put out enough fires in her life.

"Maybe you don't need any of these"—he paused, waving his hands vaguely—"special spells. Maybe you already have enough."

She shook her head, hair falling into her face. "It's not enough. I'm not enough, not against Afrith."

"You *are* enough," Vaelor said, reaching over and sweeping a strand of hair behind her ear. She looked up into his eyes, her chest rising.

"And I'll take care of Afrith," he added, his words practically a growl.

"I'd like to see that," Fig said, her heart racing. "I just don't know what else is waiting for us in Nithe."

Picture yourself in the Gold Wood, Emrah said a few hours later. She was at the back of the ship now, where no rogue flames would come near the sails, throwing flames over the side into the growing dark. Silver eyes from the midship told her Vaelor still watched her practice.

Though she was no closer to figuring out how to harden her flames or shoot an arrow, a few hours of practice with Emrah had brought her spirits up.

The dragonet landed on the rail near her and continued, *If my presence affects you that much, just pretend you're in the Gold Wood whenever I'm near. Expect the amplification.*

Fig nodded. "Of course, it makes sense when you say it like that," she muttered.

Emrah snorted. *Well, I've lived in the Gold Wood for a long time,* he said.

Does it affect your fire at all? Fig wondered.

He snuffed and shook his head. *No, it's always the same for me. The trees only seem to affect you mages.*

Fig pressed her lips together.

Go again.

She twisted her wrist and released the flames so they flowed out the back of the ship over their wake. Vilvan had assured her they were far enough from any ports or shipping lanes that no one would see them.

She pictured glittering gold all around her, as if she were again surrounded by the aurans. She played with the size of the flames, adjusting her expectations before trying something new. Twisting her hand, she separated the flames into two ribbons, then sent them in different directions. It was basic fire magic, but keeping anything unexpected from happening was the true aim of the exercise.

Emrah flew away, perhaps to catch another fish. She kept up the flames, gradually getting up to eight small strands before wondering if the dragonet was coming back.

Did you fall in or something? she asked him.

A snorting sound came through their connection. *No, I'm seeing how far away I can get before it affects your magic. Has it wavered at all?*

Not at all. She stared at the eight ribbons of flame trailing from her fingers. They looked the same. She wondered if she could divide them into sixteen strands.

Suddenly Emrah swooped up from below, coming close to her flames.

"Woah!" she called.

Focus!

She returned her attention back to the flames, but they had only briefly flared up, and she suspected that resulted from the surprise more than Emrah's proximity.

That was great, Fig! Emrah cheered.

She carefully let the flames drop, and as her eyes adjusted to the darkness once more, she asked him, *How far away did you get?*

Far enough for the test, I think.

She shrugged, giving herself a small smile. She had barely lost focus, and her flames hadn't bloomed much larger at all with his nearness.

A door opened midship, and Fig turned to see Ziggy poke her head out. "Dinner?" she asked, though it didn't sound like much of a question. Fig had eaten all of her previous meals when no one else was in the galley, and apparently that hadn't gone unnoticed.

Fig couldn't say no, and surprisingly, she felt no need to. Maybe all of her practice with Emrah had burned away her disappointments—at Mairead's departure and at her own abilities. She followed Ziggy and Vaelor into the captain's quarters, where Quinnetra had started setting up. Emrah landed on Fig's shoulder with an affectionate head bump to her cheek.

Though Vilvan stayed at the helm, and these were technically his quarters, it was clear he had no need for them. They appeared as fresh as the cleanest tavern room, the crisp bedsheets untouched and dust on the built-in bookshelves.

Fig wasn't surprised that the dryad would shun an indoor space. What *did* surprise her was the food the Fienn-Da had provided for them. She hadn't expected homemade Bard's pie aboard a ship taking an illegal voyage to the Hollow Isles. Steam wafted from the mashed potatoes, carrots, and ground shafra meat when Quinnetra set a plate down in front of her.

She blinked up at the woman who peered back down at her. "What? We're smugglers, not animals. That doesn't mean we all have no taste in food."

Ziggy yanked out the chair next to Fig, saying, "Spend a lot of time cooking on ships then?"

"My fair share," Quinnetra replied. "We all do what's fair."

"Fair for mages, though, it seems like," Ziggy said, pulling her own plate closer as soon as Quinnetra set it down. "How come Evandahl didn't tell us his organization was made up entirely of mages?"

"He's our leader," Quinnetra said, placing another plate in front of Vaelor, who was on Fig's other side. Squashed between the two silverswords, she knew she'd have trouble managing her silverware at the small table, but she wasn't about to complain. Quinnetra took her own plate and sat across from Fig, while Emrah took off to land on the shelf facing the windows.

Moonlight glittered across the water in their wake, making the ripples appear like broken glass. Fig tucked into her meal, and upon the first bite, wondered how ship food could possibly be as delicious as what she'd eaten back at Resbrok. Her heart clenched, remembering their time in the *solanse*, and her gaze slid to Vaelor. He caught her eye with a soft smile, and she looked back down at her plate, heart racing.

Suddenly he felt a thousand times closer, the skin of his arm a thousand times warmer when she accidentally brushed against him when using her knife.

Emrah looked like he was about to curl up and go to sleep. Fig didn't blame him, after all of the flying and fishing he'd done while she practiced magic. She longed for her own lumpy hard bunk, which had done her no favors last night.

But the food was delicious, and when Ziggy ribbed Quinnetra into bringing up a bottle of Tysainian wine, the company became more boisterous. A feeling of warmth filled Fig's core, and she realized that it outweighed the heavy feeling that had settled on her chest after the library job. Vaelor, Ziggy, and Emrah were here; she wouldn't have to face Afrith alone. And though she didn't expect them to assist them with Dev's rescue, Quinnetra and Vilvan represented the support of the Fienn Da. Emrah, despite the racket, did indeed fall asleep, and they all spent a moment admiring the curl of smoke that came out of his nostrils.

Fig shared a glance with Vaelor, her heart doing another little flip when she met his silver-ringed eyes.

She tore her gaze away and seized her wineglass. Sure, he was here, and sure, he was handsome, but he was just a silversword pledged to Dev; that had to be the only reason he had stayed.

But then his large hand suddenly covered hers, feeling like golden sunlight on her skin. "Goldfire, I—"

A dark red stain spilled across the tablecloth, and Ziggy yelped, reaching for her wineglass. Fig leapt from her seat.

"Bard's quill, 'sword," Quinnetra complained with a smirk. "Aren't you supposed to be better at everything than the rest of us?"

With the wine clean up underway, Fig decided to get some air. She said her farewells and left Emrah snoozing by the window—she doubted Vilvan would care if the dragonet slept there—and went up on deck.

She sensed Vaelor's approach before he joined her at the rail.

"I was just thinking about the library," she said, seizing a topic at random. Though Vilvan dutifully manned the helm, it felt as though she and Vaelor were the only two in all of the Hollow Sea, the blanket of stars a velvety expanse above them.

"Hmm." He rested his elbows on the railing, looking out at the water.

"I...I'm glad we got the seed, but I wish I hadn't..." She paused, clearing her throat. "I could have killed any of you. I was lucky no one was in the way."

"But we weren't," he said. "Only those briigards of Afrith's."

No matter how often she tried not to think about it, she was frequently plagued with intrusive thoughts of the night librarians or bleaks discovering their bodies amid the flames and ash. Though she hadn't killed them, it felt like she had.

She sighed, still not looking at him.

"I feel like I'm a brand-new mage again," she confessed. "Since bonding with Emrah, or whatever this is, everything is so strange."

"I felt...a similar way after my crossover," he admitted slowly.

"What was it like for you after?" Fig asked quietly.

"Like everything had changed, yet somehow it was still so similar to how it was before. For a long time, I felt like..." He paused for so long, Fig was sure he wouldn't finish the thought. The only sounds between them were the lapping of water on the hull and the wind in their ears.

"I felt like I wasn't me," he finally said. "I was changed. Never to return to my old life with my family, no longer worthy of happiness or peace. No longer worthy of anything good." His voice broke.

She opened her mouth in indignation and finally turned to him. "Vaelor, you deserve goodness in your life." She reached out and grabbed his hand as her eyes met his. Her breath hitched, and a strange tightness hit her chest. "You deserve—"

But his lips were on hers, the space between them obliterated. A spark rippled through her, and she responded with equal force, moving her lips in unison with his. The sharp scent of steel in her nose was not unpleasant. Warmth filled her core, even though she knew her fire magic was safely contained. His lips crushed against hers, his hand moving to rake along her jaw.

They broke apart, gasping. Fig couldn't take her eyes off Vaelor's. She was still holding his hand. Her face warming, she started to pull away, but he stopped her.

"Don't," he said, curling her hand into his. His gaze locked on her as if she might disappear if he looked away.

The next kiss was gentle, pushing all thoughts of rogue fire magic and the briigard Afrith from her mind. Yet she couldn't help but think she was dealing with something far, far more dangerous.

CHAPTER

45

Dev stepped onto the black sands of the Hollow Isles for the first time in thirteen years. Green moss and rolling hills towered above them past the beach where they had landed. The last time he'd been here, he'd come with his mother and Shadryn. They'd been mere boys at the time. Their mother had shown them around the different islands, taking them high up to the Falls of Aerinsur, then down to the meadows to watch the goats frolic about on the ancient stones littering the island of Nithe like an overturned marstone board. Stopping by the farmhouses in the village for meat pies and to harry the shafra in their fields.

But now the little village on the valley floor was run-down, with gaunt, tired faces disappearing the moment he spotted them. No goats or shafra roamed the streets or gnawed on grass in their pens.

Even the grass and moss seemed less green, although that might be the result of the cold front that had settled on the island, far too brisk for this time of year. Dev shivered in his coat, arching up his shoulders. If he fought his cuffs, he could generate some heat, he thought facetiously. He glanced over at Afrith, who walked beside him wearing a new emerald-colored cloak, its collar lined in black velvet. The man had also brought a staff Dev hadn't seen before; it had a matching green emerald within a bold cage of gold set atop it. Dev had spent their brief stay in Tirnalore locked in a tiny basement, but apparently Afrith had done some shopping, among whatever nefarious plots he'd set into place. Dev had heard lots of footsteps and muffled voices from his basement confinement.

Dev looked up from the valley but couldn't yet see the castle. "Can we do away with the restraints now?" Dev complained. "You got me here—I'm on Nithe. But I'd like to enter the halls of my forebears unshackled."

Afrith considered it for a moment, then, surprisingly, flicked his wrist. The cuffs disappeared.

Dev closed his eyes, allowing himself half a second to savor the blissful feeling. When he drew his hands apart from one another, it was as if a magnet still kept them together. Pulling them apart was a slow affair, almost as if the muscles had begun to resign themselves to the position for the rest of his life.

Well, let's hope my life goes on a bit longer, Dev thought as they passed a group of stones set in a circle around a stone monolith.

It wasn't lost on him that he could now perform his own magic. Unfortunately, he was sure that Afrith was on the alert for that too. And he had to admit, he *was* curious about what lay ahead.

He tore his gaze from the towering monolith. Who *did* sit on the Hollow throne? Could what Afrith said possibly be true, and not the inane scribblings of the Bard on scraps of paper, only to be tossed in a great celestial fire like so many other dead ends?

It took almost no time to traverse the short valley, with no farmers stopping to greet them and no bleating animals in their way. No, the farmers were shut up in their farmhouses, pathetic plumes of smoke rising from their chimneys in weak attempts at fires. There were no delicious scents of stew or pasties baking, only a horrible sense of dereliction. *They've been blockaded and sanctioned for so many years,* Dev thought.

But had all this been the result of his father's actions? He shook his head. No, this was something else. The Hollow Isles had been a vibrant country, supporting themselves with their farms and fishing. *The blockade didn't do this. Preventing the island of Kildaria from trading their renowned metalwork didn't do this.* The emptiness of the island felt strange, and a hollow pit formed in Dev's stomach.

The ground hardened, and the air became colder the higher they climbed. As they trudged up the dirt path, they watched a fog roll in and cover the bottom of the valley, distorting their view of the beach. Black sands gave way to dark earth, once rich with minerals. Now the grass looked dead, frostbitten. No birds flew anywhere.

It wasn't until he saw the castle that he first spotted the ice, black as night and splintering in icicles from the outcroppings of rocks on the path to the castle steps.

He clenched his fists.

They walked up the steps, where he and his brother had played while Mother had discussions with her great-uncle, who ruled the Hollow Isles back then. Black icicles covered the black rocks, jutting out in points at every turn of the staircase.

They passed through black doors that swung open with ease, making almost no sound.

Hollow Castle.

It wasn't large, by any means. He could see the throne from the door, but it was far enough that he couldn't make out the face of the man sitting there.

A chill bit through his clothes, and his breath clouded before him as they walked forward. Suddenly everything in Dev's body told him to flee, to use his magic, to run.

But he had to know. Afrith led him forward, and the icy chill sank deeper into his chest with every step.

The man on the throne stood, a scepter in his hand—no, a spear—with black ice encrusting the metal tip. A swath of dark brown hair surrounded his no longer handsome face.

"Hello, brother," the man said.

On the morning of his brother's crossover, Dev had evaded his tutors and snuck through the servants' halls in the castle, hoping to find a back way into the Red Chapel before the ceremony started so he could watch. Dev would also be going through the crossover in a few years, and he had only heard rumors about the transformation. It was ludicrous that even his brother, the crown prince, hadn't been told what the process entailed. But Dev wanted to be prepared, and he didn't trust Shadryn to impart the secret knowledge to him once it was over.

Dev had already picked out his weapon to be Welded to, even though he was only twelve and would need to wait six more years. The Verrence Armory held a curated collection of weapons for anyone of the Verrence line to choose from. Dev had chosen a sword. Not the most unique item, but it was familiar, and it was a lifetime commitment. Besides, swords were powerful, and that was exactly what he wanted enhanced.

Finally, Dev found what he was looking for. Niel Ganivan, one of the castle brats, had led him back here the other day, and Dev thought it might lead near the Red Chapel—a back hallway with discreet slivers of windows looking over the main chapel area, where he could see in and not be seen.

The large fount stood at the center of the otherwise empty grand stone room, in a well of its own at the bottom of several steps. Even here, at the seat of the Rayvan throne, the fount resembled a stone well, as it did in every other chapel. Dev always found it strange that there was no further prestige in the red sisters' worship. Didn't their goddess deserve more devotion than a stack of stones in a circle to hold her most holy of water?

Dev shook his head. He would be bound to Morgha once he'd crossed over as well.

A door slammed inside the chapel, and Dev leaned closer to the opening he had chosen, hand upon the ledge. A thrill ran through him. He was breaking the enclave's laws and must not be discovered, but he had to know.

His brother Shadryn paced into the empty room, hands behind his back, head down in thought. Dev wondered if pre-crossover solitude was a requirement or if his brother had decided to come to the chapel early.

He was just glad he wouldn't have to beg Shad for secondhand details. Every silversword who'd crossed over suddenly became too good to divulge anything about the process, even to the princes. Well, that was about to change for Dev. He'd taken matters into his own hands.

Shad continued his pacing, his normally calm-if-pretentious features becoming more anxious by the minute. So much for the great speech about becoming a man Shad had given him last night before bed.

Finally, Shad went over to the fount, staring at it ponderously for several minutes. Dev could see the surface of the water reflecting his brother's face.

Then Shad reached out a finger to touch the water, and Dev's mouth hung open at the sacrilege. Curiosity, perhaps?

Except the surface of the water had frozen over, blue ice splintering out in spiderwebs across the surface.

Ice. Magic.

"What?" Dev mouthed, incredulous.

The sound of voices carried into the chapel, and in the next instant, the door burst open to reveal their father, King Haemond, who greeted his son solemnly. Behind him trailed the top members of the enclave and a column of red sisters. It was time.

In a panic, Dev looked at the surface of the water, but the ice was gone. It had disappeared. He stood still, his hands once again behind his back, as he waited for the 'swords to line the stone steps on one side and the sisters on the other.

"No," Dev whispered, hands scrambling along the ledge as he tried to get to his feet in the narrow passage. *No, he can't.*

He had to get inside the chapel. He had to stop them. Mages couldn't be turned silversword. Everyone knew that. Including Shadryn.

His brother knew he was a mage and was doing it anyway.

"I have to stop them," Dev said silently to no one. All the silverswords said Svoran blood was cursed, right? There must be a reason for it. "I have to—"

But the ceremony had begun. One of the red sisters used her dagger to slice open Shad's palm, and Dev couldn't tear his gaze away. How would he even get to the chapel entrance from here? It would take perhaps ten minutes, and by then...

"I should stop him," he repeated. The sister poured holy water into Shad's palm, mixing it with the blood. Then she dipped her finger into the bloody water to write a series of runes down his chosen weapon—a spear, like he'd always favored. It was to the point and deadly from afar.

But when the head of the enclave took up the spear with its bloody runes and thrust it into Shadryn's chest in a killing blow, Dev knew he was far, far too late.

Shad fell onto his back, the spear sticking out grotesquely. But no one in the chamber faltered or showed any interest other than the one sister who inspected the runes written on the spear in blood and holy water. She knelt beside him—the crown prince of Tytan, dying of the spear wound—and did nothing about it.

Dev's fingers clenched the ledge so hard bits splintered off under his fingernails. Was this it? This was the ritual? Or had they discovered he was a mage and killed him for it?

How *did* a silversword become Welded to their weapon?

That was what he had come here to find out.

Sweat fell down his brow as he watched. Was this supposed to be how it went? Shouldn't they be trying to heal Shad with the holy waters?

The king's face was impassive but proud. Dev knew his father had no love for the head of the enclave, some bloodthirsty briigard always calling for war. He must not want to show any weakness in front of the man. He had made a perfect speech last night at their small family dinner about all the wonderful things Shad would accomplish now that he was joining the long line of Verrence silverswords.

Seconds dragged on into minutes, and Dev saw his brother's hand fall limp to the floor.

Two red sisters approached him with ladles full of holy water. Another two placed their hands on the weapon and pulled. They began pouring the holy water over the wound, laying their tattooed hands on the bloody mess. Dev's heart pounded. Red glowed from the backs of their hands, and more water was doused. Blood and water ran down the steps as they poured and poured and poured.

Nothing.

Had they waited too long? Was it...

Tendrils of black began to snake up his brother's arms, and several sisters let out a gasp, one of them scrambling away from Shadryn's body.

The king stood, his hand on his own weapon.

"What is this?" Rhivven demanded.

"Keep pouring," the king commanded. "You haven't healed him yet."

The sister who had scrambled away went back to the fount, like the others, but after several minutes of more blood and water, it became clear. Shadryn wasn't coming back.

Dev stared at his brother's body, realizing that the black tendrils were actually his veins—his blood... What in the name of the Bard...

"Mage blood," one of the silverswords spat. "There's no other explanation."

"It has to be something else," the king said, his chin high as he stood over his son's body. "That's impossible."

Two of the red sisters were whispering to one another, and finally the older one, her gray hair streaming out from under her red hood in long swaths, approached them. "Is it not possible, Your Majesty, that it came from...your departed queen?"

Cold gripped Dev's heart. How? How could Shadryn *have* Svoran blood?

And why, *why* had he willingly done the crossover when he'd already known?

Dev had known, and he hadn't stopped him.

Could have stopped him. Could have shouted from his hidey-hole here, despite breaking the enclave's laws about crossovers. Could have found a way to the front of the chapel, burst in, and told them all...what? That Shadryn was a mage?

Their mother...

As hot tears carved their way down his face, he stared at his brother's body, knowing he could have stopped this.

And he would never be able to set down that guilt for as long as he lived.

Dev fell to his knees, digging his fingers into the fabric at his thighs. *No. Yes. His brother Shadryn was alive...or...*

Black veins stood out at the edges of his pale white face and ran along his pale muscled arms. He wore a crown of jagged black ice.

"Brother," Dev choked, "y-you're here." His first words were the stupidest that could have come from his mouth.

"In the flesh," Shadryn said, holding his arms out, one of which carried the very spear that...

"How? *How?*" Dev demanded. "I-I saw you die at your crossover. You knew you were a mage, and—"

"Oh, you knew about that, did you?" Shadryn said, a hint of the old mirth in his face as he paced slowly toward Dev. "Yes, I died. That's what happens when you cross over. It just took longer for me to come back than the enclave and sisters expected with my Svoran blood complicating things."

"But I—"

"Father refused to believe Mother had Svoran blood, and so, after everyone was gone, he dragged one of the sisters back in to try to revive me. It took a little longer, and then Father whisked me onto the next boat out of Tytan with my new friend, the old woman who'd brought me back to life. She, of course, couldn't be allowed to let anyone know what an abomination I had become. Her words, not mine, after we left Tytan."

Shadryn stood only eight feet away now. He was dressed in all black like the ice surrounding the castle, black boots were laced to mid-calf, and a shining black crown sat upon his head. "Stand, Devryn. Get up."

Dev, still gaping at his brother, realized he was kneeling on the floor. He hastily got to his feet and cast an incredulous glance at Afrith. Had he known all of this? And for how long?

"And...and what happened to the red sister?" Dev asked, his mind working fast. He had a thousand questions, but he kept them simple...for now.

"Oh, she came with me to Nithe. But without regular replenishment of the holy waters, it was hard to keep her alive. Age and everything." He shrugged as if they were discussing the theories of life in their chambers at Rayva. "We were, of course, abandoned by the rest of the continent."

And then Dev realized the crown his brother wore was no crown at all, but black ice protruding directly from his skull in the shape of a crown.

Dev clasped his hands behind his back to keep them from shaking. He wished Fig and Vaelor were here.

Selfish, he thought. *By the Bard, I wish them as far away from here as possible.*

His brother cocked his head, and his eyes flashed—not the usual silver ring of a silversword, but a blackish silver like the armor of the Tysainian soldiers he'd seen in passing. "But of course," Shadryn continued, "the enclave had to provide a reason why the crown prince's crossover hadn't gone as planned, so they blamed mother and tossed you into the Carriage House."

"R-right," Dev said. "It was a year or so before my powers manifested."

"Yes," Shadryn said with interest. "Afrith tells me you have air magic? The two of us, air and water. A perfect set. I've always wondered what Mother would think of it. She was water, too, you know."

Despite learning his long-dead brother was alive, despite the creeping feeling that there was a good reason why Svoran blood shouldn't be mixed with silverswords, and despite his own terror about what this meant for Dev and why Afrith had brought him here, the revelation that his mother was a water mage brought burning tears to his eyes.

Shadryn frowned in what looked like solidarity. "I eventually found out from the people on the islands. Had to track down the last of our relatives, though they could hardly be called that—friends of the family, actually—and I got it out of them."

Nodding, Dev swallowed the lump in his throat, not wanting to know how Shadryn had gotten the information out of them.

"It's good to know," he agreed, with a glance down at his feet. Black frost was creeping toward him along the floor, almost as if Shadryn didn't realize he was doing it. Could he control it? Did he want to?

Dev suppressed a shiver. Then, he gathered what little courage he had left, hitched up his smile, and said, "I hope you have better accommodations for your brother than *this one* gave me." He jerked a thumb at Afrith.

A slow smile lifted Shadryn's pale cheeks, and he said, "Of course, brother. I have great plans for the two of us."

Acloak of fog wreathed the beaches of Nithe when the *Trevena* sighted land the next day at dusk. The island's famously black sands were invisible among the rolling clouds, and a chill in the air met them. In the distance, they could see peaks of snow-capped mountains and the Falls of Aerinsur, which Fig had only heard of in poems.

She pulled her coat closer, shivering.

"I visited once, as a child," Quinnetra said. Only the two Fienn-Da and Fig stood on the deck to greet the land. "Before—you know—the blockades. At least those ships are long gone." Fig had heard all about the Tytan ships blockading the islands, forbidding anyone from trade.

"I've only ever seen paintings," Fig told her. "Back at the Carriage House."

Dev had shown her. The Carriage House had a small library open to all mages, student or master. On one of those warm summer nights in the Gold Wood, they'd cozied up in the library as he showed her a book filled with illustrations of the Hollow Isles. He'd spoken only of the places and not of his childhood visits or his mother. Fig had asked no questions, only told him how beautiful it all was. And it truly was beautiful.

"Want me to move the fog?" Quinnetra asked, lowering her

telescope.

"No, no," Fig said, shaking her head. "We don't want to alert anyone. It's good cover."

"Of course," Quinnetra replied. "I didn't know if you wanted to go in fire blazing, or..."

"Definitely not," Fig said, with almost a chuckle. "Let's treat it like the library job. Except Dev is what we're after, and we have no maps, no schedules, no nothing."

Quinnetra blew out a breath. "Not my kind of job," she admitted.

"I understand," Fig said. "And of course, you're welcome to stay on the ship—"

"I didn't say I wouldn't go. As much as Vilvan hates the ship, I'm leaving him here. Not his type of job, either. Evandahl said I could leave you on the shores and turn back. But I'm not going to do that. Not after what you did for us in the library. You didn't even know what it was we were after, but you committed. The Fienn-Da could use someone like you. *Mages* could use someone like you."

Fig nodded tightly. "Thank you."

"That it?" Ziggy swaggered up next to them. "You know, Quinnetra and Vilvan could blow away the fog, right?"

Fig snorted quietly and explained again that the plan was stealth.

The 'sword rolled her eyes and said, "Fine, fine."

Emrah landed on her shoulder as Vilvan lowered the anchor. "We'll need to row over," she told the dragonet. "Mind scouting out the beach for us?"

With a chirp, he took off, green and gold scales dull in the foggy sea air.

Tell me if you see anything, and come right back, Fig instructed.

Yes, mother, he replied.

Her face warmed, but she didn't care.

"Oh, that looks much better on *you*," Ziggy was saying.

Fig turned to see Vaelor coming from belowdecks, wearing one last surprise from Evandahl: blackguard armor the Fienn-Da had stashed in the ship for them. Fig ran her eyes up and down the black-brushed plate armor; her chest filled with tightness again as she remembered those fingers brushing her jaw, sending a shiver down her back.

It seemed like forever ago that Vaelor had lost his silversword armor in the Nova Istra Bay, but whenever Fig thought about it, memories of tearing off the armor and clinging to Vaelor in the fiery bay swamped her. Her face warmed.

"Y-you look good," Fig told him.

Ziggy pouted. "See? He looks better in it than I do."

Fig lifted her gaze from Vaelor and smiled at Ziggy who was wearing her own blackguard armor. "Well, you're just more suited to silver, I think," she said. "You sure looked good in it when you saved us at the Notch."

Ziggy beamed, and Vaelor snorted at the obvious compliment.

All clear on the beach, came Emrah's report.

Great, come back, why don't you, Fig said, her eyes lingering on Vaelor's for a second.

And the next thing she knew, Fig was in the rowboat, watching Vaelor bring them closer and closer to Nithe. Time seemed to be acting strangely in quick bursts, bringing her toward the thing she simultaneously longed for yet dreaded most. She swallowed and looked up at Vaelor.

"You ended up rowing us to Nithe after all," Fig told him.

He looked at her quizzically through his helm.

"When the *Narrow* was blown up, I said it was too bad you couldn't just row us to the Hollow Isles."

He gave her a look, but she could tell from his eyes that he was smiling, which unfroze her insides a little. Suddenly she longed for a few more days on the ship. A week. A month.

By the time they hit the beach and she felt the black sands under the rowboat, all thoughts of weak jokes and those few Bard-blessed minutes on the deck last night were dashed from Fig's mind. Ziggy leapt out and made quick work of bringing them up the beach and out of the waves, where the rest of them climbed out.

"We'll hide it here," Quinnetra said, lifting a hand to manipulate the fog with the tiniest hint of red wind. A dense patch of fog settled over the rowboat, hiding it in the shadow of an old, rotted dock.

There were no footprints on the beach, no people at all. Fig supposed there wasn't much need to maintain the old port anymore. Not when anyone caught visiting the Hollow Isles would feel the wrath of Tytan.

After twenty minutes of walking the black sands, they saw another ship. Fig's insides did a flip. Fear surged through her, but also a measure of relief. Dev was here—he must be.

What do you reckon? she asked Emrah.

I'll fly ahead and find you a path, he answered. *To the castle?*

To the castle.

A shower of light green sparks drifted down on them as Emrah departed. They followed, a trail of sparks guiding their way.

Two silverswords, an air mage, and a fire mage. Normally, that would be a deadly combination. But she hadn't learned how to harden flame or shoot flaming arrows.

What she had would have to be enough.

When the black sands gave way to half-frozen ground, black icicles jutting at random from the landscape, Fig's insides began to writhe in doubt at her decision not to try learning something more difficult during her brief time training.

Vaelor walked beside her, watching the path for light green sparkles as Emrah led the way. The green sparkles were the only thing that kept her going as they found some stairs, which they could only assume led to the castle housing the Hollow throne; it was so thoroughly cloaked in fog, they could hardly tell where they were. Black ice jutted from every corner, matching frost rimming every stone.

Suddenly, Fig's feet went out from under her, slipping on the ice. She couldn't catch herself on the railing, which had black ice shards jutting from it. A strong arm steadied her, and she nodded thankfully at Vaelor.

He's here! Emrah called.

Fig's heart leapt, almost slipping again, but Vaelor retained his protective grip. *What? How do you know?*

Windows at the top, Emrah said. *And someone else is in there too.*

Vaelor's grip tightened at the words. He released it and unsheathed his sword. "Well," he said, "That means we keep moving, doesn't it?"

Fig swallowed the lump in her throat, nodding. "Right," she croaked. "Right. We're going in after him."

They had reached the top of the stairs and found themselves face-to-face with a set of grand double doors, also rimmed in black frost. Careful to avoid the ice protruding from the flagstones at their feet, Fig stood still while the others filed in behind her.

"I don't suppose there's a back door?" Ziggy said. "This doesn't feel as stealthy as you said—"

"I know, Ziggy," Fig said tiredly. "But Dev is in there, and it could take hours to find another way in. Busting in 'fire blazing' it is."

"Are we certain—" Quinnetra began.

"Look," Fig said, "if it's just some musty old noble on the throne, hopefully, we can talk. But with all this ice, if it's a mage..."

"Fire blazing," Ziggy said with a throaty chuckle as she unsheathed her weapon. The scent of copper permeated the air, and Fig glanced at Vaelor's sword, ready beside her. Welded to its master, the weapon enhanced the person. What would happen if the person was already a weapon?

The third option she hadn't voiced, Dev's long-dead brother...

"Bard bless it," Fig muttered and yanked open the door.

Emrah landed on her shoulder. His claws felt comforting as they sought a steady hold. *Stay with me,* she told him. He nudged the side of her head with his snout.

Inside was a nearly empty throne room. Resplendent in more jagged black ice, Fig knew deep in her bones that this throne wasn't held by some musty old noble, but a person far more troubling. If it was who she thought it was—

Without warning, a pinnacle of ice appeared almost as if it were bursting out of the black marble floor. Fig dodged to the left, narrowly missing it.

She heard the sound of crashing armor.

A terrified shriek.

A gut-wrenching scream of pain.

Quinnetra's feet were dangling inches from the floor, her dress fluttering in the last breeze it would ever touch, her body impaled upon a massive shard of ice. She reached out, blood gurgling from her mouth as her eyes sought Fig's. Then the light inside them went out.

Fig's gut clenched violently, but she kept from retching, instead bringing flames that spit sparks to her hands. She scrambled to stand with her feet apart, ready to fight. With Emrah still on her shoulder, she focused on the flames. She imagined she had a piece of the Gold Wood with her.

Figures moved down by the throne, silhouetted by the mullioned windows at the back wall. Three men. And among them…

"Dev," she gasped.

He was dressed in a beautiful black coat, his hair perfect, and his boots shined with blacking. The only thing out of place was the look of pure deadness in his eyes.

"You may stand down, Fairaleigh Veil," the man she didn't know said.

Almost a copy of Dev, but with deliberate mistakes. His hair, darker. His skin, paler. Of course, she had never seen anyone with veins of black cascading down their arms and neck before either. The jagged crown on his head told her everything else she needed to know.

She let her flames burn out a little.

"What happened to 'fire blazing'?" Ziggy demanded from behind, steel in her voice.

Fig ignored her, keeping her face pointed at the man on the throne. She nodded her head back at Quinnetra. "And what of our companion?" Fig called down the length of the throne room. Hatred seethed on the tip of her tongue as she watched Afrith lean in to make a comment to the third man.

"I have no plans to offer you the same fate," the man said. "Yet."

"And why is that?" Fig called back. "If you know who I am, you know I'm here to take back our king. Return Devryn to us, and we'll leave in peace."

Hollow laughter echoed down the room. "There is no need," he said. "Tytan will have a Verrence on the throne once more."

"He's not saying…" Ziggy said.

"He is," Vaelor hissed.

"How?" Fig called, her voice quaking.

He waved an impatient hand. "I don't feel like explaining again. But for now, I might have need of you, Fairaleigh Veil. A good mage is a priceless commodity. And with a pet dragonet at your beck? Come. Come forward."

Fig faltered, but Vaelor took a step in preparation.

"No, not you, 'sword,'" the man on the throne said. He tossed out a casual hand, and black ice burst from the floor.

"No!" Fig shrieked, throwing her hands out, flames dripping from them. But the ice didn't impale him. Instead, it enclosed him and Ziggy in individual cages. Black shards of ice enclosed them from all angles; Ziggy slammed her pommel against the bars to no avail. This was not regular ice.

Her palms hot as coals, Fig let her hands drop by her sides. Her throat was raw. She forced herself to turn around and put one foot in front of the other to reach the throne. To reach Dev.

"*Goldfire, no,*" Vaelor called quietly.

"I have to," she whispered, knowing that he could hear her.

She focused on Emrah's weight on her shoulder as she took one step after another toward the throne.

Drakioryn's breath, Emrah swore. *What is that on his head?*

Her steps slowed. A crown of ice, jutting directly from his skull. The skull of Shadryn Verrence. Just by looking at his face, she had already marked the resemblance to Dev. Yet his was a hideous mask lined in black veins and wreathed in a crown of ice. He was skinny, pale, and bore only a ghost of his former beauty. The rightful heir to the Rayvan throne.

Sparks gathered at her fingertips, and it was impossible not to let some sputter and fall as she came to a stop about eight feet away.

Shadryn's mouth twitched. "Afrith told me all about you, and this fascinating creature you've bonded with. You know, of course, fire and ice make thrilling connections, thus why I got along so well with Afrith when he came calling. And why I think you and I will get along just as nicely."

Fig said nothing, wondering if she had moved too close to the man. He held a spear—no doubt his Welded weapon—its tip wreathed in the same black ice as everything else.

It was no wonder the silverswords said mages had cursed blood. If they turned into *this*.

But how had he even survived the crossover? It was clear the change had done far more than the usual transformation. The all-encompassing black ice was proof of that. She had seen *nothing* like this from other water mages. She stifled a shudder, thinking back to Estill using her blood. Fig could only hope that wasn't something all water mages could do. Shadryn had an obvious affinity for ice; she hoped it was his only specialty.

Shadryn clapped his hands together, making Fig jump. "Everything's falling into place. I'm just waiting on one more guest to arrive before I can set things into motion. Afrith will lead you two somewhere more comfortable while we wait."

"But—" Fig gave a panicked look toward Vaelor and Ziggy, still stuck in their frozen cages.

Afrith used an emerald-topped staff as he walked and shot an expectant look at them to follow. Shadryn sank into his throne, pressing his fingers to his temples.

"Let's go," Dev urged, pushing her a little.

Her chest fluttering so hard she thought her heart might burst through her skin, she gave instructions to Emrah to relay to Vaelor.

Don't provoke. *Be safe.*

Her eyes burned with tears as she let Afrith lead her and Dev from the room. The relief at getting away from Shadryn was tempered harshly by having to leave Vaelor and Ziggy behind.

And Quinnetra was lost forever. How would the rest of them escape the same fate?

Fig slipped her fingers around Dev's arm as they followed Afrith. She searched for any way out, but the hallway was narrow, and she didn't see any other direction they could turn. Fig's other hand went to Emrah's scales, patting them in reassurance. At least no one had tried to take him from her. Shadryn had seemed interested, but what use had he for a fiery dragonet that had already bonded with Fig?

She stared at Afrith's green-clad back in hatred. "Nothing to say this time? You had plenty of things to say back in the *solanse*." She clenched her sparking fingers, thinking back to those hated green flames that had enveloped her friends and taken Dev from her.

"Oh, I've much to think about," Afrith said gravely. "Changes are in motion that will affect the power balance in Svora for centuries, much as Tesvier the Relentless did when the dwarves revolted, and he claimed their Mountain. The promise that Shadryn holds is a thousand times more potent for our futures. The future of mages, that is."

"You're disgusting," Fig told him. "Kidnapping Dev and—"

Afrith scoffed, drawing to a halt and facing them. "Bringing him right where you had intended to take him in the first place? And delivering him into the arms of his long-lost brother? Devryn should be thanking me."

Fig glanced over at Dev, but he made no comment. He still had that dead look in his eyes, but he had allowed her to keep her hand on his arm as they walked. Emrah's claws dug a little deeper into her shoulder.

"No one's thanking you just yet," Fig spat at Afrith. "Oh, and especially not your mages in Tysaine. Well, not that any survived, anyway."

The only indication that Afrith was bothered by her statement was a slight twitch of his neck, which he covered by brushing his hand over his hair. "Yes, well, things happen for the cause."

"Things happen," Fig repeated. "A lot of things happen around you. Care to explain what's happening here?"

He whirled around, his hot breath going right into her face. "Listen here, Fig. We stand on the precipice of a better life for mages and everyone in Tytan—the whole of the continent even. Don't fight it just because you can't comprehend it yet."

Fig narrowed her eyes at him. "I thought you were different."

She let the comment fall and stuck out her chin, waiting for him to lead on.

With a *clunk* of his staff on the frosty flagstones, he spun around and brought them to the end of the hallway. Dust covered whatever the frost didn't, but the door Afrith led them through worked well enough, if a little creaky at the hinges. Afrith pushed them inside and slammed the door shut with a *bang* and a *click*. Fig went to check the door but yanked her hand back before touching the doorknob; it was hotter than coals. Slamming her shoulder against the door did nothing but vent a fraction of her rage. The entire door was hot, so she backed off.

Dev stood by the narrow window, his arms crossed over his chest. The window was much too small for either of them to get through, though Emrah might fit. A crazed memory of Emrah's tower in the Gold Wood surfaced in her mind. If only they could have stayed there...

The narrow window looked into a small courtyard surrounded on all sides by more castle walls. It must have once been beautiful, a stone fountain in the center and a towering sycamore tree beside it. The tree was dead, its bark mottled with black ice and its limbs long barren. Dead branches littered the courtyard—one had even broken a significant chunk off the fountain.

Fig sighed, then turned to Dev. "It's good to see you, Dev. I'm just sorry we couldn't have found you sooner."

Dev leaned forward and crushed her into a hug, burying his face in her shoulder. "It's not your fault. I just wish...I don't know. I don't know anything anymore. What to do, what to believe. I saw him *die*, Fig."

"What?" she whispered.

She felt the breath shudder from him. "I hid. To watch his crossover. I saw it. Do you know how they Weld a weapon to a silversword? They kill them with it, and then bring them back using runes and water."

She swallowed hard, suddenly picturing Vaelor's sword piercing his chest on some highland battlefield, blood pouring from the wound.

Slowly, Dev withdrew his arms, then started pacing around the small room. There was a bed and a broken crate in the corner, and that was it. There wasn't much room to pace. Fig positioned herself on the dusty bed, knees drawn up to her chest.

"I saw his veins turn black," Dev continued, "and the silverswords said it was cursed mage blood, and that was that. And the worst part?

My father *knew*. He helped revive him and banished him here. To get rid of him. He never told me...never told me..."

"We'll figure this out," Fig said shakily. "We'll find a way out of here."

He shook his head, and Fig realized he looked years older than when she'd last seen him, even though it had only been a little over a week.

"He wants to take back Tytan, Fig, with me by his side. Except he wants me to cross over first."

CHAPTER

47

They huddled together on the dusty old bed for hours, whispering everything that had passed since Dev was kidnapped. Dev was trying to remain on Shadryn's good side, though there was nothing his brother said that Dev agreed with. So far, the ploy had worked.

Emrah left through the courtyard window a few times to try to scout around the castle, but every time he went out, Fig paced nervously around the room and asked for updates repeatedly, until he got annoyed and stopped doing it. She just couldn't help but picture Shadryn trapping him in an ice cage somewhere, and Fig never seeing him again. Emrah was able to report that another boat arrived on the beach and that Vaelor and Ziggy were still imprisoned in the throne room. He couldn't find any reliable passages out of the castle besides the main doors. The effects of weather, time-worn nature, and ice blocked every other possible entry point.

Sparks kept her hands warm, as she rubbed them together in the frigid air.

The door opened with a slam, and Afrith's haughty face leered in. He had his new staff by his side, the hue of the emerald reminding Fig of his green flames. "You have been summoned," he said.

Fig had Emrah relay their movements to Vaelor and Ziggy, though she felt bad that they couldn't respond. Ziggy, in particular, probably found the one-way conversation torturous.

The castle was small, meant to support only the royal family and a few servants, nothing like the castle in Rayva. Cobwebs stretched across the ceiling and corners, which were thick with dust and pierced by the occasional icicle. It looked like the place hadn't been occupied in years, except Shadryn had been here since his crossover. He obviously had no use for most of the castle...or servants, for that matter. Had he lived alone? All these years?

No wonder he seemed a little mad, though she didn't know what effect the botched crossover had on his senses. And yet the islanders seemed to surrender to his rule, as detrimental to the Isles as it was.

"Like playing fetch for your master?" Fig jeered quietly as Afrith led them back to the throne room.

"I do what is required of me," he answered simply. "I wouldn't expect you would understand. You can hardly stick to what's expected of you, Fig."

She scoffed. "Nice try. And too bad for you, I've finally found a cause worth sticking to." She glanced at Dev, who furrowed his eyebrows at her.

Me? he mouthed.

She nodded with half a smile. Her stomach, however, was in a painful knot that felt as if it would never unravel. They were almost at the throne room, the temperature dropping every second and black ice coating nearly every surface. How in the name of the Bard were they supposed to get out of this?

Vaelor and Ziggy were still in their prisons twenty paces away, but a newcomer in a red cloak was kneeling by the throne. Fig stiffened. Whoever this red sister was, it meant that Shadryn's plan was about to be set into motion.

As they got closer, Fig realized the figure wasn't kneeling; she'd been thrown to the floor by Shadryn's feet. The red hood was drawn back, revealing long red hair. Mairead.

No. Fig gasped and strode past Afrith, coming to Mairead's side. She picked up the girl's arm. "Mairead, are you hurt?"

Mairead looked up at her, her eyes swimming in tears and rimmed in red. She shook her head. Fig glanced between her and Dev, who was walking hesitantly toward them.

"The final piece," Shadryn said with emphasis. "Afrith brought me many gifts from his travels. We can now ready my brother for greatness, just as I received greatness from my own crossover. Together, we will be unstoppable in reclaiming Tytan."

Fig inhaled a painful breath. There was no way she could let that happen. Even if Dev didn't die, she would not let him turn into...*this*.

It was Mairead who spoke up first. "B-but...but sir, I can't—"

"You can," Shadryn said. His voice displayed no emotion. "And you will. We have holy waters, enough for the crossover. And Afrith tells me you've performed it before."

Fig clenched her fists. *Emrah! We have to stop this.*

Just say the word, Fig. He danced nervously on her shoulder.

They could attack Shadryn with fire, but then what? Afrith would fight back. Shadryn too. She hesitated. Shadryn's magic was fast and deadly no matter where he stood.

Mairead was no fighter. And Dev's air magic was no match for Shadryn and Afrith. Could she and Emrah defeat both of them? Or at least hold them off long enough so the others could escape? How long would it take to break Vaelor and Ziggy from their cages? Mairead still crouched, terrified, on the ground, tears rolling down her face.

"There's no time to waste," Shadryn said, clapping his hands together. Specks of black frost exploded from his hands, evidently delighting him. "Every minute we linger, that traitor Rhivven sits on the throne. Our throne, Dev."

"I...I know, brother," Dev said placatingly. "But...we can take it back. That was why I fled Tytan for the Hollow Isles in the first place, and I...I didn't even know you were here." His smile didn't reach his eyes, but Shadryn didn't seem to notice. He tightened his grip on his spear.

"Right. And first thing, we need you to cross over. We need to make your magic stronger."

Dev's throat bobbed as he swallowed. "Actually, I—"

A clang sounded from the ice cages, and Fig saw Vaelor hammering on the bars with his sword. *Clang. Clang.* Fig could feel the strength of the blows reverberating down to the floor and up into her toes. Ziggy was trying to wrench apart the black ice with her hands; her normally formidable strength could rip apart massive wooden beams if she tried, but even a strike from her powerful, gauntleted fists did nothing but chip away a small amount of ice. This ice was *not* normal.

Fig clenched her fists even tighter, fingernails digging into her skin. Every second, she almost said the word to Emrah. But every second, she hesitated. Shadryn could kill any of them instantly. Mairead, who had no place even being here. Vaelor, trapped in a cage. Would she and Emrah even be able to melt the black ice?

Shadryn sighed. "Let us away from here. I'm only holding those two should they wish to serve the real Tytan. I know one of them is bound to you, Dev. But I haven't much need for silver*swords*. The fount is in the courtyard. The red sisters were unconventional here— no real chapels like Tytan had."

Mairead still didn't get up; her hands splayed on the marble floor as if she could cling to it with her fingers and stay there. Shadryn's impatience burst out in a surge of growing icicles all around them— jutting up from the throne, the floor, and the nearby wall.

"Dev," he said shortly. "I believe you know this girl? Tell her to do her job or I will make her."

And with that, Shadryn stalked from the room, leaving Afrith to hover over them like the pompous, traitorous mage he was. Fire crackled at his fingertips where he clutched his staff. "Hurry. Get her up," he insisted. His eyes revealed a hunger Fig had never seen before.

Or had she? Buried memories from the Carriage House, recently riffled through as she and Dev had reminisced back in Viren, rose to the surface. Learning from Afrith and seeing that look in his eyes whenever they'd discussed a particularly unique piece of magic, reports of discoveries made at Tirnalore, news brought to the Carriage House by returning mages.

Power.

She glanced at him in disgust. "What do you get out of all of this?"

she hissed at him.

Dev crouched down to speak with Mairead, whispering in her ear.

Afrith ignored Fig and banged the bottom of his staff on the cold marble. "I said hurry."

Fig went over to help Dev with Mairead. "Listen, Mairead," she hissed as quietly as she could into the girl's ear, "we're trying to prevent this, trust me. Just get up before Afrith gets any ideas or Shadryn comes back."

The look Mairead gave her cut straight into Fig's gut. Her green eyes swam in tears, red rimming her eyelashes. "I can't, Fig," she said, her voice hoarse. "I can't do it again."

"A crossover?" Fig asked.

Flames wreathed the floor around Mairead, and she scrambled to her feet with a squeal.

"Go," Afrith said, lifting his staff menacingly at her.

Mairead's throat bobbed, and she gave Fig a terrified glance, her hands shaking as she adjusted her hood and turned toward the door.

This is bad, Fig told Emrah. *Wait! You stay here in the throne room and try to free Vaelor and Ziggy, all right? I'll try to distract anyone from noticing you're gone.*

Emrah clenched her shoulder. *I should stay with you. Shadryn is the most dangerous. I don't want you facing him alone out there.*

No. Free them, and we'll have a better chance. Besides, I'll have Dev with me.

Before Fig passed through the archway leading outside, Emrah slipped from her shoulder and took wing. Afrith, blind with the promise of powerful things before him, had stalked ahead with Mairead and Dev, and didn't even notice Fig coming out behind him.

Shadryn stood by the fount at the center of the courtyard, in front of the dead sycamore tree. Black icicles began to form on the branches above him. She wondered if he even knew he was doing it. He clutched his spear casually, but the black ice wreathing everything around him was anything but casual.

The ice isn't melting, Emrah reported. Fig closed her eyes painfully. *No! Wait!* Emrah said. *It's just, really, really slow.*

Of course it is, Fig replied grumpily. *Hurry!*

A snarl wove through her mind in reply.

Do your best, she amended. *Please.*

"Come along now," Shadryn was saying. His darkened eyes had more life in them than earlier. Fig kept to the back, partially blocked by the tree, her body half turned away, and hoped no one would notice Emrah's absence.

Hurry, hurry, she thought to herself. Her hands were behind her back, a ball of nervous sparks between her palms.

"Wait, brother," Dev said, when everyone was there.

"I'm afraid we don't have time," Shadryn said again. "We can take the next tide out of Nithe if we hurry. I know you're afraid, but with our same blood—"

"It's not that," Dev said. Fig's chest hurt at the sight of the bold defiance on his face, and her respect for his bravery grew a thousand times. "I haven't selected a weapon. Perhaps this isn't the right time. I wouldn't want to rush such an important decision."

Shadryn looked dumbstruck, staring in disbelief at the fount. "How could I have possibly... You're right. And you can't be Weld to any rusty old sword or pathetic dagger. Strike it!" he cursed, slamming his fist down on his thigh in a burst of anger. Knee-high black ice jutted from the cobblestones, and Fig had to leap out of the way to keep her leg from being impaled.

Mairead backed into the fount, letting out a little yelp as she caught herself on the weathered stones.

But Shadryn didn't seem to notice or care about his outburst. He went on, "I do have some weapons here, but you know what, brother? We need something more powerful for you." He lowered his voice, as if afraid of insulting Dev. "Air...can be a little too light, you know? You need something that will raise you up more. Perhaps in the Verrence Armory we can find something..."

Dev was nodding, but Fig saw the tears in his eyes.

Afrith cleared his throat expectantly. Shadryn looked up from the nearest icicle he was studying, as if he'd only just noticed it was there. "Oh, yes, Afrith. You should go first, anyway, since we currently only have one crossover to go by."

Fig found her jaw dropping as Afrith lifted his chin and strode up to the fount. If Afrith crossed over, and became even more powerful...

Emrah, how's that ice melting going? she thought urgently toward Emrah.

I'm working on it! I've got through one bar, but this 'sword' of yours is a big man, and he's not going to fit through some tiny gap.

Well, hurry it up, please! Shadryn let Dev pass on the rite, but Afrith is up next.

Shadryn pushed a ladle into Mairead's hand. It looked as weathered as the stone, but it would hold water. Mairead wiped her cheeks again with the sleeves of her robe. She must have picked up new robes at the Narndian, but they already had a rip in them.

"An interesting choice, my friend," Shadryn remarked, gazing at the staff Afrith had brought with him. "You do realize...a killing blow..."

Afrith nodded tightly.

Shadryn gestured vaguely. "Well, someone else..."

Fig and Dev shared a look of pure panic. A killing blow.

Surely Mairead wasn't about to bludgeon Afrith to death with that regal staff, but Fig had never killed anyone before either—even if he was about to be brought back to life. But that wasn't guaranteed in this situation.

She couldn't do it. Despite all her years in the underbelly of Tytan after quitting the Carriage House, she'd never...

"Fairaleigh," Shadryn said suddenly. "You seem to...despise him. Why don't you do the honor?"

The staff was suddenly in her hands. Had Afrith put it there? A massive emerald sat on top, caged in gold filigree. A killing blow. He had to die for the rite, in order to cross over.

And by the Bard, how she had dreamed of it ever since their fight in the *solanse*. For taking Dev from them and dropping them into this frozen nightmare. For betraying mages and seeking power. For drugging Emrah and keeping him from her. She stared into Afrith's eyes, her chest burning in anger, her fingers whitening around the hard wood of the staff.

And yet...after everything she had worked to build for herself. All that time digging herself up out of the muck on her own.

"No," she heard a voice say. "I'll do it." It was Dev.

The staff was pulled gently from her fingers, which felt like they'd hardened into claws around it.

"I owe him for the kidnapping," Dev said in a would-be casual voice to Shadryn.

Shadryn made no apologies for his part in such a thing, but merely shrugged, his attention now on the waters of the fount.

"We'll need the runes first, of course," Shadryn said.

"Oh," Mairead said, her voice still hoarse. "Right." She turned to the fount, trembling a little.

Suddenly Shadryn was in Mairead's face, his cold breath clouding between them. "And if anything goes wrong," he said quietly, "just know that there's no one left in the Hollow Isles to heal you."

Mairead pulled away with a shaky nod, dipping the ancient ladle in the fount, and placing it carefully on the edge. Shadryn made no move to withdraw, lurking over her shoulder. She stared at Afrith's hand. "I'll need..."

"Ah, of course," Afrith said, pulling out a dagger. He sliced open his palm and held it out to her.

Blood dripping down the tip of her finger, Mairead went over to the staff in Dev's hands, and drew a series of runes along its length. Fig recognized some of them from the red sisters' chapels and tattoos. Others were completely foreign to her, intricate intersecting lines, simple slashes, and circles intertwined.

Then Mairead traced over the blood runes with water from the fount. Each one glowed briefly as she drew the second set, leaving the marks painted in blood and water. Fig could feel a deep magic thrumming in the air. The smell of blood wasn't quite the strong harsh scent she usually associated with silverswords. Not yet.

Afrith appeared solemn, but his eyes burned with the look Fig recognized. Power. It would soon be his if his rite went like Shadryn's. Mairead backed toward the fountain, and dipped the ladle once more, ready.

Now it was Dev's turn. His eyes looked deader than ever.

After the first blow, Fig looked down at the black-frosted cobblestones. She could hear Afrith fall to his knees, then to the ground. She couldn't block out the sounds of each blow from the staff. Afrith's grunts of pain. How many strikes would it take?

Four. To get the right hit in the right place, or enough damage to fell him. Four strikes until Afrith lay dead on the cobblestoned courtyard, the smell of ice and blood permeating the sea air.

Mairead scrambled over, ladle dripping, silent tears streaming from her eyes. She applied the waters to the wound—his head, of course. Dev had drawn back, mouth open in horror, the bloody staff limp in his hands. Fig's chest swelled, and she wished could go to him, but no one had noticed Emrah's absence yet, and she had to keep it that way.

Water. Laying of hands. Muttering of prayers. Repeat. Mairead dashed back and forth from the fount, applying the waters, the tattoos on her hands glowing as she called on the help of Morgha.

But would the mother reach out with hands of death or of healing?

Fig stared at the scene without blinking. Afrith's boots, which he must have shined that very morning, stuck straight into the air from the bottom of his robes. A funny detail to notice, Fig thought in a detached way.

"Keep at it!" Shadryn urged when Mairead stopped, pulling her hands away from Afrith's skull. "It will take longer with mage blood. You must keep trying. They thought I was dead when I crossed over."

She kept trying. Though water soaked the frosty cobblestones, staining the bottom of everyone's cloaks. Though Afrith's head looked healed on the outside. Though his chest did not rise.

A strange pallor began to creep over his skin. Not like the black veins that spiderwebbed across Shadryn but a consuming ripple that flashed over his skin, shades of black writhing underneath.

They looked like...flames.

Shadryn gasped. "More, more!" he called, frantically waving for Mairead to bring more water.

Mairead acquiesced, again slamming her knees to the cobblestones as she poured more water on Afrith's head.

Fig watched as the black flames under Afrith's skin writhed sickeningly, then went out.

"Stop."

It was Fig who said it. Shadryn raised a hand—she wasn't sure what he intended—but she pressed on. "Flames. Black flames, didn't you see?" She pointed at his skin. "They've gone."

"He could still make it. That might just be..." Shadryn trailed off, staring at her. "Wait. Where is your dragonet?"

She cursed herself; she'd involuntarily taken half a step forward. Shadryn's black-silver gaze flicked toward the throne room behind her.

The bottom of her stomach dropped out. Flames, the likes of which she had never summoned before, burst from her hands, and she flung them at Shadryn. She had no other choice. Vaelor and Ziggy were in there, and Shadryn could kill any one of them in an instant. Afrith was dead. And it was time to go.

She stumbled backward, pushing her flames between her and Shadryn. Mairead scrambled behind her, either trying to get away from the fire or from Shadryn. Now they just needed...

"Devryn!" Shadryn called. "Take her air away or something, will you? I still want her too."

Fig kept the flames up, but when an icicle almost impaled her from below, she threw one of her hands toward the ground, guarding from below.

"Run!" Fig told Mairead. "Get to Vaelor and Ziggy!"

The red sister ran. Fig kept the flames up as long as she thought of Dev and Vaelor and everyone who needed her. They would not end up like Afrith, dead on the ground. She and her flames were the only thing between them and Shadryn.

CHAPTER

48

As Fig entered the throne room, a massive crack of ice sounded and reverberated up through her feet. She leapt to the side in terror, her flames going out as she rolled away on the cold floor. When she righted herself, she looked around frantically for a protruding icicle, but the sound had come from the other end of the room. A large bar of ice lay shattered on the floor. Vaelor was hacking away at the remaining ice around the melted opening, slamming his sword pommel with a massive force into the ice bars. He bashed his shoulder into the weakened bars.

"Get to Ziggy!" Vaelor told Emrah, slamming his sword again; Emrah flitted over and let his flames fly over Ziggy's bars. "Fig!" Vaelor shouted.

"It's Fairaleigh, though, isn't it?" Shadryn's cold voice slithered in her ear. She froze in place, ice covering her feet.

How had he gotten so close? Her flames...she'd let them go when she rolled to avoid an ice blast that never came. How could she have been so stupid?

She felt an arm around her throat, gentle but unwelcome, and Shadryn's breath in her ear. A wickedly sharp point pressed into her side. Ice or steel, it didn't matter; either could kill her.

"That silly nickname of yours was given to you by my brother, wasn't it?" Shadryn said. She said nothing; she didn't think he expected her to.

"Shad," Dev said, from behind them, a note of pleading in his voice.

Fig's insides had frozen, too, but she knew that Shadryn wasn't directly responsible for that. His breath was on her neck, the smell of ice and death thick in the air.

"Afrith wasn't as strong as you are," Shadryn said in her ear. "Clever and controlling. But your flames are magnificent. And I'd bet the Bard's ink stores that your familiar was too far away enough to even help bolster your magic that time."

Fig's neck muscles seized at the mention of Emrah.

Ice shot out at the other end of the room, shards forming a circular cage around Emrah that dangled high on a black shard of ice. He flapped his wings, trapped.

Emrah, Fig called. Her eyes stung. Stupid. She was so stupid. She hadn't prepared enough to save Dev or themselves. They should have realized Afrith was telling the truth about Dev's brother being here on Nithe, should have realized they would be dealing with something far worse than a single fire mage.

Shadryn continued. "Which is why you'll make an excellent silvermage—that's what I'm calling it, anyway." His voice purred like a creature made of shadow.

She felt like she was going to throw up.

"What—" She choked the words out. "What do you want me for? I'd only be more powerful, a threat to you, even—" What was she saying?

A dark laugh rang out, and she could feel his chest rumble.

"Brilliant," he said. "I told you fire and ice are compelling companions. We'll be brilliant together. Come, I have a dagger from the Kildaria ironsmiths that would be a fitting weapon for you to Weld with. Sorry, Dev," he added in an undertone. "I'd let you take it, but she's more fitted for the quick and stealthy weapon."

"Shad." Dev spoke again. "Are you sure? Like she said...she's already powerful enough. Do you really want more mages like you?"

"More mages like me?" Shadryn said. "Of course not. Well, not *too* many. That was where the silverswords went wrong. Crossing over anyone and everyone to make an army. An army has a thousand heads. A thousand snakes. Like Rhivven and his dog Djuren."

"Djuren?" Dev asked. "You didn't mention him before."

"Yes, it's because of that greedy briigard that the coup went all wrong."

"What?" Dev pressed. "You...had something to do with the coup?"

"That's what I've been *saying*, brother. The Rayvan throne needs a Verrence, and the silverswords—"

"There *was* a Verrence on it," Dev said in a dead voice. "Did you—"

But Shadryn was done with the conversation, gesturing sharply with his spear toward the ice cages. A squeal rang out from behind Ziggy, and Mairead came out into the opening between the cages, a black icicle jutting up after her. She rubbed her thigh and came forward.

"Little red sister," Shadryn called, his elbow clutching more tightly around Fig's throat. "We require your services again. In the name of Morgha, of course. I won't hold Afrith's death against you. That was his failing."

It looked as if it took everything Mairead had to take those steps toward them, her hands balled into fists by her sides. Her eyes were still puffy and red, but she was no longer crying.

The ice around Fig's feet began to recede. She started shaking.

Suddenly, Shadryn whirled her around, and the ice melted in an instant. The sharp point at her side turned out to be the blade of his spear—steel sheathed in ice—which he still aimed at her middle.

"Don't worry," Shadryn said, lifting his ice-crowned head with a hollow smile. "You'll be thanking me after."

But through the doorway to the courtyard, Fig could see the body of Afrith on the cobblestones, and she very much doubted that.

He pushed Fig toward the courtyard, and a sharp crack rang out, followed by a crash. It reverberated through Fig's feet, shaking her to the core. Fig glanced around in panic for another ice shard, but no, it was...

Vaelor. Charging forward in blackguard armor, his sword raised. "You touch her again and die," he called.

They had seconds—perhaps even less than seconds—before Shadryn would act, so Fig did the absolute stupidest thing she could and reached for his spearhead, her hands hotter than coals. She yanked her hands back after only a second, before the metal met her hands. She'd managed to melt the ice around his Welded weapon and sufficiently distract him.

Behind her, Fig heard the bursts of flame crackling. Emrah was trying to melt his cage, but it would take forever, and Ziggy still wasn't free.

Shadryn threw up a massive wall of black ice in front of them, like a wave of death. Vaelor crashed into it within moments. He began hacking away at it with his sword, his only weapon, a part of his soul.

Now Fig really knew what it took for a blade to become linked to the one who wielded it, what he had gone through, what they'd all gone through. She'd had her suspicions over the years, but hearing it from Dev and seeing the botched crossover...

A sharp pain stung her hand. Shadryn grabbed her wrist and yanked her hand up, palm now bleeding. He hooked his spear in the crook of his arm and held up a dagger for her to see.

Vaelor's strikes against the wall of ice reverberated up through her feet. *Clang. Clang.*

"Well-crafted isn't it?" Shadryn said, turning the dagger a little. "We can do the crossover right here if you like. I'll just bring the holy water to us."

Shards of ice rained down on them and a black shadow dropped in front of Fig. Vaelor, in his blackguard armor, sword raised. He'd climbed over the wall of ice to get to them.

Shadryn twirled the dagger lazily, and a shard of black ice burst forth. Vaelor slashed through it with his sword. A horrible ringing pierced their ears.

Another shard; another slash of his sword. Vaelor's speed matched Shadryn's in a dance of ice and death. Though Fig wanted Vaelor as far away from Shadryn as possible, the silversword held his head down, doing everything he could to get to her.

Fig began to gather fire in her hands.

"Enough!" Shadryn shoved her bloody hand away, knocking her off balance as he stepped back. Ice shards surged out of the floor around her—not intended to kill, but to entomb her—going all the way up to her neck where the sharpest points surrounded her throat. Her bloody palm lay on the outside of the ice prison, her arm trapped as it was.

Vaelor let out a war cry and slammed his blade down on the ice entombing her. Then a terrible scream rent the air.

The sound of something shattering, then clanging to the floor.

Vaelor's sword. Which was now in pieces.

His scream died, echoing horribly around the frozen throne room. The silence that followed seemed almost deafening. Fig stared at his sword, her eyes pricking. Vaelor crashed to his knees.

"Pity," Shadryn said slowly. "Should have chosen your weapon a little better, I suppose. But you can't expect much from a Virenish war crossover." He shoved Vaelor with the blunt end of his spear, pushing him aside.

And Vaelor let him. He cradled what remained of his sword in his hands, then scrambled to pick up the pieces like a dying man trying to stuff his guts back inside his body.

Because that's exactly what this was. The sword that had killed him had brought him back to life. It was intrinsically linked to him—his heart, or body, whatever the rumors said. Without it...

He stared at Fig's ice prison, his eyes unseeing yet filled with rage and sadness. Like he still felt the emotions but didn't know why.

"Enough of this," Shadryn said. "I'm tired of waiting. He waved a few fingers in the direction of the courtyard, and then froze, staring around at Dev. His eyes bulged.

A faint amethyst glow surrounded Shadryn's head, robbing him of air.

Shadryn coughed and choked, a look of betrayal on his face. "Brother," he gasped, reaching vaguely toward him.

"I'm sorry," Dev whispered, tears in his eyes.

Shadryn grunted, dropping the dagger, but he still had his spear. Free hand wrenching upward, black water seemed to leach out of the floor and rise up around Dev, curling around him in a twisting vice. The edges of the water began to freeze, spiderwebbed shards of ice wreathing Dev in blackness.

"No," Fig said. "No!"

And even though her palm was bleeding freely, she could still use it as it jutted out of her ice prison. Flames shot from her hand. They weren't precise and calculated like Afrith's nor did they use any special technique. They were wild, and full of rage and pain. They were bold. And broken. And they burned.

She aimed right for Shadryn.

He fell back, dropping the ice whirling around Dev. "Enough, enough!" he choked.

When the flames subsided, she saw that Dev had been drawn into Shadryn's icy grip, the spear trained on his ribs.

"Devryn, I'll forgive your outburst if you put this one down. It's her or you. I can't have both of you betraying me when I return to Tytan. She would make a powerful ally, but it seems she would rather align herself with the same kind of 'swords who killed Father."

Dev glared at his brother. "You had a hand in the coup. *You* had Father killed."

Shadryn scoffed, waving his spear tip vaguely. "Devryn," he said tiredly, "there is more than a coup to assassination. I don't expect you to understand it, having been pampered in your mage's castle all those years, instead of learning statecraft."

"So you did?" Dev demanded, struggling against his brother's grip. "You admit it?"

"I didn't order for Father to be killed," Shadryn said. "Djuren and Rhivven betrayed me."

"But a coup is a coup," Dev insisted. "How in the Bard's name were you planning on deposing him? No, I don't believe you. You wouldn't ever ascend to the throne if Father was alive."

Fig blinked heavily at Dev. So Shadryn had initiated the coup, probably with Afrith's contacts, but the silverswords had their own agenda. Well, it was all the same, wasn't it? A bloodthirsty briigard on the throne.

Dev's struggles turned nasty when Shadryn used the butt end of his spear to jab him right in the stomach, making Dev double over in pain. The staff of the spear came down, heading toward the back of Dev's head.

The motions Fig had practiced in the Fienn-Da basement in what felt like years ago sprang to life. The spark, as she connected to her inner flame, darted along her synapses. A burst of flame, and then they were surrounded by a ring, the flames as high as her shoulders. It encircled all of them. Mairead had scrambled over to Vaelor and the two of them were huddled behind Fig in her ice prison.

A devilish laugh rang out from Shadryn. "And just what do you think that will do for you?"

Fig glanced down at Vaelor, his eyes dead-looking; Mairead, the tears dried on her face; Dev, a spear jabbing further into his side. She took a shaky breath.

"Oh, you're about to find out," she said, reaching out with her senses to the rest of the throne room. *Ready, Emrah?*

Nearly!

Faster than last time, she dipped into her inner fire and sent the spark out again. Another ring of flames flared up, this time so small that it only circled her, its flames licking the prison of ice she was trapped in.

A chirp from above was all she needed. Flames exploded from her skin, blasting the ice prison with her strong intent. The ice cracked and broke, already weakened by the flames circling it at the bottom. Her limp hand fell, and she cradled it to her chest, blood running down her arm.

Shadryn stumbled back as the fires bloomed outward, and she crashed forward. But he stopped when he hit the shoulder-high wall of flames encircling them and released a shriek of pain. The black veins edging his face seemed to dance in the firelight. Fig spat at the ground.

Water and fire were *not* allies.

"You're not crossing anyone over," she snarled. "And you're not taking Tytan."

She stalked forward, pulling back the flames so they only wreathed her hands and arms. *Emrah, help Ziggy*, she called.

Red sparks sifted down as Emrah darted back over the remains of the ice wall. At the same time, Fig lunged forward. But she went for Dev—to both brothers' surprise—and he let out a little yelp. Though Fig's arms were wreathed in flame, she hadn't burned him. That little control, she could manage.

She wrapped an arm around him and walked backward away from Shadryn, saying nothing while continuing to stare in his black-silver eyes.

When they reached Vaelor and Mairead, Fig kept one flaming hand on Dev, and used her other to help lift Vaelor. He acquiesced with little enthusiasm, as if in a waking dream. He cradled the shards of his blade safely in his hands.

When she turned her head to look at him, she saw the silver rings around his eyes were wreathed in red. She blinked and gripped him even harder, focusing all her energy on not burning them all. But as long as they were wreathed in her flames, they were safe. That was all she knew. Shadryn lurched forward but seemed to think better of it when Fig cast a wall of flames in front of her.

Fig and the others finally turned their backs on Shadryn to run down the length of the throne room, leaving him in a circle of raging flames that blazed in the coming light of dawn. If Shadryn couldn't summon ice from inside the flames or her blaze was too hot to wield water, she would never know.

Ziggy burst through her prison with a final flourish as they ran past, Fig's flames still wreathing them.

"I finally get out and we're already leaving?" Ziggy called.

"Shut it, Ziggy," Fig said. "Let's go!"

Ziggy turned around and guarded their exit, Emrah circling overhead.

But no ice came, and the golden flames raged into the dawn.

Their footsteps beat across the black sands, and then they were in the rowboat within seconds of finding it. Ziggy rowed while Dev tried to speed their progress with a little help from the wind. Fig watched Vaelor worriedly; he clutched the sword pieces carefully but seemed responsive enough.

Finally, they rowed into the shadow of the *Trevena*. Fig screamed when an amethyst wind lifted up in the air and onto the ship.

Fig found her feet and steadied herself on the deck, then she lurched to the railing to look below. *Emrah, get Vilvan*, she told him. He zipped off to find the dryad. Mairead was flown to the deck a moment later, her hood coming off her head, and her red hair fluttering about her face. Her eyes were wide as she glanced at Fig, then both of them rushed to throw their arms around each other. Mairead pressed her head deep into Fig's shoulder, her body trembling.

"Don't you even think of trying that with me," Ziggy's voice threatened from down below.

Fig and Mairead broke apart with tearful chuckles, and they looked over the rail.

Dev sailed himself up and landed on the deck with a little more accuracy than he'd given Fig. She watched as Ziggy guided Vaelor up the ladder first, after helping him carefully tuck the sword shards into a pouch behind his plate armor.

Fig's nerves buzzed as she clutched the railing, watching the two silverswords climb the rungs. As soon as their feet were on board, she turned to see Vilvan hurriedly working the ropes to lower the sail.

"Where's Quinnetra?" he asked, when he tied off the rope and dashed toward the wheel.

"She didn't make it," Fig said through clenched teeth.

"She didn't..." Vilvan said, jaw dropping. "Ah." He put a hand to his mouth, glancing back at the island. Finally, he said quietly, "It'll take a lot longer to get the ship going with just me and the wind."

"Dev can help, right, Dev?"

Dev stared blankly at the sail, but Vilvan hauled him over by his side and began hurriedly explaining. A wind from the highest peak of Nithe had begun to howl down the valley, swirling the morning fog, and Fig imagined creatures of shadow bearing down upon them. Perhaps they really were.

The *Trevena* creaked and swayed, but finally got underway with a lurch. Fig's eyes bulged. She raced back to the rail, retching repeatedly over the side.

Coughing, choking, and spitting. She hadn't had any issues with seasickness on the way here, she thought as she pulled her hair away from her face.

She spit again, her gaze landing on the fog-wreathed castle of Nithe.

Mairead had brought her a skin of water, and she rinsed her mouth, spitting it all into the Hollow Sea.

Would Shadryn pursue them?

There was no doubt his sights were set on Tytan, but had he survived the flames?

She wiped her mouth with the back of her hand and turned around when she heard Emrah chirping. He settled on top of the main sail.

"You made it," Ziggy said quietly. "You're alive, and you did it, right?"

"Right," Fig said. "And almost everyone got out," she added bitterly.

"You did your best," Ziggy said in her best big sister voice. But if Fig were being honest, the words hit her so hard it made her want to cry. She had tried *so hard*.

And even though she hadn't mastered magic as well as Afrith, they had managed to avoid getting caught in Shadryn's plan for crossovers because they'd all worked together—not just due to Fig's fire magic.

"Where to?" Vilvan called.

Everyone looked at Fig. Including Dev. She jerked her chin in his direction. "It's your call."

"My…" He scoffed. "My call? After I just got myself kidnapped and found myself unequal to battle a brother I thought long dead? No, it's your choice, Fig. You're—"

"Me?" Fig demanded, her chest suddenly growing hot. "You're the one who dragged me into this, Dev! I was minding my own business at a tavern outside the Gold Wood when you two briigards showed up!" She gestured at him and Vaelor, who Ziggy had gotten to sit down on some crates.

"Yes, but you're—" Dev began.

A twin burst of flame came from her hands unbidden, but she didn't care. They had all almost died. She and Dev could have been turned into monsters like Shadryn. Or ended up dead on the frozen cobblestones, covered in blood and water.

"Don't say I'm your best advisor," Fig grumbled, her rage spent on the flames. "I'm probably the worst in the history of all Svora."

"And I'm the worst crown prince," Dev said, shrugging. "I've just had my title usurped by my dead brother."

"We make a bloody pair, don't we?" Fig said weakly. Suddenly she felt dizzy, like she ought to sit down. She remembered the skin of water in her hand and took another swig.

"We could go back to Tirnalore," Ziggy suggested. "The Fienn-Da would take us in."

"And just as soon slit our throats," Fig muttered.

Tytan. Tirnalore. The *solanse*. No matter where they went, they weren't safe, and they would bring darkness down on whoever sheltered them. It was no longer just the silverswords they had to fear.

Fig curled in on herself, then decided to sit before she fell down. She lowered herself to the deck, clutching her knees to her chest. Vaelor sat directly across from her, staring back at Nithe, or perhaps at nothing. Fig's heart constricted. That bloody Viren, rushing in to fight for her and Dev...breaking his sword to defend her from the ice prison.

"We need to heal Vaelor," Fig burst. "His sword—"

Vaelor looked up at the sound of his name, and his eyes made her breath catch. She remembered seeing the smallest amount of red around silver. Would it get worse? Would the separation from his sword weaken him? Kill him over time?

"He hasn't dropped dead so far," Ziggy remarked, evidently thinking along the same lines. "I've always wondered. You mostly only hear of 'swords getting killed the normal way."

Fig frowned, thinking. *The normal way.* Death and blood and more death. "Mairead, would the sisters at the Narndian know anything? With that impressive hospital of theirs?"

Mairead shook her head. "No, they've entirely denounced the silversword practice in Tysaine. That's why I..." Her breath hitched. After a long pause, tears began streaming from her eyes. "I didn't want to...didn't want to do the crossover, but they made me..."

"Shh," Fig said, coming closer to Mairead and grabbing her hands. "I know. I wish we could have—"

"No, not them," she said, jerking her head back toward Nithe. "Back in Nova Istra. The mother at Mar Nevan said I wouldn't have to do any crossovers in the first couple of years. There were other chapels in Nova Istra. But Maelchior and his friend forced their way into the chapel and demanded that I perform it. They had sprung a fighter of some kind from the cells they wanted to add to their ranks."

Fig hung her head, thinking back to the altercation with Maelchior in the chapel and his disdain for Mairead. "I'm sorry, Mairead."

Mairead shook her head. "No, you don't understand." She spoke in a whisper. "*They made me kill him.* Run the sword through, covered in runes, sinking it into his body and then pulling it out again.

And then they made me go to the fount."

Fig's mouth was open in horror, and she quickly closed it. "I'm so sorry they put you through that."

And Shadryn had just forced her to do another crossover, resulting in a real dead body this time. No wonder she'd wanted to stay at the Narndian, enjoying a peaceful life of healing, surrounded by the sisters who'd accepted her.

Mairead sniffed, using her robe sleeves to dry her eyes. "I sent inquiries to Mar Nevan about the statutes, or anything. Certainly the holy mother wouldn't approve of a sister being forced to...strike a man down. Well, the next thing I knew, they sent the letter branding me.

"It was Maelchior and the others at the barracks, they thought I had tried to get them in trouble with the enclave, and they complained."

"Would the sisters at Mar Nevan heal Vaelor?" Ziggy asked.

Mairead studied him. He was watching Fig but hadn't spoken a word of his own since his sword had broken. "They might," Mairead said finally. "If anyone would know how, they would."

"So we take him there," Dev offered. "He's the reason I'm alive thrice over."

Fig frowned. "Dev..."

"What?"

"I don't think you should go."

"What?" Dev demanded, just as Emrah asked, *Why not?*

"Shadryn is going to try to take back the Rayvan throne. He's down one ally, but if he didn't survive that fight, I'm the Bard. We barely got ourselves through. Imagine if he goes straight to Tytan after licking his wounds. You need to find a way to take back the Rayvan throne before he does. And take him down in the process."

An uneasy laugh coughed out of him. "That's all? Where do you think I should go, then?" Dev said, crossing his arms against his chest. "Who's got an army that'll take on an enhanced psychopath mage who should be dead?"

"Go to Tirnalore," Fig said. "Like Ziggy said, the Fienn-Da would take us in. They might not have an army, but they have mages and a network. Their leader, Evandahl even said he would offer you aid, since we helped him steal the auran seed."

"And we can trust them?" He narrowed his eyes, evidently not forgetting her earlier comment about throat-slitting.

Fig shrugged. "They're your only hope of getting any sort of help to take back Tytan. Or uncovering Afrith's network of spies in Rayva."

Wait a minute, Emrah said. *The seed that Evandahl wanted? Didn't you say those were Afrith's mages at the library?*

Recognition clicked in Fig's mind, and she stared out at the ever-brightening sea. "You're right," she said quietly. "He knew about the seed. But was it for Shadryn or himself?"

Dev shook his head. "Shadryn didn't mention anything of the sort while I was there. I think the only thing he tried to hide was his role in the coup in the first place."

Fig frowned, nodding.

"But," Dev went on, "I also wonder if he had deluded himself into thinking that he hadn't had anything to do with that part. He genuinely seemed to think he just needed to get the throne back."

"Afrith had a hand in a lot of things," Fig said, her nerves rattling. "If he was playing a side game outside of Shadryn's plans for that auran seed, who knows what else he might have set into motion."

"I'm not sure we'll ever know," Dev said. "But that seed... It's safe with the Fienn-Da?" Fig nodded. "So that's it then," he went on. "We're going to Tirnalore?"

Fig looked down at the deck, clenching her hands tighter around her knees as the sun began its golden ascension over the horizon. "Actually, I...I'm going with Vaelor."

To her surprise, no one objected, not even Dev.

Vaelor lifted his head again and finally spoke. "To Mar Nevan?" he croaked.

Fig nodded.

"I imagine his sword will need to be mended," Dev said. "But that reminds me... Do you remember that sword the dwarves mentioned?"

"Yes," Fig said, the thought making her uneasy. "The Sword of Morin."

"Well, I think we might need to speak with them too. An unbreakable sword of legend might be just what we need to defeat Shadryn. But first—Emrah, would you be willing to circle back to the beach and set fire to some ships?"

The River Fienn was bathed in the light of the half moon when Vilvan anchored the *Trevena* along an empty stretch of riverbank to let off two passengers.

The former crown prince of Tytan and a silversword, the oldest descendant of House Ashbrok, fled into the night. The air tasted of the green river grass, and nothing like the magic he was used to in the *solanse*.

The dryad left a coded message for his leader in a cache hidden in a hollow hill, then lifted anchor and set sail for the place he knew best: home.

In the *solanse*, they could find respite if only for a moment. None of them would stay long. The fire mage and her *drixia*, the healer and the broken silversword. All would find their ways on the long paths that needed treading.

But like him, they were unable to plant their roots just yet. Such was the painful promise of home.

THE END

GLOSSARY

FAIRALEIGH VEIL	Also known as Fig, a fire mage with gold flames who no longer trains at the Carriage House.
DEVRYN VERRENCE	Heir to the Rayvan throne, an air mage with amethyst colored magic.
VAELOR RESBROK	A silversword in the employ of the Verrence family, from one of the last clans to fall during the Slaughter of Viren.
RHIVVEN	A bloodthirsty silversword who led the Silver Slaughter.
EMRAH	A dragonet with a possibly shaded past.
NIEL GANIVAN	A silversword from Thornkill.
LIESS ASTOR	A silversword from Southmarch, Weld with a formidable axe.
GAN WROGHSLEY	A silversword Weld with a shortsword.
QUEEN EILEIGH	Deceased, mother to Devryn.
BRUNA	A paper mage who Fig lives with.
COLLIS	A dwarf of the Feijowa clan.

FIRTH	A dwarf of the Feijowa clan.
MAIREAD JOIROS	A Sister of Morgha.
MAELCHIOR	A silversword posted in Nova Istra.
FENRA	A swamp dryad of the de Wald gathering.
ELDER ELIZARETH	An elder of the de Wald gathering.
VILVAN	A swamp dryad of the Lokin gathering. Friend of Fenra. He is on his pilgrimage out of the swamp.
ZULA RESBROK	Vaelor's grandmother.
AIDIENNE TASKOR	Tutor at Resbrok Manor.
PERRIN RESBROK	Adopted son of Zula, he is technically Vaelor's uncle.
MARLOWE	A dwarf who works at Resbrok Manor.
MASTER AFRITH SENAKA	Fire mage with green flames who taught at the Carriage House.
ELFIE	A svorcat, Afrith's pet.
ZIGGRUNE ASHBROK	Also known as Ziggy, a silversword who was turned at the end of the Silver Slaughter.
VINNIEL	A silversword posted in Viren.
SISTER STERINWAIT	A Sister of Morgha with a fount in Verindas.
ELFRAR	A swamp dryad, Fenra's brother.
LADY ATRICIA	A noble of House Griveen of Viren.
LORD ONALDE	A noble of House Weirbrook of Viren.
LORD ELESTE	A noble of Viren.
CAPTAIN FELRAS	A silversword posted in Viren.
ISHI AND EVVY ASHBROK	Ziggy's younger sisters.
FANGALORE	Also known as Fang, part of the Fienn-Da.
URSA	Fang's dog.
THOMAT EVANDAHL	The leader of the Fienn-Da.

KING ARTAXIS	King of Tysaine.
QUINNETRA	Part of the Fienn-Da.
KERAFINA	Part of the Fienn-Da.
ALLIFREY	A knife mage.
ESTILL	A water mage.
KING BAILEMOR	Historic Verrence king, who took the Gold Wood for the crown.
TESVIER THE RELENTLESS	Historic Verrence king, who took the Mountain for the crown.
MOTHER SAVIDAH	Head of the Sisters of Morgha.

PANTHEON

MORGHA	The goddess of healing and death.
THE BARD	He records the story of everyone's lives to share with the gods.
DRAKIORYN	In dragonet lore, a mighty dragon god.
CORAVA	A Virennish goddess.

FLAURA & FAUNA

VIRRENISH EIFDALES	A large horse breed originating from Viren.
AFFERVATZ	A type of stone.
LYRESTONE	A type of stone.
AURAN TREES	Endangered trees with gold bark and gold leaves, which emit gold sparkles in the right light. It is said they enhance the powers of mages.
VORSE EAGLES	A large brown and white eagle breed.
WHORLTHORNS	A bush with thorns in the shape of spirals.
BLOODRIL	A type of stone.
SVORCAT	A gold cat, originally native to the Gold Wood.
TAGOR	A large and vicious swamp reptile.
SILVERSAP	A healing plant.
VIRAGROVE TREES	Native to Viren, they only grow in the water of the salt swamps. Natives make a strong tea with the leaves.
ANDISIA MOSS	An invasive air plant from Andisia, which grows easily on any surface and favors the trees of the salt swamp.
KAFYE	A drink made from hard beans that grow on bushes, originating from Kafyetta in Tysaine.
FIREMOTHS	Green glowing insects in the salt swamp.
ILDERBERRIES	Purple berries found in the salt swamp.
SHAFRA	Woolly creatures kept by farmers for their fur and meat.
FOLI-LEAF	A Virennish plant which is not safe for animals.
ETRU	A Tysainian plant that is a mild sedative.
ASHBAR	A plant for smoking.

Virennish Language

Solanse	"so-lonse"	The salt swamps
Voixage	"voy-yahj"	A pilgrimage that the swamp dryads take out of the solanse for fifty years
Grimazir	"gree-ma-zeer"	Grandmother
Mazir	"ma-zeer"	Mother
Brozir	"broh-zeer"	Brother
Ida moz'n	"ee-dah moe zin"	I'm here/I'm with you
Visat	"vis-sat"	Is that
Mo desz	"moe dess"	My god
Mo der	"moe dehr"	My dear
Va	"va"	Yes
Meve	"meh-vee"	Maybe
V'rai	"vray"	An exclamation of surprise or awe
Vir dan	"veer-dahn"	A greeting
Mir	"meer"	Look
Merda	"mare-da"	A curse
Drixia	"dree-sha"	A dragonet

ABOUT THE AUTHOR

Liz Delton writes and lives in New England, with her husband and sons. She studied Theater Management at the University of the Arts in Philly, always having enjoyed the backstage life of storytelling.

World-building is her favorite part of writing, and she is always dreaming up new fantastic places.

She loves drinking tea and traveling. When she's not writing or reading, you can find her baking in the kitchen, out in the garden, or narrating books on her podcast, Fictional Bookshop.

Visit her website at **LizDelton.com**

ALSO BY LIZ DELTON

LEGENDS OF GOLD AND SILVER
Flames of Gold
Fires of Ruin (Prequel short)

REALM OF CAMELLIA
The Starless Girl
The Storm King
The Gray Mage
The Starlight Dragon
The Fall of Azurite

SEASONS OF SOLDARK
Spectacle of the Spring Queen
The Mechanical Masquerade
All Hallows Airship
The Clockwork Ice Dragon
Seasons of Soldark Novella Collection

EVERTURN CHRONICLES
The Alchemyst's Mirror

FOUR CITIES OF ARCERA
Meadowcity
The Fifth City
A Rift Between Cities
Sylvia in the Wilds